NAKED DESIRE

Regina had never seen a man's body unclothed. His lines were fluid and beautiful. There was whipcord strength beneath his skin, his stomach flat and hard. She found herself wanting to touch the muscles there, probe them.

"You haven't a stitch on, MacGregor. Cover yourself."

"I want you." MacGregor's deep rasp slid across her damp skin as he rose and padded slowly toward her.

The firelight cast orange ribbons across his tall body, lashing at the width of his shoulders and streaming down the narrow length of his hips. Aroused and walking toward her, MacGregor did not shield his need.

"You can't have me!" Regina backed away.

MacGregor loomed over her in the shadows. "I don't intend to debate the matter, ma'am. You're my woman from now on. I'll be easy, but I intend to stake my claim."

Wild Dawn

❦❦❦❦❦

Dear Reader,

At the end o review of a dazzlir w *York Times* bests *Genuine Lies*. It's honestly her best.

We hope you agree.
The Publishers

WILD DAWN

CAIT LOGAN

DIAMOND BOOKS, NEW YORK

This book is a Diamond original edition, and has never
been previously published.

WILD DAWN

A Diamond Book / published by arrangement with
the author

PRINTING HISTORY
Diamond edition / June 1992

ISBN:1-55773-732-0

Diamond Books are published by The Berkley Publishing Group,
200 Madison Avenue, New York, New York 10016.
The name "DIAMOND" and its logo are trademarks
belonging to Charter Communications, Inc.

PRINTED IN THE UNITED STATES OF AMERICA

10 9 8 7 6 5 4 3 2 1

Dedicated to the Native Americans and the new West frontier, a blend of nations and of hearts.

Thank you, Maureen Walters (my agent), for making my storytelling possible.
Thank you, Hillary Cige (my editor), for your support and expertise.
Thank you, Kerry (my daughter, my sunshine and rainbow delight).
Thank you, readers, for allowing me to share my stories. This book is my gift to you. Enjoy.

WILD DAWN

PROLOGUE

Colorado Territory, 1867

THE mountain man adjusted his buffalo robe to better protect his four-month-old son from the October wind. Tucked against MacGregor's lean side, little Jack slept in his fur-lined pouch and suckled in his dreams.

MacGregor scowled at the gray clouds drifting low on the Sangre de Cristo Mountains. Sweeping through big game country, the English had taken his Indian wife and a baby he never knew existed. MacGregor was married to Singing Bird while he was drunk, and he left her the next morning. Unaware of the marriage, he'd discovered the birth of his son at the same time he'd learned of his wife's death. Lured by the Englishmen's promises, Singing Bird had left him a strong son to raise.

Jack. With his Indian heritage written in his black hair and dark, rosy skin, Jack would be safer in the high mountains.

MacGregor had learned how to survive as an orphan shoved into a mission school. Then in the War Between the States, some called him a hard man who made his rules along the way. By MacGregor's rules, the English owed him; a man took what was due him . . . a wife for a wife, a mother for a mother. Take one he would. Raised by mountain men, he knew how to corner his prey and set the trap.

MacGregor had come from the hell of the Civil War to find the West ripped apart by the Sand Creek Massacre

of Black Kettle's Cheyenne. Red Cloud's Sioux to the north
thrust at the soldiers trying to lay forts along the Bozeman
Trail. The railroads pushed westward, and the Sweetwater
gold rush fever ran high. Quanah Parker, the half-white
leader of the Kwahadi Comanche, fought the Kansas Medicine Lodge Treaty.

Sweeping through the bloody grounds, English sporting
nobility shot buffalo and left them to rot while they drank
afternoon tea from china cups.

MacGregor rubbed his son, soothing him and thinking of
the woman in the cabin just an hour's ride from him. In his
experience, women needed a man to do their thinking, to
provide for them. He intended to use a gentle but firm hand
on the woman who was his by rights. Marriage by necessity
was often the case in this rough country, and the female
would choose him rather than dying on the mountain.

Mist clung to MacGregor's weathered skin and beard as
he thought of the Englishwoman, kidnapped and deserted in
the cabin. He'd watched her when he scouted the English
camp; she had spit, plenty of backbone. But she'd be hungry
and freezing now, willing to bargain. She had no choice:
Lady Regina Mortimer-Hawkes was his.

"I will survive. I always do." Regina smoothed
away a tear from her bruised cheek. She hated feeling weak;
weakness was worse than the freezing cold. Leaning against
the cabin's logs, she sniffed and shivered and forced herself
not to cry.

Wearily she fought the hunger gnawing at her stomach
and the painful bruises inflicted by the kidnappers.

As a child, she'd dreamed of King Arthur and his knights
rescuing her from her father. A gallant knight would ride
out of the English mists with his lance poised and great war
horse pawing at the earth. He'd carry her off to safety and
court her with flowers and sonnets.

But she wasn't a child any longer. The protective knight
hadn't ridden into her life.

Using all her strength, Regina forced herself to think of
surviving. The freedom of the American wilderness lay

just beyond her reach. There were new settlements in the sprawling lands where she could begin anew. . . .

Lifting her chin, Regina forced her stiff English pride to return. Perhaps she'd gotten that pride from her father's people, or from the dark, moody Bedouin blood of her grandmother. How her father had hated his daughter's dusky skin, despite his gift of the Mortimer-Hawkeses' amethyst eyes. Mocking her, he had taunted her with the name "Pagan." As a child he had hurt her, but she was free of him now.

The marquess would soon discover that she had left colored glass in the family vault, taking her Bedouin inheritance with her. Now the jewels nestled in the leather horn of her sidesaddle.

Regina straightened her back against the cabin's cold logs, arranging her tattered skirt over the rags that covered her bare feet. When Lord Covington had proposed to her and offered the hunting trip to the American wilds as an engagement present, she'd accepted immediately, making plans to escape and lose herself in the new country.

Alfred Covington was weak and spoiled and had gambled away a fortune. When her father had offered Regina and her money, keeping the jewels for himself, Alfred had immediately become her suitor.

Closing her eyes, Regina remembered Lord Covington's bloated, enraged face after their argument; her kidnappers had frequently whispered his name, linking him to the deed.

The wind howled around the corners of the cabin, and Regina gathered her torn shawl closer.

The men had made a mistake. . . . They'd let her live.

But now the mountain and winter waited to claim her. Closing her eyes, Regina forced herself to dream of hot, sweet English tea and scones.

Then a horse whinnied and Regina's heart stopped. She opened her lids and listened intently before she scrambled to her feet.

ONE

"HALT there, I say," Lady Regina Mortimer-Hawkes ordered as she stepped out of the log cabin. She pointed her empty dueling pistol at the man's heart. Peering through the ghostly gray mists that preceded the mountain night, she lifted her chin. There were men like her father who could smell fear, feed on it. Whoever this frontiersman was, whatever he wanted, she would not display the fear snaking wildly through her.

She swallowed, forcing moisture down her dry throat, and straightened her shoulders. Pressing her lips together, she tightened her finger on the trigger of the empty pistol; her free hand swept a long, rippling strand of raven hair away from her cheek.

Had her fiancé, Lord Covington, sent his men back for her?

Would she survive another attack at their brutal hands?

The tall man adjusted the buffalo robe carefully around his chest, the edges skirting his knees. Tied to an aspen branch a stone's throw from the cabin, his mottled horse whinnied. The man turned his head toward the three horses and two loaded packing mules.

Poised for danger, the man's hand tightened on his rifle and lifted it all in a single motion. He moved with an animal grace, as though he had walked through hellfire and survived by his keen wits and not the kindness of man.

Turning slowly, the stranger faced her. A wash of dead leaves caught on the winter wind, slashed between them.

Swishing through the pine branches, the wind sounded like the keening of a faraway banshee.

A wolf howled in the distance, his pack joining him in a chilling chorus. The eery sounds hovered between the tall man and Regina, causing the hair at the back of her neck to rise. Caught by the wind, a dead leaf tumbled along the wooden planks of the porch and scratched at her legs above the rags. The shreds of her petticoat, wrapped about her feet, lacked the dignity of her buttoned, heeled boots.

Regina straightened, the strands of her hair escaping the loose knot at the crown of her head. Her body craved the warmth of the man's fur robe; she could almost feel his heat throb inside it, like muscle sliding within sun-heated skin. Draped in the shreds of her torn dignity, Regina squared her bruised shoulders.

Her fingers shook around the small gun as she fought the fear ricocheting through her. "I ordered you to halt."

Shadowed by the wide brim of his hat, his deep-set eyes narrowed down at her. Taking two long strides toward the cabin, the man stopped.

His dark, piercing gaze cut through her like an icy sword. Her hand clutched tighter at the shawl, the pulse at the base of her throat pounding. . . .

"Ma'am," he said, dipping his head slowly and watching her with piercing eyes. "I'm a blunt-spoken man, but fair. I reckon you deserve to hear where I stand." His lips moved slightly as though tasting his words on his tongue before allowing them to slide free in the deep raspy tone.

He shifted his arm beneath the fur cape, the wind lifting the edges about his calves. "My son, Jack, is under this robe. He needs that cabin tonight, and I'm coming in. That fancy little gun won't go through buffalo hide. The chambers are empty anyway. . . . Tuck it away."

When she stared at him blankly, he nodded and took a deep breath. "I'd appreciate you asking me in. I've come a long way for you."

Long legs shifted restlessly beneath the buffalo cape. "The Indians know you're MacGregor's woman—that's me—MacGregor. I'm needing a woman for Jack, ma'am, and you're the choice cow of the herd."

"Cow?" she repeated blankly.

"Female . . . woman," he answered impatiently. "You'll find I'm not good with words."

Stunned, Regina's gaze slid down the tall man's body, shrouded by the cape down to his buckskin leggings and boots.

A cold chill ran up her spine before she straightened her shoulders. Fear danced over her flesh like icy sleet. The mountain man had no claim on her; his arrogance caused her to remember her father.

"I'm a blunt-spoken woman," she tossed back at him. "I haven't heard of you, nor am I 'your woman.' If you have a child in your robes, show him to me and you may have shelter for the night."

When he spoke the wind rose, penetrating the rags covering her feet. MacGregor's black eyes sliced at her, and his voice reminded her of a castle mastiff's growl. "No one doubts my word, ma'am. Jack's tucked in snug enough, and I'm not bringing him out until we're in the cabin. I'm done palaverin'—talking."

He lowered his head deeper into the mass of buffalo fur. "I'm tired and my son needs that cabin, ma'am," he said roughly. "We're coming in. You've got the night to think about living or dying. . . . The way I see it, you have four choices: You can freeze in that cabin this winter—alone . . . let the Indians turn you into a tribal squaw . . . or maybe some trapper will set you up as his property in a back room and hire you out . . ."

Then he added quietly, " . . . or you can marry me."

The proposal caught Regina broadside, winding her. He must be a lunatic, she decided, taking a breath to compose her thoughts. The wind whistled around the cabin corners, and she shivered, her torn dress exposing her shoulders to the wind. She gathered the lacy shawl closer against the cold, her finger growing numb on the steel trigger.

"I am an engaged woman, sir," she shot back hotly, pushing back a wind-tossed curl from her cheek. She drew her shawl around her shoulders as though it were a shield against him. "I'm having a rough patch, but—"

The man's low voice slid over her chilled flesh like a cold steel blade. The easy drawl sharpened. "Rough patch," he repeated harshly. "You cost me ten plew—beaver pelts. Swift Foot of the Kiowa had already claimed the first time on the blanket with you. You've been corralled up here for three days."

"How did you know that?" Fear slammed into Regina, her eyes widening.

"I scouted Covington's camp, picked you out for my own. I'm not one of the men who left you here, but I'm claiming you just the same. . . . Now, like I said, I'm done palaverin'. Step aside."

Dry aspen leaves crackled beneath his boots as he moved like a mountain cat, suddenly standing over her.

Dark eyes took in her long, disheveled hair and torn skirt before he spoke quietly. "They call me MacGregor. A quarter Indian, the rest is white. I'm needing a woman, and now I'm claiming you. You're needing a man to take care of you. We'll strike a bargain for Jack's sake, or in the morning I'll leave you to die. Winter is coming to the mountains, and it will be a hard one. I'm taking my boy to my valley—one hundred and sixty acres—and you can come as my woman . . . my wife," he corrected. "That's about the size of it."

Regina's eyes widened, rage slashing through her. "If you knew I'd been kidnapped, you should have stopped them. But no man claims me."

His gaze ran down her again, and Regina curled her fingers into a fist, fighting the urge to hit him. "You'll last less than a week without me," he said without feeling.

MacGregor's beard blended with the fur, leaving black eyes framed by the dark skin of high cheeks. His gaze flickered over her taut face, challenging her.

"How gallant, sir," she managed stiffly. "How chivalrous . . . a true gentleman. You come in here like some dark knight home from the Holy Wars, claiming the castle and the damsel in distress as though it were your right. . . . I don't think I like you very much, Mr. MacGregor."

He nodded curtly. "Never asked a woman to like me."

Beneath his long lashes, he traced the tear trails down her dirty cheeks. She could feel him searching inside her wounds and fear, probing for the right words to soothe her as though she were a frightened child. "Whites call me a hard man, and Indians call me Two Hearts. I know how to hunt and trap, but I don't know much about soft words for females." He inhaled deeply, then continued in a low voice as though he were taking a vow. "I'll keep to my side of the wedding vows, ma'am. Won't bring other women to our marriage bed, and I won't beat you. In return, you'll help me with Jack and do the woman work. Seems like a fair offer to me."

Her fingers, torn by searching for roots and bark, clutched the light crocheted shawl, crushing it. MacGregor needed a woman, did he? She'd fought men wanting something from her for years. MacGregor had proposed his demands to the wrong woman. "Baby under your cloak or not, you are to leave. Now."

One corner of his mouth moved upward, though the warmth didn't reach his eyes. The westerner's gaze touched her face—a small oval-shaped face beneath a heavy tangled mass of long hair. An arched lift of black brows and the thick mesh of lashes, spiked with tears and shielding eyes that changed from dark blue to purple with her emotions. Her lips pressed together tightly as he lingered, tracing the generous wide contours.

"Ma'am"—the stranger's relentless stare rose to meet hers—"like I said, I've got a four-month babe under my robe. I'd appreciate you asking us inside. Otherwise, I'm coming in anyway."

A thin mew sounded on the freezing wind, and the mountain man asked again, this time his deep voice held the growl of a dangerous bear. "Can we come in, ma'am?"

Stunned by fear and hunger, Regina watched as the tall man stepped past her into the stark cold cabin. His size filled the empty room, a huge man staking out each corner with a hunter's eyes. She barely reached his chest and realized painfully that with a flick of his hand, he could snap her neck. Or take her on the floor against her will.

Her stomach contracted painfully, and she rubbed her palm against it. Swallowing a measure of her pride, she asked, "Could you spare food . . . please?"

The buffalo robe swirled around his long legs, tangling with the fringes of his leggings when he turned toward her. "Get in," he ordered gently. "Close the door. I'll answer your questions later . . . after Jack's warm and fed."

She stared at him, hating his strength. "You leave me little choice."

Inside, the man towered over her. With every ounce of her strength she forced her knees to lock, boldly meeting his intent stare as he leaned his rifle against the wall.

Straightening, he studied her quietly, taking in the rags wrapped about her feet. "You're scrawny, but there's still plenty of spit in you. . . . You'll do," he stated quietly, easing back the buffalo robe from his arm.

Lifting an infant swathed in soft skins from the pouch crossing his chest, he searched the tiny, sleeping face. "My son—Jack," he said softly, reverence threading the gravelly voice. "He'll be needing a fine woman like you."

"Oh, my goodness," Regina finally managed. Slowly she forced her gaze to the baby, who nudged a fold of tanned skin, searching with his mouth. Under a cap of glossy straight black hair, Jack's tiny face was round and dark-skinned.

"His ma died," the man rapped out gruffly. "Didn't want him anyway, I reckon. He's half Ute and half mine . . . Jack's all mine now," he corrected. "Can you hold him while I get wood?"

He moved quickly, taking the pistol from her and easing the mewing baby into her arms all in one motion. The mountain man's calloused hands moved over hers, helping her support the tiny body. The baby searched her torn clothing, finding the softness of her breast, nudging it hungrily.

Tiny and vulnerable, the baby needed shelter and care to survive. The baby, an innocent bit of humanity, nestled and comforted her in the lonely wilderness. Like a flame, the fierce longing rose to protect the child, tearing at the cold and fear deep within her. She wasn't alone now, if just for an instant with the tiny body cradled against her. Instinctively she gathered him closer, and the man's hands slid away.

The baby smiled in his sleep, and for a moment she forgot MacGregor's demands. The sweet warmth of the innocent child ensnared and soothed her.

"I've got airtights—tins of milk," the man murmured softly, watching her wrap the skins more closely about the infant. "He can wait a minute while I get firewood. Jack squalls to beat high hell when he's hungry."

His fingertip trailed down her cheek, leaving a warmed path. "Soft as Jack's bottom," he murmured softly.

Regina forced her eyes up to the man. Despite what she had been feeling for the infant, she didn't owe his father. His heat tantalized her chilled body. She resented him then, the overlord male pawing through the crumbled castles of her dreams, her desperation. She resented wanting to rip open his cape and snuggle to the hard warmth of his body. "Mr. MacGregor, your son does need shelter for the night, and you are both welcome. As for your bizarre offer of marriage . . . I refuse. The idea is absurd. However, I would care for the baby until you take me to civilization."

His eyes narrowed down at her, tracing the taut contours of her face. For an instant the wrinkles at the corners of his eyes deepened with humor. Then he lifted her chin with the tip of his finger as though she were a child who amused him and needed reminding of his strength. "You don't have much to bargain with, ma'am. You've got choices. Go or stay. Live or die."

She met his stare. The taut moment passed slowly, her fury licking around her like flame. "Dark blue eyes, almost purple. Slanted at the corners," he murmured slowly. "The color of wood violets."

"Damn you," she said between the edges of her teeth, her anger giving her strength. "You thrust a poor helpless baby in my arms, torment me with his needs, then demand my hand in marriage. You don't actually expect—"

His eyes ran over her mouth, and Regina shivered, unprepared for the need to wrap herself around him, taking his heat and strength. Then MacGregor looked down at Jack, nestling cozily against her. "I don't want anything happening to my son, ma'am. You'd better sit down now," he offered gently as he wrapped his robe around her and settled her in a corner by the flickering fire.

When he stood, Regina looked up. Frozen, near starving, and frightened for her life, she hated the man. She gathered the robe closer about her and glared at MacGregor's broad shoulders rippling beneath his leather jacket. The leggings had been split to his calves to reveal blue cloth trousers. A yellow stripe flowed straight into his tall, worn boots.

He'd been in the War Between the States. A foolish war that England would have smothered before it began.

The scarred wooden grip of the gun escaped the worn holster lashed to his right thigh, the dull sheen of cartridges lining the wide belt.

MacGregor shifted slightly, resting his hand on the butt of the gun as though it were an old friend. "Army issue, a Smith and Wesson. Weighs about four pounds. If you pointed it at me instead of that peashooter, I'd have worried. Peashooters won't go through smoked buffalo hide."

She caught her bottom lip between her teeth, a habit she'd gotten into in the past four days. What right had this man to march up to her doorstep, issuing his notorious four choices?

"Your feathers are ruffled—you're riled. Out here it's make do and live, or don't and die. . . . If that helps," he added in a soft low rasp. After watching her glare up at him a moment, he patted her roughly on the shoulder and strode out of the cabin, closing the door softly behind him.

Regina settled the baby closer to her, and he quieted, dozing. As the warmth of the robe seeped into her, she lifted back a fold of doeskin from the baby's round face. She traced the tip of her finger over his cheek, wondering how such a small baby could survive in the wilderness without his mother. *How could she survive?*

Why had she wanted to throw herself at MacGregor? Why had she wanted those long arms to wrap around her and hold her as gently as his son?

The heavy fur brushed her cheek, and Regina remembered MacGregor's touch. Hewn from mountain rock, he had touched her softly, almost reverently.

Pain ripped through her again, tearing at her heart. *In her lifetime not another man had touched her cheek as gently.*

The baby nestled closer, his tiny hands reaching out with long fingers.

A baby! Regina breathed lightly as she watched him. As a girl, she'd wanted a whole brood of children tagging after her, and the emptiness stung her like a nagging sore. Now, abandoned in the great American wilds, a rough mountain man presented her with a baby.

Regina smiled whimsically. "No doubt you'll grow up to be a scoundrel just like MacGregor, arriving on a poor unsuspecting woman's doorstep and demanding her hand in marriage, but for now . . ." The baby was a soft, warm piece of civilization nestling sweetly in her arms.

While Jack was sweet, MacGregor lacked chivalry. The choices he'd offered her were not appealing. Whoredom or marriage to him.

"Marry him?" she asked Jack in a whisper. She stroked his plump cheek with the back of her fingers. "Impossible . . . MacGregor's woman, indeed!"

She eased back a silky strand of hair from the baby's forehead, stroking it gently. Regina cuddled Jack's little body against her and nourished her dreams. With each dawn her hopes had risen, only to fade by afternoon. Her fiancé's henchmen had chosen the cabin well. "I don't have a chance in Hades to wander out of this wilderness."

Closing her eyes, she sighed slowly, too tired to stir her dreams of a warm English hearth and the knight sweeping her to safety.

A shot rang out, and Regina tensed instantly, her arms tightening protectively around the baby. The sound sliced through her like a cold, dull knife. Was the man dead? Had he killed? Were the kidnappers coming back for her now, the mountain man's body stretched out on the frozen ground?

Her quickened heartbeat lifted the fur near the baby's face, and the infant squirmed slightly. She forced herself to breathe slowly, waiting for the fear snaking through her body to still.

Then the solid thud of an ax chopping wood sounded outside. The rhythm of a familiar sound comforted her slightly. Jack yawned, exposing toothless gums and raising a tiny arm as he stretched. Regina gently tucked the baby's arm beneath the buffalo robe. "Marry me," she repeated, smiling softly at the baby. "The idea. He's hardly my dream of a rescuing knight saving a lady. Your father has a lot to learn about the proper mode of courting a lady. If he weren't your father, sweet one, I would call him a brainless, mountain-size oaf."

Oddly content with the little body sharing the lush fur warmth, she rocked the baby. "When you're grown, don't go about demanding marriage from every lady in need."

Suddenly the door crashed open, and the mountain man entered the cabin, bearing a huge armload of wood. Regina noted the way those long legs moved like a hunter stalking deer. Or men. He kicked the door shut, and the baby jumped and began to wail, thrashing his tiny limbs.

She rocked the infant against her, quieting him. She resented MacGregor interfering with the only peace she'd felt in days. "You blackguard," she said quietly, scowling up at MacGregor. "Your baby was sleeping."

MacGregor's intent stare skimmed her rigid face, then he drawled almost pleasantly, "You remind me of a setting hen ready to defend her nest. Jack will go back to sleep. He's used to noise."

"Well, I am not," Regina snapped, rocking the squirming, crying infant. "I am certainly not used to being compared to a chicken—"

"Setting hen, ma'am. One who takes good care of her chicks." He crouched, stacking the wood on the stone hearth carefully. Lady Regina had never been ignored in her life, but as she watched the man's large hands tend the growing fire, she decided not to confront him. After all, there would be time enough later, when the blessed warmth seeped into her bones. . . .

Jack's small lips worked in a sucking motion, causing a twinge of piercing emotion to race through Regina.

MacGregor pitched pinecones on top of the coals and stirred them, then turned toward her. He stared at her, a strand of waving black hair crossing his broad brow. "Females always have questions, woman. I've got a feeling you've got more than most. What are they?"

The tone of a lordly male addressing a servant slid along Regina's neck like the scrape of nails across slate. "In good time. My first question will be why you scouted Lord Covington's camp and why you didn't appear to save me from those brutes—"

"That's two questions, ma'am. The answer to both of them is that I do what suits me."

"What suits you!" she snapped just as Jack began crying again. Without thinking she rocked and kissed him, and the baby instantly quieted. Over the little cap of straight black hair, she whispered fiercely, "This poor child. I suggest you get him a proper home. If left to you, he'll have no idea of sanity or of a gentleman's behavior."

MacGregor lowered his brows, staring at her intently beneath them. "Maybe I know that, ma'am. Maybe that's what I'm wanting him to learn from you."

"Good Lord," she managed after a moment, trying not to startle the baby.

A muscle high on MacGregor's cheek contracted beneath the dark skin. "I know women who'd want me and Jack. But they . . . they're not what I'm wanting for my boy. The kind of woman who'll take any man for two dollars or a good plew. I'll teach Jack what I know . . . hunting, trading, surviving. But the country is changing, and he'll need to change with it. You'll teach him . . ." MacGregor swallowed. "I'm wanting him to know something I don't. Something that will make him fine and special. Has to do with the soft things. Like talking to a fine woman without offering her two dollars' blanket money. Then he can take a settler woman, make a home for himself—when he's old and hurting."

MacGregor's deep voice was quiet, and Regina caught the wisp of regret lingering in the silence.

He shrugged, watching the flames. "I'm not fancy with words. I've talked more to you than most, trying to explain how it is . . . how it's going to be. A mix of white and red blood, I've lived hard, and now I'm doing the best for my boy, staking you out. In the mountains a man lays out a woman's path for her. Just like I'm doing for you. It'll work out."

He snapped a dried branch easily, the crackling flames lighting one side of his face in the shadows. A sheen the color of polished leather slid along the high bones of his cheek, his jaw hard and shadowed with a black beard. "My boy likes you," he murmured quietly, turning back to the fire.

"Mr.—MacGregor," Regina began helplessly, sensing his deep commitment to his idea of claiming her. "If you would just escort me to the nearest settlement, I'll tend your child on the journey and see that you are well paid. However, your demands for marriage are—"

"Jack needs a woman's soft body holding him."

MacGregor placed wood on the fire, then rose to his full height, studying Regina and the child. "He likes you," he repeated softly, as though satisfied. "That's good. Jack's had a hard time. You just sit there while I settle the animals and bring in my packs."

Regina's muscles stiffened instantly. "I resent being ordered about. . . ." she began.

Walking over to her, MacGregor let a warm finger trail down her cheek again, the gentle touch stilling her protest. "I know," he said quietly. "Your tongue throws out fancy words like flaming arrows. Those purple eyes are spitting mad, ready to fight."

His finger slid across her lashes and over her brows. "Black as a crow's wing, tips catching the light like blue fire."

He reached into his pocket, and then handed her a brown paper parcel. "Food. You'll be hungry, I expect. It's jerked buffalo, so don't eat too much . . . or your belly will hurt. There's a fresh deer kill outside."

Her stomach knotted as she carefully unwrapped the hard, dried meat with one hand. Regina clamped her teeth on the leathery strip and tore off a small piece, chewing with effort. The tough salty meat tasted heavenly.

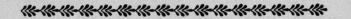

TWO

"CHEW a while before you swallow. I'll bring in your things," MacGregor said quietly, watching her.

"My things?" she repeated slowly around the hard lump of meat.

"Picked them off the bushes when I followed the men back to the Duke's camp." He paused as though placing his thoughts in order. "Had to shoot those three men, miss. They got liquor and supplies . . . started back for you." He shrugged, and the fringes bordering his long arms danced. "You wouldn't have wanted to . . . keep them company."

"You murdered three men—" Regina managed around the meat, her eyes wide.

"Shot them, ma'am. There's a difference between hitting a man in the leg and in the heart. I've never gut-shot a man in my life."

MacGregor's face darkened, his eyes snapping at her. "I said it was a fair match. Told them to leave you alone, that I just wanted your things—my woman's things," he corrected, then shrugged. "They wouldn't turn back. Gave them an honest chance on the draw." He rolled a broad shoulder slowly as though it ached.

The dried meat stuck in her throat, and she coughed. Moving quickly, the big man crouched to pat her on the back. "You get used to gunfire out here, ma'am. But you don't have to worry. I've always been fast."

Unable to speak, Regina covered her mouth with her hand. MacGregor glanced at his sleeping son, then back

19

at her. "You've got real soft ways about you. You'll be good for Jack."

MacGregor touched her hair, moving a strand back from her face. He touched the colored bruise on her jaw briefly, his expression grim. "They didn't have to do that," he muttered, rising to his feet. "I'll fix Jack's milk. Then if you'll feed him—use your finger, a cloth, and a spoon— I'll set up camp."

"Outside?" Regina's breath caught. MacGregor reminded her of a fast, dangerous wild horse racing across the mountains toward freedom.

"No, ma'am. I'll be sleeping near my boy and my woman," MacGregor stated quietly. "You and Jack need a few days' rest, then we'll be moving on before hard winter sets in."

Despite the warm robe and the glowing fire, her flesh raised with a deep chill. Was her destiny to live as a white captive on the American frontier? Instinctively she cradled Jack closer, and the baby nestled to her, giving a long, contented sigh.

"I could use the rest myself. Jack wakes up in the night, hungry as the devil. He's tough, though, and he's mine, the same way as you are . . . if we agree on the bargain." MacGregor's fingertip slid down her throat and away in a heartbeat.

She raised her chin, meeting his eyes. "I haven't agreed to your proposal, MacGregor. There's little chance that I will."

"You will," he said with that deadly certainty. "I always get what I go after." He gripped the edges of the robe, gathering it closer to her throat. His hand swept down quickly, tracing the slope of her breast, easing the fur away from Jack's face. "Don't be scared, ma'am," he murmured gently, cradling Jack's head in his palm. "The way I see it, there's those behind you who want you dead or worse. You can't go back—so that leaves me . . . if you want to live."

Too hungry and worn to fight him now, she closed her lids. "Leave me," she whispered wearily.

Regina stared at the fire, unable to move from the warmth surrounding her like a velvet blanket. Dozing, she was startled when MacGregor eased Jack from her. "His milk is ready, ma'am. I'll feed him."

She rubbed her eyes and yawned. "I can do my part, MacGregor. After all, you've been quite busy." She had awakened to a warm cabin and the enticing aroma of food—a huge roast sizzled over the fire, dropping fat into the flames. Her mouth watered, but she stiffened her shoulders, her pride returning. "I'm quite capable of feeding the baby—Jack."

MacGregor allowed her to resettle the baby, setting the airtight tin beside her. He nudged Jack's small lips with a cloth saturated with the warm milk. Instantly the baby tensed, his mouth searching. MacGregor's large fingers moved over hers teaching her how to tempt the baby with milk on her finger, then on the cloth. "A big, strong son," the westerner whispered reverently. "When there's a woman who will take pay for her milk, Jack likes that fine. But he's already taking milk from a spoon sometimes and a little gruel, too."

The baby grunted and sucked greedily, his tiny hands lashing the air. He gripped Regina's little finger tightly. MacGregor smiled, running his finger across the baby's small tight fist and across the back of her hand. "Like I said, Jack likes you."

"I return the feeling. Such a warm, cuddly lad." She quickly tore off another piece of jerked meat, then continued to feed Jack. Chewing slowly, she watched as MacGregor stirred a small iron pot over the fire and unwrapped his packs. The man struck quickly, a featherlight touch running across her flesh. As though he were tasting her. . . .

Escaping the mound of lace and silk held in MacGregor's large hands, her silk pantalettes slithered to the rough-hewn floor. For a moment MacGregor stared at them as though they were venomous snakes ready to bite through his boots. His rough features shifted, a reddish tint rising beneath the darkly tanned skin.

"Fancy women's things. Wouldn't hold in a strong wind," he muttered uneasily, carefully placing the clothing next to her. A shred of lace clung to his large dark fingers and MacGregor ran his thumb over it slowly, reminding Regina of the gentle way he had touched her cheek. "They tossed all your things from the trunks into the bushes. I gathered what I could along the way." He rose and turned toward the fire. "The men . . . soiled them."

In a moment of panic, Regina remembered the hard blow to her cheek and the way the three men had run their greedy hands over her breasts and thighs.

"I wanted to study a flock of Navajo sheep, and Lord Covington arranged for the men to take me on the expedition. With crossbreeding perhaps they could toughen my strain. Suddenly the men were tearing at my clothes . . . forcing me to run after the horses until we reached here—"

"IT'LL just take a minute, Sam. I want to taste that prime English meat. . . . Me first. . . ."

"Nah. We'll keep her here, then come back after we get rid of that duke. From the looks of her, we wouldn't get back for our money soon enough. Wait . . . then we can take all winter breaking her."

"But, Sam—"

"Plenty of time later. The duke wants us back now, and he's paying hard dollars—"

"He's a mean seven-sided son of a bitch, killed that good horse for getting snake-scared. That buzzard is done with her—so why can't we poke her a little?"

Dazed and lying on the cabin floor, Regina had heard the bone-shattering blow and a man's weight hit the floor. "What I say goes, Krebs. We'll have her fancy bones all winter. She can be your maid, old man. Wash your drawers." Sam's fiendish laughter rang out before the cabin door slammed.

" . . . I cooked a haunch on the spit," MacGregor was saying, crouched at the fireplace. "Made some broth and some hot water for tea. English ladies like tea, don't they? I got some at the settlement store when I bought drawers for Jack."

"There's a settlement near here? Oh, please—"

"No, ma'am. Big Hawk's Grove is in the other direction. We're headed for north country across the Sangres and the flats to my place . . . you and me . . . and Jack. There's nothing to the south or the east but trouble."

She shivered, fighting against her tears. She had planned and come so far. . . . "I'd rather die here," she whispered carefully.

His lips pressed into a straight line. "You just might. Comanche, Sioux, Kiowa, Cheyenne are fighting soldiers, settlers, and miners for the whole territory. A woman like you would be prime blanket makings for red or white."

MacGregor's long hard fingers tightened on his thigh. "You've got the night to decide. Why don't you rest now?" His question was darkly ominous, and Regina breathed quietly as she met his gaze. The mountain man could only be pushed so far, and in his way he was warning her. . . .

With the jewels in her hands, she could pay for safe passage . . . Tucked into her saddle, they would pay for her new life. "Did you collect my saddle from the men?"

"No, ma'am. That fancy bit of leather wasn't with them. You'll be needing a proper saddle."

Tiredly she cuddled the baby against her breast and closed her eyes. She rubbed her throbbing temple with slow, circular motions, wishing the nightmare would dissolve. She'd planned so carefully, storing the jewels in her pommel and tormenting Alfred into the hunting trip into the wilderness. . . . she needed that saddle, and then she would be free. "MacGregor," she began warily, "I have to get my saddle—"

"You want to count coup—take your revenge, I'd say by the look in those stormy eyes," he murmured in that low, soothing tone he used for Jack. "Give you a day or two, and you'll be right back up to the fighting spit-fire."

Her lids flew open. How could the mountain man possibly know anything about her?

MacGregor pilfered through a large sack, dragged out a clean cloth, and placed it over his broad shoulder. "Do you want me to take Jack? He needs his back rubbed now. Cries if his stomach hurts. In just a minute he'll be asleep, then we can take care of you."

"What? What do you mean, 'take care of me'?" She'd had enough of men's rough hands pawing at her; she'd fight him with her last breath.

MacGregor shrugged, then rubbed his shoulder slowly. "I like the way you don't flutter about. Speak your mind plain. . . . You'll be needing to eat and clean up some. Then you can sleep all you want. You'll need the rest for our trip—when you decide to live."

Regina's fingers tightened on the baby. Her father and Lord Covington had criticized her for speaking her mind and because she didn't "flutter about." Yet a crude mountain man admired those traits?

MacGregor leveled a dark, serious stare at her. "I'll wait until you see it my way—"

"What?"

"Females have their ways of letting men know when the time is right, that's all."

Sputtering a moment before she found the right words, she snapped, "How crude! You can wait until Doomsday. I shall never . . . never—"

MacGregor tucked the cape over Regina's cold feet and held each foot with his hands, warming her. He rubbed her arch with his thumbs, following the high arc slowly as though scouting new territory. Placing her foot on his hand, he studied the contrast. "Small, narrow—like a child's. . . . Mating comes natural, ma'am," he offered easily, patting the robe. "It wasn't necessary for them to take those little fancy shoes of yours. They weren't any good anyway."

When Jack began to squirm, Regina raised him to her shoulder to run the flat of her hand up and down his small back. "Mating, indeed. As if I'd—" She looked away from MacGregor's dark eyes, the wrinkles deepening with humor as she blushed wildly. Thoughts of his large body moving over her slighter one caused her to shiver. MacGregor would be whipcord lean and hairy and hard and . . .

She ran her tongue along her suddenly dry lips, forcing herself to stare back at him. His finger strolled down her hot cheek, testing it, and she jerked back.

"I reckon we can manage the mating part fine, once you're back in prime and feeling sassy," he said in a low, husky voice that caused her to shiver.

Regina stared at him, her heart pounding. Something hot and dark gleamed beneath his thick lashes, a look of stark desire that no man had thrown at her.

Something just as stark and wild went scooting down her body, heating it. Regina swallowed, fighting the urge to move into the safety of his arms.

She shivered, fighting the impulse of her body to press against his, to savor his lean strength. He was a hunter and a taker, and she was in danger of falling into his grasping hands. She would be no more free than in England. "I'm not going with you, sir. But you are welcome to rest for the night here," she managed evenly. "Please reconsider my offer to look after Jack until we reach civilization."

Jack burped and she nuzzled his black hair, cuddling the warmth of his small body against her.

"Civilization," he repeated bitterly. "The countryside is red with blood. I told you, my boy is half Indian. . . . That's why I'm taking him into the mountains—to keep him alive until he's learned enough to survive by himself. If something should happen to me, there are folks that will keep him. Right now I'm doing the best I can—getting a woman like you."

He breathed deeply, spreading his hands and studying them intently. "We'll palaver again, when you're feeling better. I expect I'll have my hands full with you and Jack. He's about worn me out." MacGregor deftly arranged a woolen blanket into a pallet near the fire. He folded several other blankets, carefully forming them around the pallet. "Keeps the cold air off Jack," he explained as though he hadn't been talking of "mating" a moment ago. "He's sleeping now. Let me have him."

Placing Jack on the pallet, he began to change the baby's wet cloths. The tender, clumsy way MacGregor's dark hands patted cornstarch on the tiny buttocks entranced Regina. She watched quietly as he covered the baby and gave him a gentle pat on the glossy black head.

"Old Jack likes petting," he explained almost shyly. "I didn't get any loving when I was a youngster, and I want my boy to know how it feels—the touching. . . . Do you know what I mean?"

He hesitated, gauging her reactions. As though he weren't used to revealing any part of himself.

Oddly, Lady Regina Mortimer-Hawkes knew exactly what the rough frontiersman meant. She'd had little or no tenderness in her life, following the strict social codes of her set—a miniature lady with perfect manners.

"I've got water heating . . . for baths. There's plenty of good soap for you and Jack this winter." MacGregor foraged in another bag and carefully extracted her china cup and saucer. He placed them on the floor and poured the hot broth into the cup.

The sight of the dainty violet-patterned cup sliced through her uneasy control. She'd packed the china set for high tea during the expedition. Suddenly tears heated her lids, oozing through her lashes.

MacGregor breathed harshly, kneeling by her side and wrapping his hand around her neck, smoothing it. "You're like Jack . . . you'll feel better with something in your stomach."

Regina found herself leaning against his hand, the tears coming faster. The silvery trail slid across the back of his hand before he lifted it away. Rubbing the damp spot slowly, he cleared his throat, looking out into the night. After a moment he held the cup and saucer up to her. "Broth. You can have meat when you're feeling stronger."

He placed the saucer on her lap, taking care to see that she held it firmly. "Drink up, Lady Hawkes." Easing her fingers around the cup, MacGregor cradled her hand to lift the rim of the cup to her lips.

"How do you know my name?" she managed after a burning sip of the broth. The nourishing taste curled around her tongue, and she savored the warm slide of the liquid down her throat.

Her stomach contracted instantly and she grimaced. MacGregor reached beneath the cape to rub her sunken stomach as though he were tending his infant son. The broad warmth of his palm traveled slowly across her body until it brushed her breast.

He paused, staring down at her pale face. Then slowly, his palm covered her breast, resting warm and heavy over her flesh. "You're small," he whispered softly. "Your heart is beating like the wings of a trapped bird."

Unable to move, Regina inhaled sharply. MacGregor's lean fingers tightened slightly, cupping her softness, his thumb rubbing the inner perimeter in a slow caress. "It's been a long time—soft," he said in a low, rough tone that caused her heart to pound heavily.

Regina breathed lightly, watching the dark flickering gaze holding hers. MacGregor's thumb ran quickly across her breast, leaving a taut nub in its passing.

Something live and hot passed between them, MacGregor's features hardening instantly. Inside her, a fierce need to stroke his hard cheek rose, her body trembling with an excitement she didn't want to feel.

She looked away, easing her body from his hand, and heard him inhale sharply.

When she looked at the mountain man again, his expression was grim. "There wasn't enough of you to start with. They should have left you food."

"There's no need to fondle me like a cow on the auction block," she said, trembling as his fingertips found her again with that soft gentling touch. No man had dared touch her until she had been kidnapped. Regina breathed in sharply, fighting the urge to hold his hand flat on her stomach. "Take your hands off me."

His fingertips slowly circled the perimeter of her breast, then slid away. "You're touchy. That's good. A man likes to know his woman hasn't been on too many blankets."

"Good Lord, man," she hissed, a sudden heat moving through her body. "Don't you know anything about gallantry and chivalry? A gentleman doesn't—"

"Gallantry and chivalry?" MacGregor's rugged face caught the firelight, a muscle contracting high on his cheekbone. "Saw plenty of that in the war when the officers—gallant, chivalrous gentlemen—raped a countryside and killed harmless people. . . . I told you flat out that I don't know much about sweet talk. That's why Jack needs you. So he can mix with your kind. And have some of me in him, too."

Between her teeth Regina said quietly, "The first thing you must learn, MacGregor, is that a man doesn't talk about a lady . . . being on blankets."

In the shadows his eyes gleamed. "Huh. How does she know when he wants to?"

"Do what?" she finished, realizing as the words left her mouth that MacGregor was speaking of his "mating." Regina had images of MacGregor's hard body moving over hers—she swallowed, helpless as the hot blush rose from her neck to her cheeks. "There are other ways, I presume."

For a long moment their stares locked. Then MacGregor tracked the rapidly beating pulse in Regina's throat. He placed a fingertip over it, and she jerked away, still staring helplessly at him.

"They'd be slow ways to please a man," he said roughly. Taking her rag-covered feet between his hands again, MacGregor massaged warmth into her. When Regina weakly tried to draw her legs free, MacGregor circled her ankles within the span of his hands, gently shackling her. In a low tone that reminded her of a wolf defending a fresh kill, he said, "You wanted to know. . . . I've been scouting your trail for three weeks, Duchess. Started right after I heard that the English would pay anyone to kill you and make it look like an accident. I don't hold with wasting a woman anyway. . . . If they didn't want you, I did. What there is of you . . . you're not much but a pile of bones," he added after mulling the thought over. "And dirty as a well-used whore."

"A whore!" Her open hand slashed toward his face, and MacGregor's fingers wrapped around her wrist.

He eased her arm down and covered it with the robe. "I'm not calling you a whore, ma'am. Those are just words," he murmured quietly, watching her.

"I'd be a whore if I went with you," she shot back hotly. "A gentleman doesn't use the word when he's with a lady." She hated the tears crawling down her cheeks, the need to curl into a ball and force the world away.

MacGregor nodded solemnly, his thumb wiping away her tears gently. "See? Those are things I want my boy to know. . . . I'm offering the marriage bed and a house, not a soiled dove's crib behind a saloon," he said quietly, huskily. "We'll be married as soon as we can find someone to say the words. We've talked enough, go on to sleep now," he said gently in the tone he used for the baby.

Regina tried to stare back at him, but her lids closed slowly. "By Jesus, you look like a scrap of a half-grown girl," he muttered roughly before freeing her.

She wanted to lash out at him, but the warmth of the meat broth had filled her, the smoky scent of the heavy robe drawing her down into its depths. Unable to keep her eyes open, Regina slipped deeper into the lush folds.

MacGregor tugged gently at the robe to cover her face. When she snuggled in the luxurious warmth, MacGregor chuckled and patted her bottom as affectionately as he would his sleeping son.

Unbidden, her fingers slipped out to find his hand. She touched his calloused palm, then drifted into sleep.

THREE

MACGREGOR leaned against the cabin wall, stretching his long legs before the blazing fire. Jack slept and made suckling noises as the wind howled outside the cabin.

The thin dog nestling against the woman had come scratching at the cabin door two hours ago. Catching the scent of her mistress, the sleek English greyhound had followed MacGregor at a distance. Inside the cabin she had cowered against the woman's sleeping body, whining when MacGregor placed the pan of cold broth and a deer leg bone nearby. He had talked quietly to the dog, noting the long whip marks crisscrossing the thin body. The dog rose shakily to lick the broth, her eyes watching him fearfully.

Now the dog snuggled to the woman's side, a pitiful creature watching MacGregor with distrust, jumping at the slightest sound.

The bitch had the look of a captured, tortured soldier, MacGregor decided, settling his back against the log wall. He grimaced, the pain reminding him of the bullet lodged just beneath the skin. Turning his shoulder carefully to protect the new injury, MacGregor sighed deeply. One of the men he'd wounded had managed the shot before MacGregor's bullet slammed into his other leg.

Probing the painful area, MacGregor frowned. He'd carried lead before; the bullet would work itself out. And if not, then later, when his boy and the woman were safe, a friend would cut it out.

31

The fire crackled and the dog jumped, watching him for a long moment before settling her muzzle over the woman's legs. MacGregor recognized the look of wild-eyed fear in animal or man as they fought sleep; he'd seen it often in the war.

MacGregor stared into the fire. War would always reach out bloody tentacles, snagging his thoughts. Before Jack, MacGregor's sleep ended in nightmares of cannon shot and missing limbs, of the human vultures ripping away at the dead's clothing and jewelry. Before he could stop them, his men had torn a half-grown girl apart, raping her after winning a minor skirmish. He'd killed a good fighting man over the incident and took a flogging himself. He closed his eyes, listening to his son's smacking noises and sleeping sighs.

Jack had eased the nightmares somehow. MacGregor didn't understand the comfort his son had given him; he just knew the boy needed him. The woman sleeping with her dog needed him, too.

Shifting his shoulder to ease his healing wound, MacGregor slid his Bowie hunting knife through the cooked venison haunch. Bringing the meat to his mouth, he bit off a chunk, chewing it slowly and washing it down with hot coffee.

The meat's nourishment seeped into him, and for the first time in years MacGregor allowed himself to relax fully. Beside him Jack slept, healthy and warm, and a woman to care for him rested nearby.

Wiping his sleeve across his mouth, MacGregor stared at the fire. The wind howled, threatening him with winter, the sound reminding him of the screams of dying men on the battlefield. Wanting to see the world, he'd gone East to be caught in a war that tore families apart. He'd wanted to run back to the mountains after his first taste of the bloodied fields.

But he'd stayed and killed until his hands were red. Was it four years or an eternity until the war ended?

He ran to the mountains like a lost lover, losing himself in the sweetness of the pines and the clear streams.

But death lurked there, too. The Cheyenne and Arapaho who were his friends had fallen before howitzers at the Sand Creek Massacre. Settlers had died by Indian and renegade hands.

He'd had his share of death. Jack's Indian heritage was a dangerous one, and MacGregor wanted to protect the boy. A man could cut out a safe spot in the high country and live quietly as the red and white wars swirled through the lower lands. Renegades on both sides ripped at the survivors like buzzards tearing at a fallen buffalo calf.

But he had to have a woman for Jack. The Englishwoman with her soft skin and husky lilting voice belonged to him now; she would come to trust his care.

Closing his eyes, MacGregor leaned his head against the logs, trying to remember the Indian woman who had been his wife. Drinking whiskey until he couldn't stand, he'd allowed the Indian marriage and spawned his son that cold October night.

Waking with an aching head and a woman he didn't remember, MacGregor left camp before the others. He'd headed out for the rugged mountain peaks to hunt and trap. He needed the cleansing streams and the wind keening through the pine boughs. He needed to find his soul.

Upon MacGregor's return to the Indian camp thirteen months later, Pierre had greeted MacGregor heartily, then cleared his throat. Stepping inside his tepee, the Frenchman had emerged to hand MacGregor a squalling baby. "He is your son, *mon ami*. Singing Bird, she is gone."

The handsome trapper had spit out a stream of tobacco as though to rid himself of a bad taste before he continued. "Followed the English dogs for whiskey. That one, Jack Ryker, he take her. . . . They killed her. I, Pierre, your friend, say this is so. The boy, he is yours. Pierre watch when she leave him for wolfbait. Pierre take."

Because of pride, or maybe it was the war still waging in his blood, MacGregor had tracked the English hunters. They had a mountain man with them, an experienced guide selling his country for money. With Jack Ryker as the leader of the pack, they had slaughtered a swath through the mountains, killing enough game to support the entire Indian nation.

Then just before MacGregor had decided to call the tracker out, he saw something he wanted.

IN the cabin the fire crackled, and tossing a broken limb into the fire, MacGregor turned his head to look at the woman. She was rightfully his now. . . .

He'd been in the woods two weeks ago, surveying the camp that day when the Englishman and woman had raced to the crest of a small knoll beyond the aspen trees sheltering him. Riding sidesaddle, the woman slid agilely from the horse before it stopped completely. Ripping her gloves from her hands and tossing them to the ground, she faced the Englishman, who had dismounted more slowly, his rifle in hand.

MacGregor had straightened away from his tree, watching the man's thin face twist in anger. Listening closely, the mountain man couldn't understand the words, but the argument was no light matter. The man had missed a trophy bighorn sheep because his horse had shied, and he wanted to kill it.

Her head back, anger ran through the lady like a taut bow string ready to snap. The prairie wind swept her clothing against her taut breasts, her petticoats a white skift against the dark green velvet skirt. Beneath her large hat, her long hair had caught the fall wind. The heavy mass lifted around her like a rippling flag catching the sun in a blue-black sheen. Then she had struck the man, dashing his ornate rifle to the ground.

A sour taste rose in MacGregor's mouth when he remembered the way the well-dressed man had slapped her with his open hand. Her hat sailed away in the wind as she fell to the ground, the massive plumes tearing free. Scampering to her feet, the woman had jerked a pistol from the man's waist to point it at his face. With her free hand she had soothed the greyhound nestling now at her side. Then, taking the man's riding quirt away, she'd beaten him to his knees.

A woman of steel and velvet, he'd thought as she tossed the quirt away and motioned for the dog to run to camp.

Admiring her steel, MacGregor had watched the fine line of her shoulders and breast, the way the velvet strained across her taut, uptilted breasts. An eye for an eye, MacGregor had decided when the woman had mounted and raced away, leaving the man to follow on foot. The woman pleased him, her untamed blood could equal the wild mountain country.

He rubbed his hand against his thigh, remembering the soft feel of her breast in his palm.

Woman-hunting wasn't his best skill. As a breed, they were too treacherous, wanting pay for their services.

But this one had fought for a horse, faced a man down with a gun, then whipped him to his knees. Eventually MacGregor had found the horse with its throat slit, and then he'd heard of the offer to kill the woman.

By the end of the first week he'd decided to take the woman.

Now he watched her settle deeper within the folds of the robe. Sipping his coffee, MacGregor studied her face intently.

Nestled in the lush fur, her features seemed childlike. Her lashes were lush crescents across her pale face, shadowing the warm flush of her cheeks. Her mouth looked moist and velvety soft. . . . MacGregor felt something odd turn inside him. He'd never held with men who needed young girls.

But she wasn't a girl. He'd seen her up close earlier, saw the lines of fatigue run along her cheeks and between those fine brows that lifted like wings. Her hollowed cheeks had caused her purple eyes to seem large as a child's, but there was a fierce look about her that only a woman could have.

The woman had forged steel running through her, and MacGregor liked that. When a man chose a mate on the frontier, he'd better get one that wouldn't run from bad times.

Her breast was so soft, barely filling his palm. He'd wanted her badly then. Wanted to sink into her woman's flesh and forget his pain in the hot, sweet fever.

He chewed on the cooked deer meat, his body slowly absorbing the nourishment. The woman needed time to mend. Time to set her mind to the new life with his son and himself.

MacGregor ran his hand across the hair on his chest, frowning. He liked the way she'd taken to Jack, nestling his small body against her. He had tested her then, watching her carefully handle his son. MacGregor had seen white women captives turn from their half-blooded children. But Regina cuddled Jack as though he were hers. MacGregor rubbed the ache in his shoulder, glancing at the woman hidden by the fur.

Mothering was a female instinct, and that was what Jack needed now. But the woman needed someone to do her thinking, take care of her, MacGregor thought, drawing a fur over him to sleep. He half turned on the floor, curling his warmth around Jack.

The woman disturbed him like a breeze riffled the dead leaves clinging to a tree. He didn't understand why, but when her slender fingers lay upon his open hand, the touch had locked him in place.

He rubbed his palm roughly against his thigh, trying to erase the lingering brush of her fingers. They were soft, he remembered, pale and fragile lying against his palm. . . . "Don't reckon I've ever had a woman touch me there, Jack," he muttered softly to his sleeping baby. "Unless she wanted to be paid."

With his right hand on his son's back, and his left on the handle of his pistol, MacGregor allowed himself to sleep.

THE mewing sound awakened Regina, and she snuggled deeper into the glorious warmth of her bed. She allowed herself to sink into the security of the dream . . . The family's country estate was marvelous in the winter, blanketed by snow. Huge blazing logs filled the wide stone fireplace. Laden with plum puddings, roast pheasant, and hams, the dining table gleamed with a fresh coating of beeswax.

With plum puddings and hot mulled cider, the holidays would soon begin, filled with guests and presents—

. . . Jennifer crying, begging Hawkes to be gentle to his child.

. . . Jennifer, whispering on her deathbed, "Take the jewels, my child, and run for freedom."

The mewing sound grew louder, demanding. Her dog whined at her side, sharing the bed with her.

Venus whined again, nuzzling her hand free of the coverings. Rubbing the dog's ears, Regina listened as a baby began to wail.

A baby!

She swallowed, listening to the odd noises enter her drowsy warmth. A man spoke quietly, sleepily. Outside the wind howled, and the hard floor was not her feather mattress. Forcing her lids to open, Regina watched as the tall mountain man rose out of his bedding.

Talking quietly to Jack as the baby's cry became a frantic demand, the man sank a thick blade into a tin of milk. He thrust it into a pan of water beside the blazing fire.

Noting the morning light skipping through the thinly scraped skins covering the window, Regina watched the man who had entered her life last night. *MacGregor.*

In the dim light of dawn and fire, MacGregor's tall body dominated the room as he moved around in his buckskin-fringed shirt. During the night he had drawn off his leggings, and the yellow stripe slid down the length of his blue trousers. He crouched beside the baby and talked quietly in that low comforting drawl. If she hadn't known he was a madman, the drawl would have soothed her back to sleep. "You're wet, Jack. You run a steady stream from your mouth to your drawers."

MacGregor changed his son's clothing, then lifted the baby at the same time he lowered himself to lean against the wall. Pouring the tinned milk into a cup, he cradled his son in the crook of his other arm. A tiny arm flailed about and caught the mountain man on his nose. He chuckled deeply, tugging the tiny hand with his lips. "You're a tough old bear, boy. Should have named you Ephraim for mountain bear. Mr. Bear—leaky britches," he soothed in that raspy, deep voice as he reached for a spoon.

At first the baby sucked frantically, then slowed to a drowsy acceptance of the spoon nudging his lips. After the baby fell asleep, MacGregor eased wood into the fire and, watching it, leaned back to rest.

"You're awake. I can feel you think, woman," he stated without turning from his task. "It's warmer here. Drag your pallet to the fire," MacGregor ordered quietly.

Regina longed to stay where she was, but the cold began to slide into the robe. When she hesitated, MacGregor glanced at her. "If you're wanting to step outside to pi—ah, take your ease—slip on my boots," he finished roughly, turning his attention to the baby again.

Regina lay still for a moment, thinking of his horses. Once she left the cabin, she could steal one of his horses—

"Easy now, Jack," he murmured, his gaze skipping across the shadows to her. MacGregor's raspy voice clawed at her, the tone deeply masculine and laden with male authority. How she resented that tone. . . . And she resented his ability to make her feel like a girl fluttering over her first love.

"You're hatching some plan to run off," he said, as though he owned her, flesh and blood, heart and soul. She let the hatred simmer within her, the old scars opening anew. "I'd catch you," he said quietly. "Tie you up if I had to. Just do your business and get some more sleep. You're not fit to travel now."

She shivered, feeling the cold slip deeper into her robe. How dare he try to understand how she thought!

"You're arrogant, MacGregor," she managed finally across dry lips. "You couldn't possibly know what I'm thinking." Rising to sit, Regina wrapped the robe about her shoulders.

A dog whined at her side, and Regina turned to see her greyhound. Pleasure rippled through her like sweet spring rain. "Venus! Oh, my love, my beautiful—"

Running her hands along the dog, Regina giggled as the dog's tongue lapped at her cheek. "Steady on, my beautiful. . . ."

Her fingers discovered the ridges on the dog's smooth pelt, and looking at them carefully, Regina traced the brutal whip marks. "He didn't have to hurt you, my lovely," she murmured, caressing the dog's maimed back.

"The dog will heal. She wouldn't let me touch her last night. You can put some salve on her later," MacGregor offered softly.

Regina wiped the back of her hand across her damp eyes. "How horrible. My poor Venus."

"She's moving like she's taken a boot or two in her ribs, but she'll heal fine. Just take her outside with you when you go."

Regina rose slowly, painfully aware of her weakness as Venus whimpered by her side. Rubbing her hand across her eyes, she wrapped the fur about her and walked to stand before the fire. Venus whined, cowering behind her skirt.

Patting Venus, Regina forced her head up. Deserted in a foreign country with nothing except her pride, she would survive. MacGregor was obviously mad, wanting to marry her. Weakened and unable to survive the wilderness alone, she hadn't a chance . . . at least just now, she corrected as Venus whined again.

"Come now, Venus. Mr. MacGregor is quite right. We both need a trip outside and more rest. Show him that you're not afraid, my darling." Gingerly bracing her hand against the wall, Regina slipped one dainty foot into the huge worn boot.

Placing her other foot into his boot, she tried an experimental step. She discovered that when her feet moved, the boots did not and served to unbalance her. MacGregor's large hand shot out, gripping her waist to steady her for a moment. His dark eyes gleamed beneath his heavy lashes, and she caught the flash of his teeth. "A woman needs a man to take care of her," he drawled; the arrogant knowing tone caught on her nerves.

Regina looked down at him haughtily, daintily removing his hand with her thumb and index finger. "I can manage. Thank you, MacGregor."

She lifted her chin higher, shuffling toward the door in the huge boots while holding the cape. She hadn't liked the dark gleam in his eyes when he had balanced her, not a bit. Nor did she like the way her flesh heated at his touch. Lifting the latch, she turned with as much grace as she could manage and said, "I shall be back soon. Come, Venus."

She thought she heard a low chuckle just as she closed the door. " 'A woman needs a man.' Damn his bloody hide, Venus," she muttered, walking toward the trees. "But I shall have my day. I promise."

When she returned to the cabin, the baby was sleeping and MacGregor had prepared her breakfast by the fire. A low flat pan held chunks of bread, and her china cup was filled with steaming meat broth. He had placed wedges of freshly cooked meat on her saucer. Regina's stomach contracted at the sight, and she exclaimed, "This looks lovely, MacGregor!"

When she sat, carefully arranging her skirts over her crossed legs to take the food, he watched her. "The dog stays away from Jack. I left a good measure of meat on the bones, and there's water in the corner."

Regina nibbled the bread, sampling it to discover the tangy taste. She slid a glance at MacGregor as he rubbed a stone along the ax blade, sharpening it.

The light was better now, settling over him like a mantle as he bit off a chunk of meat and chewed it slowly. His hair reached his shoulders, a thick glossy mass of waves. His nose had an odd angle to it, as though it once had been broken. The heavy beard covered his jaw and cheeks, but his complexion was very dark, tanned by the weather.

Lounging against the wall, MacGregor was possibly the fiercest man she had ever encountered. She'd seen frontier men from a distance—dirty, fierce men. Yet MacGregor's hair and skin were clean, his body lean. From the hole at the tip of his stockings to the deerskin shirt, he was nothing but hard angles of muscle and bone. She could have easily fitted twice into his shirt as it stretched tightly across his broad shoulders. A wave slipped across his brow, softening the angular width. Working peacefully at his task, he glanced at his son when the baby stirred.

Regina's gaze returned to MacGregor's chest, where the fringed deerskin shirt opened to reveal his red woolens. Escaping the undergarment was a heavy thatch of dark hair that curled at the base of his muscular, tanned throat.

She closed her eyes, trying to force away the image of black glistening hair covering a wonderfully broad, muscular chest. A lady didn't want to run her fingers through the hair covering a man's chest!

Regina's fingertips tingled, and she swallowed, moistening a suddenly dry throat. MacGregor hadn't concealed his need for a woman when his fingers skimmed across her breast.

Regina gathered her arms around her tightly, trying to quell the sudden surge of longing to simply move into his arms.

His arms moved, muscles and cords sliding beneath the leather shirt, his long legs stretching out before him. He was too powerfully built, much too large. He would surely tear her. . . .

She shivered, trying to force her thoughts away from the mountain man.

Picking up his huge hunting knife, MacGregor spit on the stone and caressed the shining steel across it. He ran his thumb across the blade, testing it. As though feeling her questioning gaze, he said, "Eat. Then sleep some more. It will heal you."

Licking her dry lips, Regina suddenly remembered Venus. "Could you spare your salve for my dog?"

For an answer he scooped a flat tin from his saddlebags and rolled it across the floor to her. After finishing her meal, Regina carefully placed her china aside, then pried open the tin. She wrinkled her nose, the pungent odor filling the air. "What on earth is in this?"

"Good enough for man or beast—grease, sulfur, leaves. Your dog will heal fine," he answered without looking up from his task of sharpening a long, thin knife. He moved, settling his shoulder more comfortably against the wall, then settled back down to his task.

After rubbing the ointment on Venus, Regina tried to stay awake. She dozed and then the big man eased her to the floor, settling her within the fur robe gently. Drowsily she touched his hand. "You can't really expect to keep me, MacGregor . . ."

Again he patted her bottom as though she were his favorite mare. "You're mine and Jack's now. You'll do just fine," he answered just as she slid off the velvet edge of sleep.

When Regina awoke next, the afternoon light was dying, the shadows slipping around the cabin. Venus nuzzled her hand, urging Regina to pet her.

MacGregor stood in his stocking feet, studying the fading day from the window. He'd shed the leather shirt, and the red woolen material outlined his powerful back as it tapered into the blue trousers that cupped his buttocks.

Regina's fingers smoothed the dog's pelt as she watched the mountain man. Thick glossy waves rippled down the back of his neck, and the heavy muscles padding his broad shoulders slid beneath the red cloth. She wondered briefly how his skin would feel on her fingertips; how his muscles would slide beneath her touch.

She hadn't touched a man's body in her lifetime, exploring it. Yet MacGregor's tall body reminded her of the beautiful Greek statues standing in her father's sculptured gardens.

He placed a heavy cloth over the thin skins covering the open windows, a protection against the cold. "You're awake, then," he said without turning from his task.

"Yes, I am." Luxuriating in the fur, Regina continued to pet Venus. The cozy cabin locked the howling, fierce winter outside. Steam rose from the pot hanging over the fire, and an assortment of food tins and sacks of flour and sugar were neatly arranged on a shelf. Covered by a large cloth, a pan rested on a flat rock near the fire, and the soft bulge beneath suggested rising bread.

Her washed clothing dried on pegs placed into the log walls, and he'd cut wood. Her teacup and saucer perched on her heavy traveling chest.

She yawned and stretched, feeling better than she had for days. "You must think I'm quite lazy, a lie-abed, sleeping like this," she ventured, slowing rising to her feet.

Brushing the wrinkles from her skirt, Regina tried to arrange her hair and her scant dignity. The rest and food had strengthened her, yet she knew she couldn't match a man who wrapped danger around him like a shroud. Except when he looked at his son, there was a flat look to his face. As though he'd faced hell and it had claimed his soul. When he didn't answer, she padded to the fire, watching the orange flames lick at the blackened stone. The sight reminded her of the family kitchens—

England. A continent and an ocean away. How stupid of her to trust Covington after shaming him. Wrapping her arms about herself, she glanced at the sleeping baby, whose plump cheeks moved rhythmically as he dreamed of his milk.

MacGregor loved and would protect his child, however rough his methods.

IN England the Marquess of Fordington, Nigel Mortimer-Hawkes, crushed the colored glass covering his desk with the butt of his pistol. In a sweep of his large hand he sent the glittering prisms sailing to the Persian carpet. His amethyst eyes darkened beneath their blond lashes, his handsome mouth pressed into a thin, cruel line. "So, my proud beauty. You've finally proved me right. Thievery runs in your blood. So much for promises to wed an honest Englishman. I shall have to teach you a lesson once more, Pagan."

He folded a thin strip of morocco leather and struck the teak desk, causing the remaining crushed glass to dance within the black velvet. Pulling a bell rope, he summoned a servant, then told the man, "I'm taking a trip to the Colonies."

After a quick list of needs, Mortimer-Hawkes dismissed the man with a flourish of his hand. He splashed stout Irish whiskey into an elegant glass. "So, Pagan. You're making a run for it, are you? Just like your mother tried and failed.

I always brought her back. I broke her finally, as I will you, my loving daughter. . . ."

He studied the amber liquid in the glass, thinking of the legend Mariah had whispered to him long ago. "The man who holds the woman of the Mariah Stone will have the power of kings as long as she lives."

Scanning his great estate, built after his marriage, Mortimer-Hawkes knew that he could not let his daughter escape him. He had thrown weak suitors at her, knowing that he alone would rule her power. Covington could be easily managed and cast aside if necessary.

But Pagan and her power were his.

WATCHING the sleeping baby, Regina decided she needed rest . . . then she'd leave, claiming her jewels from Lord Covington's camp.

Suddenly the skin on the back of her neck seemed to lift, like Venus's hackles rising when danger approached. Regina straightened, refusing to show the fear racing through her as she sensed MacGregor standing behind her. She shivered beneath the light shawl, knowing that he could easily strangle her with one large hand. His heat warmed the length of her backside, the fire crackling before her.

"You're thinking about running from me. About how to count coup on the duke," he drawled softly.

"He is an earl," she answered flatly, angered that he had tracked her thoughts perfectly. "My father is a marquess," she lashed at him, then closed her eyes.

"Is that so, Duchess?" MacGregor asked after a sound that could have been a chuckle.

Nurtured in the wilds, MacGregor had no concept of nobility, nor the savage games they played. She'd escaped them now as she would the mountain man. But first she needed one thing from her old life. "I need my saddle."

His hand rested on her arm, and Regina shifted away from his light touch. "Hate can eat a person's insides," he said darkly. "Turn them into what they hated. There are other saddles—"

"Revenge?" she interrupted sharply. "I can manage that myself, thank you, Mr. MacGregor."

Gripping the shawl tighter about her, Regina opened her eyes to stare at the flames. The coals glowed like the rubies, the sparks like a shower of tiny diamonds . . . her payment for freedom.

Taking her shoulders in his hands, he urged her gently aside, then bent to stir the thick soup with a wooden spoon. Replacing the cloth covering the bread with a heavy lid, MacGregor placed the pan into a corner of the fireplace. Scooping coals onto a flat board, he placed them carefully on the lid.

She wanted that raspy low voice to curl around her loneliness. "You're baking bread," she remarked, prodding him to speak.

After a moment his silence grated. She nudged a stick with her rag-covered toe. "Of course you're baking bread. You're obviously engaged in making a meal," she snapped.

MacGregor nodded. "Sourdough. Not hard if the starter doesn't die." He reached for a large pan and settled it on the floor. Then he took a bucket filled with Jack's soiled cloths, dumped them into the pan, and poured another bucket of hot water over them.

This man had shot three men and provided for her needs while she slept, then he laundered the baby's things. How nice, she thought—a henchman and a maid and a nanny, all rolled into one tall, rough-looking man. When she tried to smother her giggle, MacGregor turned on his haunches to look up at her.

Covering her smile with her hand, Regina offered, "Well, it is strange to see a man like you tend a baby."

MacGregor rose slowly to his full height. When he stood near her, Regina stepped back to meet his eyes. "No one has laughed at me since I was a boy. I don't like it," he stated slowly. "You'd do well to remember that, Duchess."

Refusing to give way to her fear, Regina pressed her lips together. "I've been threatened all my life. You might as well kill me now, MacGregor. Make short work of it, if you will. Because I intend to laugh as I desire."

Beneath his beard, his jaw shifted. The deep-set eyes warmed, traveling over her proud stance from head to toe and back. "You're a fiery little broody hen," he said slowly, the wrinkles at the corners of his eyes crinkling. "Jack will need that."

"You said that before. What Jack needs is—" Regina could feel the wild temper she'd kept stored for years begin to simmer. Keeping a leash on her anger, she said between her teeth, "I am trying to be pleasant."

"Pleasant," he repeated slowly, as though tasting the word. "I watched you whip a man to his knees."

"I was deeply angry—" Regina frowned. "The only time I touched a whip to a man was when Covington . . . You saw?" she gasped, realizing now how he had scouted the hunting camp and witnessed the scene.

"We'll eat soon," he offered, folding his arms across a chest that blocked the rest of the room from Regina's vision. He shifted his weight over those long legs as though he could wait until Doomsday. "You'll feel better with a full belly. The book says females and babies are like that."

"Book?"

He nodded slowly, moving his long legs apart and tilting his head to one side. "I can read. A Black Robe . . . a Spanish priest . . . whipped it into me at the mission."

His lazy drawl caused her to want to rip into him. Regina wrapped her fingers in her shawl, straining for control. "Of course you can read. And your book . . . what does it say about women? That the only way to get one is to waylay her?"

"Haven't read it all, ma'am. Just some parts to help me with Jack." He shifted again, rubbing the flat of his hand across his upper arm.

"And women?"

"Yes, ma'am. When I decided to go woman hunting for Jack, a settler's wife gave it to me. Has recipes you'll be needing, too. Cooking and such. She wrote me how to make bread, the loaf kind with fresh butter and honey melting on it. Soon as we reach my place, you might get started on it."

Tethering her growing anger, Regina swallowed, gripping her upper arms tightly. Her head went back, the cords running along her neck tightening with tension. "You can't treat me like your son, MacGregor. Telling me what's best. You may choose what's best for your child. But not for me."

The wrinkles radiating from his eyes deepened, a sparkle beginning in the depths of the dark eyes. "That's what a man does—tell his woman what's best for her," he answered easily. "The way I figure it—about raising Jack—is we'll have to work at it, like two mules pulling in harness."

"Oh!" Regina stamped her rag-clad food. "Perhaps if I give you a good thrashing, you'll come to your senses."

"Yes, ma'am . . . anytime you're ready. I reckon as your husband, I'll have to take the edge off that temper a time or two. If you don't beat me too hard," he agreed easily. "Better eat. It'll settle you down some. Go on now, take care of yourself outside, and then we'll eat."

Regina's cheeks burned, her fists knotting in her skirt with the urge to fly at him. She'd managed to slide through threats smoothly in the past years, untouched by the savage anger she'd suddenly discovered with Covington. The mountain man could bring temper writhing out of her like a viper from hell. "I want you to know," she began slowly, picking each word and sliding it between the edges of her teeth. "It wouldn't serve you to anger me. I could be dangerous when aroused."

"Uh-huh," he agreed too easily, dismissing her threat as though it were a clinging leaf. "But the bread will be done soon, and we'll eat then. I like hot bread with my meal."

For a moment Regina glared up at him. "I hate you, MacGregor," she stated slowly. "And if I were you, I'd add a measure of soda to Jack's wash. From the stench of it, it needs sweetening."

Later, after the savory venison and barley stew had warmed her, Regina was still angry. MacGregor's smug look, that of a hunter who had caught his quarry, nagged at her.

Satisfied, was he? she stormed silently, fighting the impulse to dump the remainder of her stew over his head. But he'd taken her advice, setting the wash aside to soak as they ate. Venus gnawed on a bone near the corner, and Jack awoke, wailing in hunger. MacGregor was instantly alert, placing his tin cup of coffee aside to prepare Jack's milk.

Tall and dominating the small cabin space, MacGregor was lean and muscular, a certain grace touching his movements.

She'd seen sharks before, almost admired the leisurely manner they approached their prey. MacGregor had that same grace. He was dangerous, possessed with the idea of having a wife and mother for his son. When he settled Jack in his arms, the tenderness in MacGregor's expression tugged at her emotions.

Feeling better, she examined the contents of her traveling chest. Delving inside, she traced the small bump hidden in the satin lining. Her ruby eardrops were still safe; they were the only part of her inheritance her father had let her keep. He wanted to torment her, dangling the rest of the jewels in his grasp.

Regina smiled—the jewels weren't tucked away in the family vault. . . . If she could just manage to escape the mountain man and get back to her saddle—

The small sewing box lay within the trunk, and Regina inspected her drying clothing. Her linens had been torn, the fine French lace damaged, the buttons loosened.

The dark, lonely feeling came stalking her like a cat seeking a plump mouse. In the trunk a velvet riding jacket was torn at the sleeve, a reminder of when Alfred had slapped her. A loosened ruffle streamed from her best blouse, worn for teatime on the American plains. Her French silk pantaloons were tattered, the lace and ribbon shredded.

Suddenly chilled inside, Regina threw the clothing to the floor. Covering her face with her hands, she shuddered, fighting for control. How her father would have loved to see her frightened, cowering like the helpless female he wanted her to be!

Swallowing the last of her quiet sobs, she straightened her shoulders. Clutching the shawl around her, she thought of her father. Hawkes tried to create his daughter, an only child, into a malleable woman. Through Regina, he would have his heir and control over his dead wife's jewels—her marriage dowry, and a legacy from her grandmother. But Regina had refused his selection of suitors. When she took a husband, it would be on her terms.

Her jaw ached, her teeth clamped together tightly. Warmth slid along her side, seeping into her chilled flesh. "Go away, MacGregor."

Raju stepped back to admire Machrajan's smile. "You have my word of honor, Machrajan, I will not run into...

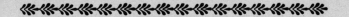

FOUR

"I'M tying your hands now, ma'am," MacGregor said quietly beside her.

Regina's heart jumped frantically when she looked up into the shadows, meeting his quiet stare. Her fingers twisted in her skirt, bunching the dirty fabric. "Why?"

He lifted a heavy eyebrow at her before answering too patiently. "Jack's needing a bath. And you might take a queer notion into your head. He might get cold while I'm messing with you."

Regina's eyebrows shot up, her expression indignant. "Messing with me?"

"Mmm, you might get some silly female notion—"

"I have had enough of your ideas of women needing to be led and tended like sheep. You sweep in here and decide to claim me whether I want to marry you or not . . . oh, of course I have several choices ranging from tribal squaw to being used in a trader's back room. Or I could choose dying here in this cabin."

She tapped her forehead. "I have what is called a brain and a soul. . . . I use them just as any *man* would. Do . . . you . . . understand, Mr. MacGregor?" she asked slowly, spacing her words.

MacGregor's low chuckle filled the cabin. "I savvy, but you're still getting tied."

Regina stepped back to gauge MacGregor's size. "You have my word of honor, MacGregor. I will not run into

51

the wilds just yet. But you will not tie my hands. I will fight you—"

"Females," he muttered, then bent and in one smooth motion picked her up, carrying her to the fire. Before Regina could lash out, her wrists were neatly tied by a leather thong. MacGregor wrapped a fur about her, tucking her feet beneath a fold. Crouching beside her, he grinned at her furious expression and tapped her on the nose with his finger. "Stay put."

Blowing a strand of hair back from her face, Regina glared at him. "You realize this is quite unbecoming of a gentleman, MacGregor. I should call you out for damaging my honor. But I'll forgive you if you untie me . . . now." She thrust out her tied wrists.

When she raised her arms higher for his inspection, the torn edges of her sleeves fell back, and his expression stilled. Taking her wrists in one hand, he turned her pale arms gently until the bruised inner sides were exposed to the firelight.

MacGregor's large thumb ran across the purple mottled patches, lightly testing them. Watching his hand skim across her skin, Regina held her breath and gathered her strength to fight.

His thumb slid slowly along her wrists as he studied the pale flesh and the reddened nail scratches put there by harsh hands. The brush of his skin chilled her, made her ache to scream, the gentle touch more frightening than the rough, determined hands.

When she trembled, MacGregor slid his other hand along her neck, his fingers gently easing aside the snarled strands. His touch skimmed across her sensitive flesh, warming it. He breathed unevenly, and the soft sound tore at her nerves. "If you're quite finished—"

She closed her eyes as he urged her chin higher, running his fingers across her swollen jaw and down her throat. He shifted, and she braced herself to fight.

"Jack put up a squall when they brought you here— had to settle him down before I closed in on the cabin. He squalls sometimes at the wrong time. . . . By then the men were gone and you were moving around—mad as a wet hen—looking as if you wanted to strip the hide off the first man who showed himself."

He looked away, the flames running a red pattern across his cheeks and catching in his black beard. "Maybe they had time, the three of them. . . . If you're with child now, it will be mine. Any child you drop will get the same treatment as Jack." MacGregor's large hand eased upward, lightly tracing a path to her temple. Lifting a heavy wave aside, he examined her forehead. She winced as he lightly probed a large bruise.

"Drop," she repeated flatly. "You mean like a cow drops a calf?"

"Yes, ma'am," MacGregor said softly, arranging the fur more closely around her slender neck. "No offense. But when I'm done with Jack, you need a wash."

Regina turned her face to the fire, ignoring him as he crouched beside her. "You could allow me privacy, MacGregor," she said quietly.

"Privacy won't help the festering. You need tending," he returned as quietly, turning to test the water placed near the fire. "You're having a wash next."

Lifting Jack carefully into the large pan, MacGregor quickly bathed his son. He chuckled as the baby splashed, the deep pleased male sound at odds with the baby's gurgling. Regina watched, fascinated as MacGregor's large hands fashioned a clean cloth about the baby's bottom and gently wrapped him in a warm flannel gown and a small embroidered blanket. His expression warmed when Jack struck him in the nose. "There now, Jack."

Forgetting her anger for a moment, Regina looked closely at the pattern of daisies and bluebells stitched across the blanket. Jack's black shock of hair, a reminder of his Indian heritage, contrasted the delicate pattern. His father caught the flailing fist in his lips, staying the baby. MacGregor's hard mouth tugged playfully at the tiny hand as he folded Jack close against his chest. Taking the tin from a pan of warm water, MacGregor eased a milk saturated cloth into his hungry son's mouth.

As she watched, father and son exchanged a long look that tore at her heart. Regina looked away from the intimacy into the fire, uneasy with the memories of her father.

"The marquess's power feeds on your hatred," Jennifer had crooned years ago. *"Your day will come, and then he'll be frightened of losing everything. Remember the legends, my lass . . . remember. . . . "*

A spray of sparks shot from a pinecone and Regina frowned, her head throbbing. Whispers clawed at her without words. Like the wind, the whispers slid around her, beckoning her. What were the stories?

Looking into the flames and hearing Jack's suckling noises ease, she swallowed the dry wadding of emotion in her throat. "I am so tired," she murmured, fighting the tears burning her lids.

MacGregor eased Jack into his warm nest, covering him carefully. "Easy, boy," he murmured softly, watching his sleeping son take one last shuddering sigh.

When the westerner gently freed her bound wrists, Regina realized she had been dozing. The fire blazed now, heating the room against the howling winds.

"Time for your bath," he said gently, tugging away the fur. Watching her quietly, MacGregor reached to unfasten the first button of her dress. When she jerked back from his touch, he nodded toward the steaming pan of water and his flannel shirt, neatly folded on a hearthstone. "You're next. I'll do your backside—"

She swallowed, instantly awake. "Oh, no, you're not. I'm perfectly capable of taking care of my own needs. Thank you."

MacGregor eased open her top button, watching her. "You have a choice—undress by yourself, or I'll do it for you. But I want to see every inch of that scrawny white hide myself before we get on the trail."

Struggling to her feet, Regina looked down at him, her eyes narrowed. "Scrawny white hide—you oaf! I can tend to my toiletries without you leering like some laughing—"

MacGregor lifted a heavy brow. He stood slowly, reminding her of his great size. Placing his hands on his lean hips, he tilted his head to one side and studied her as though she were an unruly child.

"Woman, you've got a fast tongue. But I'm seeing what they've done to you myself."

Regina backed away a step, kicking her skirt out of the way. "Very well, you have pushed me to the edge of my endurance. I shall have to tutor you in a manner you understand—violence. You ought to be ashamed, MacGregor. A man your size—" She glanced about the room, searching for a weapon. Finding none, Regina glanced at him, reached down to sweep up the back hem of her skirt to draw it through her legs, fashioning loose pants. She lifted her fists in front of her. "Come on, then, fight me. I'm told I'm quite proficient—"

"For a flea." MacGregor smiled then, his teeth showing whitely against the black beard. When he chuckled, Regina lashed out a foot, catching the back of his knee. Locking his legs and widening his stance, the mountain man crossed his arms over his chest unmoved by her attack.

Regina thrust out a finger, poking him in the chest. Beneath the shirt, there was no yielding, flabby flesh. Nothing but muscle and bone. She swallowed and continued, "I spent a summer with the French Basque shepherds—foot boxers, champions."

Amusement deepened in his flashing eyes as he tucked an errant lock behind her ear in a lightening quick movement. "Uh-huh. You're taking a bath, ma'am—"

"You're toying with me as though I were a child." Her foot shot out again, striking his flat, muscled stomach.

"Ooof!" MacGregor stepped back, grinned wider, and began unbuttoning his shirt. When he exposed a thick patch of black hair covering a tanned chest, Regina's mouth went dry. Over the hard muscles the crisp hair formed a vee down to his navel. . . .

Her heart racing, she faced him. The mountain man circled her slowly, forcing her into a dark corner. He reached out, and she chopped his forearm lightly with the side of her hand. The blow, meeting hard muscle and sinew, jarred her to the shoulder. Her fingers slid away, brushing the twin scars covering his chest. "MacGregor, truly you have been kind, but—"

"Yes, ma'am?" he asked politely as though he had all the time in the world. "Truly?"

She ignored his mockery. "I . . . might need bathing. But I am no small child. I can tend to myself," she finished weakly. "Perhaps you could look after the stock until I finish."

Sidestepping her next kick, he wrapped a hand around her ankle. While she balanced on one foot, he said, "You have my word that I'll treat you just like Jack, ma'am. But I want to see—"

"My scrawny hide. As though I were a plucked chicken for the stewpot," she finished for him, balancing precariously as he lifted her foot higher.

MacGregor's large thumb swept slowly along her ankle as though testing the smooth skin. "Yes, ma'am."

She eyed him warily, struggling for balance. He was teasing her, his thumb sweeping her insole playfully. She ignored the ticklish sensation, scowling at him. "MacGregor, no one has bathed me since I was a child. I insist upon privacy."

The long hard fingers tightened on her ankle, and MacGregor's tall body was suddenly too still. "No one?" he asked softly. "At your age?"

Hopping aside, Regina glared at him. "What do you mean, 'at my age'?"

He released her ankle, and she stood free, trembling with anger. "Hell. You aren't exactly a spring chicken," he stated flatly, looking at her more closely.

Glaring at him, Regina walked to the fire. "Of course, I'm not. But I'm not in my dotage, either. Stop staring at me as though you've just seen a dinosaur."

Watching her thoughtfully, MacGregor scratched his chest, fingers rummaging through the coarse hair. In a quick rippling movement he stripped his shirt and tossed it aside. Covered with hair that veed down to his trousers which hung low on his waist, MacGregor's chest was broad and heavily muscled. His flat nipples peeked through the crisp black hair and shifted over the muscles as he ran his fingers across his skin. Layers and ridges of muscles ran across his flat stomach, his dark skin gleaming. He shifted, legs apart, and the trousers slipped an inch lower to reveal an untanned strip of flesh.

Regina forced her eyes to meet his. Within the folds of her skirt, her fingertips moved restlessly against her thigh. With an effort she forced her nails to bite into her leg. "If you will step outside for a moment, MacGregor, I can bathe by myself."

"No. I want to see every inch for myself—"

Regina's chin went up as she finished his sentence again. "Of my scrawny hide. You are so complimentary. Heavens, you would make the ladies at court swoon with delight—"

Moving toward her, MacGregor grinned. "Take off your clothes."

She thrust out her open palm, staying him. "If you touch me again, I'll cheerfully geld you."

Chuckling at her, he reached into his bags to extract a tin. Opening it, he thrust it beneath her nose. The pungent smell shot up her nostrils, causing her to grimace. "Smell that. Butterfly root, leaves—Indian cure-all. You need it painted on those scratches, or you'll get the fever. I've seen marks like those take a good man down after days of being out of his head. You drink Indian tea to go with it, and you'll be fine."

Regina shifted uncomfortably. She rubbed her hand down her bruised arm, the scratches hot beneath her touch. "Very well. I can see the difficulties of an infection in the wilds."

Placing the tin aside, MacGregor poured more steaming water into the large pan. Bending slightly, his trousers tightened on firm haunches and heavy thighs. When he straightened the fabric cupped his bold masculinity, and Regina's thoughts scooted back to the marble statues, their sex clearly molded amid the leaves of the family garden. Firelight traced a firm ridge of muscle sliding down his arm.

Inhaling sharply, Regina closed her lids. MacGregor wasn't a statue in her father's garden; every inch of the mountain man threatened emotions deep within her.

Shivering slightly, she forced her attention to the salve, sniffing it. "Hmm. Hardly rosewater, then." Regina looked at Jack's warm soapy water, desperately wanting to bathe. She hated the feel of the men's hands roaming her skin— yet to have a man look at her without clothing . . .

She turned to MacGregor, leveling a hard stare at him. "I have your word, then."

Nodding solemnly, he reached out to take a small twig from her knotted hair. He tossed it into the blazing fire, then took the huge Bowie knife from its sheath at his waist and handed it to her. She gripped the handle, the heavy weight uncomfortable in her hand. "You have the word of MacGregor . . . but if I can't restrain myself, I'd prefer you used a good sharp blade to cut me. Or geld me."

Regina ignored the taunt and lifted her chin. "Turn about, then, while I disrobe."

He nodded slowly at the knife held in her hand. "I'd take it kindly, ma'am, if you wouldn't try to use Old Hugh in my back."

Regina lifted the blade, running her thumb along the honed edge. "Old Hugh?"

When he nodded, she averted her head to hide a quick smile. So the black knight had named his sword "Old Hugh," she decided, examining the leather-wrapped handle.

"I shall try to restrain myself, MacGregor. Though the thought has certain appeal. Turn about." When he turned slowly, crossing his arms, Regina's breath caught. The scars of a bullwhip crisscrossed his broad back. On his upper shoulder a circle of reddened flesh surrounded an angry, puckered wound. Her fingers stretched out to trace a deep ridge lightly. "Gads, you need attention yourself, MacGregor!"

"Woman, are you part chattering magpie?" His shoulder shrugged away her light touch. "Get on with it."

Her fingers trembled as she undressed quickly, shivering despite the flames at her back. Grabbing his clean shirt, she held it in front of her. "You may turn around. But remember your promise."

The sight of his back held her. She'd seen oxen mistreated like that by her father. Watching his face as he turned, she trembled as his gaze stroked down her body.

His eyes darkened as he looked at her shoulder, bruises mottled the smooth slope forming the shape of a rough hand.

Taking the soapy cloth, MacGregor began to wash her. He gently cleansed a long scratch running from her throat downward to her upper breast. Easing the shirt aside, he patted the cloth along a bloody ridge.

Closing her eyes, Regina forced herself to breathe slowly, dragging the air into her lungs. No man had ever seen her fully undressed, and the humiliation of her helpless struggles against the three men returned.

Would their unclean touch remain forever? she wondered, averting her head.

Kneeling before her, MacGregor gently tugged on the hem of the shirt. When she held it firmly, shaking her head in denial, he continued to wash the nail marks on her inner thigh.

The marks were deep, infected, and as he bent close, patting the soapy cloth lightly, she tensed. "Easy now," he reminded her softly, inspecting the wounds. "They're festering."

When his fingers pressed against her thigh gently, urging her to spread her legs, Regina breathed sharply and clutched his shirt desperately. She had been shamed enough by men's hands—"No. That's enough."

MacGregor took her fingers, holding them. His thumb ran across the back of her skinned knuckles. Looking up at her, he said slowly, "There's a deep gash running around your leg to your backside. It's festering."

Fighting years of hiding her body, Regina fought also for control. Waiting, MacGregor began to apply salve to her upper body. When he returned to her thighs, Regina forced her legs to move apart. His fingers worked gently at the scratches between her legs, and she inhaled softly when his warm breath slid across her skin. She hadn't expected her body's moist heated response to his light touch, nor the need to touch him.

For just an instant she wanted to feel his arms hold her safely as he had held Jack. But she wanted more . . . to rummage her fingers through the dark crisp hair covering his chest, to stroke the scars on his back, soothing him. MacGregor had seen hell, and she wanted to erase that pain. She closed her eyes, fighting to remember that the man wanted to claim her as he would a lost cow.

MacGregor worked quickly, efficiently dabbing the salve on when he was finished. "Turn around."

Regina gripped the shirt tightly when he dampened the cloth, dabbing lightly at a wide patch of scraped skin where she had been dragged by the men. Her grip on the knife tightened. He breathed roughly once as she sidled from the cloth, the fiery pain soon eased by his salve. "That place is bad," he murmured.

He bent to unwrap her feet, tossing the rags aside. Taking her ankle, he placed her foot in the warm soapy water to wash it thoroughly. Unbalanced for a moment, Regina placed her hand on his shoulder. Tendons and muscles slid beneath her touch, warm and steely, working smoothly beneath the surface.

With his head bowed MacGregor cleansed and dried each foot, then slid them into his large stockings. After tugging the heavy knitted tops over her knees he stood and placed his hands on his hips. "We'll have to do that again tomorrow."

He swept a glance at her legs, then turned away. "Ah . . . you might want to scrub a bit more . . . privately."

The intimacy of his request caused Regina's cheeks to heat. Regina lifted his shirt and, using the cloth, cleansed herself of the men's hands before she looked at him again.

The flames lit his face; hell blazed in his eyes, hidden beneath the thick shield of lashes. Then the moment was gone.

After lifting her hair free of the collar, he turned to scowl at the fire. Pitch exploded in a small cone, and a flurry of sparks shot out onto a hearthstone. MacGregor watched the tiny coals, a vein showing in his temple. Regina watched the primitive beat of his blood throb beneath the weathered skin. His large hand reached out to settle upon his empty leather scabbard as though searching for the Bowie handle. "Fresh water is heating in the bucket. There's mud in your hair. Needs a washing."

Regina's hand shot to her hair. She remembered falling behind the horses and being dragged by her hair. She shuddered, remembering the coarse laughter. "Of course."

After refilling the basin with fresh hot water, he stood aside and waited for her to kneel. She glanced up to see his eyes crinkle at the sides. "Looks like a bird's nest," he said, the deep voice touched by humor. "Makes a man wonder why women have so much of the stuff. Or Indians, either. Though theirs is some neater."

"My dishabille is not my fault, MacGregor," Regina returned stoutly. "And for your future information, a lady does not like to be reminded that she is . . . mussed."

He chuckled again, that low unused sound like the purring of a Bengal man-eating tiger. When she sniffed and began plucking out her remaining pins, carefully placing them on a stone, MacGregor eased down to his knees. He took a strand, running his fingers down the length, gauging it.

Taking care, he eased the strands apart, stopping as she winced. "Ouch!"

Patting her head gently, MacGregor said, "This is worse than burrs in a horse's tail. We could cut it off," he suggested when she shot him an angry glance.

"I will not use my good brushes on dirty hair," she stated haughtily. "Nor will I cut my hair. I can manage."

When she began plucking at the snarls, MacGregor shook his head and delved his fingers into the strands, patiently easing them apart.

There was tenderness and safety in his touch, and she knew why the baby quieted when being handled by MacGregor.

She turned aside, tucking her chin within the folds of the shirt. She hadn't asked him to help her, and his kindness hurt her as surely as a wasp's sting. To conceal her pain, she lifted her chin and said coolly, "You know, once I saw apes preening each other. Picking lice and eating them. I do hope you're not expecting me to return the favor."

His fingers stilled, then began working again. "You're not at the lice stage yet, ma'am. And I've already had my food. Hold still."

Regina blinked back the tears she'd held for a lifetime. "You're heavy-handed for a maid, MacGregor," she lashed out at him, arching away from his hands.

"Settle down. I'm not doing any more for you than I would my horse." She noted a new tiredness in his voice, the thought stilling her.

Finally the heavy mass tumbled down her back, and he lowered her head forward over the pan. MacGregor eased the wild strands into the water and began to work quietly, methodically. His large hands scrubbed a bar of soap along the strands and mopped her face dry every now and then as though she were Jack. Then he poured more warm water over her head, and Regina came up struggling for breath. "You are trying to drown me!"

He laughed outright, placing a clean heavy cloth over her head. Rubbing it briskly, he ignored her indignant cries. "This isn't a laughing matter, MacGregor!"

When Regina finally struggled free of his grip, she realized he had been playing with her like a grizzly with a cub. She tossed the towel to the floor, stamping her foot and shaking her damp hair down her back. "You did that on purpose, MacGregor. You purposely tried to drown and suffocate me. Tried to kill me!"

His mouth turned up, and for a moment the wrinkles fanning from his eyes deepened.

"If you weren't such a woolly-faced scoundrel, I could tell if you were laughing," she accused hotly. "As it is, behind that bush, heaven knows what you're doing! I should shear you like one of my sheep."

"Yes, ma'am. But with winter coming a man likes his face warm."

"Oh!" Snatching her brushes from her case, Regina sat

cross-legged in front of the fire and began brushing her hair.

She was suddenly too tired for the task, soothed by the feeling of being clean and the warmth of the fire. When MacGregor took her brushes and handed her a cup of tea, she studied the leaves swirling in the bottom of her cup. "Mr. MacGregor, you'll do well to remember that I have a nasty temper. And at the moment I would very much like to lift that thick black scalp from your arrogant head."

"I'll remember," he said quietly.

She half-turned, studying him over her shoulder. He held the brushes awkwardly, one in each hand as he waited. The shadows beneath his eyes caused her to turn back to the fire. The mountain man was deeply tired, needing his rest. Yet he would see his task through. "Start at the ends and work up," she ordered softly.

MACGREGOR stirred in his furs, instantly awake when Regina rose from her pallet. The woman stood over him like a shadow. He breathed quietly, feigning sleep when she bent to lift Jack into her arms.

"Your father is a black devil, little MacGregor," she whispered in hushed, lilting tones, moving away from him to the fire. "With a beautiful son," she added, nuzzling Jack's dark head. "Such a sweet baby you are, my lad."

In the hours hovering between night and dawn, Regina changed Jack and prepared his milk, adding fuel to the fire. MacGregor lay still, watching her tend his son, rocking the tiny body against her. Feeding Jack near the fire, Regina wrapped them both in her fur robe.

She talked softly to the boy, and Jack cooed back at her, the sounds blending into a music that soothed MacGregor as he lay listening.

MacGregor knew she was curing herself, making her medicine. Holding Jack had done that for him, too. When she lifted Jack to her shoulder, Regina kissed the baby's cheek, and MacGregor's heart skipped a beat.

Long ago a lost child lay sobbing in a cold, dark cell, stripped of clothing to shame him and needing the closeness of a mother's touch. MacGregor pressed his lips together. He was no longer a child, begging for scraps from the priest's well-stocked table. But he wanted everything for his son—food and the warmth of a mother's arms holding him in a fever.

The Englishwoman whispered and sang a hushed lullaby, rocking the baby. Wrapped in her thoughts, she was unaware of anything but his child. She laughed softly, a low wispy sound, and Jack cooed in response. "You know, poor child, I thought your father was the black knight, rising out of the moors. He is fierce-looking and very much in need of manners. I will thrash him soundly when I'm stronger," she confided softly to the baby. "He's hardly the knight I dreamed about as a girl. Every young girl dreams the same, you know . . . waiting for her knight to sweep her away on his mighty steed, taking her to his castle to live happily evermore. . . ."

MacGregor closed his eyes, listening as she began to sing in a high clear voice. The words were unfamiliar, mentioning a lost love and the music of Greensleeves, yet beautiful as a mockingbird's trill. The pleasant sound floated over him, soothing him as her fingers had soothed his scars.

She'd frightened him then, stunning him with the lightest touch and making him ache for more.

MacGregor turned, reaching out a hand to touch her empty pallet. The heat of her body still warmed the furs.

He was damned tired, he decided, running his palm over the lush pelt. His shoulder ached, and the years weighted him now. A muscle tightened along his jaw, coursing down his throat, the bile rising in his mouth. Of mixed blood, Jack wouldn't be forgotten in a missionary school as he had been—

Her laughter rose sweetly behind him, and MacGregor listened, entranced by the sound that reminded him of water coursing through a rippling stream, sunlit and bubbly.

He'd chosen Jack's new mother well.

When she tucked Jack in his nest and returned to her pallet, MacGregor allowed her to remove his hand from

the fur. He liked the touch of her slender fingers on his
wrist, easing it upon his chest.

He sighed then, turning away from her to the fire.

The screams of the dying came creeping after him in
the night, and then he waited for the dawn to chase them
away.

LORD Alfred Covington strode across the Persian
carpet covering the prairie grass. His whip beat the crimson
wall of his tent rhythmically. Then he threw himself to his
bed of buffalo robes covered by Irish linen. The whip struck
dully against the pelt of a Bengal tiger as the earl stared at
Krebs.

"He should have wounded you higher," he shot at the
man rubbing the bandage on his thigh. "You surely have
no need of your manhood when you can't even complete
the murder of a woman."

"She ain't ordinary female flesh," Krebs returned in a
surly tone. "Took three of us to drag her off her pony."

"That bitch isn't dead, is she, Krebs?" Covington asked
too quietly, the whip thudding ominously against the pelts.
He threw it against an ornate Turkish incense burner, then
studied the dark red coals. They reminded him of Regina's
ruby eardrops and the fortune her death could bring him.

"No, sir," Krebs answered in a whine. "A wild man came
out of the trees just like Old Ephraim—"

"Old Ephraim," Covington repeated the mountain man
phrase carefully. "Mountain bear?"

"Aye. Mean he was. With black, glittering eyes."

"A bitch and a bastard, then," Covington said, picking
up the whip to poke the coals. "I needed those eardrops as
proof of her death, Krebs."

"He can shoot, sir. Knew where to place bullets so as not
to break bone, he did. Took a shot in the back like it was
nothing."

"Filled with mercy, was he? I'm not feeling that par-
ticular tenderness myself now, Krebs." Covington turned
on his henchman, who shivered in fear. "As the fiancé of
the only legal Mortimer-Hawkes child and granddaughter

of that foreign woman, I am entitled by her death to half her family inheritance. Lord Mortimer-Hawkes would fall heir to the remainder."

The earl frowned, the cruelty in his long, thin face sharpening as he poked the scented coals. "By fathering her child, I could have had the entire fortune at my disposal after the marquess's death. . . . I would have enjoyed watching her whelp. She needs reminding of her proper place."

"Yes, sir." Krebs shifted toward the tent flap, watching the Englishman's face. The hired man had killed the other two men after the mountain man rode away. If Covington were to discover how they had planned to keep the woman—

"Bring me her ears, Krebs. With the rubies in them. And kill the bastard with her. But make him pay first," Covington ordered tightly. "Send in that Indian squaw as you leave. She needs me to remind her of her place, just like the Lady Mortimer-Hawkes."

The whip lashed at the Bengal tiger pelt again. "I've changed my mind. The lady can wait. Ryker can track her easily enough with those purple eyes and raven, curling hair . . . though with that ugly dark skin, she'd pass for a squaw. I want to take a few more days clearing out the buffalo. Once I have her ears, I'm heading for England and that damned Bedouin bag of jewels that Mortimer-Hawkes keeps throwing at me. Without it I wouldn't have stained my good name with that savage-tempered bitch."

FIVE

MacGregor awoke instantly, his finger tightening on the pistol's trigger. Shifting beneath his buffalo robe, he turned toward the sound and slowly opened his eyes.

The woman sat with her legs crossed, her back to him as she faced the blazing fire. Water heated in the metal buckets, her china cup delicate against the flat stone of the hearth.

The bare light coming through the cloth covering the window touched her, framing her from the shadows. She dipped the cloth into the water, soaping and rinsing herself in languid, graceful movements.

Regina's long hair flowed down her bare back and MacGregor's palm moved restlessly, remembering the rippling mass. She had washed it again, the damp strands forming curls at her hips. In the daylight it would be blue-black as a raven's wing catching the sun.

Something stilled him as he watched her, the flickering light playing about her dark, feminine outline. The soft slope of her breast ran down into a small waist and MacGregor began to harden. He'd never watched a woman bathe, and the sight fascinated him.

There was beauty in her movements, the gentle sway of her hair as she moved. Like white doves, her hands floated over the rippling strands that shifted, tantalizing him with the curves of her body. Firelight danced across her skin, licking at her long, thick curls. She lifted and spread the heavy strands, the movements seductive, revealing and taunting him with the sight of her body. She moved like a willow swaying in the wind, the sinewy rippling of a cat.

One that needed petting, he decided as the firelight flickered on her body. She moved, lifting, swaying, turning, stretching slender arms high. MacGregor wanted that pale body weaving, stroking his, hip against hip.

Dressed in her drawers, the woman reminded him of the greyhound, Venus. Sleekly formed, with soft breasts and haunches. The rounded curve of her hip moved slightly, and MacGregor rubbed his palm against his chest.

She was soft. That woman scent filled the cabin now. The light scent of wood violets blended with a deeper musk that stirred and tantalized him. He closed his eyes, remembering the heady scent of cinnamon and woman as he'd bathed her spread thighs.

The wind had risen, howling outside the drafty cabin. He should be checking on Jack, but the sight of the woman bathing bound him. He moved slightly, positioning for a better view of the Englishwoman seated before the flames. In profile her eyes were closed, her arms moving gracefully as she cleansed the length of her throat. The water glistened on her skin, the muffled sounds of her bathing almost like music.

There were soft sighs of pleasure as the water streamed down her body; a drop clung and shimmered on the very tip of her breast.

MacGregor's fingers moved through the lush fur covering him, remembering the silky skin.

The firelight danced on her skin, outlining her body. With the dark cloud of damp hair sweeping down her back, her skin was light as a fawn's.

Old Hugh rested across her lap, the steel blade glistening in the light.

Was she praying? He knew there were those who had a god. In the war they had called out to him for help. But their answer was shot and cannon.

He'd learned long ago that the world was a lonely island, filled with pain and hunger. He'd fought the loneliness as a child, then as a man found himself leaning into it like an old friend.

Then there was Jack and now the woman, whose swaying, graceful movements reminded him of a cat.

She was cleansing herself, distancing herself from pain and fear, and drawing on her inner strength. There was a hard curve to her mouth, and MacGregor studied her intently. Yet her touch had run softly across his back, tracing the scars. Her fingertips had brushed his palm in her sleep.

She'd frightened him then with her soft touch. Like a butterfly's wings brushing across his back. And he'd responded how he knew best, by lashing out at her.

The humming stopped and she stood slowly. MacGregor's heartbeat slowed as he watched, his mouth drying for the taste of her. She was pale and thin, more like a girl than a woman, her hipbones prominent when she loosened her drawers and they fell to the floor.

Pale buttocks shimmered and shifted slowly, the soft flesh just waiting for his palm.

MacGregor skimmed her long legs, remembering the silky feel of them beneath his fingers as he applied the salve. Once his hand brushed that soft nest of curls at the top of her thighs and he'd caught that musky sweet fragrance rising from her flesh.

The firelight danced on the upward tilt of the woman's breasts. They were small and shimmered as she bent, the tips pointed—his hand trembled, curling into a fist.

Just above the soft rise of her buttock, dimples created small shadows that he wanted to trace with his fingertips. In the shadows behind her knee the softest patch of skin enticed him. . . .

Stirring restlessly, he forced himself to quiet. He was hard, needing her, shivering with a painful heat that wouldn't be smothered.

When he wanted a woman, it was a quick toss beneath the blankets or furs. He'd taken his ease and not lingered past his paid time. Yet the Englishwoman's small body excited him more than the lush weight of a full-blown woman.

Regina turned slightly, pointed the blade at the fire, and drew a line down the center of her body.

MacGregor understood instantly and frowned. The woman had taken an oath for revenge.

She'd have to fight getting away from him first. It wouldn't do for his woman to go man hunting.

Placing the blade on a stone, she stood and began to bathe quietly, running a cloth down her body. The slender waist curved into narrow hips and the line of her thigh. . . . She bent, spreading her legs to let the water run down her inner thighs.

MacGregor swallowed the dry wad of longing suddenly lodged in his throat. She was too slight, her breasts barely filled his hands. Closing her eyes, she ran the soapy cloth down her flat stomach, rinsing the curling nest below. Then soaping the area, she parted her legs, resting one on the hearth as she bathed herself intimately. A soft length of thigh glistened damply and MacGregor's blood started heating. He couldn't remember the last time the softness of a woman's thighs gripped his hips, accepting his plunging body.

The women he'd known worked for pay and spent little time at the game, accepting a quick, rough ride as their due. MacGregor swallowed tightly. There was something soft and new in the Hawkes woman, her violet eyes clear as though she hadn't known a man. He thought of them darkening with anger and softening as she touched Jack.

Her skin had quivered beneath his touch, her body tense. He wondered how she would feel moving beneath him like heated silk. Instinctively he knew the woman hadn't known many men, nor let them touch her. Nor let them watch her bathe—

The thought that he'd be holding her, touching that rippling skin, and seeking out her moistness caused MacGregor to tremble.

Desire skimmed across him, torching his skin; his heart pounding heavily within his chest.

She was his woman, wasn't she? He gritted his teeth, recognizing the hot need riding his body. He'd made up his mind to marry her, and a ceremony would come as soon as they could find a preacher.

A strand of black hair caught on her breast, webbing a fine mesh across the soft, glistening skin until the dark tip peeked through. She turned her back and presented MacGregor with a slender, tapering line to a tiny waist and surprisingly soft rounded hips flowing down to long legs.

MacGregor's muffled groan swept down his taut body. He'd been without a woman for a year, finding that prostitutes couldn't cure his chilling nightmares.

After her bath Regina drew on his shirt, rolling the sleeves back to fit her. She glanced at him and found him watching her intently.

"You've been spying, MacGregor. In Malapor the rajah would have your eyes put out for such a trespass," she whispered huskily.

"Blood-thirsty little witch, aren't you?" he answered mildly, throwing off the heavy fur.

Her eyes widened, flowing down his hard body. Lying amid the furs, his dark length blended with the buffalo pelt. His beard gave way to the black hair spreading across his chest and tapering down his flat stomach. For a lean man, his thighs were heavier, his pale legs long and covered by a rough surface of hair.

Regina had never seen a man's body unclothed. His lines were fluid and beautiful, the muscles shifting beneath his dark skin as he rolled his wounded shoulder slowly. There was whipcord strength beneath his skin, his stomach flat and hard. She found herself wanting to touch the muscles there, probe them.

She shivered, angry with herself. She'd just been mauled by three men. "You haven't a stitch on, MacGregor. Cover yourself."

"I want you." MacGregor's deep rasp slid across her damp skin as he rose and padded slowly toward her.

The firelight cast orange ribbons across his tall body, lashing at the width of his shoulders and streaming down the narrow length of his hips. Aroused and walking toward her, MacGregor did not shield his need.

"You can't have me!" Regina backed away a step and instantly realized her mistake. MacGregor's tall body had forced her into a drafty corner. Desire throbbed out of him, burning her flesh.

In the cramped space she couldn't move, her breath tight in her chest. MacGregor loomed over her in the shadows. "I don't intend to debate the matter, ma'am. You're my woman from now on. We'll be married as soon as we can. But until then, we'll just have to make things do. Later there'll be time for knowing, but not now," he said rawly, his gaze shooting down the unbuttoned shirt. "I'll be easy, but I intend to stake my claim."

Gathering the shirt against her, she muttered, "Of all the nerve."

"Yes, ma'am," he agreed easily, taking a step nearer. "Won't take a minute, and then we can be on our way."

Her eyebrows lifted sharply. "You are an oaf! You actually expect me to submit to your animal urges?"

His finger reached out suddenly and skimmed a warm trail down her throat to a point between her breasts. "Yes, ma'am. Plenty of deals are made on the blanket. This is an honest one by my way of thinking. I like to stake my claim on what's mine and keep it."

"Oh! You're talking about me as though I were a horse needing branding!"

His broad palm slid down the front of the shirt, catching the hem and tugging it gently aside, despite her fists wrapped in the fabric. "I'm wanting my woman. It's as simple as that," he said quietly, scooping her up in his arms and carrying her to his pallet.

MacGregor's weight trapped her beneath him before she could slip away. He quickly stripped away the shirt and tossed it aside, then held both her wrists in one hand.

She wanted to scream, to fight him and the other men who had pawed her. But MacGregor's size and strength easily captured her. He thrust intimately against her inner thigh, a sheathed blend of silk and steel. When she bucked against him, trying to dislodge his grip, MacGregor's harsh breath swept across her hot cheek.

Fear went slithering through her like a snake; a brief memory of the smell of rotted teeth and unwashed bodies swept over her, and she shuddered.

Breathing quietly, she brought herself back from those men and their hurting hands. Lying beneath him, she struggled for control, accepting his greater strength. . . . MacGregor had not hurt her. His scent was of wood smoke and soap. His hair had caught the fragrance of the mountain pines and cold, crisp air.

His desire ran between them, hot and terrifying. He couldn't know how frightened she was of being taken, the forced submission more costly than his intrusion into her body.

"I am bloody well angry with you, MacGregor," she said between her teeth, breathing heavily.

Easing his weight away from her, MacGregor rested on his elbows, his hard thighs clamping hers still. His desire beat upon her like hot waves, his face harsh with the passionate need.

His heart thudded against her breasts, the rough hair covering his chest brushed her intimately. His hips rested against hers, the hardness probing her thighs gently. He was taut, holding himself from entering her, his eyes glistening with the primitive need.

"What do you want?" he asked harshly, brushing a wet strand away from her face with his lips. "Tell me."

She thrust against him, furious at being weaker, as she had always been in the plans of men. Her father—her mind calmed suddenly, apart from herself and the man looming over her. MacGregor had said there were bargains made on the blanket; perhaps she could strike an arrangement with him.

Fighting a fine edge of fear, Regina thought of a bargain and explored it. Of course she was afraid; this mountain man would be her first man.

With a sense of jumping off the edge of a cliff, Regina inhaled sharply. MacGregor was a kind man to his son and to the animals. She'd have to keep that thought close to her.

She was like any other woman whose time had come to lay with a man. Life had a way of thrusting itself in her face, and now surely she could deal with this, too.

"Loose me, MacGregor," she snapped, balancing her thoughts against the increasing pressure on her leg. The bargaining moment was at hand, she thought warily. He wanted and she wanted . . . an exchange of needs, fairly met would serve them both. "A gentleman doesn't tear at a woman like this. The very idea—I haven't even had my breakfast tea."

The barb caught him broadside, she noted with a small measure of satisfaction. "If you're wanting a bargain to soothe your guilt," she continued, watching his eyes darken, "I can't ride without my favorite saddle. It's a treasured keepsake, and I can't possibly leave without it. If you want me, you'll have to help me get my saddle."

His lids narrowed, his eyes roaming her upturned face. "You're not handing out orders to me, Duchess," he said roughly. "I'm claiming you, simple as that. A woman can expect that from her man. You can squall later, and I'll give you all the foofaraw you want. I'll get you a saddle." He moved slightly, and the tip of his manhood rested against her intimately.

Beckoning slyly, her flesh moistened and softened as if licking at him. Waves of heat ran through her, her thighs softening against his hard ones.

"Foofaraw?" She shifted and realized that he had slipped smoothly into the feminine valley between her legs. Breathing rapidly, Regina closed her eyes, remembering women's stories of tearing flesh beneath grunting, sweating males. She accepted the fate she had fought—she would distance herself, absorbing the pain, and leaving her body as he hurt her. . . .

Fear clawed at her stomach, and she forced herself to concentrate on the gentle way his hands had moved over the animals and Jack.

But she was a woman lying beneath a man for her first time, not a horse or a baby.

"Foofaraw—pretties, gifts women like. Maybe money after I sell my spring furs," he explained rawly, his hot face finding the soft curve of her neck and shoulder. "Let me in. . . ." he asked quietly, waiting for her response.

Against her, his large body trembled, and she found her hand smoothing the scars covering the taut muscles of his back. How vulnerable this rugged man seemed now, how needing. . . .

Regina struggled to keep her emotions away from the task ahead. She was striking a bargain after all and couldn't let a momentary softness interfere.

"Then I claim my saddle and you can have me. This once. Then you'll take me off the mountain." Trembling, Regina knew she had sold her body, but the rough mountain man knew the wilderness, and he could complete her task. Once the jewels and her safety were assured. . . . She could feel his blood pound into her, the raw need driving him, trembling through him, barely leashed.

She . . . would . . . not . . . be . . . afraid. She thought of beautiful poetry and lover's warm words and the romantic knights of King Arthur. She had dreamed of her first time being a sweet, sweet song. . . .

Perhaps Lady Guinevere had the leisure to be afraid, but Regina dealt with reality.

He rubbed his chest against her, a luxurious, slow movement that caused him a sigh of pleasure. The deep male sound swirled about her, the aching need woven about it. "Done," he whispered. "You'll have what you want."

Regina swallowed uncomfortably, realizing that for some odd reason, her lower body had gone as soft as velvet. Sheathing his hard length between her legs, yet without him entering her body, she began to melt. Damp and warm, a fullness ached and needed tending in her lower stomach and trembling thighs.

Of course she could fight him, make him pay painfully. But he'd have her finally. Or would he? There was something waiting in him, waiting for her to yield or to fight. She sensed that with a word she could stay him from his course.

In her lifetime she'd seen little male tenderness, yet now the heat of his eyes was only for her. Once she'd wanted that look and found no man looking at her as though he adored her.

His firm lips had a tempting curve she wanted to experience against her own. . . .

"Are you so set upon this course, MacGregor?" she asked in a husky whisper that barely resembled her voice.

"Yes, ma'am," he answered adamantly, trembling against her. "I think . . . I'll die if I don't have you now." The admission was roughly spoken, but Regina knew the strength of his feelings.

Regina closed her eyes, inhaling his fresh scent blended with smoke and pine. "I'd prefer a gentler approach, MacGregor. Then, of course, you can expect to be killed later . . . if you don't keep to your gentleman's word. I'll start by shooting off your toes and then working my way upward. . . . Perhaps I'll scalp you like the heathen you are. Perhaps I'll tan your pelt and nail it to the cabin door. . . ."

Nuzzling her skin, MacGregor's mouth moved against her, causing her to shiver. "I'm hungry for you, not words. Can we do it, so we can get about our business?"

His beard slid across her flesh and a strange aching need fluttered delicately within her.

"I have no idea how to go about this, sir. And if I did, I would do so, then finish you off. Why, you haven't even kissed my hand, much less my mouth, and here you are—"

MacGregor raised over her, his eyes oddly gentle beneath the fierce eyebrows. "Kissing is for children. I'm for the other. At my age I know what I'm about. A hard fast ride takes the poison out of a man—"

She blinked, disbelieving. "Egad!"

Regina shook her head, blushing furiously beneath his warm perusal. "You may be ready to. . . . Kissing is . . . part of courting. Though we're in the wilds and you've proposed . . . I think we should keep to the customary order of events."

"Could we do that later, ma'am?" he asked as his gaze

slid hotly down her body to touch her breasts nestled against his furry chest. He moved slightly, like a big mountain cat nestling to a warm sunny branch, adjusting to the feel and the sway beneath him.

"The kissing first," she began adamantly, then the words drifted away as MacGregor carefully lowered his broad chest to her softness.

He eased against her, flattening her breasts gently as his eyes closed as though he absorbed his pleasure, savored her body flowing against his hard one. "Where?"

Astonished by his question, Regina found herself looking hungrily at his mouth. After all, if he was going to force her to accommodate his mating practices, she should accept with style becoming a lady. And then she would have her saddle, of course. She would keep her part of the bargain. "I've never been adequately kissed on the lips. That would seem a good starting point. Perhaps you could say a sweet word or two along the way."

"Words are empty, it's the bodies that do the loving—"

"Yes, loving. Words like that," she whispered, then moistened her lips with the tip of her tongue. He followed the movement as though he were dying for the taste of her.

What an odd pleasure, she mused. MacGregor had somehow kept her warm and safe and had caught her in a strange, exciting game.

His mouth pressed hard against hers, quickly, then was gone. "Now?" he asked roughly, raising his hips slightly and rubbing himself against her intimately.

Frowning darkly, Regina glared up at him. She might have made a practical bargain, but romance should be kept involved, too. "You're the man. I should think you would have more experience in matters of the heart. Kissing on the lips is supposed to be . . ."

She looked away, shy with her emotions and the dark, lean man who so badly wanted to enter her body. "Sweet. Like a love sonnet. Or tasting jams."

He arched a brow, a slight curve to his hard mouth. "Or honey?"

"Well, yes." Meeting his eyes, Regina swallowed tightly. "Then I'll keep my end of the bargain."

"Foolish." Yet his gaze washed across her hot face, gauging her intently. Then, taking a deep, longing sigh, MacGregor carefully placed his lips over hers. Looking into her eyes, he rubbed his mouth along hers softly. The caress was so light and sweet that Regina closed her eyes, her lips lifting to the warmth of his. Instinctively she knew he was taking care not to harm her. In a tender play she brushed his mouth, pleasure seeping into her as he inhaled sharply.

MacGregor breathed roughly, his eyes glittering beneath his lowered lids. Carefully he shifted, and Regina found him gently probing her feminine opening. Arching away, she found herself warming, flooding damply around his hardness.

He kissed her again, and this time his lips roamed hers, asking sweetly.

Lost in the heady sweet sense of being cherished, Regina allowed her lips to part and meld with his firm ones. Closing her eyes, she enjoyed the slow tasting of his lips against hers, sinking deeply into the gentle taking.

MacGregor's thumb moved slowly across her inner wrist. "You're soft like doeskin. Or like your silk ribbons,"

Before she could protest, the tip of his tongue prowled across her lips to enter her mouth. Catching her breath, Regina watched his dark scowl deepen as he gently probed her mouth, tasting her. The intimate gesture caused heat to flow through her. His hard hips moved slightly between her legs, and she found herself trembling. His tongue flicked again, and feminine muscles deep within Regina contracted suddenly, startling her with pleasure.

The cords within her started heating, her body melting when he entered her gently. A movement of his hips brought him sliding deeper into her moist softness. He let out a deep, ragged groan, his great body trembling over her.

She hadn't bargained for her skin growing taut, her body accepting and dampening at his gentle probes. Realizing the depth of her submission to his powers, sheer terror jolted through her. MacGregor was playing games, taunting her, waving his male arrogance at her. Her head went back, and she glared at him, "Your tongue in my mouth was uncalled for, sir. Truly indecent."

After a moment's silence his voice was low and uneven. "Sorry, ma'am. I just started thinking how sweet and warm you are between your legs and wondered what your mouth would taste like. Can't say I've ever wondered that about a woman. . . . Like I wanted to crawl in and taste and get fever hot—"

"Sweet and warm between my legs? A gentleman would not have said such a thing." Regina tried to swallow, tried to look away from the hot glitter of desire in his eyes. She trembled, her legs feeling as though they were weak, his warm, rough thighs burning against her inner knees.

"It's true," he whispered huskily. "You're so soft and sweet there, too." He shuddered, closing his eyes briefly. "So tight and soft . . . hot."

He slid deeper, and Regina went taut. She'd heard of the blood and pain—yet she was softening, stretching, and allowing him to enter with only the slightest discomfort. "That's enough," she whispered shakily, arching back from him. "I've changed my mind. . . . You're hurting me."

"No, I'm not. You're soft and hot here, wanting me . . . opening to me like rosebud petals to the sun. . . . I liked the kissing," he whispered back gently. "Haven't ever kissed a woman when I was in the saddle before."

"Egad! This is horrible," she whispered, feeling him slide deeper within her. Her body had accepted him, encased him tightly, throbbing against his strength. She ached for more, trembling, wanting to feel his mouth on hers. "Egad, MacGregor," she whispered shakily. "What are we going to do?"

For an answer MacGregor's mouth settled gently over hers. Taking his time, he tugged at her lips with his, running the tip of his tongue across her bottom lip until she parted for him. Thrusting deeply within her mouth, MacGregor suckled her tongue, playing a sweet game that Regina found herself returning.

She wanted to touch him, her fingers moving restlessly as he held her wrists.

MacGregor groaned roughly against her throat and trembled as though staying a beast within him. Gently, pushing a small way deeper within her, he sighed and Regina found herself heating, seeking his mouth hungrily as she stretched to fit around him.

"So I am the first . . . and now you're mine," he said roughly, running a broad, rough hand down her body. The raw male possession caught at her, binding her as his hand covered her breast, his eyes locking with hers. He pressed the soft mound gently, and she fought the groan of pleasure rising out of her. Her hips lifted to his sweeping touch down her thighs.

"My God!" he exclaimed roughly. "I've never—"

His eyes closed, and his skin stretched tightly across his cheekbones. Regina couldn't keep from lifting her hips, fitting her knees to his hard hips as he slid deeper within her.

The first shock of waves hit her, swirled her around in the dark passionate waters, pulling her from her rock of safety and taking her into the heat of the night.

Throbbing around him, Regina watched, stunned as MacGregor's black eyes darkened, then blazed brightly. "You feel it, too, don't you? The mating?" he demanded unevenly. "Hot . . . deep in the blood."

She moaned as he held himself tautly above her, straining to remain still as Regina lifted her hips to him. The wings of hunger beat at her, pulsing and taking him on a dark, sweet flight.

He moved roughly against her, claiming her fully and quickly.

Regina trembled and ached, wanting more. "Kiss me, you oaf," she muttered between her teeth.

Obeying her, MacGregor settled deep within her. His lips moved sweetly, leisurely across hers as she swirled through the clouds, cradling him and tugging him deeper within her. She'd seen mating birds fly against the sky, and the soaring heat shot through her as though he'd swept her to the sun. There were colors and heat . . . Her light cry echoed softly against his cheek as she drifted back gently to the furs.

MacGregor closed his eyes, feeling the tight woman-muscles closing on him, keeping him when he was past his time.

He wanted that desperately—the tender enclosure when the moment was gone. Beneath him, Regina breathed rapidly as though she had run a long hard race. And she kept him close.

She'd drawn him into the fire her first time, caught him, and made him weak.

Still sheathed within her, he frowned against the mass of sweetly scented hair ensnaring him. Her small breasts rose and fell against him delicately, and MacGregor found himself waiting for the brief touch.

She'd held him as closely as a knife in a sheath. Wanted him. And had only asked for her saddle and a kiss.

MacGregor shifted, suddenly uneasy with her softness about him, beneath him.

He'd wanted her quickly.

She'd taken him to a place he knew he'd never forget.

Now she stared at him, looking stunned and helpless. And so soft.

He had to kiss her. Her mouth moved softly beneath him, answering the aching need within him.

Against his mouth, she whispered raggedly, "Loose my hands, MacGregor."

When he obeyed slowly, he realized he must have hurt her in his passion. Her hands skimmed his shoulders lightly, caressing him. He wanted that touch, craved the slender fingers flowing across his shoulders like leaves drifting down a slow stream on a hot summer day.

"My dear," she whispered unevenly against his ear. "Are we quite finished?"

He swallowed, suddenly as weak and exposed as his son. He wanted to slide into her warmth and forget his past of pain.

He wanted the throbbing sweetness, the hot velvety sheath tight around him, and the low moans as she fought her passion.

Trembling, fighting the new emotions within him, MacGregor stared at her helplessly only to find two dark purple eyes meeting his own.

A slender pale hand reached to sweep back a strand of his hair gently. The light touch caused MacGregor to feel as though he stood on the edge of a high cliff, and the earth began crumbling slowly beneath him.

"There wasn't much to that after all," she whispered huskily. "And now that it's done, shall we prepare to leave? I want to ride properly in my saddle."

AT midday Venus crouched against Regina, shivering beneath the weight of the buffalo robe they shared. Gathering the dog closer, Regina tightened her legs around the Appaloosa gelding as he picked his way across a rocky path.

Snow crept beneath the robe MacGregor had tucked roughly around her, the freezing wind almost burning her cheeks until she burrowed deeper in the coarse fur.

Leading, walking beside his horse, MacGregor turned back to glare at her. When she had demanded leaving immediately to get her saddle, he'd thrown the furs back angrily. "You'll have it, by God. Though I should end this foolishness now."

Now Regina pulled Venus closer to her, whispering to the dog. "MacGregor is certainly in a terrible state of mind. Moody. Even his horse, Kansas, is acting out of sorts. Poor Jack is such a sweet child, despite his father's black moods."

Venus whimpered, thrusting her long nose out into the cold air. Regina tucked the lush fur around her pet. "When we get to civilization, he'll be rid of us. That should make him even happier."

Walking ahead and leading his small train, MacGregor was outlined against the dark, ominous sky. His robe swirled about him, the baby safe in a sling against his hard body.

The long rifle was gripped in his hand, the metal catching the dull light like the steel of a knight's lance.

"I didn't like being ordered about this morning like a simpleton, Venus. Not a bit. The man has much to learn about treating a woman with . . . dignity. Etiquette is very important, even in the wilds."

Regina shifted on the saddle, adjusting to the uncomfortable aches in her body. She had not expected her loss of virginity to be so painless. Nor to have the burning, exquisite ache. Actually, MacGregor with his rough style was more careful than the men of the women she had heard talking.

Her lips pursed softly, remembering his kiss. She had no doubt that the caress was new to him. But the way his brows drew together as though concentrating solely on her mouth was somehow . . . endearing.

"Posh! I merely accommodated his animal needs so that we could be on our way. One has to make sacrifices. With the storms coming we would have been trapped in that cabin until spring."

MacGregor had shot dark, menacing glances at her after leaving the pallet and jerking on his trousers. Draped in his long hair and beard, and stalking about the cabin, he left no doubt that he was angry. But he had carefully prepared new water for her bath and had stepped outside as she cleansed him from her.

Closing her eyes, Regina remembered the dark concern in his eyes as he had returned to the cabin with wood. She was sipping her tea and holding Jack, enjoying to the last minute the safety of the cabin.

He had glared at her as he eyed her torn velvet riding dress. "You'll be wearing my clothes. The wind will cut right through those duds."

In the end he helped her roll up the trousers and fasten them with a thong. Tugging up his woolen stockings, Regina found him kneeling at her feet. MacGregor had fashioned small moccasins for her, turning the fur side inward. Slipping them on her foot, he adjusted the laces, then wrapped a sheath of fur around her calves up to her

knees. His large hand had brushed her thigh and had opened
to rest momentarily on her. Then MacGregor jerked his
hand away as though he was not aware of touching her.

In preparing to load the animals, he had snapped at her,
"You keep that pouch of food slung across you, miss.
You'll be needing nourishment before we stop."

When she'd asked about the mottled horses, his answer
was curt. "Appaloosas. Nez Percé ponies. You'll ride
Fleetfire, a gelding. My horse is Kansas, and Blood is
that bad-tempered broomtail carrying your chest. Mules
are Daub and Ned."

The strong horses had stamped and whinnied, excited as
MacGregor checked the packs. Marked by white across their
rumps and loins, their chestnut coats caught the shimmering
mist, their nostrils shooting steam into the freezing air.

Pausing, he had looked up at her. "We're going across
the mountains, and it's hard traveling. You'll have to hold
the dog. She can have some food, too, I guess. I'll tend
to Jack."

Now MacGregor's robes swirled as he turned to her, the
rugged mountains behind him covered with deep snow. The
wind swept through the pine trees, the branches swishing
softly.

So he was angry with her, was he? She hadn't incited his
attack. When they reached civilization—

Regina frowned, gathering Venus's warmth closer to her.
"Lord Covington and his henchmen will pay. So will my
father."

By the late evening Regina's head drooped, her body
aching. She felt herself being lifted down from the horse,
a man's deep voice soothing away her protests as he placed
her on the ground and covered her with another robe.
He tucked a flap of the pelt across her face, warming
her.

When she awoke, she discovered that MacGregor had
fashioned a lean-to around her and was feeding Jack outside. A small fire licked at the damp wood, and snow lay
like a thin white blanket across the clearing in the pines.
Wolves howled in the distance, and a deer haunch sizzled

on a spit. Strips of meat cooked slowly over another green branch braced against the spit. The remainder of the deer he'd wrapped in canvas hung high from a tree, anchored by a rope tied to a lower branch. MacGregor had heated water in a pot, and the tin of tea leaves waited on a flat rock.

Regina yawned, feeling as though she could sleep for days. She stretched beneath the layers of furs, surprised by the warmth surrounding her. By using pine boughs, blankets, and furs, MacGregor had made his lean-to warm and snug.

"You're awake, then," he said roughly as she wrapped a robe about her and sat beside him. He studied Jack's fat cheeks intently. "Ah . . . if you need help in the bushes, yell."

"I can manage quite well, thank you," she returned stiffly.

"There's Indians here. Until they know what my woman looks like, you be careful."

"Your woman! You are daft!" she hissed, rising and sweeping regally from the camp. "Come, Venus," she ordered the greyhound, who looked at MacGregor.

"Go with her, dog," he said gently.

"You don't have to take orders from that oaf," she hissed as Venus trailed after her, looking back longingly at the warm camp. "After all, he's been well paid and will have more, once we get my saddle."

When she returned, she stamped her foot near him as he lounged, watching the fire. Jack rested lengthwise on MacGregor's long thighs, happily nesting in the warmth. Regina's legs weakened as she thought about the strength of his legs within hers. She curled her fist against her side, fighting the odd tide of emotions sweeping over her. "Perhaps we should get the traveling arrangements in order, MacGregor. We are simply making do until we reach civilization. I can pay you well for your trouble, and then you can go on your merry way—"

He tossed a sourdough biscuit at her. When she caught it, he ordered mildly, "Better eat. You're scrawny enough already. On the blankets your bones stab a man until he aches."

She caught the swift look of pain in his black eyes, and then it was gone. "You look no more than a child," he muttered in disgust.

"I'm thirty-one years of age," she shot back hotly. He certainly didn't have to test her bones and complain about them! "How old are you, MacGregor?"

Rocking Jack gently within his thighs, the mountain man answered warily, "Near as I can figure, I should have about thirty-nine or forty summers behind me."

"Then I should think," she gritted from between her teeth, "that a man your age should have acquired a few ideas about the delicacy of a lady—"

"You mean like not staking a claim on my woman?" he demanded too softly. "You're a sore measure at that. Rangy as a scrub cayuse pony."

Regina took a deep breath and found her mouth watering for the bread. "We'll see," she answered stiffly.

How could she possibly have felt any tenderness for him earlier as he lay sprawled upon her? He'd caught her broadside and winded her, that was all, she answered silently. Weakened by her experience, of course she was susceptible to anyone who would take her to safety.

Tearing off a chunk of biscuit, she glared at him as she carefully swept the robe aside to sit. Jack hiccuped in his sleep, his fat cheeks working as he dreamed of his milk. MacGregor's hard face softened as he drew a warm pelt about his son.

He tossed a biscuit to Venus, who grabbed it in the air and settled next to the mountain man. MacGregor adjusted part of Jack's fur pelt across the dog, rubbing her back. "Good dog."

"Venus, you traitor," Regina accused drowsily as she reached for a pan of roast meat. She chewed it slowly, staring at the fire and letting the juices strengthen her.

"You're getting worked up again, aren't you, woman?"

The low question cut across her thoughts. "I'd like to kill them," she said slowly, meaning every word.

"And me, too, along the way?" he asked roughly, handing her a tin cup of hot tea. "Packed your fancy dishes away so they wouldn't break."

He caught her wrist, turning it carefully within his large hand to examine the new bruises. His expression darkened. "Them hurting you, then me."

"Perhaps. But I struck a bargain with you, and I expect you to hold to it." She sipped the tea, noting that he drank coffee. Jack cried in his sleep as MacGregor lifted and carried him into the lean-to. When he emerged, he carefully draped a pelt across the opening and anchored it at the bottom with a rock.

Regina watched sleepily as MacGregor checked on his horses and mules. Then he was standing over her, holding out his hand. The broad, upturned palm lined with calluses seemed so safe—

"Ma'am?"

His hand drew her upright, then settled possessively on the small of her back as they entered the lean-to.

SIX

MACGREGOR opened his mouth to yell at Smythe, who had just stepped into the sniper's line of fire. Smythe's blond head exploded, a fine spray of blood and brains hitting MacGregor's blue uniform coat.

MacGregor froze in midstride, the sound of Smythe's scream echoed through his brain. . . . A woman cried out softly in the dark, a high-pitched keening sound like a child. "Don't hurt me, Papa," the girl begged, whimpering. "Papa, please don't hurt Jennifer."

A cold wind pelted snow against MacGregor's nose as he awoke completely. He was fully dressed, as was the woman twisting on the furs beside him. A heavy robe covered them both, and she fought it with hands and knees. Jack slept quietly in his warm, furry nook.

A small snow flurry brushed MacGregor's face as he sought her face, a pale oval shape in the night. In the darkness her enormous eyes held the terror of her nightmare. "Don't hurt me. . . ."

MacGregor's heart pounded against his side, his stomach turning at the woman's whimpers. "Wake up," he whispered softly so as not to wake up his son.

When he edged closer to her, her eyes widened with fear. Backing against the wall of branches, her lips formed a silent "No." Caught by the dark side, terror washed the woman's face.

He'd seen soldiers awake from sleep, tangled in their nightmares. Trapped by his horror, another man had fired at a sleeping soldier in his blankets, killing him.

"It's all right," MacGregor whispered as he held very still, watching the wide, dark eyes slowly lose their wild glaze. "Shh."

Huddling against the lean-to wall, she shivered, her teeth catching the softness of her bottom lip. "MacGregor?" she asked softly, warily.

"I'm here and Jack is sleeping in his nest."

She shivered again, her eyes wide in the shadows. He wanted to hold her. To stroke that small quivering body and smooth away her fears.

He watched her long lashes close slowly and thought of the new, strangely soft hunger to linger with her. Even now he wanted to slide closer to her, holding her against his chest as he would Jack.

But he wanted that small tight body heating his, holding him and clinging desperately to him as if he were a part of her. In his lifetime he had needed no one; the thought that the woman he had chosen was also his need settled uncomfortably on him. . . . "I can't sleep. You were making noises," he muttered darkly, drawing the pelt higher on his shoulder.

He'd lived without kindness in his life, knowing that when he took a woman, it served a need. Distrusting the softer elements brewing within him, MacGregor held his body taut and ached.

His palm ached to slide beneath her clothing and rest upon her small breast. Just to touch her, feel the beat of her heart like a wild, trapped bird, and to smell the exotic, spicy scent of her skin. . . .

Trembling over the planes of his face, her fingers followed the hard bones and dark heavy brows. Her touch floated over an old scar and retraced the broken angle of his nose.

"MacGregor?" she asked softly again, easing a strand of hair back from his forehead. Smoothing the hard line of his jaw, searching out the taut muscle as he ground his teeth, her fingers trembled.

"Go back to sleep," he ordered harshly. Aching for her

softness, he found himself afraid. He'd heard of men losing their souls to women, ruled by a soft touch and a warm bed. He was long past an age for cuddling in the night. When he wanted her, he'd take her. . . .

Glancing at Jack, she pushed a clinging tendril away from her cheek. "I must apologize . . ."

Then MacGregor's fingers sifted the silky strands, easing them from around her neck. A vein throbbing rapidly slid down the smooth, pale column, and he wanted to place his mouth over it. To taste the heat and the life within her. In the shadows she looked back at him, vulnerable as a fawn hidden by its mother. He'd never wanted to place his mouth on a woman's skin before, wanted to taste the sweetness lingering there—"Go back to sleep," he urged more gently.

"I should have braided my hair," she offered hesitantly and glanced at him. MacGregor's black eyes had glimpsed her frightening past and hadn't laughed. "What time is it?"

Husky with sleep, his voice wrapped softly around her. "Two more hours before rising. You'd better rest."

"I want to see Lord Covington's face when we take the saddle. If you're as good with a gun as you say you are, there should be no problem." Regina sat upright, crossed her legs, and tried to gather her hair into her hands. MacGregor lay back, his arms crossed behind his head as he watched her futile efforts to control the strands flowing down her body.

He toyed with the end of a curl, bringing it across his mouth and catching the tangy, spicy scent. "You'll follow my orders and stay put, Duchess. Or we'll stop right here. . . ."

"You made a bargain." Regina's pale face turned to him in the darkness. "And I am not a duchess."

"I keep my bargains. But you stay behind with Jack while I collect that saddle you're so set on. If I hadn't read in the book that women had to have their special things around them to be happy, we'd be headed for my cabin now."

Her mouth opened as though to argue, then closed quickly.

Nibbling on her bottom lip, she fretted with her hair. Spilling over her graceful, slender hands and nimble fingers, the elusive silky locks defied her efforts. Somehow a fat coil had twined around his finger, trapping him. MacGregor ran his thumb across the curl, testing its silky, clean texture.

Closing his eyes, he let himself drift back to the bargain. She caught him to her, the mass of hair flowing around the pelts, entangling him. *Who had snared who?*

As part of her body, soothed by her hands skimming across his shoulders, the torment of his soul had eased. She lingered when the mating was done as though she liked touching him. As though she were as contented as he, to remain a part of him. . . .

"Oh!" she whispered, frustrated as the strands danced around her, shimmering in the half light. "I'm cutting it."

"Shh." His fingers moved gently in her hair, catching and weaving the strands into a single braid. Beneath his touch, Regina closed her eyes. His heat flowed along her back, and she wanted badly to move into his arms, terrified of dreaming again. Her long uneven sigh blended with the sound of the wind outside.

MacGregor tied fringe torn from his coat around the end of her braid, then gently smoothed the length over the shape of her breast. His fingers lingered on the heavy braid, sliding to brush against the heated skin of her throat. "Lay down. You need to rest."

Reluctantly Regina settled by his side and glanced uneasily at him through the shadows. If he knew of the jewels, could she hire him to take her to a settlement for the winter? Would he forget wanting her as a wife?

"You know this isn't unlike an African hut," she whispered conversationally. Had he heard her screams? What did he know of the nightmares that had plagued her since she was a child?

He lifted a dark brow, mocking her. The steady look set her mind humming back to the previous morning and the bargain. She shifted against the furs, stretching her legs to be more comfortable, and he frowned. "Are you hurting?"

"Hurting?" she asked, understanding what he meant.

He shrugged, his gaze tracking her hot flush in the shadows. "I've heard that women newly opened sometimes can't walk. You spent a whole day in the saddle."

In her lifetime she had been abused, and only Jennifer had cared. Uncomfortable with the thought of this frontiersman entering her intimate thoughts and feelings, Regina settled for a quick dart of anger. "We've made a bargain, and I kept my word. Tomorrow I'm walking, too." Her lower stomach contracted with heat as he continued to study her in that slow, dark manner, probing into her secrets until her cheeks flamed.

Then suddenly his hand was beneath the robe, gently massaging the soft mound above her legs. She squirmed beneath the light, persistent touch, tightening her thighs against his seeking hand as it slipped lower. "What exactly are you doing?"

"Tending you." The curve was there on his hard mouth, mocking her attempts to dislodge him. She gripped his thick wrist with both hands, only to find his long fingers firmly lodged between her legs, rubbing the gentle twinge there. Regina caught her breath, feeling herself beginning to melt and dampen her drawers.

"MacGregor," she managed shakily, "when I was a child, I killed a man who tried to touch me as you are doing." A quick picture of her father's drunken friend leering over her childhood bed flashed before her. "I stabbed him through the heart with a kitchen knife."

In a quick move he grasped her hand, lifting it above them to study the pale fragile lines of her fingers. "With this small, soft thing?" He turned it in the bare light. "Why, it looks like a white dove. Or a new white rabbit. Look how pale and small it looks against mine."

MacGregor's heavily calloused palm fitted to her smaller one. His dark skin against hers reminded her of their bodies joined and moving together.

Jerking her hand to safety, Regina rubbed her palm on the rough pelt. His touch caused her to shiver, not from cold but with a lingering ache to caress his lean body.

Taking her long braid, he lifted it across his chest, toying with the tamed strands. He raised it to his nose, smelling the thick rope of hair like a new spice, and the intent expression of his face caught her. After a long moment he murmured huskily, "I liked that foolish kissing."

The simple statement jarred her, caused her lips to part softly, remembering the gentle play of his mouth on hers. To defend her emotions she snapped, "With that great black beard around your mouth, it's a wonder any woman would kiss you."

"None have," he answered quietly after a long moment, running the braid along his cheek slowly. "No woman has held me after. Nor tortured me by kissing before."

Regina turned her hot face away, then curled from him. She had acted scandalously, craving him to stay with her. Wanting the warmth and security of his arms wrapped tightly around her. Wanting the sweet cherishing of his lips against hers and the warmth building between them. "It won't happen again."

"The kissing or the other?" he asked softly against her ear as he moved closer, pressing his thighs against the back of hers. His hand swept from her shoulder to her waist, sliding to rest on her jutting hip.

The raw ache in his voice reached out to snare her, and she shivered. MacGregor could be one of the sneaky ones, set upon ruling her with more devious methods than her father. She jerked the robe higher on her shoulder. "You're set on tormenting me out of the last bit of sleep this night. Go away."

His breath swirled round her ear, his lips pressing a spot just behind her ear. Regina jumped, tingling deep within. She rubbed the kiss away, settling a distance from him.

Sliding against her, he whispered roughly, "For a kiss, ma'am."

"I'm not passing out kisses on whims, MacGregor." She began as his long length pressed warmly against her backside and his arm slipped across her, drawing her back.

"We could do the other, then," he said firmly, his hand roaming the bulky robe to find her chest. "I thought about these all day yesterday . . . like two strawberries on cream . . . I thought about the taste. . . ."

She swatted at his seeking hand, her blood suddenly racing as she remembered the gentle sweep of his palm across her bare flesh. MacGregor had touched her as though she were made of spider down, a tender seeking. "I don't want to hurt you, sir. But I can."

Captured her wrists gently, rubbing them with his thumbs, MacGregor lay his hot cheek against hers. "I'm . . . sorry about the way I marked you, ma'am," he offered roughly. "I got to thinking about the other and forgot. Being in your saddle was just about the sweetest thing—"

"Saddle? You are crude. . . ." Regina thrust against him only to have him catch her deeper in strong thighs and arms. Against her buttocks the solid press of hardened muscle nudged insistently.

"A woman's saddle can make a man forget anything," he whispered unevenly against her cheek as he turned her beneath him. One heavy thigh lifted over hers, his stocking foot nudging her insole. "Especially when she's so ready. . . . I don't know why you're so riled—"

"Because you have no idea at all about . . ." she hissed, twisting against him.

"Are you going to kiss me or not?" he demanded with an arrogant edge to his voice. "Just like a female to go messing with things, then change them."

Turning her head, Regina found her lips next to his.

"It won't happen . . . again. . . ." she whispered slowly, entranced by the way his eyes slid over her mouth. As though she were a sweet he had to taste. She swallowed, her throat suddenly dry.

MacGregor inhaled sharply, closed his eyes, and found her mouth. For a moment Regina watched his thick brows draw together as he concentrated on the task. Then her lids closed as she savored the sweet desire running through him.

He brushed his mouth against hers, following the contours from corner to corner. Then taking his time, his lips traced her cheeks and jaw, leaving a heated trail. "So soft," he murmured huskily, returning to her mouth. "Ah, ma'am, do you think you could push your mouth against me like you did before? Like you were hungry for me? Wanting to taste me a little bit at a time?"

"I did not," she began, only to have her lips lift and part to his firm ones.

Breathing lightly, she hadn't known a man's mouth could be so achingly tender. His big hands rose to frame her cheeks and lift her face to his lips.

In the slowest of ways he fitted his mouth across hers. For a butterfly's heartbeat he rested, then experimented with another soft, tantalizing kiss. Then he suckled gently, as though he were drinking nectar and savoring the taste.

When she clung to reality by a shred, wanting to move against his warmth, MacGregor slowly opened his eyes. "I like that," he repeated raggedly against her mouth.

Regina licked her bottom lip and caught MacGregor staring hungrily at the moistness. He touched it with the tip of his tongue, and she couldn't resist sucking him gently inside.

Moving over her, MacGregor rested on her lightly. He breathed deeply, thrusting his hips against hers.

Stiffening against him, Regina tugged at his hair, found it clinging to her hands, and found her fingers rummaging through the crisp waves. "We're not doing . . . 'the other,' " she ordered firmly.

He scowled down at her. "One in the same," he said, unbuttoning his trousers with one hand.

"It is not! They're completely different," she snapped trying to keep his hands from her trousers.

"You keep this game up," he gritted between his teeth as she applied a quick and painful thumb lock on him, "and Jack is sure to squawl."

"Jack surely wouldn't want his father raping a woman," she spat out, glaring up at him. "A fine example of a gentleman you are. Kissing is different. And we made a bargain the last time we . . ." Embarrassed, she let her words drift into the wind.

"No offense, but I like the other. And I never raped a woman. . . ." His dark cheeks flushed suddenly as he looked down at her accusing expression. "Damn it. You've never been opened before. Any man would have hurt you."

"I've never had a man before," she repeated firmly. "You caught me when I was tired and weak. You played on my sympathy."

"And all the time you were jabbering about kissing. Wasted time about it, too. You set your bargain between us, and you'll have that fancy saddle. What do you want to trade this time?"

"You are a brute," she stated carefully from between her teeth, eyeing him. "An animal set to rut."

Clenching his jaw, MacGregor whispered tightly, "A man does the same thing as animals, ma'am . . . mate. As soon as Jack and you are snug, I'll get that damn saddle. But I sure as hell can't see staying off you meanwhile."

"Oh!" She squirmed beneath his weight. "You really are a ruffian."

"Woman, you are making me—" he warned as Jack started crying softly. "I should just kiss you until you're all weak and wet for me and then climb on and ride."

Regina's open palm struck his hard cheek, and Jack began to cry hungrily. "I shouldn't try that if I were you, MacGregor. You'll find Old Hugh lodged safely in your drawers."

"Pah!" he snorted as he lifted himself free of her and tramped outside. "Females!"

MacGregor wanted to brawl with the toughest man in the mountains, then drink himself blind. The mountain men before his time drank the bile of a freshly killed buffalo for liquor; MacGregor scowled at a bighorn sheep bounding on a high rocky butte. "Let a good buffalo cross my path now, and I'd kill him in a minute."

He hunched his shoulders, running a free hand across little Jack as he held the reins with his other hand. If he wanted softness, he sure as hell had chosen the wrong woman.

She was *his* woman. She had fought him in the lean-to, and he had barely kept himself from taking her. "Men set the rules to protect women because they are weak," he muttered darkly. "This one is scrawny *and* muley."

The icy wind clawed at him, and MacGregor turned to check on her—his woman. Following his path in the snow, Regina looked like a half-grown boy dressed in his clothes.

His hand tightened on the cold leather reins, remembering the silky heat of her body flowing beneath his, opening and accepting him.

Walking for three straight hours while Jack slept quietly in his warm sling, MacGregor deliberately set out to prove her weak. Prove that she needed him.

Now, those dark purple eyes met his evenly, daring him as she trudged through the knee-deep snow.

Turning back to the path, MacGregor scowled, fighting the ache in his body. She could turn on him like a scalded cat the minute he opened his mouth.

Bending, he lifted a broken fir branch from the rocky trail and threw it aside. He smelled smoke; the old rendezvous camp was nearby. His child and the woman needed the warmth of a good fire. Walking down the treacherous, snow-covered path, MacGregor glanced back at her as Ned slid a few precious feet off the trail. The mountain man held his breath as he tugged at the animal's reins, cradling Jack with his other hand. Leaning her slight weight into pulling the mule, Regina sang softly. Stroking the mule's long ears, she whispered and Ned suddenly calmed. Before MacGregor could fight his way back up the trail to her, she was leading the mule again. When he stood a few feet from her, she glared at him. "Is there a problem?"

Jack cried softly and Regina swept aside MacGregor's robe to caress the infant's cheek. She smiled lightly, tucking a tiny fist back into the skins. "He'll need changing soon," she said, carefully covering his son.

She had the mothering touch, he thought, reading the sudden softness in her eyes. A man could fall into those eyes, fringed by heavy thick black lashes, MacGregor decided sullenly. He'd made a poor bargain, but one that he'd keep to get her blasted saddle. Right then he'd have promised his soul to . . . "We're coming to a rendezvous. Jack will be warm and fed, but you're another matter," he growled, uneasy with his thoughts.

Her eyes widened and MacGregor found himself leaning down to her. "The men catch a whiff of your skin, and they'll be after you like a pack of dogs. . . . They're randy, ma'am," he added carefully, wanting to make certain she understood.

"Posh. And you're not? Here you stand, dillydallying while Jack needs changing and food. I understand perfectly. You've got a boy traveling with you, not a woman." Taking care to tuck her braid beneath her shirt, Regina skimmed the snow-covered valley below them. "Shall we go?"

"Ma'am," MacGregor gritted between his teeth. He didn't like her throwing his need back in his face. Back-fighting wasn't his style. He'd made his bargain with her outright. "After we're married proper, I'll see that you learn a thing or two."

Lifting her winged brows high, Regina tossed her head. "I can manage. See that you don't forget our bargain."

"It was a poor bargain at that," he growled. "Not enough meat on your poor bones to keep a man warm."

Her lids narrowed. "You really are a crude man, you know."

MacGregor cupped her face between his thumb and fingers. "Violet, I'm your man now. We're getting married as soon as the preacher shows up. You could be carrying my child now," he added, wanting to place his mouth on her softly parted lips.

Fear danced in her eyes, swallowing her. A sudden pain went skittering through him like a rabbit running for the brush. Maybe she didn't want his baby bouncing on her lap. The thought hurt. "Mating makes babies," he stated roughly. "You should have thought about that before you agreed."

So she hadn't wanted his child, had she? The thought went cutting through him. To cover the ache, he added hoarsely, "Jack will be needing a brother or a girl baby, too. Once you fill out some, we'll have to see about spending more time on the blanket." He caught her hand before it hit his cheek.

"You . . . are . . . evil," she said, her face paling beneath the silky soft skin. "I did what I had to do then. Your bastard child wasn't in the bargain—"

"Bastard?" he roared, and an animal went scurrying through the brush. "I'd be the rightful father of the child. Your husband. Any children we have will be on the right side of the blanket. Woman, we are having a preacher say the words as soon as we can."

Her lips trembled, the purple eyes blinking away fat tears. In the next instant MacGregor found his lips tasting the quivering softness of hers. When he lifted his head, her mouth lifted slightly as though she wanted him, too. "You're mashing Jack," she whispered, her eyes wary.

"Jack's warm. I'm hot."

"Why did you call me Violet earlier?"

He frowned, trying to remember. "Because you've got purple eyes like violets deep in the wood, that's why."

"That's almost poetic, MacGregor," she whispered softly, her eyes widening before they lowered to a deer crossing the winding stream in the valley. She traced the path of hoof marks in the smooth snow. "I did what I had to do," she whispered cautiously. "Don't make more of it than it was."

Running his thumb down her cheek, testing the silky texture, MacGregor knew she fought her pride. On an impulse he bent his head and tasted her mouth again slowly.

When he was done, she looked drowsy and warm, tasting of hunger. Leaning against his side, she fitted neatly into the crook of his arm and hadn't noticed how his palm had fitted to her trim backside, smoothing the curve. His thigh had slid between the softness of hers, and the smooth muscles had moved against him. MacGregor smiled softly, tasting her sweet mouth on his lips and the nestling warmth of her body against his side. "I could get to like this kissing business. Been wanting to nibble at the corners of that mouth, see if there's more honey there or inside where it's hot."

"Posh," she managed huskily after a moment in which she just stared at him, her cheeks pink. Then she stepped free.

The camp was a mixture of crusty mountain men, Indian women, and children. They moved around the newcomers, who slapped MacGregor on his broad back and peeked at his baby son. A huge man, draped in furs and crowned by a tuft of feathers, moved through the crowd like a bear through kittens. Dark blond curls flowed about his shoulders and down his back; his handsome face was smoothly shaven. A gold earring caught the sun as he petted Venus. "That your son, too, MacGregor?" he asked in a booming voice that carried across the snow-draped camp. "How's my baby boy, eh? That Jack?"

The man's large hand stretched out to take Regina by the nape of the neck, playfully shaking her. Her teeth chattered, and she fought to keep her balance in the mud and snow. The mountain man chuckled and grinned. "This is one scrawny pup, my friend."

"The boy isn't mine, Pierre. But if he were, I'd be shoving my blade across your fingers right now," MacGregor said in a low quiet tone.

The giant's hand left Regina immediately and she glanced at MacGregor's dark scowl. "Aye, you're touchy, my friend. Perhaps the boy is a lover, *n'est-ce pas?*"

MacGregor's teeth shone whitely within his dark beard as he tossed the reins of his horse to the giant. "I'm not as desperate as you, Pierre."

"Wah! I take women to the blankets. With big bouncing breasts," the giant roared, shoving Regina toward MacGregor. "Here, perhaps your friend needs a nice fat squaw to warm his skinny bones. Full Kettle," he called, beckoning to a young girl, her round face shining with grease. "Come, be nice to this boy."

"The boy stays with me," MacGregor said, lazily cutting a piece of meat from the spit and handing it to Regina. "We're needing a lean-to for the night."

Pierre clasped him on the shoulder and Jack wailed. "Give the baby to a squaw and come drink with me, my friend. We have stories to tell each other, *mais oui?*"

MacGregor glanced at Regina's hot face, averted into her furs. "We need rest and food first. My son needs a warm fire."

Pierre's black eyes shot from MacGregor to Regina. "Let the boy take care of the baby. Come, we have fine whiskey, good meat. Buffalo tongue and hump bread. We drink ourselves blind like in the old days, no?"

Jack wailed louder, and an elderly Indian woman tugged at Regina's buffalo cape. Her black eyes sparkled like beads in a leathered face. "Come. Warm fire. I bring food and a woman to give milk to Two Hearts' son."

MacGregor nodded, and Regina followed the stooped woman to a small hut with smoke coursing from the top. Jack wailed steadily, and within moments a young woman entered shyly to feed him. Regina fell to the fur pallets as MacGregor chuckled deeply.

When she awoke, MacGregor was snoring softly beside her, his arm wrapped around her. Despite the huge fire outside the hut and the drunken laughter, MacGregor slept, fully dressed. He roused when she turned slowly, wedging space between them. Stretching out his arms, he drew her back to the cove of his body, his hand sliding beneath her shirt to rest on her stomach. "Pierre is keeping you and Jack safe while I'm gone, Duchess. I'll have the saddle back by nightfall tomorrow."

Trying to dislodge his hand, Regina squirmed around to face him. Somehow his palm now rested on the bare curve of her buttock. MacGregor looked down at her in the half light, his eyes sparkling. Grinning, he gently squeezed her buttock. "You need fattening up. Winter is almost here."

Narrowing her eyes, Regina twisted against him, and he chuckled. "Want to bargain again?" he asked huskily, managing to insert his heavy thigh between hers.

For an answer Regina brought her knee up sharply. He took the intimate blow, cushioned by the robe between them. "Feeling fiery, are you?" he demanded, scowling at her. "Here we are, going the wrong way down the mountain—one we've just now gone up—after some damned useless saddle, and you're acting like a stubborn mule dragging an overloaded pack."

"I shall scream," she stated quietly between her teeth when he captured her flying hands. "There are men out there who will defend my honor."

His eyes widened as though she'd delivered a full blow. "You're my wife now."

"Wife!" she threw the word back at him. "I simply did what was needed at the time. Don't be drawing grand pictures in your mind, my good man."

MacGregor took a deep breath, glaring at her. He wanted to sink his lips onto hers and see if she really tasted like honey. "You'll feel better after you've eaten," he offered warily. How could something so soft and willing change into ice?

AROUND the night's huge bonfire the trappers talked of old times and the wasteful killing of animals by the English "feriners." Lifting their "John Barleycorn" jugs, they drank and mourned the old ways before the settlers and the forts. Indian women and children moved like shadows around the men.

A small man draped in furs patted his wife's back affectionately as she passed, serving from a pot of beans. He adjusted a baby on his lap, making way for two other toddlers.

Pierre held Jack, crooning softly to him while the baby dozed. Wearing a gray hat of the rebel south, a trapper named Tall Tom drank steadily from his jug and eyed the newcomers. A wild shout went up nearby, followed by bawdy male laughter and a woman's giggle.

Seated on a log next to MacGregor, Regina kept her eyes down as she ate from the wooden trencher. Shooting dark looks at her, he growled, "Eat that grub like a hungry boy, not a female picking at crumbs," he ordered in a quiet aside.

Cursing him, Regina grabbed a slab of meat and tucked it into her mouth. The lump of roast elk was tough, and chewing it grimly, she met MacGregor's amused eyes. He clapped her on the back roughly, "That's right, eat. Food is good for a growing boy. Right, Pierre?"

Stealthily he tugged the knit cap she wore downward, covering the braid. When MacGregor leaned past her to slice a chunk of meat from the spit, Regina hissed, "I don't believe for one moment that these men are dangerous."

Turning, he stared at her over his shoulder. The look was too arrogant, nettling her. "Be quiet," he ordered tersely.

"What are you 'friends' "—Tall Tom leered, sliding a nuance into the word—"Whispering about? I always knew you blue bellies preferred boys, MacGregor. But hell, I should have known . . . you're never with women. Except that squaw I heard you took." The rebel laughed coarsely. "Or did she have to get you drunk just to get close to you?"

"You're drunk, Tom. Settle down," MacGregor said quietly, watching the other man.

Tall Tom surged to his feet, scattering his jug and food upon the frozen earth. "Hell!" he roared. "You Unioners think you can ride over anyone, don't you? Well, not me, you carpetbagger scum."

Tossing aside his buffalo robe, Tom drew his long knife from its sheath and crouched in a fighting stance. The blade flashed in the firelight as he tossed it neatly hand to hand. "Let's do it."

Pierre raised Jack to his shoulder and whispered, "He is mad from the last time you threw him in the creek."

"The idea that MacGregor and I—" Regina began hotly, cut short by MacGregor's dark scowl.

"Stand back," he ordered quietly, one hand raising her up by the nape of her neck and setting her aside as though she were a kitten. "Take Jack and go to the hut."

Bristling with anger, Regina parted her lips to argue just as Tall Tom stomped toward them. The man was enormous, hate and fury in his face, his blade weaving in a figure-eight design. Towering over her, he laughed wildly as she looked up. "A boy. Only MacGregor would take a stripling to his blanket."

"You, sir, are most offensive," Regina stated hotly before

MacGregor shoved her aside. Drawing his blade, he tossed her his pistol. The gun was heavy, much larger than her dueling pistols.

"Pah! The bear defends his cub," Tall Tom roared, thrusting out a massive hand that landed flat on Regina's chest. The hard width hit her right breast, covered by MacGregor's shirt and a heavy buffalo robe.

Without thinking, Regina raised the pistol slowly, facing Tall Tom. Holding the weapon with two hands, she slowly pulled the hammer back. "Stop bullying. I shall shoot you dead if you don't step back."

"Get your finger off that trigger," MacGregor hissed behind her. "Get out of the way."

"MacGregor got himself a boy," Tall Tom taunted, weaving and crouching in front of her. His blade flashed next to her shoulder and a tuft of buffalo hair floated away. The fire danced wildly behind him, the crowd quietly watching.

He took a step toward her, and just as MacGregor's arm came sweeping out to shove her aside, Regina pulled the trigger. Tall Tom looked down through the sulfur fumes to his foot. "Damn me," he muttered blankly. "There goes that toe."

Blood spurted into the mud as Tall Tom faced MacGregor, a smaller, leaner man. "I'll geld your sweetheart later, MacGregor," he snarled. "And peel that sickly dog like a grape. But first you'll feel my blade."

MacGregor slashed a dark look at Regina. "Go."

Stunned by the crimson blood staining the snow, Regina looked up at the raging giant and managed, "Oh, I'm so sorry, Tall Tom."

The mountain man roared, his eyes rolling wildly.

"Go!" MacGregor ordered as Tom's knife slashed through the air at her. The hissing sound cut through her shock, and she danced aside just as MacGregor's fist shot past her to stun Tom. "I said scat!" he commanded tightly, thrusting her aside.

His fist slammed into Tall Tom's belly, and the giant staggered. When he glanced at her, MacGregor's expression was sheer fury.

Thinking better of arguing at this point, Regina allowed Pierre to sweep her away to the safety of the hut. Wild, excited shouts volleyed through the camp when she took the baby from Pierre. Then he was gone.

Venus whimpered, crouching close to her.

"Savage beasts," Regina whispered to Jack, who regarded her sleepily. She sat and rocked him gently. "Your father is out there now. No doubt he and Tom are gleefully carving large chunks off each other. . . . Savages, the both of them."

Shivering with emotion, Regina hugged the baby closer. Another shout went up, then a drunken round of laughter. Jack slept peacefully through the noise, and Regina carefully placed him in a warm nook. "Poor lad. With a father like yours and friends like his, you're going to need—"

A large hand swept open the fur covering to the door as MacGregor stooped to enter the hut. Glaring at her for a long moment, he picked up a jug of whiskey, braced it on his shoulder, and drank deeply. Wiping the back of his hand across his mouth, he glanced at Jack, who slept quietly in his bed of fur.

Reaching down, MacGregor grabbed the front of her shirt. He tugged her to her feet, holding her like a rag doll in front of him. Thrusting his face down at her, he gritted, "Tall Tom is nursing a broken leg and a lost toe. . . . When I say scat, woman, I mean scat," he growled savagely.

"Of course you're angry. Perhaps I could have handled the matter better," she said after a quiet swallow. In this mood MacGregor was frightening, his black brows jammed together, his eyes blazing fiercely in the shadows.

Mud covered his cheek and neck, matting his hair against his temple while a thin long scratch oozed blood on his beard. "You need to bathe," she whispered. MacGregor looked as if he wanted to tear something apart. . . . What if Tall Tom had killed him?

Visions of MacGregor, sliced by Tall Tom's knife, danced behind her closed lids, her stomach knotting.

"Wash?" he repeated roughly. "You just shot a toe off a man and let me tidy up your mess. Then you tell me I need a wash?" he roared, incredulous.

Regina caught her bottom lip in her teeth. "Perhaps I'm not being kind," she admitted huskily as MacGregor loomed over her, his heat burning into her. "Perhaps this isn't the proper time to be firm about cleanliness."

Trembling, she knew that with one move he could easily snap her neck. Yet she needed to make some gesture of good will, since he'd clearly assigned himself to the duty of protecting her. "I could shave you," she offered in a wispy voice when he continued to glare at her. "Then tend that nasty scratch."

He digested her offer as though chewing on tough buffalo hide. "Let's get this straight now, woman. When I say—"

"Scat," she interrupted with a nod, "I will scat."

To her horror, her bottom lip quivered and tears burned behind her lids. She hated weakness and crying, fought it with all her strength, and was devastated as a single tear slid down her cheek. She blinked her lids, and suddenly there was a steady flow.

Her knees threatened to give way, and her arms wanted to reach for MacGregor. Looking up at him through tears, she managed helplessly, "Oh, MacGregor . . ."

He stared at her for a long moment. Then his fingers trembled slightly on her neck, his thumb sliding gently across her damp cheek. She shivered beneath the light touch, wanting to move into the safety of his arms.

"Hell." MacGregor folded her carefully into his arms and held her until she stopped shaking. His hands caressed her back, his jaw pressed tightly to her forehead as he rocked her.

When she began to calm, MacGregor leaned outside the hut and yelled, "Pierre! Get me hot water."

Then he turned back to her, his dark eyes gleaming. "I could use one of those sweet kisses."

Regina slid her arms around him and lifted her lips. She needed to feel his hunger, to know that he was safe.

MacGregor swept her against him, pressing her full length against his taut body. His kiss was hot and hungry, his hard body moving against hers.

She opened her mouth to his tongue and suckled it as his hands roamed her body.

Then she lay on the furs, MacGregor's hardened body resting over hers as he trembled in her arms.

At first she didn't hear Pierre's call. MacGregor's hand sought her breast as cold air swept into the tent and Pierre stood over them, grinning widely.

MacGregor tensed, turning slowly to glare up at Pierre, who shrugged. "I brought the water," he said, placing two buckets near the fire. "My friend, she is a beautiful woman with her cheeks hot with passion, her mouth like red crushed flowers from your kisses."

MacGregor jerked her shirt closed, his big hand resting at her throat as he ordered stiffly, "Get out."

"Ah, this time is different, is it not?" Pierre asked, amused. "I fear she has caught your cold heart in her soft hands, my fierce friend."

"Get off me, MacGregor," Regina ordered shakily when Pierre swept out of the hut.

MacGregor cursed Pierre, his dark eyes cutting at her as he rolled away. He lay looking at her, his hands bracing his head. "I want you," he stated unevenly, his gaze sweeping down her body as she stood.

She trembled, fighting the emotions racking her. And then Jack cried.

"You want me, too," MacGregor added quietly, following her hands as she shakily arranged her clothing.

SEVEN

Two mornings later MacGregor lay on a small knoll overlooking the earl's hunting party. His neatly trimmed beard was damp with the cold mist preceding snow; he'd wanted Regina's fingers touching him and had suffered her embroidery scissors snipping away near his jaw. Concentrating on her task, her bottom lip caught between her teeth, she hadn't noticed as he brought her astride him. He'd nearly gone mad, her hips bouncing on him intimately as she turned and twisted.

His shoulder ached now, the bullet lodged deeper into the sheath of muscle. Behind him the ragged, snowcapped peaks of the Sangre de Cristo mountains glowed in the coming dawn. Pink streaks began to shoot out across the gray sky, clawing at the night. The faint light allowed MacGregor to study Regina, who snuggled warmly to his side.

She looked more like a child than the woman who had washed his wounds, her fingers gently probing his scalp. As she'd tended him, MacGregor had closed his eyes, inhaling the spicy scent clinging to her skin. "My dear," she had soothed softly when she'd finished. "I am so sorry you were hurt."

The next morning he'd awakened with a cry in his mouth and Smythe's head exploding behind his lids. The brush of a slender finger across his lips caught his cry. Like a diamondback rattler heading for the safety of rocks, the nightmare slithered away into the darkness.

She'd tenderly kissed Jack and placed him in Pierre's arms on the other side of the trader's pass. Venus had whined but stayed near the Frenchman. Riding behind MacGregor on his Appaloosa, Kansas, Regina had absorbed every new sight with delight. She'd exclaimed as they passed the tumbling waterfalls that cut through the deep ravine bordering the traders' pass and the high trees. They met an old mountain man coming up the pass on their descent, and she kept to MacGregor's side, eyeing the seasoned veteran warily. Moon Jerkins sighted her wide dark blue eyes on him, and his yarns grew wilder. " . . . Chased that injun for two moon afore I snared him. Turned him gutside out just as a lesson for other redskins messin' with old Moon Jerkins."

He'd approved of the way she'd taken a plug of his "tobacci" and missed the way she tucked it into her pocket. While Regina mimed chewing, Moon checked his mule's saddle. "Good boy, yer bringing along there, MacGregor. Make sure Old Ephraim don't get him . . . though 'bar is gettin' scare hereabouts. By the by, passed some redcoat sports back a piece, shootin' buffaler and lettin' 'em rot. Deer, too. Don't seem to know that the whole Indian nation is stirred up from the Smoky Hill route down along the Purgatory. Cheyenne taking up the war cry with General Custer on their heels. Kit Carson is headed to Washington with the Ute. Some half-breed's been disowned and is butchering whites on the Taos Trail. Injuns don't want settlers, nor miners. In the middle of it all, the railroads are moving in . . . varmits are taking gold dust and hairy money—good beaver plew—to let a body pass over the old trails."

Moon had spit a stream of tobacco juice into a sagebrush. A badger hissed, then waddled away into the reddish rocks. "Eat that, old son," the mountain man crowed, his grin showing missing and blackened teeth.

He swung up on his mule, placing his musket across his arms. "Won't hurt those fancy redcoat backsides none to have a Kiowa arrow outfit it, I reckon. You still smoking the pipe with redskins, MacGregor? Walkin' twix the nations?"

MacGregor nodded curtly as Regina's eyes slashed to him. Moon spat again, kicking his mule. "Going to the high country to sit this fandango out. You'd best do the same till things simmer down. My woman and brood are there now . . . for the winter."

After Moon's mule and heavily loaded burro disappeared around a rocky embankment, Regina touched MacGregor's arm. "Gads, MacGregor. I had no idea. All the Indians made us welcome and—"

She'd caught her lip with her teeth, looking away. "He bartered with a few guns and powder, always promising more. Whiskey and beads, too. I see now why we were so safe," she added softly, then was quiet.

"From what I saw, the duke's party was too large and well armed to be taken easily. Several tribes are already on reservations. Others are fighting the government's reins."

At sunset they walked the horses, and Regina swung a sagebranch along her thigh. She had turned to MacGregor and stopped, her eyes luminous in the dusky shadows. "I realize now how dangerous our bargain was to us both. I respect you keeping your word in the face of grave danger. When I am able, I will repay your efforts highly."

MacGregor had found himself grinning, then startled by the sound of his laughter. "At your service, Lady Hawkes," he had said gallantly, enjoying the fine blush rising from her collar into her cheeks. He'd tucked a finger into the opened collar and tugged her closer. "You can begin torturing me now with one of those foolish kisses."

Closing his eyes, MacGregor had leaned down near her face, waiting. The sagebrush branch slapped against his chest, and he enjoyed the fine swagger of her hips as she marched away from him.

Now, nestled against his side and sharing his buffalo robe against the night chill, the Englishwoman slept quietly. He traced her small face, framed by the lush fur. Black tendrils clung to her skin, her lashes dark crescents beneath high winged brows. Softly parted, her soft lips taunted him . . . reminded him of sweet, lingering kisses that tempted and haunted. Dressed as a boy, she shifted slightly, and her thigh slid between his legs.

The woman's softness ran beneath the leather and fur, fitting the rounded contours snugly against his hard frame. Her scent rose around him, slicing through the heavier smells of leather and smoke with the daintiness of a silken feather.

The first morning birdcall sounded in the stillness; brush rattled and MacGregor turned slightly to see the dull pattern of antelope rumps glowing softly in the faint light as the herd grazed quietly. The sagebrush glowed with frost, daintily taking the dawn.

Regina sighed, nestling closer. Her small body had tightened suddenly, and he whispered, "You're awake, then."

"I'm terribly excited," she returned when he tucked the fur more closely around her face.

In the half light her eyes were huge and mysterious, and MacGregor found himself leaning closer. The color had changed to the dark blue of a deep mountain snow lake. In the still, cold dawn he wanted her close and soft. "We traveled hard yesterday, crossing the pass. You could sleep another half hour."

Regina shivered, returning his gaze intently. "I feel marvelous . . . as though I've waited my entire life for this moment. Today should be much more thrilling than . . ."

She smiled slowly as though a thought delighted her. "Today shall be my coming-out season," she finished firmly, watching him. "Much more thrilling than being presented before the court."

"They've been drinking. We can move in and escape without notice . . . I moved the horses last night while you slept," he returned, suddenly aware of the warmth between them. "You're owed the blooded stock. We can pick them up at the base of the pass. Passed a Cheyenne they'd beaten and left to die. Gave him all the horses but the blood stock. Figured they owed him. There's about twenty sheep bedded down just beyond that rise. A mean-tempered mongrel almost gave me away."

"Yes, certainly. I agree that payment should be made. . . . About my sheep, MacGregor." Regina scanned the rise he had indicated. Turning back to him, she frowned. "I'm dreadfully sorry not to have told you this before, but I must have those sheep. I bred the Merino and a Leicester Lincoln cross with a Cheviot ram, Hercules. The Cheviot is an agile strain from the borders of England and Scotland. They're easy lambers and good milkers, perfectly suited for the American wilds."

"Sheep," he repeated flatly, trying to track her thoughts while watching her soft lips. "Woollies."

"Yes. Marvelous wool for weaving." She closed her eyes, smiling dreamily. "From what I've heard, the mountain alpine meadows would be perfect for sheep, with lovely carpets of flowers much like the heather of Scotland. I can't wait to begin."

Her eyes opened, the heavy fringes of her lashes framing the bluish-purple depths. Golden shards danced around the black irises, his reflection captured in the depths. MacGregor shifted uncomfortably, startled by the thoughts of sunflowers and wood violets catching the sun.

"Heather. Weaving . . ." he repeated, lowering his lips to hers for a light kiss.

"Heather, wonderful heather—tiny purplish-pink flowers. And marvelous weaving." Her mouth clung for just an instant, lifting to his like the petals of a prairie flower warm from sunlight. Taking his time, he rubbed his lips across hers to taste the sweet, moist flavor of her mouth. This time her lips parted slightly, and she closed her eyes, breathing quietly.

MacGregor eased her closer, folding her carefully against him, taking his time not to frighten her.

Resting along his length, she was strong as a green willow and soft as rabbit's fur.

He moved closer, seeking the heat that lay beneath the surface, and found her arms sliding up to draw him near.

"You look wonderful in a trimmed beard. I would so love to see that jaw shaved." She kissed his cheek, and MacGregor's heart stopped. "When we have time, let me cut your hair a bit."

Slender fingers slid through his hair, easing the waves gently away from his forehead, and MacGregor's eyes closed. The feathery, warm strokes held him as surely as strong hemp rope. She kissed the scratch on his throat, following it upward to his cheek and the bruise on his forehead. "I am so sorry Tall Tom hurt you, my dear," she whispered against his skin, holding him fiercely against her slight frame.

MacGregor barely breathed, savoring her possession. No one had ever held him as close, nor as sweetly.

"Come here," she murmured huskily, drawing his lips back to hers.

He shivered, forcing himself not to frighten her. Holding his body taut, MacGregor tried not to crush her against him, straining for the sweet taste of her skin, her mouth.

"Yes, like that," she said, sighing against his lips, flowing beneath him like silk, tangling her arms and legs around his larger ones. The word came again, sliding like warm honey against his mouth. "Yes, quite."

Soft kisses pressed a heated trail to his ear, nibbling daintily on the lobe. The warmth of her breath flowed around his ear, swirled in it, and MacGregor's throat went suddenly dry.

Then she was apart from him, sitting up and stretching her arms high. "What a lovely day. The sagebrush smell is wonderful, so clean."

Taking the ruby eardrops from the small pouch at her waist, she fastened them in her ears and grinned down at him. "For good luck. We shall need it, don't you think?"

MacGregor groaned, fighting the need in his body.

Regina leaned closer, studying him intently in the dim light. "Gracious, what a dark scowl, MacGregor. You haven't changed your mind about keeping the bargain, have you? About reclaiming my saddle?"

"I'm thinking about saddles, all right," he stated flatly, fighting the taut desire riding his body.

"It's lovely morocco leather and should be kept with the rest of the leather goods in the tent nearest the horses." Regina tucked her braid into the woolen cap and tugged it low on her head. Her enormous eyes skimmed his face.

"My. What a dark look, MacGregor. Are you still hurting from that Tall Tom person?"

"I've felt some better," he returned, his body aching and hard.

She shivered, rubbing her small hands together. "I am so looking forward to . . ." She grinned again, her teeth flashing in the half light. " . . . to counting coup this morning. But, oh, how I would love a cup of good English breakfast tea. Oolong would be lovely, too."

The antelope moved away slowly, and Regina's hand rested momentarily on MacGregor's chest as she followed the white rumps disappearing into the dark shadows. "Lovely creatures . . . graceful." She inhaled deeply and sighed. "Smell the sage. It's wonderful. So clean."

He wanted to throw her to the ground, sink into her, and forget everything but . . . Regina grinned at him again. "Oh, MacGregor. This is so much more exciting than I believed. I feel as if I . . ." Her eyes caught on his dark gaze, holding it for a long moment.

"My dark knight," she crooned softly, stroking his lips with the tip of her finger. Looking down tenderly at him, she smoothed his hair away from his face, and MacGregor found his breath trapped in his lungs. "You've rescued me from a certain death. . . . Here we are on this magnificent day, preparing to count coup and salve my wounded pride. I'm beginning a new life because of you rescuing me from the cabin. I've been thinking, my dear. For a time I'll need to conceal my identity. . . . So from this day forth my name will be . . ." She hesitated and grinned impishly. "Violet. The beautiful name you gave me."

In his lifetime MacGregor had never been touched as tenderly, as magically. She smiled, her fingertip tracing the shape of his ear and down his throat. "You have over-powered all the stories of the knights rescuing the damsels trapped in the castle, my friend. When I was a girl, my dreams were of the dark knight, rising majestically out of the mist to save me—"

In another instant she flung herself on him. Her lips were hot and seeking on his, startling him as her small tongue slid into his mouth. Her hips moved against his, unskilled and abrupt, her hands skimming down him to find him full and aroused. Holding him within the cloth of his trousers, she whispered unevenly, "Please don't be angry with me for not acting like a lady, but I'm so very excited. I'm . . . kiss my breasts for good luck. Do it. . . . Do it, now, MacGregor. . . ." she urged, taking his hand and placing it over her small breast.

Above him, her eyes were enormous, pleading. "Please. Just this once. I need that savage feeling as if nothing else matters."

Trembling and watching him like a hungry doe, Regina laughed nervously. "How unlike me. Did you mean it when you said my breasts looked like strawberries on cream? Did you?" she demanded huskily, unbuttoning the cloth shirt to slide his hand inside her camisole to the soft, yielding flesh. "No one has ever said anything so marvelous, so poetic to me before. As if I were Helen of Troy. Or a heart's own true love. This morning, poised for revenge on Lord Covington, I feel quite unlike an English lady."

MacGregor blinked, trying to find his heartbeat as her hand followed the shape of him intimately. She rose against him then, her eyes dark and mysterious, asking for his touch.

In the dawn her breasts were white, peaked with cold, as she lowered herself to his mouth.

He kissed the crest of one silken breast while keeping the other warm in the palm of his hand. "Aye, like that. . . ." Her hips moved urgently against him.

When he tasted the sweet nub, licking it with his tongue, Regina bolted against him. "Egad, MacGregor!" She shivered, sighing breathlessly.

She stared down at him with startled eyes. In another moment she flung herself full length on him, holding him tightly against her.

Her cheek was hot against his, her body trembling in his arms. Her mouth brushed his ear, her uneven breath filling it with warmth. "Thank you," she whispered, clinging to him for just an instant. "My dark knight. So bold, so wonderfully gentle."

Then, easing herself away, she straightened her clothing briskly as though finishing a satisfactory task. "What a lovely morning. Oh, I'm so excited. When can we begin?"

MacGregor sat slowly, his body aching for release. He felt he'd been caught in a Missouri tornado and tossed into another territory, then flattened on the ground by a steam engine. But the excitement dancing in Regina's eyes bound him, the pink dawn catching on her cheeks as she giggled and tossed a cold biscuit to him. "My dark knight. Ready to reclaim my honor. What you need is to wear my colors."

She searched through her pockets and withdrew a bit of purple ribbon torn from her pantelettes. Nibbling on her bottom lip, Regina tied the ribbon around his upper arm with a flourish and grinned. "There. Wearing your lady's colors for luck, you should be safe, my dear."

Running his finger slowly across the ribbon, MacGregor couldn't remember when a woman had marked him as hers. The gesture reached deep inside him and smoothed an ache he didn't want to acknowledge.

Trying to track her moods, MacGregor ate slowly, watching her scan the English camp, her color high. One sign of fear from her, and he'd have thrown her over his shoulder, packing out for the high country. "You're just as eager to count coup as any Indian on a warpath now," he said slowly as she tipped the canteen for a drink, then wiped the back of her hand across her mouth.

"Lovely feeling. Not at all like having to go to court or dress for a ball. And much more fun, I should think." She held the biscuit higher and grinned, looking like the young boy she portrayed. "Once we get to civilization, I shall make certain that you have a supply of jams before you go on your way. A toast to victory," she said, offering the canteen to him and patting his knee as though he were her brother. "Don't be frightened. You're wearing my colors, so you'll be safe. I won't let anything happen to you."

MacGregor swallowed quickly, shoving aside dark thoughts of Regina treating him with a bribe and a pat and sending him on his way.

She leaned against him and lowered her voice as though sharing a secret. "I find Pierre's earring to be rather dashing, don't you agree? I mean, no proper gentleman would wear one, of course. But all in all, I can see where he would make a lady swoon."

MacGregor stood abruptly, stretching and easing the tension out of his body. He didn't want to hear her speak of Pierre or any other man in that tone. The sound of it riled him, and he didn't know why. "We'd better take that camp now, while they're nursing bad heads."

She stood beside him, scanning the half light for the outline of the tents. "Lovely. Just lovely."

"Lovely," he repeated, trying the word on his tongue, fitting it to the woman. Bending close to her ear, MacGregor allowed his hand to curve around her slender neck, caressing the fine skin. "I don't want anything happening to either one of us. Jack Ryker is a skunk. He can drink whiskey all night and lead a killing party at dawn. He'll wake up at the slightest noise and wouldn't hesitate to slit your throat. So listen carefully. If you so much as take one step on your own, I'll toss you over my shoulder and run for the horses. Your damn saddle will make a fine pillow for the Comanche to trade in Mexico."

Regina licked her lips, her huge eyes darting up to him. "Your servant awaits, kind sir. I will be at your side, following your slightest whim just like the knights of King Arthur."

While he scowled down at her, she grinned and kissed his cheek. Her finger ran down the crease between his eyebrows, the light touch stunning him more effectively than a war ax. "Please, don't worry so. I'm small and fast and really quite capable. Just tell me what to do."

"DON'T worry, she says . . . wearing a damn purple ribbon on my arm, stealing horses and sheep with Ryker at my backside," he muttered beneath his breath, searching through the dark tent for the saddle. With little effort he spotted the reddish leather patterned with an intricate flower design and a large molded saddle horn. Wrapping the saddle into a blanket, MacGregor tied and knotted leather thongs, quickly fashioning a sling for his back.

He stepped outside the tent to see Regina's small body outlined against a dwindling fire. Lighting a long torch, she darted to several tents, setting them on fire. "Damn, she is fast as a rabbit," MacGregor muttered, gripping his Springfield rifle tighter as she darted inside the largest tent.

He held his breath, clinging to the shadows until she stepped outside. The bundle strapped to her back shifted as she ran toward the small valley apart from the camp. A dog barked sharply, and the flock of sheep, light and shadowy in the dawn, began to flow toward the pass. Running around them, circling the flock, Regina's small body caught the pink light of dawn.

Jack Ryker's stocky body appeared suddenly, blocking Regina from MacGregor's sight. "Hell," MacGregor cursed, easing the saddle to the ground. In the instant Ryker raised his rifle to his shoulder, MacGregor was on him. The force of his body threw Ryker to the ground. As he fell, he swung the rifle butt upward at MacGregor's head. Ryker's knife hissed, sliding from its sheath too late. . . . MacGregor's knife slid between his ribs.

"You bastard half-breed," Ryker gasped, blood spurting from his mouth before his lifeless eyes stared at the dawn.

Wiping his blade on Ryker's chest, MacGregor picked up the saddle and began loping toward Regina, cursing with every step. Then the first call of fire sounded at his back, and men, groggy from drink, stumbled from the burning tents.

The sheep moved too slowly, he thought, picking his way across a prairie dog field. Bleating, moving like pale leaves on dark water, the sheep disappeared into a stand of aspens with white bark.

He caught Regina easily, grabbing her arm to pivot her against him sharply. "I said burn one tent, then light out, woman. One," he shot at her just as a dog's sharp teeth nipped at his heel.

"Easy on, MacGregor," she ordered quietly when he lifted his rifle butt to strike the mottled black and white head of the snarling dog. Through the shadows the dog's white eyes looked back at him.

"There now, my fine lad," Regina soothed, petting the dog. "MacGregor is in a temper this morning. But we're not going to let that stop our lovely play, are we?"

"Lovely," MacGregor repeated, wondering how many times she had used the word that morning. "We could get scalped or shot in the backside at any moment, and you think it's lovely?"

"Lovely," she returned, grinning up at him. "There now, laddie. MacGregor may growl a bit, but he's a friend."

MacGregor glanced back at the burning camp, then at the goat leading the sheep deeper into the pass. The dog growled at Regina's side until she pointed toward the flock of sheep. "Go."

"We can't take those sheep through the pass."

She began walking quickly after the small flock, moving easily across the rocky trail. "Come on, MacGregor. It's a lovely morning for an adventure. Lady Guinevere is a wonderful lead goat. My sheep follow her without question. They're a Highland Scots cross, perfect for the mountains and lovely for wool. Fine mutton, too. These darlings aren't intended for cooking pots."

"Uh-huh," he said, shifting the saddle on his back. Veering off the trail, he found the horses. After swinging up into Kansas's saddle, he tied Regina's saddle to the horn. Slapping his coiled rope against the horses, he urged them toward the mountain pass. Overtaking the flock, the horses circled them and slid into the first bend marking the pass. Overhead a red-tailed hawk soared higher into the pink dawn, his shrill call cutting into the morning. A grayish-brown chipmunk ran up the side of a yellow pine to hide in the thick needles.

Patches of snow clung to the shadows, and Regina stepped through them as daintily as a lady on a London stroll. MacGregor found himself tracking Regina's slim backside as it swayed gently in boy's trousers. He wished that sweet curve were tucked neatly against him in the furs. He never wanted a woman clinging to him, never wanted her breath to swirl in his ear and hear those soft uneven sighs against his skin. . . .

Walking Kansas beside her, he blinked at her wide, saucy smile. The shouts behind them grew weaker as he studied the woman he'd set out to claim as his wife.

Her breath sent up a small cloud of steam in the cold air. The dog nipped and herded the sheep, keeping them in a close pattern moving through the rocky, curving pass. She ran back to her mistress frequently, acting like a frisky pup at her heels. Regina talked to the white-eyed dog, patting and slipping her a piece of jerky. "There now, my laddie," she cooed. "They left you to tend the flock all alone, didn't they? Venus is waiting with Pierre and a baby, too."

She bent to feed the dog MacGregor's sourdough biscuit, and the pack on her back slipped. "I'll take that," MacGregor said quietly. Less than an hour ago this woman's kiss ignited a fire in his belly, and now she looked like a girl, grinning up at him.

In the first sharp light after they passed a shadowy bend, Regina's thick, gleaming braid swung free to brush her hips. She lifted the pack to him carefully and smiled up at him. "My books . . . poetry and a wonderful book by a colonist woman, Mrs. Child."

He lifted the pack, inspecting the intricate designs of the bright indigos, reds, and purples of the soft cloth and the clinging fringe.

Running her fingers lovingly across the cloth, she said, "My paisley shawl. Quite in fashion when worn with a plaid dress. The pattern came to Scotland from India by way of the trade routes. See the intricate patterns? There are legends about it. One says that it's a caliph's fist print, his signature. Another says it's a flame. Mine is of fine wool from the undercoat of ten cashmere goats, though there are muslin and gorgeous bright saffron-colored shawls. Don't you love the tiny flowers inside the flames? The design is called *buta,* meaning 'flower.' " Regina grinned up at him wickedly. "Napoléon gave Josephine an Egyptian paisley shawl, and she ordered hundreds more. I've always thought the shawls to be rather . . . seductive."

Glass clinked softly within the bundle as he tied it to his saddle horn, and Regina bent to pick up a long stick. "Please be careful, MacGregor. That's fine English brandy and Scots whiskey in my shawl."

He eased the pack open enough to lift free the bottles and tuck them carefully into his saddlebags. Shifting in the saddle, he stared at the sheep moving higher on the mountain pass. This morning Regina had come after him, touching his arousal and asking for his mouth on her skin. She'd called him her "dark knight" and marked him with her purple ribbon before the raid in which he'd killed Jack Ryker. Then here he was stroking her shawl and watching her hips sway as they herded sheep and horses across a dangerous pass. In the midst of it all, she'd taken a name he'd given her. MacGregor shifted uneasily in the saddle. He wanted her near, her arms and bosom soft against him. . . . "You can ride behind me."

She grinned widely, stunning him. "Wouldn't think of it. But perhaps you'd better check on the horses. They're probably needing a tending hand while Laddie is doing all my work. He's a fine one, isn't he? A ship brought his mother to the docks and I found her amid the fish, begging for scraps."

"The dog is a female," MacGregor stated quietly as he turned to watch smoke rise into the morning sky behind them. He ground his teeth, aching for the touch of her.

"Oh, I know. But they wouldn't have let her come if they'd known, and I've gotten into the habit of calling her a 'him'. You see, I've been planning this trip a long time, and chose Laddie even before she was born to be my accomplice. Lovely when plans are successful, isn't it?"

MacGregor urged the big Appaloosa ahead slightly. He didn't want to explore the way the dog's scent could have caused every male dog in the country to follow them. He glanced away at a beaver dam, studying the thick fur of a big male with the eye of an experienced trapper. Women of quality shouldn't know the particulars of breeding. "You'll get tired. Wave when you do."

"Why, MacGregor. I believe you're blushing!" she exclaimed, studying him intently.

"Hell and damnation, woman. A man needs his privacy," he began hotly, as glimpses of her white breast in the dawn went scooting through him unbidden.

"Women, too," she said quietly, glancing down at the rising smoke in the shadowed valley. "Will they follow?"

"Not likely this morning. From what I saw, they'll have to sleep off their whiskey first. Without Ryker, they'll have to sit it out for a while."

Her brows went up. "Without Ryker?"

"Killed him. He had a rifle pointed at that swinging rump of yours. Since I'd just kissed those strawberry breasts and you'd run your hands down my privates, I reckoned Ryker better not nick anything I wanted to play with."

"You killed Jack Ryker? Was that necessary?"

"You're alive, aren't you? Swaying your hips and strawberry breasts, enough to pull a man's eyeballs from his head." He'd taunted her, not wanting her to pursue how many men he'd killed along his lifetime.

"MacGregor! Swaying hips, indeed." Flushing wildly, she stared at him, her mouth parted. "Strawberry . . . I did not fondle your . . ." She swallowed. "You know."

"Yes, ma'am. I truly do. It was lovely having you hot and wanting me. Can't say as I've ever had a woman come at me like that. Truly. It was divine."

"MacGregor!"

He admired the soft way she turned away, embarrassed. A man didn't want to think his woman had talked or rolled with another man, and Regina reacted just the way he wanted—new to the game.

Patting Kansas's mottled neck, MacGregor sat back in the saddle. "Feels mighty fine, boy . . . having a woman get hot and skittery when you're wanting her."

When Regina hadn't turned his way in an hour, he slid his fingers along the soft shawl and toyed with the fringe. "Women," he tossed at the horses, who began following him. He glanced over his shoulder to Regina and found her playing with the dog. "Riding point for horses and sheep. Carrying a woman's shawl and waiting to bed her like a half-starved boy."

He tucked up his collar against the winds sweeping down the ravines and settled into the saddle to doze.

THE moon rose slowly over the Sangre de Cristos, lighting the small meadow where they had stopped for the night. The sheep had slowed crossing the pass, and once the goat had turned on MacGregor, charging at him. Hercules, the ram, looked on with mild interest. Finally accepting his fate, MacGregor slid the entourage into a deep red rock ravine with lush grazing grass, tucked away from the mountain wind and fed by a stream.

Though the sky was blue overhead, the small meadow lay in shadows. A mountain cat screamed distantly in the night, and the horses, tied loosely to a rope strung between pines, whinnied uneasily. In a nook against the red rock cliff the sheep grazed peacefully. Laddie lay on a fallen pine log and sniffed the damp, earth-scented air frequently.

MacGregor snared two rabbits, roasting them on green wood spits propped over the small campfire. A small light skillet caught the meat drippings; camp coffee seeped in a tin bucket near the fire.

"This is marvelous," Regina called, propping the last of the branches she had cut against one side of the stripling MacGregor had tied to the ground. Placing her hands on her waist, she grinned across the shelter at him. "I am famished."

Crouched by the fire, MacGregor tossed a handful of cornmeal into the browned drippings and added water, stirring it into a gravy. Looking more like a boy than a woman, Regina should be tired, but he'd seen her thriving energy before, fed by excitement. Once the warm food hit her stomach, she'd curl into the sleeping robe like an exhausted child. Thrilled by their success, her face was flushed by the campfire as she settled at his side.

Leaning back against the red morocco leather, Regina looked at the stars over them and stretched her arms high. "Wonderful country. Beautiful and clean. This morning was positively exhilarating."

She giggled, patting him on the thigh. "You should have seen the earl's face. Lying there with his doxy, drunk as a loon, unable to do anything but watch while I tied him to a tent pole."

At that MacGregor placed the skillet on a flat rock and stared at her. "You what?"

Her eyes widened indignantly. "There you go with that positively black look as though I've misbehaved." She straightened, ran her hand across her forehead to smooth the curling tendrils back, and lifted her chin. "I had to let him know who was counting coup on him."

"He knows you're alive now," MacGregor stated slowly. "He'll be coming for you. Before he might have thought it was Indians."

Regina's eyes leveled at him, light within their dark lashes. "I wanted him to know. It was a point of honor. He'd treated Venus badly and left Laddie and my poor little lambs to fend for themselves."

MacGregor lifted his eyebrow. "You weren't exactly sweet-talked into leaving camp."

She frowned and looked away at the sheep settling down on the thick, dry grass. "No. I understood we were going to study a nearby flock of Navaho sheep and camp for a few days while I talked with the shepherd. My dream and the purpose of these sheep are to provide a new life away from England. . . ."

The sound of the creek rippling by the camp mingled with the animals' sounds before she turned to him. Her small hand rested on his thigh, and MacGregor found himself thinking of her breasts instantly, the soft flesh beneath his lips. . . .

"I am so glad you stole the horses, MacGregor," she whispered urgently. "I couldn't bear to leave them behind. We could use them for trade with the Indians as we go. I hear the natives treat their stock well."

"Unless they eat them for winter meat. You could have been hurt." MacGregor didn't want to think of the ways she could have been hurt. He handed her a roast rabbit haunch. "You wouldn't last long as a camp whore."

Biting into the meat, Regina scowled at him. Around the clump of meat, she said, "I wish you wouldn't use words like that." She licked her fingers daintily and asked, "I've been thinking, MacGregor. Where are these dangerous savages, the scoundrels that Moon mentioned? And why are we safe? And what did he mean, 'walking twixt the nations'? By the way, I've caught two lovely trout in the stream, and they'll keep there until breakfast. I want to do my part, MacGregor."

She tossed Laddie the remainder of the rabbit and wiped her hands on her trousers. She scanned the gravy, sampling it with the tip of her finger, and smiling at him as he waited for her to finish. "Well, are you too tired to talk? Shall I tuck you in and sing a lullaby?"

"I'm waiting for a chance to answer."

"Thank you for today, MacGregor," she said softly. "For keeping the bargain, despite the danger."

"Uh-huh." On an impulse MacGregor dipped her finger in the gravy again and licked it from her, his eyes locking with hers.

"My . . ." She sighed unevenly, then cleared her throat. "What else have you cooked?"

EIGHT

LADDIE barked savagely just as Regina finished dipping the last sourdough biscuit into the gravy.

The band of Indians moved from the night like shadows into the camp, surrounding them. Draped in furs, blankets, and feathers, Little Bird's warriors consisted of Cheyenne, Arapaho, Kiowa, and a Sioux bearing the mark of Red Cloud's band. The large gold cross covering Little Bird's beaded breastplate shone in the firelight, a fresh scalp of blond hair tied to his lance glistened. He raised his hand to salute MacGregor and spoke in English. "Two Hearts. Today you raided the whites and gave our Cheyenne brother many horses. Your red heart remembers your brother, the Cheyenne, murdered in their peace camp at Sand Creek by the white soldiers."

"I remember and pray that the peace treaty of Medicine Lodge Creek will ease the hearts of the Cheyenne and Arapaho."

"Pah! Black Kettle was at Sand Creek. His first wife murdered as she fled behind him. Yet he signs the white treaty for southern Cheyenne and their Arapaho friends, agreeing to one small patch of ground—a reservation." The word bitter in his mouth, Little Bird's broad mouth turned down.

MacGregor studied the warriors and the red paint marking their faces. These men, cradling their rifles as they hugged hatred to their hearts, would not bend to any treaty. With their Kiowa allies they tormented George Custer who

127

led the Seventh Calvary under General W. S. Hancock. Custer pushed the soldiers until a few ran from their enlistment.

Yet these men were friends of MacGregor's youth, and he ached with them. "I saw you, my friends, watching the camp. I have waited for you to share my humble fire," MacGregor answered, returning Little Bird's salute. Regina stood at his side, her face pale. The fierce men towered over her, their hearts filled with grief and murder. Men who had been tortured and whipped, fighting desperately for their lands against Spanish, French, and the floods of soldiers, miners, settlers.

Several inches shorter than the men, Regina met their stony looks with her own. Steel ran through the blood of both races, and each Indian appreciated the proud lift of her head.

Pride rippled through MacGregor; his woman stood beside him unafraid. Studying the five Indians who moved close to her, she looked back at them evenly. One touched her skin and the rippling braid, tangling his finger in the curling ends. Another toyed with her ruby eardrops curiously.

"The whites are foolish, like pale slugs on the bottom of a rock, waiting for the badger to tear them out. You understand the wind and the deer, running free," Little Bird stated quietly. "For this we call you brother and allow you to pass in peace, though there is blood flowing along the Purgatory and the Taos Trail and many who do not mark their brothers."

Dressed in a blue uniform jacket, leather leggings, and a loincloth, the Indian chief turned to Regina. "Your woman can run like the wind."

The Kiowa warrior grinned. "*Polainyi*—rabbit."

Little Bird's eyes flicked down Regina, and for a moment the cruel lines around his mouth softened. "This is the one you have claimed from the mountain and the whites. She is narrow like a boy. Surely she cannot be soft beneath the furs. You may have to take another wife to get sons to play with Jack."

Beside MacGregor, Regina's blush deepened in the firelight, and she stiffened. "Mr. MacGregor and I have a business arrangement," she began hotly, then stopped when she glanced up to see him smiling.

"Whiskey?" Manti, a Cheyenne, asked in a low, guttural tone.

"No whiskey. The Kiowa, the Arapaho, and the Cheyenne fight the wave of whites and their unclean ways," Little Bird stated harshly, scowling at Manti. When the warrior looked away, Little Bird nodded and turned to MacGregor. "Has your heart chosen its people, my old friend? Will your son of two bloods be thrown into a white man's school, alone and afraid as you?"

MacGregor placed his hand over his heart. "I take my son to the high country, to safety. My woman, too."

Little Bird touched Regina's braid as it crossed her breast. "My brother, the woman is not weak. She is a prize to warm the poorest man. Many will fight to have her, whites and red blood alike. You may pass freely, you and your brothers, because you take only what you need. Others who kill the buffalo and the deer and leave them to rot will meet another fate."

At his side Regina shivered slightly, and MacGregor found his hand seeking her small one. Little Bird glanced at their joined hands, then at MacGregor.

"Once as a child you fought the priest and took his lash to set me free, my brother." He touched his chest and then MacGregor's. "We found our visions in the Sun Dance together. . . . Of two bloods, you may pass safely. Your woman, too. You take your son to safety. This I understand."

Little Bird's broad lips curved into a small smile as he glanced down at Regina, who barely reached to MacGregor's shoulder. "She is scrawny, my brother. Perhaps you would need warmer meat in your blankets. A fat woman is good in the cold winter."

"Now, see here—" Regina began hotly before MacGregor tucked her against his side, his hand resting low on her hip.

"A poor man takes what he can," he said quietly as a flush rose in her cheeks. Patting her soft buttocks, MacGregor nodded toward the sheep. "Your flock needs tending, my dear," he said quietly, pressing his hand against the small of her back to urge her toward the sheep.

Her eyebrows shot up. "My flock . . . you want to speak to your friends without me," she snapped. "MacGregor, you are dismissing me like a child to be put to bed. In England and the Colonies, men think that women can't understand politics."

Scooping up the shawl bundle near her saddle, she walked toward the sheep. Watching Laddie meet her in a patch of moonlight, MacGregor admired the sway of her hips for a moment, then spoke quietly in Cheyenne to Little Bird.

TWO hours later, after the Indians had slid into the night, Regina returned to camp. Sitting cross-legged beside the fire and sipping his coffee, MacGregor watched her sweep elegantly into camp, draped in the large shawl. The brilliant colors caught the firelight, rippling along her body as she stalked past him and turned. Unbound, her hair shimmered and danced, fanning out as had the shawl. She gripped her shawl tighter with one fist and the apricot brandy bottle with the other. "You!" Regina swept a heavy swathe of gleaming hair back from her shoulder. "You and those men are really, really rude. No proper manners at all."

Flowing around her opened flannel shirt and rough trousers, the shawl caught the firelight, shimmering with it. The shining fringes danced around her leather leggings as she stalked the length of the clearing. Suddenly too warm, she shook free of the shawl, stripped the jacket from her and tossed it to the lean-to. Flicking open the buttons of her shirt to the top of her camisole, she was unaware of the slight shimmering of pale flesh entrancing MacGregor.

Then swathing herself in the shawl, she sighted down on MacGregor, trying to see his expression beneath the black beard. He looked like a pirate, missing an earring, she thought hazily, fighting the memory of his mouth tugging exquisitely on her breast at dawn. "There I was, made to sit like some shepherd boy tending the flock, while you chatted with the men about scalping and bloods and such."

Regina lifted the brandy bottle at him as he lifted a thick eyebrow, mocking her. She leaned down to press her finger to his broad chest. "Yes, I've had a tiny sip or two. Because I am very, very upset with you." A heavy fall of hair slid down her breast as Regina stood over him. "There you sit, happy as a lark on a limb, while I am made to skulk in the shadows. MacGregor, you have a thing or two to learn about being a gentleman. One does not make a lady wait in the shadows."

He tucked the lacy camisole deeper into her shirt, buttoning the revealing edges. "We have a visitor."

Regina tossed her hair away from her face. She blinked and swayed slightly, suddenly aware that a trapper shared the shadows with MacGregor. "Humph! Our woodland parlor entertains all sorts of visitors. Your woman, indeed."

She leaned down near his face. "I see that smile lurking beneath that black beard. You leer, MacGregor. And letch. I have never met a gentleman so disposed to leer and letch. Yet you lust and drool . . . and then complain—so I am scrawny, am I? . . . Who are you?" she asked the trapper seated at his side. Dressed in leather and an ornate beaded breastplate, the big-bellied man began opening a Bible, running his finger down the lines.

"He's an old friend. A preacher," MacGregor began warily. "Buzzard Jones."

"He just happened to drop into camp"—she snapped her fingers, suddenly dizzy and hot—"just like that?"

"Do you, MacGregor, take this woman in holy matrimony?" When MacGregor nodded, Regina glared at him.

"He knew I'd been wanting a proper marriage." MacGregor omitted that after talking to Little Bird, the warrior immediately sent his fastest runner to Buzzard's mountain camp.

"Do you, Lady Hawkes, take this man in marriage?" Buzzard continued, running his finger down the tattered pages.

Regina swung to the preacher. Seated next to MacGregor's bulk, Buzzard was birdlike. Dark with grime, his face looked like tanned leather. She swung back to MacGregor, eyeing him carefully. "You have an odd assortment of friends. This man can't read. He's holding the Bible upside down."

"Are you happy with the bargain at the cabin?" MacGregor asked her softly, easing a long strand of silky hair around his finger.

"Yes, of course."

"Done and married. Sign this here paper, missus," Buzzard thrust a scrap of paper at her. "Ah . . . I'll just hold that bottle for you in the meantime."

"I am very angry with MacGregor just now. If I sign this worthless paper, will you leave camp, Mr. Buzzard?" she asked, handing him the brandy bottle, which he raised to his lips.

"Amen. Hallelujah. Yes, siree, man and wife. This day in our Lord . . ."

Regina signed the paper and snatched back the brandy bottle. "Apricot brandy is not to be swilled, my good man."

MacGregor stood and slid coins into the preacher's hand. He grinned when Buzzard led his mule from camp. "Violet MacGregor."

Buzzard called back, "She's a mean one, MacGregor. Watch your step."

"Huh," Regina sniffed indignantly. "Mean one. Scrawny. The compliments one suffers when in the American wilds." She licked the last taste of apricot brandy from her lips while MacGregor finished sipping his coffee and tucked the paper into his pocket. She nudged his boot with her moccasin, prodding him. "Would you like a nip?"

When he raised the tin cup, Regina poured a good measure into it. She grinned up at him happily. "Quite the day, wasn't it? Filled with adventure, eh?"

"You're half gone," he said, easing down by the campfire. In a quick movement he snared her wrist in his large hand and gently tugged her down to his lap. For an instant she stiffened, unused to the hard contours beneath her. For such a lean man, MacGregor seemed comfortably padded. Adjusting herself to his angles and letting him hold her warmly had certain advantages. "Egad, MacGregor. You move so quickly. You must be very fast with a gun."

Beneath her, his body was solid, tense as though he waited for her to escape. "Told you I was. But I'm finding that there's things to be done nice and easy and slow."

Regina blinked up at him, trying to remember what Buzzard had said about "the missus," then dismissed the thought as MacGregor's strong arms closed slowly, warmly around her as though he were cuddling Jack. She closed her eyes, savoring the tender emotion. Actually, a little cuddling wouldn't hurt her right now, she decided, nestling her head on his broad shoulder. "You can be sweet at times, you know. My knight in the wilds, rescuing my flock and wearing my colors. I've never been so content as this moment, despite knowing that you can be quite evil at times. A lusting, moody brute."

When he cradled the back of her head in his palm and lifted her lips for a brief kiss, she snuggled against him. "Oh, MacGregor, it was wonderful. Running across the bush, counting coup and the purest revenge, then escaping unscathed. You should have seen Covington's face." She began to giggle. "There he was, besotted and used, his jaw agape. His nightshirt up to his. thighs. . . ."

She leaned closer, whispering. "He has terribly skinny thighs. Like two white sticks. Yours are . . ." She searched for the word and grinned as she found it. She wiggled her bottom comfortably on his lap. " . . . more manly."

When MacGregor said nothing, she looped her arm around his neck and sighed contentedly. "My lovely flock is safe and so is my saddle. And you were marvelous. Running through the brush, scowling like a pirate boarding a ship . . . my colors on your arm." She ran her hand down his cheek, her eyes softening as she shifted closer. MacGregor had kept his side of the bargain, something few men in her experience had done. "All in all, you've tried to meet the bargain, despite your obsession with this wife thing."

Stirring beneath her hips, he seemed quite uncomfortable. She smiled softly, remembering how accommodating he'd been throughout the adventure. "You know, there are some gentlemen who would run away when I asked them to kiss my breasts. But you were ever so kind. Truly . . . I feel quite rosy and cheerful. Oh, certainly, I'm tired. But just a little celebration first. Right, MacGregor?"

"Lovely," he answered, lifting the cup to his lips. Mac-Gregor's hand slipped beneath the shawl to find her breast, caressing it until it hardened. She shifted experimentally over his hard lap and settled on the hardened ridge she'd remembered.

She sipped the brandy, watching him over the rim of the cup. Darkly mysterious, glowing with some magical light, his black eyes met hers and his hand tightened on her breast for an instant. Then his palm was warm against her stomach, the hard fingertips sliding lower.

When he shared her drink, she touched his earlobe. It was warm and dark, and she began to think of the other warm and dark places on his body. The hard planes and angles, hot with masculine need and trembling with the effort of being gentle with her. MacGregor's skin was so hot now, his heart beating heavily in his chest as she placed her fingertips over it. She rummaged through the rough hair covering the heavy muscles. "You know, MacGregor, you would look dashing with my ruby eardrop in your lobe. Just for now. Later you could get a tiny gold hoop like Pierre's."

The firelight caught on the cord contracting in his jaw and throat. "You damn well like his ears, don't you?" he asked tightly.

MacGregor reminded her of a tough fighting mastiff with bruised pride and needing soothing. Feeling very warm and safe wrapped in his arms, she smoothed the rough hair escaping his shirt. She wanted to make peace with him and pressed a kiss to the base of his throat. "You really shouldn't look so fierce. It's just because you're tired. Let me pierce your ear as a peace offering. Think of my eardrop as a magic talisman to keep you safe. Please, MacGregor. We're only together for such a short time. Pax?"

His lips tasted like her apricot brandy; the lovely feeling of soothing him with touches and kisses warmed her. Poor

MacGregor, she thought drowsily. He needs petting and cuddling. . . .

"You might as well get your branding ceremony over. I give you one ear to keep you quiet about Pierre," MacGregor stated warily. "Reckon that will even the score. There's not another woman who I'd let mark me."

"Oh, how sweet! If it hurts, I promise to kiss it better. And I'll clean it every day so that it will heal properly."

MacGregor scowled. "This is serious, woman. A man can't wear baubles out here without . . ."

She smiled slowly, her eyes luminous. "But my dear, absolutely no one would question your motives. You are so manly."

He shifted uncomfortably and cleared his throat. "Do it then. I'll be proud to wear your mark."

"How gallant, how marvelous—"

"Now! Before you talk my ear off instead of maiming it."

Regina squeezed MacGregor's earlobe, dimming the pain, then carefully inserted an embroidery needle disinfected by good brandy. "Waste of good liquor. . . ." MacGregor protested as she thoroughly cleaned the area, dabbing away the bit of blood with a cloth saturated in the alcohol.

When the ruby glistened in MacGregor's ear, Regina kneeled beside him to study the pirate effect. She turned the jewel to the firelight, studying her handiwork. "It looks . . ."

He lifted a heavy brow. "Marvelous? Lovely?"

Tilting her head, she whispered huskily, "I've never seen such a beautiful man." With his hair gleaming in the firelight, the rough planes of his face in sharp contrast of dark and light, he was the fresh new country, the clean winds and sweeping meadow grasses. He was the mountains, craggy and capped with snow, and the spring sweeping over the rolling green hills. She lifted a strand of his hair, tracing the texture with the tip of her finger. The smells that clung to him were clean, unlike the cloying scents of the court. She inhaled his scent, savoring it. "Divine."

She wanted him then, stretched out beside her and tasting her with the hunger of the dawn. She could feel his desire running through her as hot and strong as the brandy. Her need to answer him throbbed deep within her.

Taking care, she placed her mouth on his, tasting the sweet apricots and the darker, headier desire heating his lips. "You're a lovely man, Mr. Two Hearts," she whispered, slipping her hand inside his shirt to feel the hard pad of muscle moving there.

"Oh, my," she whispered as her open palm found a hard male nipple. Rough and hairy beneath her touch, she found the nipple's mate and explored it while he watched her, his features darkening in the dimming fire. Loosening the top buttons of his shirt, she soothed the tense muscles of his throat and shoulders experimentally, finding his heart beating hard against her hand.

She wanted her breasts fitted tightly against him, wanted his dark skin against hers. Kissing him again, she unbuttoned her shirt slowly and placed his hand on her camisole. When his broad palm moved against her, molding her softness with trembling gentle fingers, she inhaled the sweet night air.

Unbuttoning his shirt all the way, she studied his nipples intently. "Two Hearts. One on either side, I imagine."

Then bending quickly, she suckled them gently, nipping, licking with her tongue, until he let out a strangled, "Violet!"

"Well, I just wanted to see if that felt as good to you as it did to me," she returned indignantly, straightening away from him. She traced the twin scars covering the heavy muscles of his chest with her fingertips, then bent to kiss them gently. "How did you acquire these, my lord?"

MacGregor's taut body stirred restlessly. He swallowed before explaining. "Sun Dance scars—"

Her lips murmured against his hot skin. "Mmm. An Indian ritual. A man dangles by his flesh for days until he finds his vision. Poor Two Hearts MacGregor. . . ."

Taking her time, Regina stood and draped her hair over the shawl. His eyes followed the movements hungrily, and she thought of how he'd touched her breasts as though she were precious. Before their raid, his mouth had been hot, tugging and drawing the heat down her legs. "Just this once to finish the bargain," she whispered huskily, watching the desire light in his dark eyes.

Turning slowly and walking toward the lean-to, she smiled as he followed.

LORD Mortimer-Hawkes stared out into the mists shrouding his castle. Before dawn the droplets shifted and shimmered beyond the window like a dragon's iridescent scales.

The previous day he had been ordered to pay coin for farming goods, and a choice breeding bull had mysteriously choked and died. The preceding week a storage house had burned to the ground.

He swept the goblet and crystal flask from his desk with a riding whip. The walnut panels echoed his cry, threw it back at him.

"Without the Mariah and the woman, I will be nothing," he finished bitterly. "Pagan, you shall pay for this disobedience and pay well," he hissed between his teeth. "I shall pluck you from the Colonies back into my keep. The arrangements for my travel are already made."

Crushing a length of satin in his hand, he brought it to his face. The exotic fragrance clung to him, taunting him, until he threw it out the open window.

The cloth caught the mists, floating through them, winding beyond his grasp as had his daughter. "Pagan . . ." he whispered rawly.

THE morning after the raid on Covington's camp, the mists clung to the valley where they had spent the night. A flake of snow caught on Regina's lashes as she watched MacGregor talk quietly to Laddie. Then MacGregor turned to look over his shoulder at her.

Through the distance of mist and light snow, she caught the heat and possession of his long slow stare, the small pleased movement of his mouth. Lying back on the fur robe, she tugged the shawl higher over her bare shoulders. Lingering in the warmth, she remembered how MacGregor had covered her tenderly with the cotton blanket and the edges of the fur robe before leaving the hut.

He'd stroked away the wild disarray of her hair from her face, his finger tracing her swollen lips.

Regina shivered, feigning sleep when he returned to crouch over her. The tantalizing light sweep of his finger traced her brows, then her lashes. "You're awake," he whispered, and the deep tone of his voice brought back another memory too wild to think about in the daylight.

"I shall die," she managed weakly when MacGregor placed the tin cup with tea in her hand. Taking care to cover her bare shoulders with the shawl, he eased her back against him and began braiding her hair.

His silence taunted her, and she shot him a daring look over her shoulder. The ruby in his ear caught and held the bare light like a drop of blood. "Whatever are you doing wearing my eardrop, MacGregor?" she asked, frowning.

"Your wedding gift to me, my dear," he said, slipping a large hand inside the paisley flowers to find her breasts.

Regina gasped, his palm hard and rough against her before he gently caressed her. "Wedding?"

"I've a paper in my pocket that says we're man and wife." MacGregor's palm slid to her other breast, warming it.

She tugged his wrist away, trembling. She ached everywhere, her breasts tender to his prowling fingertip. Yet something warm and soft caused her to want to snuggle back on the furs, drawing him down. . . . "Stop that! Here I am in my dishabille—"

He ran the tip of his finger across her breast. "Dishabille?"

She shivered, fighting her body's instant, liquidy heat. "Not properly dressed or groomed to receive visitors."

His large hand ran across her shoulder, cupping it. "Then you'd better dress. Because your . . . dishabille"—the word rasped from him unevenly—"makes me want to—"

Struggling into her clothes, Regina slid the shawl around her head and shoulders, glaring at him. "I'm in no mood for your bloody lust, MacGregor. The sooner we're off, the sooner we can part ways."

His kiss was hard and rough, taking her back down to the fur bedding. "We've mated, and now you're my wife. There'll be no going separate ways."

"MacGregor . . ." she began, then placed her fingertips to her aching temples. "I will deal with you later," she managed weakly.

Outside, Regina turned away from the broiled trout, her head throbbing. She sipped her second cup of tea, nibbling on a hard, flat biscuit. A gray mare waited beside MacGregor's horse, her saddle gleaming in the faint light. Using every drop of strength she had, Regina washed her face in the stream and walked toward the mare.

Placing her hand on the pommel, she leaned against the horse weakly and fought for strength to mount. In another moment MacGregor's arms had lifted her onto his saddle and he'd swung up behind her. Taking care, he wrapped her in the soft cotton blanket they'd shared, tucking the shawl around her face as though she were Jack.

Hearing the horses whinny and the sheep bleat, she sank softly into sleep.

Twice during the ride she allowed MacGregor to help her to the bushes. She followed his soft whispers, drinking water from his canteen and nibbling the cold fish. Then he folded the blanket carefully around her and lifted her to his saddle.

She awakened just as Pierre, holding Jack against his shoulder, stepped out of the bushes late that afternoon. "Ho! My friend, you have another *bébé* on your lap, *mais oui?*"

Sitting in the saddle while MacGregor swung down, Regina forced her lids open. He raised his arms for her and she found herself slipping down into them. MacGregor carried her to a lean-to, covering her carefully.

When she awoke, it was night and snow had begun to fall lightly. Both men sat near the campfire, watching her come toward them. A large rack of ribs roasted on the spit, and steam rose from a pot of soup. The horses grazed apart from the sheep, and Jack nestled in MacGregor's arms, cooing softly. His small hand reached up, and the man kissed it, his eyes warm on her. A night bird flitted through the trees overhead, and sparks from a bead of pitch burst out of the fire.

Uncertain of both men, Regina tugged the blanket closer and sat on a log. Pierre cleared his throat. "The *bébé* has been good. He eats and sleeps and only cries for food."

When Regina stared into the fire, fighting fatigue and her headache, MacGregor said quietly, "She's got a bad head. Swilled apricot brandy until she pierced my ear with her mark, then dragged me into the lean-to. Tortured me, used me hard and fast, before she started snoring."

Regina's head pivoted to him. "MacGregor!"

In the firelight he grinned back at her. The ruby eardrop flashed against his dark skin, taunting her. "Yes, ma'am?" he asked innocently.

Thinking better of arguing the events of the night, Regina closed her lips tightly. They were tender, as was every muscle in her body. As though she'd strained against her limits. Bending her head, she hid the quick flush moving up her cheeks.

Venus moved close to the Frenchman, laying her gray head against his shoulder for a moment. "What is she wearing, Pierre?" Regina asked, noting the heavy skins encasing Venus's narrow body.

Pierre shrugged and served her soup in a tin cup and placed a wooden trencher of ribs beside her. "She needs a coat. I make her one. Little pants and shoes, too, for bad winter."

Warming to the big Frenchman, Regina smiled, instantly aware of the way MacGregor had tensed. She could sense his dark mood. "Thank you so much, Pierre. That was thoughtful."

Without looking at MacGregor, Regina ate slowly, picking her way through her thoughts. "This is very good, Pierre," she managed formally after tasting the gruel.

He shrugged, pouring coffee into tin cups for MacGregor and himself. "Sagamite. Hominy, meat, and dried pumpkin . . . a little dried plum for sweet."

"We're moving out at dawn," MacGregor stated abruptly, his voice low and rough as he changed Jack's cloth easily on his lap. "Pierre will take the horses to trade while we head on to my place for the winter."

Regina fought to keep the spoon moving steadily toward her lips. She ate the gruel slowly, forming her words carefully. "I'm leaving, too. The nearest settlement would do."

Pierre's gaze skipped to MacGregor, then back to her. "The settlements are not safe," he said quietly. "Big trouble. The Bozeman Trail is closed, some forts now. The Sweetwater gold miners watch their backs. Much trouble since the Sand Creek Massacre. Red Cloud of the Oglala Sioux fights for his hunting grounds to the north. There is no peace between red and white now. The English will be hunting for you."

"She'll be safe. We're heading on up to my cabin," MacGregor stated quietly as he placed Jack against his shoulder. The baby's black glossy head bobbed for a moment, then nestled down with a sigh.

He'd handled her in passion as easily as his baby, Regina thought, frightened by her emotions. "Give me back my eardrop," she shot back at him, needing his anger to feed her own. "I have the means to pay you now, and you shall have your due in the morning."

"Damned if I didn't last night," he said, ominously spacing the words. He tossed a small knife in a beaded sheath to her. "A wedding gift from Little Bird's woman."

Regina turned the beautiful beaded sheath to the firelight, studying the intricate flower designs. "It is lovely. But they are mistaken about the marriage. You must give this back."

"The hell I will," he said quietly. Rising carefully with Jack tucked in the crook of his arm, he stared down at her through the smoke. Their eyes locked, and Regina shivered as she saw the determination in his. "See that she drinks her tea, Pierre. It settles her down."

Then, his shoulders and back very straight, he entered the lean-to with Jack.

"My friend is wounded, *chère*," Pierre murmured softly. "He thinks you dislike what he offers. This goes deep in a man's pride. He can provide for you and the boy's needs.

Now you need the safety of his mountains."

"Pierre, I am going with you," she hissed. "Mr. Two Hearts has some idiotic notion—"

"He says you are married, *ma chère*," Pierre stated quietly. "I see death in his eyes for the man who touches you. He wears your mark in his ear. There is danger all around. For now you have no choice."

Regina tried to push away the sight of the single drop of blood she had sucked from MacGregor's newly pierced ear lobe. She closed her eyes, and behind her lids his dark intense expression as he moved over her in the night appeared. She swallowed, something running through her too strong and wild to deny. Looking down at her white trembling hand, Regina murmured, "Rubbish. We were simply . . ."

She glanced at MacGregor, who moved toward the sheep bedded down nearby. Laddie and Venus moved at his heels like shadows. He crouched by a ewe, running his hand slowly across her ears and head as he had explored Regina's face the previous night.

"I do not take a woman from my brother," Pierre stated simply, rising to his full height. "He protects you from all others as well. A white woman cannot travel alone here, *ma chère*. Let him care for you until it is safer for you and the Englishman's dogs are called off. By then . . ."

He shrugged, the fringe on his jacket dancing. "You stay with Two Hearts this winter. His *bébé* and perhaps the man need you more. You will be safe."

"Rubbish. Mr. Two Hearts, indeed."

"MacGregor wants his family safe, little one," Pierre murmured. "His heart bears many scars, and he is frightened a little, I think. He gives what he can, and much has been taken from him," he said before moving off into the night.

Regina sipped her tea, watching MacGregor move through the small flock and crouching beside each one. Flanking him, Venus and Laddie nuzzled his arm and licked his hands. When he had finished, he moved to the horses and began inspecting their hooves.

She'd seen men who knew animals, soothing them with gentle hands. Men who could settle a mare as she foaled or approach a dangerous bull and touch him easily. MacGregor's ways weren't hers, but animals sensed the security of him, just as she had during the day.

She thought of his hands, gently holding her as they rode through the rocky pass, or the way his body tightened as he turned in the saddle.

Wrapping the cotton blanket around her, Regina sat near her sheep. Settling beside the goat, she allowed Venus and Laddie to lie against her. Surrounded by the animals' heat, she stared up at the stars.

She didn't want to cry. Didn't want to feel small and alone, as she had as a child. She had always survived. Shifting slightly, Jennifer's fearful face slid across her lids as she dozed, fighting sleep. *"Remember the stories. . . . "*

Venus cuddled closer, whining softly. She stilled when Regina petted her.

Later, she felt herself being lifted and carried. MacGregor placed her inside the lean-to, tucking her into the curve of his body, and covering them both with the buffalo robe.

In the night he placed his hand over her breast and drew her closer. With his hard body pressed against her back, Regina dropped into sleep.

NINE

"THE wind leaves the valley and lifts over the mountains here. When it goes up, the sand drops and makes those hills," MacGregor explained later in the day as the stock drank from a meandering stream. With the high, rugged Sangre de Cristos behind them, he pointed across the flats to another mountain range lying in the west. A flat sagebrush-studded expanse, swept by freezing winds and laced with snow, lay between the rising mountains.

"To the south lays Taos. Old Bents Fort is east across the Sangres. We're headed west." He scanned smoke rising in the distance, his face grim as he turned to Pierre.

The Frenchman nodded, the two tall men placing their hands on each other's shoulders for a moment, their eyes meeting. "I will get a good price for the horses. Je t'aime will serve your woman well," Pierre said, patting the Indian pony he had given Regina. He swung up on Covington's finest Arabian mare and began moving toward the grazing herd. He waved to Regina, who held Jack, then let the mare race with the other horses, moving south into the new wild land.

MacGregor nodded, his face grim. "That will put them off the scent. Horses with lines like those are easily spotted."

The freezing wind swept around her, lifting the curling ends of her braid and playing with the fringes of her jacket and leggings. Beneath her soft moccasins the frozen sand made a crunching noise as she passed. She glanced at the canvas sheet covering her saddle. MacGregor and Pierre had agreed that the ornate lady's sidesaddle would be easily recognizable and should be hidden. MacGregor had saddled Pierre's Indian pony, a small, tough brown-and-white mare, taking care to shorten the stirrups of a western saddle for her.

Jack fretted restlessly in her arms, his round cheeks flushed. "There, there, my lad," she crooned, rocking the baby. "We'll manage without your friend. He'll come back to play with you."

MacGregor slashed a dark look at her, noting the beaded sheath at her waist. The look held and warmed, his expression softening. "You'll do," he said quietly.

He pointed toward the barren flats, and Laddie stood up instantly. The dog barked excitedly, and Guinevere bleated immediately, her bell twinkling as she moved ahead of the sheep, her udders jiggling gently.

Jack cried softly, and Regina bent to kiss his cheek, frowning at the heat in the tiny body. "Shh, little MacGregor. We're off."

MacGregor watched his friend, following the way the horses ran into the sprawling freedom of the Taos land. "I'll take Jack," he said, watching her.

"I can manage. After all, we have a bargain, don't we? Until we reach civilization?" The hot, possessive glance he threw her way tangled around her heart and stomach and left her trembling. As though he'd die to keep her at his side.

"Until I call it quits," he said flatly, watching her. "Like I said, my boy needs a woman, and you took the job."

Regina straightened, setting her shoulders back. Another man had owned her mother and had tried to break her. Whatever the mountain man was—gunslinger or tender father—she couldn't allow him to possess her soul.

MacGregor's hard profile turned toward the flats, scanning them. "We're not headed for the settlers. One look at those purple eyes, and there would be hellfire trouble. The duke's trackers would be on our heels before the trail had cooled. You're mine now. The same as Jack," he said flatly, swinging up to his horse. "Are you riding or walking?"

Regina eased Jack aside and slipped her hand in her pocket. "I want to give you this in return for my eardrop . . . payment for saving my life and helping me get back my saddle." Walking to his horse, she lifted and opened her palm.

Glittering in the sun, catching the light in colors, and sending it up into MacGregor's face, the diamond was a perfect cut, the size of a bird's egg. The colors danced on his dark skin as he looked down at her.

"Glass. Payment for taking what is due me by rights?" His deep voice was too silky, a tone she had come to recognize as very dangerous, concealing a dark mood.

"There is more. I want you to take me to the nearest fort or settlement as soon as you can. Pierre—"

"You turned to him for help?" The question was hard and flat, demanding, startling her with the intensity.

"Of course. This morning you were in a devil of a mood—"

"You've been playing up to him, sashaying around him with that damned dishabille shawl around you. A thing like that can give a man a powerful need for the blankets." MacGregor scowled down at her, his hand rubbing his shoulder.

"How coarse!" Regina trembled, wanting to slash out at him. "You're saying that I offered my favors to him. What I am offering is payment for services—" She caught her lip, wishing she'd chosen another word.

"Services," he repeated slowly, darkly, as he straightened in the saddle. "You're paying me for time on the blanket with that piece of glass?"

"No!" The cold wind sweeping across the flats didn't cool her hot cheeks. "This is an African diamond, MacGregor. Worth many times over anything you may have. I'm asking that you take me to the nearest settlement. Once I'm on my own, I can manage."

MacGregor leaned his forearms over the saddle horn and scanned the flats, tracing Pierre and the flock of sheep moving away in separate directions. Tall and rangy, his eyes shadowed by the brim of his hat, MacGregor suited the tough, dangerous country. His black eyes slashed to her suddenly, pinning her. "They'll be after you for the stone now. There will be a price on your head and men who would take it."

Jack began to squirm against her, and Regina held him closer. "I took what was mine. Lord Covington doesn't know it's missing."

"You had it hidden, then, because you didn't have it before," he finished curtly. "Either way, he'll be after you."

"It's part of my inheritance and my dowry, my wedding gift to my proper husband."

MacGregor straightened slowly, his saddle creaking as he straightened his long legs in the stirrups. His smile wasn't nice, more like a wolf showing his teeth at a helpless rabbit. "I reckon that's me, Violet. Bring my son." Then he moved off slowly, leaving her holding Jack.

Jack slept soundly, snuggled against her as she followed MacGregor and her sheep. Tugging down her cap, Regina glared at his broad back, noting the times he rubbed his shoulder. When he rode alongside her to take Jack, she glanced at him, then continued to ride, her head high. MacGregor's hand reached out to press her thigh for a moment, his voice rough and low in the sound of the wind sweeping through the sagebrush and yucca. "Like I said, you're a broody hen, tending your chick. Jack knows when he's well taken care of. That's good, because we'll be traveling hard now so we can get to the cabin before the snow is too deep."

"He's not feeling well."

MacGregor's expression darkened. "I know. That's why we'll be pushing hard. Can those sheep keep up or do we leave them?"

Regina stared at him, tossing her braid behind her shoulder. "Laddie and I can make them keep any pace you set, Mr. MacGregor."

His eyes flashed with pride, the satisfied expression of a man who had made the right choice. "That's what I thought. There's rawhide in you, Violet MacGregor, and that's what my boy needs. Steel and the softness, too."

The sleeping baby made smacking noises against her breast, and MacGregor's black eyes swung to her chest. "Now, that's a sight," he whispered roughly, reaching over to lay his broad hand on her back. "My boy taking to his new ma. I like that place myself, smells like cinnamon bark."

Was their night in the lean-to a dream or a memory? Regina wondered, shivering as she met his dark gaze for a skip of a heartbeat. She fought the sounds and the feel of his heavy body resting on hers in the aftermath of a passion. Within moments of entering the lean-to after the raid, she'd risen to frightening heat, and MacGregor had entered her too slowly, too reverently. She'd taken him savagely, running through the heat in a fever, until . . . Flushed with the memory or the dream, she followed Venus's graceful sprint after a black-tailed jackrabbit.

By evening Jack began fretting in his sleep, and Mac-Gregor quickly built a small pit fire, surrounded by rocks. While Jack's milk heated, MacGregor fashioned a hut from the brush, protecting them from the sweeping wind. Too tired to care about fighting his possession, Regina stumbled into the protection and fed Jack while MacGregor cared for the horses and mules. Venus crept into the shelter and lay against Regina's leg. "My poor beauty," she soothed, petting the greyhound as she rocked Jack.

Before dawn MacGregor lifted his son from her, talking softly. "We're heading out as soon as Jack's fed. Horses and mules are ready."

By noon Regina clung to her saddle, her body stiff and cold. The wind penetrated the cotton blanket and her clothing, and they seemed no closer to the mountains. MacGregor sighted a wagon in the distance and rode toward it, leaving her behind. When he returned, he gently took Jack from her. "They've got a meal we can share and a fire for Jack's milk. The sheep will move on ahead."

He studied Regina intently. "It's a catwagon, loaded with whores. They have their own rules, but one or two would sell their souls for that piece of glass you're carrying. One word from you, and they'll peg you. Keep those eyes down, too," he ordered grimly.

"Maybe it would be best if we went our separate ways. I could travel with them—"

He scowled down at her. "My wife traveling with whores? You think they'd take those woollies or the dogs?"

"I'm sure for a price, they'd allow—"

"For a price they'd sell you and the animals."

The ten women ran to meet them, skirts flying and gathering blankets around them for warmth. "Lawsy me!" a large black woman cried out when he swung down from the horse. "Such a pretty little child. Indian baby, I'd say."

MacGregor reached up and lifted Regina down, drawing her tightly against his length as they huddled behind the wagon to break the force of the wind. The canvas covering flapped and beat loudly against the high staves of the wagon. He handed Jack to the woman. "My son. He'll be needing his milk warmed, then we're heading out."

"I've got plenty milk, right here," the black woman said opening her blouse.

"Can't your woman feed that squawbaby?" a woman with bleached blond hair and an unbuttoned bodice asked. She moved against MacGregor, her white breasts jiggling slightly above the corset she wore over her stained red satin dress. "Can't see much of her, but she looks like a Mexican-Indian breed. You hungry for white meat?"

She reached up and flicked the ruby in his ear. "That's a nice pretty. Trade you that for a quick one right now." She thrust out her quivering breasts at him. "Bargain day, mister. Goldie is worth a hell of a lot more than that bauble."

Tucked against MacGregor's lean side, Regina shot a stare at the blond woman. "Indeed," she muttered before his hand tightened threateningly on her waist. The flat of his hand urged her breasts against his flat belly, the movement bringing her thighs around his hard one. MacGregor's thigh moved intimately against her with a rhythmic, sexual intimacy overlooked by the women.

The thought that women came fluttering around him like bees after honey angered her. Taking a deep breath, she ducked her head, frowning. She didn't want other women touching him; she trembled with fury and despised the bitter emotion.

When she tried to ease away, he held her closer, his thigh continuing the stealthy nudging. Trembling with frustration, Regina's softness began to dampen, despite her anger. In desperation she let her hand slide to his lean backside and pinched him hard. MacGregor grunted and glared down at her, allowing her a few necessary inches of freedom.

Another woman with bright red hair and painted eyes chewed her small black cigar. She eyed MacGregor from hat to worn boots. "Fancy ain't had no man since last night, mister. Your woman best drag you away fast 'cause you look like a whole lot of man to these hungry women. Bet you could sweet talk a woman right slick out of her drawers in one shake of a cat's tail."

"Huh!" Regina snorted.

MacGregor leaned back against the wagon, cupping his coffee in his hands. Looking very arrogant and male, his long legs in a wide stance, he glanced down at Regina's averted face. "My woman keeps me happy," he drawled.

She glared up at him then.

"Scrawny little thing, ain't she?" asked a big woman with jet-black hair as she handed Regina a bowl of hot beans and a tin cup of coffee. The odor of strong perfume used to cover an unwashed body filled the air as she reached past Regina to pour whiskey into MacGregor's cup.

"A man likes whiskey with his food. I like it anytime. Like my men anytime," the black-haired woman said, pushing a dirty strand of hair back. "Mister, have you married a half-grown child? Can't she talk? Or maybe your squaw is too good to mix with the likes such as us," she called belligerently, the wind throwing the words back in her face.

MacGregor stood away from the wagon, scanning the sheep who had begun to move again. A full head taller than any of the women and rawhide lean, he stretched to his full height. One woman sighed and another reached out to stroke his broad chest. His hand moved quickly, removing her touch like an unwanted, clinging weed. "She's got the infirmities. We're moving out."

The woman glanced at Venus, gnawing on a bone. "Sickly-looking dog, too. Mister, for such a man, you picked two unhealthy specimens."

"I do love a big, rough man," another woman cooed softly, her hand running up and down MacGregor's arm. "You're a mighty lucky woman, missus," she cooed. "Hell!"

The tip of Regina's bridal knife slid across the back of her hand, the light scratch seeping with blood. MacGregor caught Regina's wrist, then took the knife and slipped it into his belt. He grinned down at her, all male arrogance. "My wife wants me all to herself."

"Knife-happy savage," the woman bawled, holding her hand.

"Now, sweetheart, watch that temper. You have me all to yourself tonight," MacGregor drawled to Regina, his grin widening.

Regina gritted her teeth and nodded, tugging her cap lower. The black woman handed Jack to her. "You'd better rest a mite, mister. We been doing a land-office business right out here in the middle of nowhere. Got plenty of beans, cornbread, and whiskey to spare. Mariah Jones is my name, and I kin whup any man-dog in two territories." She nodded at Jack, who alternately nursed and fretted. "That baby is sick. 'Course, being a breed, they can live on scrub brush and cactus juice."

Beside Regina, MacGregor's tall body stiffened, and he threw his coffee at the woman's feet with two silver dollars. "We're heading out. I'll take those boots you're wearing for my wife."

Taking care, he lifted Regina with Jack in her arms to the pony. In a quick glance she saw the fury in his eyes, felt the way his fingers trembled as they brushed Jack's flushed cheek. His lips tightened as he looked up at her.

In that instant Regina knew that he'd kill to protect his child. She knew, too, that Jack needed her to survive.

Against her breast, Jack mewed softly, his black eyes meeting hers for a moment before he dozed. She tightened her arms around the baby, adjusting him into his sling.

This was her moment of choice. "I'll take care of Jack," she agreed huskily. "Until he's better."

For an instant his hand wrapped around hers, and something strong, yet tender passed between them. "You'll do, Violet," he stated roughly, patting his son's glossy black hair and adjusting the pouch sling. "You'll do just fine."

Gently, MacGregor folded the cotton blanket around her and his son, then tucked the folds beneath her bottom and legs. With deft motions, he slid her moccasins off and replaced them with the boots. The women peered from the shelter of the wagon, and the wind carried their comments to Regina. "Now, that's a man . . . got cold eyes . . . gunslinger for sure . . . takes care of that squaw as if she was a high-falootin' lady."

That night Regina watched MacGregor tend his son in a deserted adobe-brick hovel. She gnawed on dried meat and sipped her tea, which MacGregor had brewed in a small tin bucket. When Jack had been changed and fed, MacGregor held him close, his expression tender. "There now, Jack. Soon we'll be home, and you'll be warm and sassy."

Easing back against the adobe bricks, MacGregor grimaced slightly, then turned his shoulder carefully to the wall. In the shelter of the wall with the night cold and quiet around them, MacGregor placed his son on his thighs. He glanced at Regina, wrapped in a blanket. "Come here. You need tending."

She didn't want to see the dark fires burning in his eyes, nor feel his need of her in the night.

"Come here," he repeated softly, delving into his saddlebags. "The wind burned your face. You need salve."

She didn't want to go to him. Didn't want to acknowledge how tired and worn she'd become. But somehow she was next to him and his fingers were soothing salve on her cheeks. Tucking her against his side and drawing the buffalo robe around them, MacGregor rocked her gently. "Nothing is going to happen to Jack," he said quietly after a moment. "We should hit my place tomorrow or the next day."

"Did you want those women?" she asked sleepily.

He chuckled, the sound richly intimate in the night. "Used to as a boy. But now I like honey kisses and the smell of cinnamon. Purple eyes staring down at me with silky hair all around, black as a raven's wing."

Regina dozed off for a moment, her head resting against his shoulder, then looked up. She wanted to comfort him, to ease the pain he held so closely inside. "He'll be fine."

"Uh-huh. Go to sleep now," he said, urging her to slide down next to the wall.

She awoke before dawn and lay listening to the sheep and the horses graze. Jack lay in the crook of his father's arm; MacGregor's pistol lay next to him.

Needing time alone, she stoked the dying embers of the fire. She could leave them now, take her horse and the sheep, and ride south, following Pierre.

Then Jack cried softly and MacGregor's deep voice soothed him sleepily. Regina frowned as she watched the flames catch on the dry sage branches. She'd come to love Jack, and now the baby needed her. Perhaps for a time MacGregor's protection was essential to her survival. Jack cried again, and she listened intently to his discomfort. Then, standing slowly, she motioned for Laddie to take the flock toward MacGregor's mountains.

They reached the foothills of the mountains at nightfall. At dawn MacGregor began breaking a trail to his cabin in the knee-deep snow.

Jack had just begun to cry in earnest for his dinner when MacGregor, the horses, and mules passed over a small rocky ridge and disappeared. The sheep had moved easily behind Je t'aime, and Laddie kept them in a close formation in the mists.

"Home," MacGregor said quietly as they stared down at a log cabin. Built low to the ground and covered with a sod roof, the small building perched next to a stand of aspens and pine, an alpine meadow spreading out before it. A small creek, dammed by beaver, fed a large pond glistening in the last sunlight. A herd of deer slid into the shelter of the forest, and antelope poised for flight, watched them cross to the house.

In minutes MacGregor started a blazing fire in the hearth and had unpacked the animals while she held Jack. Small and musty smelling, the cabin had a rough table, two stools, and cots. A woman's torn lace corset, discolored by dust and smoke, was nailed to a chinked log wall. Various stone jugs, wooden bowls, and iron pots were stacked on the shelves. MacGregor glanced at Regina, who still stood watching him. In another quick movement he snatched the corset from the wall and tossed it into the fire. "Trappers have been using my place. Now that I've got a marriage paper in my pocket, they'll stay away." He took his son, preparing to feed him. "It's small and snug."

He nodded to the two cots laced with heavy rope. "I'll make a bigger one for us tomorrow."

Regina managed to walk to one cot and ease down carefully while Venus whined and settled by the fire.

She slept heavily and awoke to the sounds of MacGregor talking to his son. "She's a fine one. Hot-tempered and strong as rawhide, and she's a lady."

He held the baby on his lap, bathing Jack's thrashing limbs with soapy water. Regina stretched and yawned, aware that he'd slipped her jacket and boots away during the night. "I am famished."

"Stew is in the pot. You've slept right through the afternoon, just like Jack," MacGregor said, dressing his son carefully. The lines in his face had deepened, and there was a slow, rough edge to his voice, as though he badly needed sleep.

While she slept, he'd cleaned the cabin and had carried in wood. Jack's cloths were strung around the fire, the cans of food and bags of staples neatly placed on the shelves. Laddie and Venus chewed on meaty bones near the fire.

Standing slowly, Regina lifted her shawl from the back of a chair and draped it around her. She needed something of home snuggled close and soft to her, her hands stroking the vivid red-and-purple pattern as she walked to the fire and sank down between the dogs. Watching the flames, she tried to remember what had clawed at her as she slept.

MacGregor stood at her side, his height filling the small cabin. "Better eat."

When she continued to stare at the fire, he crouched beside her and tugged at the rawhide thong binding her braid, working the strands free. MacGregor traced the shape of her ear. "You dreamed about that black woman, Mariah. Screamed out her name and another—Jennifer."

"Mariah?" she asked softly, the name flickering, taunting her like an elusive feather. Then he handed her a bowl of steaming food and her china cup of tea, and the name went sailing away into the smoke.

"Jack is sleeping. I'll see to the stock," he said quietly, easing his coat sleeve up his injured arm. "The sheep and goat are bedded down in a half shed. The way the wind hits the valley, there should be some grass left for a little while."

Regina placed her bowl aside and began lacing her leggings. "I'll want to see my flock. They've had a hard time of it."

"And you haven't?" he asked quietly as he waited by the door. When she passed, MacGregor caught the shawl beneath her throat and drew her to him. "I didn't make our marriage bed today," he said, watching her closely. "I'm asking you to mate with me on the floor tonight."

His fingertip rested over the rapid pulse in her throat. "You took me like lightening and thunder last time, rode me too fast. This time, I'll know just how fast you move when you're wanting."

Regina ran out the door, leaving her shawl in her hands.

MacGregor was too big and moved too fast, she decided later as the winter winds began howling around the cabin. In the distance a coyote howled, and Laddie lifted her head, listening intently.

When Jack had quieted for the night, MacGregor inhaled deeply and rubbed his shoulder once more. She glanced up from petting Venus to see him grimace. "Damn lead. Taking its own sweet time to work out this time," he muttered, the firelight running across the high ridges of his cheekbones and coloring them with reddish tones.

Regina rubbed her hands together, studying them. "I'll take it out."

"What would a woman like you know about lead and meat?" he shot back at her.

"You have little choice. I can take it out," she returned.

"You're a lady. You'll faint dead away, useless as—"

She smiled tightly. "We shall see, won't we?" Rising to her feet, she slipped her knife from its sheath. She poured Scotch into a cup and dipped the knife in it. After placing his knife in the coals, she turned to him. "Strip down."

Watching her warily, MacGregor eased his leather shirt off and sat on a stool. Regina eased his red underwear from him, noting the bloody stain on his shoulder. His forehead was hot against her palm. "You're running a fever, MacGregor," she said quietly.

The wound had festered, his dark skin inflamed and puffy. When her fingertips probed for the hidden bullet, he stiffened and groaned slightly. "Lead works out."

"Not this one." Regina cleansed the area gently, locating the bullet, then took up her knife.

"Damnation," he swore softly as she probed beneath the bullet, working it from the band of muscle with the tip of her knife. She caught the lead pellet in her palm and dropped it onto the table, then began cleaning the deep tear in his skin.

"What happened to your back?" She ran her fingertips across the scar ridging his shoulders.

MacGregor lifted the Scotch bottle to his lips and drank heavily before answering. "The priests loved whipping the sin from themselves. When they finished, they started on the half-bloods, including me," he said between his teeth.

For the first time she'd picked a stone up from his past and turned it over to find his pain. Reaching out to stroke his hair, Regina closed her eyes and remembered her painful childhood. Somehow, his head rested against her breasts, and MacGregor sighed as he nuzzled the soft curve.

She stroked his head and neck, wanting to soothe away his pain. "Your wound is bleeding badly, my dear. I'll have to cauterize it."

He nodded. "Do it. Burn it with Old Hugh. Do it, then let me rest against you. God, I'm tired."

The Bowie seared his skin, the odor of burning flesh filled the air. Regina quickly salved the area and wrapped it with a strip of her clean cotton petticoats. MacGregor allowed her to tug his boots off and strip him while he stood.

He lifted his good arm and placed his hand on her cheek. "I could use one of those foolish kisses now, Violet." Standing over her, he'd never looked more vulnerable, more needing of her comfort.

"Do as you're told and you'll get one when you're settled down for the night," she returned, aching to hold him.

"Now." He leaned down waiting, eyes closed. She raised on tiptoe and brushed his lips with hers. "There, now, MacGregor, that's a good man. . . ."

His eyes opened suddenly, looking deeply into hers. "Lay with me tonight, Violet. Hold me like you do Jack when he's hurting."

Wrapping around her, his ache mirrored her own, frightening her. "But you're a man, fully grown."

"I'm needing you tonight, woman. Haven't ever asked a woman to hold me before," he answered tightly, straightening. Looking arrogant and proud in his fever, she knew he wouldn't ask again.

"Very well. You settle down on the pallet in front of the fire, and I'll check on Jack."

He was asleep when she slid beneath the heavy blankets, dressed in his long cotton shirt. Taking care not to touch him, she lay looking at the fire. MacGregor shifted his tall body, his hand reaching out to find her breast. Slowly his fingers closed around it, caressing the softness gently. In his sleep he eased downward to rest his head on her chest.

Big and tough, warrior and father, he rested helpless now in her arms, needing her strength.

She found herself stroking his hair, unable to stop the tears sliding down her cheeks. To soothe them both, she began singing *Greensleeves* softly.

"DAMN it, woman. You don't need to know how to shoot a gun or throw a knife," MacGregor snapped a month later. The first week of December had wrapped them in the snow-covered valley.

He tossed the cleaned snowshoe rabbits down on the table and pointed to the blanket she had placed across a rope strung between the cots. "But then, you've got fool notions for a married woman. Man and wife weren't meant to sleep apart. Damn, you're tough as rawhide when you get a fool notion inside that pretty head. You've cleaned and scrubbed everything, got me cleaning my boots before I còme into my own house."

Regina stopped reading the poetry of Elizabeth Barrett Browning and placed her marking ribbon by "Lady Geraldine's Courtship." Running her finger around the rim of the violet pattern on the china, she looked up. Neatly shaved, MacGregor's dark, strong jaw tensed with anger that had been brewing since he'd healed. "Shh, Jack is napping. I expect you to act like a gentleman and see us through this bad patch." She took a deep breath and continued, "Stop looming at the doorway like a grizzly about to pounce on a rabbit."

"A grizzly would be a mite more friendly than I feel now. You shaved me when I was sick, and I figured that wouldn't hurt me if it was what you liked. Well, I've been shaving every day, waiting for you to decide what was best for you." He ripped off his coat, glared at her, and deliberately tossed it to her cot. He pointed to his chest. "Husbands! I'm the only one around—*tell* their womenfolk how to hop. I've got the marriage paper—"

Regina rose to her full height and tapped his wide chest with one small finger. "So I signed a ridiculous paper when I was high in my cups. You can't expect me to abide by it."

"Drunk, Violet. You were drunk and willing."

She brushed her hand across her temple, trying to keep her temper. Patting the braids wound like a crown on her head, she swallowed and counted the sheep grazing in the shallow snow. She adjusted her lace blouse, her short skirt swirling around the leather leggings as she turned. Taking care to wrap a shawl she had fashioned from a soft blanket around her shoulders, Regina faced him and raised a slender eyebrow. "I may have been a little excited over our victory . . ."

MacGregor took a step nearer her and unfastened the top buttons of his red woolen long johns. In the afternoon shadows with her eardrop catching the light in bloodred colors, he frowned down at her. Regina took a step backward, her hip hitting the table. He took another step, and his hand shot out to snatch the wooden stick that had been holding her thick braids in place. "You've got queer ways. I knew that when I took you. But when a man's wife spends more time with her sheep and his baby than mating with him on a cold night, he has plenty to complain about."

Toying with her cup, she asked the question plaguing her. "If I had not been with you at the catwagon, would you . . . ?"

MacGregor's black eyes skimmed down her throat, and he placed a finger on the pulse beating rapidly at the base of it. His voice softened and deepened. "Not after you. I've an idea that no other female could tempt me with swaying hips and sweet honey kisses. You've ruined me for any other woman, Violet MacGregor. You're jumpy as a doe guarding a fawn or a rabbit set to run right now."

Catching his wrist, she looked up at the harsh angles of his face and the sensuous curve to his mouth. "But you enjoyed being fondled by those women."

His thick brows went up. "Fondled? With your blade ready to gut any trespasser?"

Placing her hands on her waist, she glared at him. "Their hands were everywhere but in your pockets."

Staring at her blankly for a moment, he muttered, "Didn't notice. Had what I wanted tucked against my side. All I had to do was to look down at you. Everything sweet and clean and loving when the time was right."

Something melted within her, warming and softening her heart. "Truly, MacGregor? You found me more desirable than all those women?"

"Truly. Hell. You're more woman than I've ever known. Is that what's been eating at you?" When she bit her lip and looked away, his warm fingertip prowled down her chest until it reached the lace bodice. He flicked open one pearl button. "I like what's under here—silky, soft sweet skin. From now on when you wash, I won't keep to the other side of that damn blanket."

In another quick movement he bent and lifted her high against his chest. "I gave you a slack rein because you'd been hurt. But you're sassy as hell now, and I'm wanting you."

"MacGregor, you have no idea how to—"

"I have plenty of ideas, Violet, and all of them have to do with those sweet kisses and the way I remember your breasts. . . ." He paused, studying the thrusting curve of her blouse. In a lower, husky tone he murmured, "There's more to you now. Can still put my hands around that tiny waist, but the other parts . . ." His black gaze strolled down her hips and legs covered by the short skirt and leggings. "Makes a man want to put his face between all that softness while he's—"

Trembling with the image of MacGregor's warm lips on her skin, Regina blushed hotly. "Oh, that's just what I mean. You go from kisses to—"

"Mating. Me in you. You holding me tight and hot and getting hotter. Feels like hot, wet satin in there, near as I can remember. You think it's easy waiting for Jack to get better and you to settle down? When you move like that?"

"What?"

"You move like a willow sways, bending, turning, looking over your shoulder at me with those purple eyes and that hair spilling everywhere but in my bed. The cabin carries your scent, and it drives me mad. At night I can see your body through your clothes with the firelight just so. . . . I'm not waiting anymore, Violet." His black eyes tasted her lips, and his arms tightened around her. "This time I'm going to ride you until you know where you belong."

She stared at him, her body aching for the heat of his. Clearing her throat, she managed, "Egad."

Against her hand his skin was hot. MacGregor's lips were hard, demanding on hers as he carried her to the bearskin pelt in front of the fire. Lowering her carefully, he placed his tall body over hers. "Now. Tell me how and what you want. Quick," he breathed against her mouth, his tongue probing gently at the corners.

"MacGregor," she managed shakily as his hand went skimming down her clothing, leaving her exposed to his mouth.

Before she could react, his head was at her breast, the hot tugging of his lips and tongue drawing her into his mouth. "Cinnamon," he whispered against her skin, his face so hot against her as he nuzzled aside the cloth covering her other breast. Licking the hardened nub gently, he nibbled around it, his breath sweeping across her skin. "Strawberries and cinnamon . . . and hot, wet satin underneath," he murmured before taking the softness into his mouth.

She couldn't move, his hands trembling as they moved over her skin. Fighting her rising passion, Regina placed her hands on his chest to push him away.

Her fingers met crisp hair, the strong muscles moving beneath the dark skin as he shifted more fully over her. Braced on his elbows and resting his hips against her, MacGregor looked down at her tenderly.

The warm look caught and tangled her senses. His fingers moved carefully through her braids, loosening them. Taking care to be gentle, MacGregor spread her hair around her head. He lifted a rippling strand to the light. "Catches the sun like a raven's wing. Blues and purples dance in the black."

Winding a length in his hand he studied the effect on his dark skin. "Sometimes at night I dream of how warm and soft this is next to my skin. Feels like warm feathers sliding on me. Smells like nothing I've ever known."

Regina blinked, trying to fight the sudden softness in her body as MacGregor's aroused weight fitted snugly between her spread thighs. Under him and shaking with emotions, she swallowed heavily. "MacGregor. You've got to stop this—"

He stared at the path of his large hand sliding gently over her breast. He caressed the soft pale weight, exploring the contours with a reverence she'd never known. His fingertip ran around the perimeter, touching the dusky tip as though it were a fragile flower. His expression softened as his fingers stroked her skin up toward her throat. "I can feel the blood move in you. Beats hard against my touch."

He slowly eased aside and stared down at her breasts. "So soft. I can fit my hand from tip to tip." He experimented, moving his palm and fingers across her skin, as though fitting her for his touch. Then sliding his hand upward, he wrapped it around her throat, stroking the taut cords lightly with his thumb. Trailing the underside of her jaw, he stroked her cheek. "Softer than doe skin, like the petals of a rose soft in the morning dew."

She wanted to fight him, to move away, but she wanted to see his face, watch the fleeting expression cross his hard features. MacGregor treated her like a special gift, wrapped and waiting just for him. His fingers skimmed her flesh featherlight, leaving a heated trail downward.

His large hand slid under her skirts to unknot the muslin drawers. Loosening them and sliding away her skirt, he studied her from her masses of black hair down to the leggings just below her knees. One fingertip traced her hipbones slowly, and MacGregor watched the trail, his eyes darkening. "Day or night," he said quietly, as if to himself. "I feel you taking me deep as a knife in a sheath. Holding me tight," he whispered raggedly, his hand trembling as he placed it carefully over the raven curls above her thighs.

"MacGregor . . ." The aching deep tone of his voice snared her, and she saw her hand stroking his cheek. "My dear . . ."

He caught her hand, pressing it harder against his skin, his eyes closing as though placing the memory inside him. "What do you want from me?" he whispered roughly, looking down at her.

"I want more," she whispered back after a long moment.

He frowned, tracing the shape of her ear. "I'm strong and I can protect you. You won't be hungry or misused. What else is there?"

She had to make him understand, bridge the gap between their worlds with carefully chosen words. "I know little of you. You love your son. You've killed and been wounded as a child. But there's more . . . there's love and sweet words."

He traced the shape of the ruby eardrop thoughtfully. "Right now, I'd rather—"

She placed her fingertips over his lips. "Shh. That word is so rough. It sounds like two animals tearing at each other in a fever."

Against her fingers his hard mouth smiled. "Felt like that in the lean-to. You came at me so fast, I was gone before—"

"MacGregor!" She stiffened as his hand flattened on her stomach. "How unlike a gentleman to mention what happened!"

He frowned, placing his hand possessively on her breast. "That's just what happened. For all your hiding behind this blanket, you took what you wanted." He grinned suddenly, smoothing her hot cheek. "Rode me—"

"MacGregor!" Regina tried to dislodge his heavy thigh, catching her clothing to her. "Oh, you are an animal. A rutting, primitive animal in heat."

He nodded solemnly. "Sure was. But you were there before me."

"Oh! Oh!" She squirmed from beneath him and sat upright in the tangle of her hair and clothing, drawing her blouse to her breasts.

"Damn, you're a pretty female, Violet MacGregor," he whispered before taking her easily beneath him. He grinned as he pinned her wrists over her head. "I might as well make use of having all these clothes half off you."

When MacGregor's hot mouth fitted over her breast, she gasped. Desire went ripping through her as his tongue laved the sensitive nub, and she groaned. In another moment he had slid deeply into her body, and she forgot everything but the blinding heat as his fullness throbbed heavily within her.

She soared high into the blinding emotions, straining to reach the pinnacle and falling softly. . . . Before she could move away from the sated aftermath, MacGregor kissed her softly, nuzzling at the tender spot behind her ear and whispering his need of her.

Then she was reaching for him again.

"You fill my heart," he whispered huskily against her cheek when they drifted into sleep.

TEN

"MACGREGOR'S his name. A métis, a white and red breed—mean as a skunk and draws like quicksilver. Quick with a blade, too," Tall Tom said after swishing Covington's prime twenty-year-old bourbon through his teeth, then swallowing the fiery liquid. "Met a preacher who married them, name of Buzzard. Says the woman was half-grown, dark-skinned, and had strange eyes. There war'n't no squawbaby, though. The woman matches the likes of the boy who shot off my toe. Never will forget those eyes . . . dark pewter in the campfire."

He wiped his lips with the back of his sleeve and glanced around the large hunting lodge. The lodge nestled against the base of the Sangres, the scent of freshly cut pine logs blending with tobacco and heavy incense. Prime antlers and horns lined the main hall, fringed rugs and pillows blended with gleaming brass and silver. The Englishman sat in a chair made of longhorns and padded with velvet.

Tall Tom eyed the heavy jeweled rings covering the Englishman's hands and the large gray pearl studding his knotted tie. "MacGregor stepped right up for the fancy little bastard—female. If old John Barleycorn and me hadn't fandangoed together, that mixed blood's hide would have been skinned and tanned proper now. Heard Jack Ryker's been taken down. Tough one, Ryker. Only a man like MacGregor would take him on. Or me. . . . They worked like a pair of mated wolves. One hamstrung me, and the other moved in for the kill."

Covington kicked aside the man who had been polishing his knee-high black boots. "Leave us, lackey," he ordered, straightening his velvet jacket and flicking a bit of dust from it. "Christmastide is this month, and I'm faced with Mortimer-Hawkes descending out of hell at any moment," he muttered.

He leaned forward in his chair, studying the rough mountain man, who lounged with his boots on the dining room table. Regina had vanished into the mountains without a sign. He suspected that once Krebs and his men left camp, they'd never be back.

Slapping the riding quirt against his tight buff breeches, he stalked to the roaring fire. "I thought I was dreaming when I saw those eyes the night of the fires," he said, as if to himself. "Yes, that heathen savage blood of hers would take to a man like the métis, MacGregor. It's a wonder Mortimer-Hawkes dirtied his title with that bitch whose grandmother was brought from Africa, even for her fat dowry."

Covington poured whiskey into a small crystal glass on a silver platter, drank it down quickly, and poured another. He swirled the drink against the sparkling glass, studying it. "They slid into camp at dawn and took the horses, firing the tents. Regina looked like a savage. She took that bloody morocco saddle and her hideous shawl."

"She's gone Injun. Should be easy to track with a squawling baby and that skinny all-legs dog. Talked to a trapper who passed a catwagon down Taos way. The whores had seen a man matching MacGregor's size with a small woman and baby. They thought it was strange the way he treated her, careful like. The woman slit a whore's hand for touching the métis."

Tall Tom tipped the crystal decanter up to his mouth and drank noisily. "I'll slit that cat from ear to ear," he said, wiping his hand over his mouth. "She shot off my toe. Marked me. He moved in then, broke my leg. Mean pair of renegades."

Covington tapped the hunter's boots with his quirt. "Speaking of the lady's ears. Did you notice rubies—red stones—in her ears?"

The mountain man thought for a moment. "No. Couldn't see nothing but those eyes, looking up at me. Black lashes all around those eyes. But the whores said the breed sported a red pretty in his ear."

"Mmm. Regina would have paid him for her passage, and her eyes are a bloody shade of purple, the mark of those savage Mortimer-Hawkeses," Covington murmured thoughtfully, then turned to the mountain man. "My good man. You bring me her ears with the rubies still in them, and I'll make you richer than you ever dreamed. Agreed?"

"Hell. I'd skin her and MacGregor for a plew a piece," Tom agreed, rubbing the ache in his mended leg. "I'll take out soon as the snow stops."

Covington turned to the flames, watching them dance along a huge log. The sight reminded him of Regina's shawl, swaying along her lithe, small body. "Wrap her ears in that bloody heathen shawl she treasures so much. Looks hideous with red and yellow flames and flowers."

His thoughts swung to Mortimer-Hawkes. The marquess had sent word that he would arrive in the Colonies before spring. As stubborn as his daughter, the marquess needed proof that his daughter was dead. In their agreement for the marriage, Mortimer-Hawkes had specifically and repeatedly told Covington that whatever happened to Regina, she was still Mortimer-Hawkes's property. The marquess was adamant that his daughter live until his death.

Covington narrowed his eyes on the orange and red flames. He'd seen men fascinated with their daughters before, keeping them for their private stock. But he'd never known a man so determined to hold his daughter's spirit. "He's obsessed with the little dark-skinned wench. Well, apparently the lady has taken another man, Lord Mortimer-Hawkes. This MacGregor may want to own her as badly as you do."

MORTIMER-HAWKES stared out at the storm-tossed sea, his ship's cabin musty and close. The small window caught his reflection, the hollow cheeks and eye sockets, his hair matted and tangled. "Pagan, you shall pay dearly," he crooned softly, watching the shade of his eyes change into dark purple in the salt-crusted glass. "You carry the family insignia, your eyes, Pagan. I shall find you easily, even in the wilds of the Colonies. You'll wear the Mariah around that slender bit of a neck like a ten-stone. That fool Covington. I should have known he couldn't control you away from my grasp. Not for a fortnight. He doesn't know what your savage blood is capable of doing. But I do. I do and I will bring you to heel as I did your mother. Then all my power will return, the estate will prosper as it did when I held you in my fist. . . ."

WRAPPED in her shawl, Regina stared at the fire running along a dried limb. With the cabin settled for the long night, and MacGregor camped near his trap lines, she was alone with Jack. The baby sighed softly in his willow crib, and Regina turned back to the fire. Sparks shot out as a bead of pitch ignited. Her lips moved around a word, tasting the memories. "Mariah."

The sound of the word brought the past skipping along her thoughts. She closed her eyes, trying to remember an elusive memory. . . . A dark-skinned woman with lustrous black eyes bent near her, smiling tenderly. . . . The woman, wrapped in gauze and veils, laughed and danced sinuously, the sound gentle and melodic as she tapped tiny cymbals between her thumb and fingers . . . the woman hugging her close and sobbing softly, her enormous black eyes filled with tears . . . her father's voice roaring with rage across time, his quirt whipping the woman who crouched at his feet. . . . Hiding behind a velvet curtain, Regina saw the woman dance for her father as he drank. Above the veil her liquid almond-shaped brown eyes were frightened, wounded. . . .

The tiny cymbals clinked softly, blending with the music of a lute as she whirled faster and faster, her soft hips quivering. The coins lining her tight bodice and girdle flashed and tinkled musically. The heavy scent of incense clung to the scene as her father stood and drunkenly swaggered toward the dancing woman. Raising her arms high, twining her wrists as her fingers kept up the rhythm, the woman stood still as his greedy hands ran over her. Then she danced away, the gauzy material clinging to her almost nude body. Her father reached out again, ripping the embroidered bodice from the woman's shimmering, full breasts.

Between the dancing, painted nipples an enormous stone, bloodred and glittering, swung from a thick golden chain.

Regina shook, opening her eyes to force away the memory of Hawkes's hand toying with her mother's nipples and the jewel before he raped her.

The flames danced higher on the log, hissing. "Mariah," Regina whispered, hugging her trembling body as the tears streaked down her face. "My mother's and grandmother's name and the name of the jewel."

A sudden chill swept into the room, and she shivered, trapped by her past.

"Come here, Violet," MacGregor said softly as he closed the door behind him. "Let me hold you when you cry. Just hold you, nothing more."

With a cry she ran into his arms.

MacGregor slammed the ax into the fallen log. Filled with frozen sap, the wood split instantly, the sound cracking like a rifle shot. He jerked the ax back. "She can't cook. Even burns beans."

He stared down at Regina clearing snow away for her sheep to graze. In the freezing air the sun hit the snow in blinding intensity to outline her small body. Dressed as a boy, she'd fitted MacGregor's big snowshoes to her, tending her flock while he ran his traps or hunted. Now pulling Jack's small sled behind her, she moved freely through the clearing bordering the pines. The fringed sleeve covering the barrel of MacGregor's Springfield rifle protruded from the bundle behind Jack's cradleboard. Regina carried it when MacGregor wasn't hunting and had recently brought home her first rabbits, cleaned for the stewpot.

She'd left before first light, taking the rifle and the snowshoes. When she returned, MacGregor was just on the point of wrapping Jack and packing out to find her.

Her grin had died when he said flatly, "There's the pot."

The violet-colored eyes had opened wide, looking enormous in her small face. "You mean . . . me cook?"

"Seems like you should be catching on to it by now," he'd said, his pride riffled a little by the way he tended the meals and baked bread while she provided the meat. "Wouldn't hurt for me to come home from two days' trapping and find a hot meal waiting."

"Lovely," she'd snapped, ripping her cap from her and tossing it to the table. Staring at him, she'd stripped off the heavy fur coat and his shirt, leaving her lacy white blouse thrust into the leather pants she'd fashioned. Taking her time, she'd worked free the single braid skimming down to her hips until the raven mass spread all along her body. "A lady isn't trained for kitchen work, my good man."

Placing her hands on her waist, she tapped the toe of one small leather-shod foot. Her hair rippled down her to her hips, and MacGregor wanted to dive his hands into it, wrap himself in the sweet perfume.

But instead, he crossed his arms over his chest. A man had to be firm with his woman, teaching her the right way. Except for the night she'd come crying into his arms, they'd squared off in the past three weeks, and MacGregor's temper was wearing thin.

"Trapping. Disgusting way to kill, MacGregor. Beastly way for an animal to die. A clean shot through the brain is much kinder."

He'd taken a step toward her, winding a soft strand of hair around his fist to draw her face near his. "I could show you beastly. Right on the floor."

Lifting her chin, Regina had met his dark stare unafraid. "Of course. Ever the gentleman, aren't you? Your way of courting is using your superior strength to overcome me."

Anger had shot through MacGregor like a burning blade. "I've never raped you. Nor mated with you when you weren't willing."

"One has little choice when one wants to survive—"

"We're married!" MacGregor's roar echoed in his ears.

"The devil we are. You don't own me, MacGregor. I'm merely biding my time until you see the reason of taking me to civilization. The times we've . . . come together have been because of necessity."

"Necessity," he repeated roughly, the word clawing at his pride. "You had to mate with me . . . so you did."

"To put it crudely . . . yes, exactly that."

"What of the babes—my children—that result?" he'd asked in a high temper.

"You can't expect me to bear your bastards, MacGregor."

"My rightful sons spawned in marriage, damn it, woman!" he roared before striding out of the cabin.

For two weeks MacGregor had kept to himself, feeling like a wounded wolf while Regina skipped happily around her flock. She'd struck at his pride, rubbing it raw. When she sang "the beautiful music of Greensleeves" to Jack, MacGregor found an excuse to leave the warmth of the cabin. He didn't want to remember the spicy scent of her skin, nor the way her breasts flattened against him softly during his fever.

Slamming the ax into the tree again, MacGregor worked furiously. He needed to rid his body of the tension that ran through it like a hot wire each time he caught the scent of her body. He taught her how to shoot the rifle as an excuse to hold her. In the evenings they worked with their knives, throwing them against a spot on the cabin log.

Learning about survival in the mountains, Regina's endless questions pursued him. MacGregor's uneasiness grew each day. . . . He'd seen men preparing to desert in the war, and Regina demonstrated those same signs.

Regina, alone in the woods, would be easy prey. The thought caused him to sweat, evading her next question.

"Women. This one doesn't know the first thing about being a wife," he muttered, trimming a branch with a quick stroke of the blade. "Wives are supposed to know how to cook and stay at home while a man traps."

Throwing his weight into the ax stroke, MacGregor studied the split wood. "They do what they're told. Wives keep their men warm in the blankets. But she wants 'more.' What the hell is more?"

Taking a deep breath, MacGregor petted Venus, who snuggled beneath a buffalo robe on the wood sled. Rubbing his palm over the purple ribbon in his pocket, he traced Regina's awkward movements in big snowshoes made from white ash and leather thongs. "She's headed out at first chance. Hell be damned."

Just then a mountain cat shifted on a limb over her ram. The cat's tawny coat gleamed in the bluish-green branches of the fir tree. MacGregor cursed, weaving quickly through the brush and trees toward the deathly scene.

The cat was on him suddenly, leaping across to another limb and down at MacGregor. A branch slapped his arm as he drew his pistol, ruining his aim. The bullet ripped across the cat's shoulder just as his fangs tore into MacGregor's upper arm. Rolling through the snow and brush with the mountain cat, fighting to keep the fangs from ripping his throat, MacGregor heard nothing but the snarling, hissing fury of the wounded animal and the sound of his fear tearing through his head.

A rifle shot cracked next to him, and the cat slumped across his chest. Huge dark purple eyes, veiled with tears, looked down at him. Barely conscious, he groaned as she shifted him to the sled. Beside him Jack fussed and dogs barked wildly. Streaks of pain ripped through him like raking knifes. . . .

"Oh, my dear," Regina crooned softly through the red haze. Her fingers soothed his hot forehead, the spicy scent of her body so near. . . .

Resting near him, feeding him broth from a spoon, she sang the lilting *Greensleeves* song.

He groaned, the fiery lashes streaking through him as she salved his throat and chest. Sounds drifted around him . . . Jack cooing and crying, Regina hushing the baby.

Her fingers were cool, brushing his hot forehead. "My sweet, dear man. Saving my ram at the expense of your safety . . . rushing through the brush like a knight charging into the fray of battle to save my precious Hercules."

From far away his voice sounded raspy and uneven. "You shot the cat?"

"Yes, my dear. And Hercules pulled you to safety on the sled. Would you like more meat broth?"

MacGregor slipped into the darkness with the taste of apricot brandy on his tongue. Near him Regina spoke in hushed tones. "Ah . . . yes, Jack, here we are. Mrs. Child's *The American Frugal Housewife* book is wonderful. . . . You see, with these dried berries we picked near the cabin today, we can make currant jelly by cooking them with sugar. Won't your father be surprised when he tastes this lovely sweet?"

Jack gurgled happily, and Regina giggled. "Yes, I like your kisses, my little man. There. You kiss me and I kiss you. . . ." Jack laughed wildly.

Her kisses were cool and sweet as summer blackberries on his lips, the scent of her hair clinging to him as he slipped down into the darkness.

The sunlight skimmed softly into the cabin filled with the scent of baking bread as Regina rocked Jack and read to him. "You see, Jack. Ladies must be treated delicately. A tender word about their hair or their dress. Perhaps give them a small present or two." Jack babbled and she laughed, the sound tripping low and sweet across MacGregor's senses.

Then she was dancing in the firelight, holding Jack close to her as she hummed a song. "Ah, yes, now you have it, my little man. Smile at your love and kiss her hand like so. . . ."

She lifted Jack's chubby fingers to her lips. "Then look into her eyes and tell her of her beauty."

MacGregor remembered her eyes, dark and purple as the small woodland flowers. Or dark blue like the clear mountain streams moving through the shadows of trees. The baby cooed and babbled, and MacGregor's lids closed slowly as he drifted back down into sleep.

Then the cabin was dark, the flames low in the fireplace. A shadow slid close to him, an exotic scent filled the air—Regina. Forcing his lids open, MacGregor found her swaying softly as she lifted her arms over her head. Tied around her waist, the shawl clung to her swaying body. She moved her hips sensuously, experimenting with the spread position of her bare feet on the bear pelt. Her hair streamed down her bare shoulders, catching the firelight as the strands slid across her bare breasts. She hummed softly, pausing and changing the tune as she rotated her hips. The cloth caught the light following the length of her legs. She repeated "Mariah . . ." slowly.

The cloth slipped low on her buttocks, dipping to reveal the rounded soft mounds swaying to the beat of the song she hummed. The slender length of an arm lifted, and the uptilted breast shimmered pale and soft in the light. Her movements brought her nearer his cot, and MacGregor caught the scent of cinnamon and woman.

Then his hand was on her warm bare thigh, the soft flesh and slender muscle trembling beneath his broad palm. Above him her full breasts quivered with the last of the dance, her hair swirling out from her like a blue-black cloak. "Violet," he whispered huskily looking up at her.

"PAGAN. You're out there, I can feel you breathing," Lord Mortimer-Hawkes whispered, scanning the coastline of the Colonies. "I'll find you, and when I do, nothing will match the power of the Mariah in my hands."

THE fever broke, leaving MacGregor too weak to protest Regina's daily reading sessions. Now his head rested against her breasts when Jack napped. She shifted the book on her lap. Her right arm rested on his shoulders as she spoke quietly. "You're at my mercy now, my fine mountain man. You shall have to listen to my favorite literature without complaint."

Braced against the cabin wall, Regina shared MacGregor's small cot, supporting him.

He sighed softly and shifted closer to the cinnamon-scented valley of her breasts. There were advantages to being weak, he'd discovered, and one of them was having

Regina soothe and croon to him. The other was the way she didn't seem to notice the way his lips rested against her skin, nor the way his hand fitted the curve of her small waist.

Closing his eyes, MacGregor let her low, husky voice waft over him like a sweet summer breeze. He let his fingers drift lower to the softness of her hip, then on to a slender thigh exposed by her short skirt.

" . . . The knights of the Round Table treated the ladies of the court with respect, as was their due. At Christmastide the halls were decked with mistletoe, and they danced and made merry. The elegant dances were much loved by knights and ladies alike. Performed to the tune of a lyre and flute, the dances provided a gentler time amid wars and rivalry. Often a minstrel would sing lovely sonnets of the lady's beauty and a heart's true love."

Just beneath the soft skin covering her throat, the pulse had quickened as MacGregor looked up.

Soft arms and warm purple eyes could snare a man just as surely as chains, he thought drowsily. Her eyes widened as he shifted, careful not to frighten her, and lifted his lips to hers.

The soft gasp of surprise filled his mouth. MacGregor's fingers skimmed around her thigh and delved gently into the warmth of her thighs. "Now, MacGregor," she whispered warily against his lips just before the tip of his tongue tasted hers.

"Sweet as honey," he murmured, trailing little kisses along her hot cheek. She quivered, her fingers tightening on his arm as his tongue traced the whorls of her ear. As he'd seen her play with Jack, he lifted her hand and kissed the back of it. When she shivered, he turned her small hand upward and kissed the very center of it.

"Egad, MacGregor," she whispered unevenly. "Egad, MacGregor," she repeated as he took the book from her and tossed it to the floor.

Taking care, he eased her down along his side. "Lay with me, Violet," he whispered, kissing the back of her hand again. "Talk with me."

Her small hand had found his chest, the fingertips smoothing the rough hair as she would pet her animals. He lifted a strand of her hair and eased it across his throat. Regina had stilled, her head resting on his chest. "I've never wanted to talk with a female. Learn about her . . . just talking," he murmured against her hair, inhaling the clean, flowery scent. "What makes your hair smell like flowers?"

The small hand on his chest paused. "You think my hair smells like flowers?" When he nodded, she whispered, "Lavender soap, milled in England."

"Mmm. Lavender?" MacGregor nuzzled her temple, letting the wayward tendrils play across his skin.

"Purple flowers, dried and . . ." She trembled slightly, looking up at him.

"Purple like your eyes . . . or violets in the deep woods, clinging with morning mist—"

"MacGregor!" Her soft startled cry pleased him.

Pressing, following her emotions like a tracker after prey, MacGregor lifted her palm to his lips, nibbling at it. "Tell me about Christmas in England."

She stiffened against him, and MacGregor continued to stroke her hair, feeling her ease slowly. "You just could be dangerous," she whispered against his chest. "I daresay that I can fight you better when you're acting like a wounded grizzly."

He laughed then, and she stared at him. "You *are* dangerous, far too comfortable and likable at the moment." He kissed her gently, just to taste the ripe, sweet moist lips rubbing against his.

"My," she whispered after a long moment. "You have your moments, my friend."

He rubbed her head playfully as he would Jack. "Tell me." Laying with her at his side, talking softly in the night was a dream, he thought lazily as Regina's head rested back on his shoulder and she gazed at the ceiling, talking softly.

"The halls of the castle were decked with mistletoe and ribbons, platters of food and drink ready for the guests.

There was music and dancing and games. Jennifer, my nanny, sneaked candies and sweets to me." She hesitated, and a bead of pitch caught fire noisily before she continued. "My father always managed to ruin the holidays. His favorite game was to punish me or lock me in the closet for hours. . . . 'Pagan,' he called me. 'Little savage.' He'll be after me. . . ."

"Hating can eat a person, Violet. And you're safe with me," MacGregor whispered against her warm skin, sensing her deep pain. To distract her, he asked, "Tell me about mistletoe, decking the halls."

Her fingers smoothed his chest, skimming across him like feathers. "Green leaves and white berries, a vine used to decorate. Kissing under the mistletoe was great sport, though the plant was said to have been prescribed by the Druids for . . . female infertility. The Scandinavians thought mistletoe was a plant owned by Frigga, goddess of love," she finished drowsily, nestling closer to him.

Sighing deeply, she rubbed her cheek against his chest. "Do you really think my skin isn't too dark? . . . My father said it was dusky as a savage's. . . ."

Running his fingers down her smooth arm, MacGregor tried the new fancy kiss to the back of her hand, and she moved closer. "Pretty as pale doeskin, bleached in the sun. Soft as down and warm as Jack's. Tastes like gold honey made from purple clover flowers. . . ."

"Really? My, you say the oddest, most lovely things. . . ." she whispered sleepily. MacGregor slid his hand inside her blouse and found the soft mound of her breasts just before he slept.

REGINA clapped her hands and laughed when MacGregor finished playing *Greensleeves* on his Indian flute. "What a beautiful Christmas present!" Seated on MacGregor's lap, Jack sleepily explored the two-foot-long instrument with chubby fingers.

"It's an Indian courting flute. Traded it from a Mandan." Recovered from his wounds, MacGregor lounged next to the fire in the evenings, sharing a cup of tea with her. He was wearing only his trousers, and the puma's claw marks crisscrossed his wide, dark chest. "*Wi oblu'spa yun'kan*," he finished before beginning another song. The melody reminded her of the wind swishing through the pines and skimming the blue snow lakes.

When he finished, Jack slept, nestled against him. "*Wi oblu'* . . ." she repeated. "What did you say, MacGregor?"

"*Wi oblu'spa yun'kan.* That's Sioux for 'when I was courting.' " He began to play again, the plaintive melody filling the cabin over the sound of the wind. When he was finished, MacGregor smiled at her and began talking quietly. The deep, rough tone of his voice entranced her. "There was an Indian maiden at the marriage age, Bird Who Flies Away. The maiden's hair was long and sleek, black as a raven's wing. Many warriors wanted to catch her eye, and if she smiled at one, she would be taken, and in the morning the bridal price of ten horses would be tied to her parents' tepee. But the girl found fault with each suitor. There was one who caught her eye, Many Horses. But he looked away from her and played his flute by the lake." Placing the flute to his lips, he played another melody, sweet and quivering, reminding her of the wind whistling through the reeds in the moors.

"She walked by him, dropping a pouch filled with dried meat to show him how fine she could cut the buffalo," MacGregor continued in that soft, rough purr. "Yet he played his flute to no one. Dressing in her finest shift, she oiled and braided her hair and painted her face and crept to the lake to see if he played his flute to another woman. Finding the warrior playing his music alone at the lake, she smiled at him. 'Who do you play the courting flute for, Many Horses?' she asked. The warrior stopped playing and stared at the lake, nodding to it. Curious to see the maiden he courted, Bird Who Flies Away leaned over the water and stared at her reflection. Many Horses leapt to his feet and captured the maiden, stealing her for his wife."

The desire in his black eyes slid over her, warming her. Caught by his story, she'd moved closer, drawn by the quiet sound of his voice. "What a beautiful Christmas present,

MacGregor!" she exclaimed, staring at him.

"I know what I'd like for a present," he whispered, running a finger along the softness of her bottom lip and startling her.

He'd become quite dangerous, suddenly in front of her when she turned, his hand brushing her breast as he reached past her. He wasn't above patting Jack's head as it rested on her breast, a long finger foraging across her skin. He'd taken to kissing the back of her hand, fitting her palm against his.

Suddenly he was too near, stalking her. Jack rested in his willow cradle, and MacGregor had reached out a big hand to snare her ankle. His thumb caressed her skin lazily, and her heart skipped a beat as she glimpsed the fully aroused length of his body beneath his trousers. "You're wearing my present. The ruby eardrop. I've decided to let you keep it when we part."

His palm cradled her calf, rubbing it gently. "My wedding gift from you. I want you wearing my mark, but my baby would be just fine. We're not parting trails, my dear." His smile wasn't nice, reminding her of a wolf waiting for a rabbit to drop between his paws.

In another instant he slid her down beneath him. "Let's pretend we're kissing under your English mistletoe," he whispered against her lips. "Long sweet kisses that taste like July blackberries dipped in warm honey."

He brushed her lips lightly, his fingers working her braid loose, easing the strands free. Pushing her hand against his broad chest, Regina stiffened. "Gracious, you move fast. . . . Now, MacGregor. We're not married. . . ."

He nuzzled the soft spot behind her ear, sending little tingles throughout her body. "Sure feels that way. About the sweetest time in my life."

Before she could react, his fingers went skimming down her bodice, opening the tiny pearl buttons. His mouth was hot against her breast, nibbling at the crest. Regina fought the heat waves skimming through her, the way her body had suddenly softened to his. Snaring her wrist, MacGregor drew her astride his lap.

His mouth opened on hers, his tongue playing with hers before she could gasp. One strong arm bound her to him, while his free hand moved quickly between them. She gasped as his arm tightened and her breasts met his hard chest. "Put your arms around me, Violet, like you did that night. Hold me as if you'll never let me go. . . ." he whispered roughly against her cheek. Gently caressing the sweep of her back with his broad hand, MacGregor pressed her against his chest, his eyes closing slowly. "Ah, love," he whispered unevenly, "like that."

"Love?" The word struck at her senses, stunning her.

"Come here. . . ." Then the tip of him pressed against her, and he lifted her hips with one hand, rhythmically thrusting her against him.

"MacGregor," she managed shakily as she softened and dampened, accepting the tip of him.

He shuddered, broad shoulders rippling beneath her hands. Hot and damp with the effort of taking her slowly, he raised his hips and filled her. "Oh, my," she whispered as the constrictions began circling him, tightening, throbbing.

Her breast filled his hand, the long fingers gently caressing her. He lay back, holding her above him. Gently lifting her hips, he adjusted her to the full hard length.

Jack cried softly, and the sound slid into Regina, stilling her. "Gracious, MacGregor, you move fast for a big man," she whispered, scampering up and to her feet.

Almost at the same time, he was on his feet, angry and looming over her as he kicked free of his trousers. The firelight licked at his lean body, outlining his powerful thighs and the aroused shape between them. "We're married proper. A man has a right to have his wife."

Trembling, her legs weakened by desire, she adjusted her clothing and fought to keep her eyes above his shoulders. "You're a hunter, MacGregor. You know how to stalk your prey, then take it without asking. I'm offering you that diamond and more if you'll take me to civilization. Surely Lord Covington has given up the search by now."

He slammed his palm against the table. "Violet Mac-Gregor, you have odd ways of treating your husband. Warm him with soft sighs and big, soft eyes . . . let him sample, then dance away."

MacGregor's finger trembled as he pointed to the bed. "We'll be finishing that—we're bound legal and proper. Though you're a scrawny, ornery excuse for a wife. Can't cook—"

"When I marry, MacGregor, it will be a gentleman of my choice. One who will court and cherish me . . . not sneak up like a wolf about to devour an unsuspecting rabbit—"

His thick eyebrows soared. "Court you? Cherish you?" he asked indignantly. "From your books. Dreams of a girl— and you're a woman full grown and almost past your prime. 'A heart's true love . . . beating heart . . . joined souls' . . . Damnation, a man doesn't talk to his woman that way. I married you, didn't I? How could one woman with a mouth like warm honey and a body that dances across my dreams be so—" He scowled down at her, placing his hands on his hips. "I've chosen you to be my woman. Bear my sons—or girls—so that Jack will have a family and won't be alone. What more can you want?"

Tugging up her lace bodice, Regina glared at him. There he stood, looming over her and as bad-tempered as a wounded grizzly, when a moment before he was playing the courting flute and telling her romantic stories. The taste of his mouth still burned her lips and the back of her hand. She shook, her legs weak as though part of her had just been torn away. She wanted to walk into his arms and have him comfort her with those sweet, long tender kisses. Her body was empty and ached for him, but not on his terms. . . . "I want to leave. And I shall."

TALL Tom stripped off his long birch snowshoes and stepped onto a log as he studied MacGregor's cabin, nestled in the valley. The morning sun caught in the snow and blinded him for a moment, then the small figure he'd been tracking crossed a meadow. "The métis's woman has taken to the shoes, then," he muttered gathering the buffalo robe around him as protection from the January wind.

"Safe enough to get her now. MacGregor lit out at first light like a scalded pup, running his traps. When he comes back, I'll take his ear and the bauble. Stick it in the woman's ear afore I butcher her." The slight figure called to her dogs, and they obeyed, scampering and sliding across the crust formed on the deep snow. Downwind from the dogs, Tall Tom eased under the shadows of the tall firs to watch the woman practice on the small rounded snowshoes. "So she's got the breed waiting on her, does she? Making shoes and buffalo robes to fit her scrawny bones," he snarled, easing along the log, tracking her.

Taking the protective sleeve off the rifle she carried, the woman turned slowly to study the surrounding trees. "Buffalo gun," Tall Tom whispered, noting the heavy length of the firearm.

Holding the pine branch aside, he watched her pour gunpowder from a buffalo horn slung across her shoulder, then tap the patch and ball down the barrel of the powerful gun. "Damn female."

In the next instant she'd lifted the gun to her shoulder and sighted in his direction. Before he could step behind the shelter of the pine trunk, the roar of the blast echoed in his brain. The long splinter lanced his eye and hot blood spurted on his skin. Staggering back against the tree, leaning against it for support, Tall Tom cursed as he jerked the splinter free and tossed it away. "Damn, there goes that eye," he growled, struggling to gather his snowshoes and run through the deep snow.

A trail of blood marked his blind struggle away from MacGregor's.

In the valley below Regina sat in the snow where the blast of the gun had thrown her and rubbed her shoulder. The dogs frolicked around her, licking her face until she giggled and rolled in the snow. "MacGregor said to leave the gun alone, that it would knock me on my butt—buttocks—and so it did. I shall have to hurry to see if Jack woke from his nap and bake MacGregor's favorite bread in case he discovers anything amiss. . . . What a marvelous adventure, my beauties!"

ELEVEN

IN the lambing quarters Maude's new lamb stood shakily and wagged his tail. Delighted with the newborn animal, Regina giggled and hugged Laddie. "What a lovely sight! Shh. Maude won't want us around now with her baby so near."

The other ewes nestled in the warm, dry cave blocked from the weather by a wall of lodgepole pine. MacGregor had built the shelter while in his scowling mood, muttering darkly about "females and babies underfoot." Yet he'd helped with the ewes, soothing them with whispers. Hercules followed MacGregor now, pulling the sled loaded with wild grass foraged from the heavy snow. Strapped to MacGregor's back on the short trips, Jack slept comfortably in his furry nest. Regina watched over the lambing, often sleeping in the warm shed.

The cave was protected by a door fashioned from pine limbs lashed together by leather thongs. Laddie barked furiously as the door slid aside, and a man said, "MacGregor Two Hearts does have a woman spending the winter with him."

Moving through the shadowy space, a huge man draped in a buffalo robe loomed over Regina. "I'm"—she searched for a name warily; the man could be Covington's envoy— "Violet," she announced firmly, as though announcing a title.

"Aye, sure you are, sweet tail." The man's hand, grimy and foul-smelling, reached out to touch her breast beneath the leather jerkin. "Full-growed Injun gal, if'n I ever saw one," he rasped coarsely, moving a step nearer and squinting down at her face.

"Ah . . . Mr.—" Regina backed against the rock wall.

"Old One Ear Mose, they call me. See?" He lifted a flap of the pelt covering his head to reveal a missing ear. "I'm not purty. But I know how to take care of females. I'm asking you nice to lay with me now. You'll get a piece of nice foofaraw and me to boot."

Taking a step aside, Regina fitted her palm over the knife handle at her waist. Before she could move, the man's huge paw reached out and snatched her wrist. "There now. You don't want to stick old Mose, do you, gal?"

Drawing her steadily to him, Mose bent over her, leering. "Won't hurt MacGregor none if we play a bit, gal."

Regina's kick to Mose's belly struck low, and the mountain man doubled over as Laddie bit his thigh. With a sweep of his hand the man rolled the dog aside. When Laddie yelped, Regina slid through the opening.

She hit MacGregor's tall hard body at a run and almost fell before he lifted her by the nape of her neck. Mose roared, rushing through the opening after her.

"She's my woman, Mose," MacGregor said too softly, almost purring. Placing her behind him, MacGregor patted Laddie's head gently. "A little rough on my livestock, aren't you, Mose?" he asked as the huge man started around him toward Regina.

"Don't like getting kicked in my privates," Mose snarled, jerking a long, wide blade from his belt. "Back off, MacGregor. I mean to have the woman."

MacGregor's long legs locked at the knee, and he hooked his thumbs in his gunbelt. Despite his easy half smile, his tall body was tense. "My wife's not up for taking," he stated easily, widening his smile.

Mose squinted one eye at him. "Wife? As in married proper?"

MacGregor touched the ruby in his ear. "See that? It's the mate to hers."

"Don't mean nothing." Mose reached for Regina. The

sound of bone and flesh crashing together echoed through the cave, and Mose staggered back heavily.

"So that's how it is." He grinned, wiping the stream of blood away from his mouth. "Always liked a good fight, MacGregor. I'd be safe with you. You're not the kind to bite off my other ear."

"Thanks," MacGregor stated quietly, taking off his gunbelt and handing it to Regina. He cradled her cheek in his palm, brushing her skin with his thumb. "Jack should be waking up now from his nap. Mose and I will want a cup of tea when we're finished, Violet. Go on down now and start the water boiling. Mose will want to spend the night."

"You're sending me away while you sort out this affair, aren't you, MacGregor?" Regina asked sharply, stepping between the two tall men. "Two noble male beasts establishing their lordly power?"

Over her MacGregor's jaw tightened ominously. "I'm going to beat the vinegar out of Mose. He needs that every once in a while, or he feels that nobody cares. Get out of the way, woman."

Mose crowded toward her, his chin jutting out at an angle to equal MacGregor's. "She can stay, you cocky, half-grown pretty child. No lawful man shaves his jaw in the full bloom of winter. You're looking like a peeled onion, boy. Maybe Miss Violet"—he stopped and grinned widely down at her before continuing—"appreciates a good fight and a good man. I figure she'd taken to me if you hadn't showed up."

She tapped MacGregor in his flat stomach. "I won't have you upsetting my ewes by crashing around like two dancing bears in a small cage. Why don't we just go to the cabin and chat over a nice cup of tea?"

"Tea!" Mose snorted in disgust. "Leaves and bark and such for sick people. Give me good rum or whiskey."

"Violet, Mose wants a fight right off the first time he sees me, woman or not. It's a hell of a lot easier giving it to him than sidestepping his offers. Settles the dust—"

"But you're fighting over me. I have a say in the matter."

"She's a talker, ain't she? Any good on the blanket?"

MacGregor glanced down at her startled expression and grinned. "Fair to middling. But her feathers get ruffled when you talk plain about it. Married folks keep that to themselves."

"Married," Mose repeated, squinting one eye at Regina. "Proper?"

"Buzzard said the words," MacGregor answered quietly.

"Good grief," Regina muttered, looking up at the two men. "You're talking about me as though I weren't here. Mose, you may have your silly fight away from my sheep. You are not to hurt MacGregor. He's just recovering from being mauled by a mountain cat. If you harm him, I shall have to hurt you."

Mose stared down at her blankly, his thick lips parting. "Me hurt MacGregor? Damn, haven't hurt him since he was a pup. Innocent as a lamb, I am."

"Fine. Since you understand the rules of this . . . this silly match . . ." She sniffed, looking up to see MacGregor's dark eyes gleam. When he looked at her that way, her stomach tightened and her heart fluttered. "Brawl to your heart's delight. I'm going to tend Jack. Remember what I said, Mr. Mose. MacGregor has been very ill, treat him kindly. I shall expect you for supper. We're having freshly baked bread. MacGregor, please check on my ewes before coming inside."

Leaning down to her, MacGregor whispered solemnly, "Yes, ma'am. You think I could have a little good-luck kiss?"

Mose guffawed, and she blushed. "Shoo. You're embarrassing Mr. Mose." Then she kissed him quickly before running to the cabin.

"TEA ain't so bad, once you figure it out. Slithers down to your gullet. No bite when it hits bottom," Mose remarked as they sat in front of the evening fire. Venus had adopted the rough mountain man, laying her head on his leg to be petted. "Damn fine dog, this skinny bag of bones," Mose muttered.

He probed his swollen lip and closed eyelid experimentally. "Tea goes right nice with freshly baked bread and that damn fine jam. Reckon I'd like to spread my robe near this fire, Miss Violet, and turn in for the night."

"No need to do that, Mose," MacGregor said as he changed Jack's swathing. "We've got an extra cot for company. A north snow is coming down." He met Regina's widened eyes evenly. "May as well be comfortable until it blows over. Won't hurt you to help Violet and me with the animals in the meantime, will it?"

"A snug, dry bed," Mose repeated in a huge yawn and looked longingly at the two cots. "My old bones are needing a rest. Which one? You two use the big one, huh?" he asked, standing and stretching. "Reckon the little one is mine, then."

Regina narrowed her eyes warningly. "MacGregor . . ."

"Mmm?" he asked, his expression innocent.

WHILE Mose snorted and coughed, muttering in his sleep and the wind howled beyond the cabin, Regina tried to keep her body from touching MacGregor's hard length on the small cot. His shirt that she had been using for a nightgown twisted around her thighs. "This is impossible."

"Shh." MacGregor's lips brushed her temple, startling her.

"We didn't need to share a bed. He could have slept on the floor. . . . You haven't a stitch on, MacGregor. You could have shown some decency," she hissed, shifting her hip from the bold nudge of his masculinity.

"Uh-huh. Mose will spread the word that you're fighting my reins, and every man-jack in the countryside will come sniffing around here." His fingers rested on her bare thigh, easing up the cotton shirt. Regina brushed his hand aside, groaning when he turned and it rested on her waist.

She gasped and turned, only to find her breasts nestled against his flat stomach. "Stop squirming," he ordered in a rasp, fitting her closer against him as his arm slid under her head.

Forcing inches between them with her hands on his chest,

Regina stared up at him through the shadows. "You're grinning, MacGregor. Pleased with yourself, are you?"

"Not half as pleased as you could make me," he whispered unevenly before finding her lips. "Think of the beating I took today, even if you threatened Mose."

"Yeow!" Mose's scream shattered the night, and Regina sat up. Jack began to wail, and MacGregor groaned.

"Damned moray eels after my other ear like it was vittles!" Mose screamed in terror, and Laddie and Venus began to bark.

"Damn!" MacGregor slid out of bed and stalked to Jack, picking him up. The baby stopped crying instantly and lay his head against MacGregor's throat with a last shuddering sigh.

Standing in the firelight fully aroused and frustrated, MacGregor stared at Regina, who smiled sweetly, trying to keep her eyes above his waist. "You invited him to stay," she whispered before burrowing beneath the blankets. "He's your friend."

"Eels everywhere!"

Between his teeth, MacGregor muttered, "Some men drink. Other men let women drive them crazy."

THE third evening of the blizzard, Mose cuddled Jack on his lap and petted Venus with his free hand. "Maybe I'll be getting me a wife and settling down, MacGregor. Seems like you got everything a man could want here. First winter I seen you without that woolly beard. Look like a half-growed boy."

"Uh-huh," the younger man agreed, glancing meaningfully at Regina, who was mending Mose's woolen underwear, and then at the cot.

"Yep. Didn't like the bath much, but the clean clothes does make a man feel new. Thank you for washing and patching them, Miss Violet."

"You're quite welcome, Mr. Mose. MacGregor and I are very grateful for your help these past days. I'm sure you've gathered enough grass to last the sheep until spring. Perhaps you'll stay with us until the snow melts."

"I'll deal with it. By the way, Miss Violet, look in the bowl under those berries I picked for your jams."

"You picked those berries last summer, Mose," MacGregor interrupted darkly. "Dried and cached them for winter."

"MacGregor, the thought is so nice," Regina said, reaching to delve into the bowl of dried blackberries. "Oh, my!" she exclaimed as she lifted a small leather-wrapped packet. "Is this for me, Mr. Mose?"

Mose held Jack, who was jumping on his lap, and grinned widely. "A purty for a purty woman, ma'am."

MacGregor snorted and continued to sharpen his Bowie on a stone. He spit on the stone and glared at Mose as Regina opened the package to find a string of Indian beads. "Oh, my. How lovely!" she cried, placing them around her neck. "Aren't they lovely, MacGregor?"

"Divine," he muttered, and Mose looked at him sharply.

Holding MacGregor's hard stare, Mose said, "If'n I could, I'd get you some fancy fixins', like a doeskin dress and moccasins with beads. You'd look right purty dancing around the cabin in an outfit like that. Not that you ain't pretty, ma'am. What with your big purple eyes and long black hair. Got a voice like an angel in heaven, too," he added for good measure as MacGregor's lips pressed against each other tightly.

Regina smoothed the beads along her chest and rose to kiss Mose on the cheek. "Thank you, Mr. Mose. The beads are just lovely."

"Lovely," MacGregor repeated, holding the gleaming blade up to the light.

"The purple beads matches her eyes," Mose returned easily. "Mighty nice meal you cooked, Miss Violet. Never ate a bird stuffed with bread before. Was real good. Tell you what . . ." Mose placed Jack in his willow crib and drew a Jew's harp from his pocket. Placing it between his lips, he experimented with notes, then began a lively tune.

Regina clapped when the song ended. "That was marvelous."

Mose played another tune and grinned when Regina

tapped her toe to the music. "Looks like we got a hoedown coming, MacGregor. Want to dance with your woman while I play?"

MacGregor glared at him, then threw the Bowie into the cabin's log. The handle quivered and stilled. "Pressing your luck, aren't you, Mose?" he asked ominously.

"Could be," Mose agreed easily. "Maybe the old goat can teach the young one a thing or two."

Regina stared at one man and then the other. "Whatever are you two talking about?"

"Laughing Dove," Mose said innocently and roared with laughter when Jack started bouncing and cooing on his lap.

"Laughing Dove?"

"Pretty little Injun gal. Wintered with MacGregor some years ago. She got to liking me better than him."

MacGregor grimly stared at the older man. "Starting trouble, Mose?"

"Me?"

"MacGregor often takes women for the winter, does he?" Regina asked, jabbing her needle into Mose's torn shirt.

"Man has to have a woman to keep him warm in winter," Mose stated easily while Regina's soft lips pressed together firmly.

MacGregor stared at Mose for a long moment. "How would you like to go hunting with me all day tomorrow, Violet? Mose can take care of Jack."

"I'd love to!" She turned to Mose. "Oh, do you think you can manage, Mr. Mose? Really, I've been plaguing MacGregor to take me hunting all day, and now he's offered and I really want to go. Would you please take care of Jack?"

MacGregor smiled at Mose. It wasn't a nice smile. Rather like one wolf showing his teeth to another.

MACGREGOR lifted his face to the freezing wind, the snow stinging his skin. He needed the burning sensation to wipe away the thought of Regina's creamy breast where Jack had innocently caught the fabric away. The sight of the soft, sweet curve had plagued him since dawn. There was something about leaving a sleepy-eyed woman holding his baby that made his heart ache.

He inhaled the cold air, and it cut through his nostrils. Regina didn't look like a settled-down married woman. She didn't hop to please him but turned on him like a spitting cat if he came too close. On the day of their hunt, he'd tried to get close to her, but she'd danced around him, delighted with every new skill.

Studying the ice clinging to a fallen limb, MacGregor ignored Mose's curses as he found an empty beaver trap. Regina's angles had rounded out on her face and body. Deep in those purple eyes there was a mystery. What was it?

Squatting beside him on the stream bank, Mose drew his fur-lined hat lower around his face. He rolled the fresh beaver plew tightly and added it to the ten they had taken that day. "What's chewing on you, boy?" Mose asked slowly. "Your craw's been full of something since I came."

"About time you moved on, isn't it, Mose?" MacGregor asked, looking at the low-hanging snow clouds. "Could get caught in this next blizzard. Wouldn't want to—"

"Hell, boy. I'm getting to like white bread and tea at your place. Miss Violet knows how to make a man feel welcome."

MacGregor's body tightened. Regina hadn't made him welcome in their bed.

Mose slanted a look at the younger man. "She's got you ready for the warpath. Only a woman could do that to you, MacGregor. If'n you're going to keep this one, you'd better start treating her fine."

MacGregor stood suddenly, scanning the low-hanging clouds. "She's warm and well fed. Those damned sheep of hers get more attention than I do."

The older mountain man rose slowly, rubbing a nagging ache in his lower back. "This one is different. You're going to have to play her game to keep her."

"We're married. She isn't going anywhere."

Mose eased aside a leafless sumac branch and started

up the stream bank, following their footprints in the snow. "Then you'd better change your ways, pup. It will take more than Buzzard's words and an earring to keep a woman like that. Snapping and growling at her heels when you figure she's done wrong . . . like hunting on her own . . . won't make her want to roll on the bear hide with you. If'n she wants to dance a bit on a cold winter night, won't strain you none to dance with her."

"Damn it, Mose," MacGregor exploded, tramping after him. "I'm still doing the cooking, except for the bread and those fancy little sweets she makes, like jams. A man has his pride."

"Reckon I'd cook for a woman like that," Mose said simply.

LORD Mortimer-Hawkes stared at meat sizzling on the inn's fireplace spit. "Colonials," he muttered, sipping the rough ale in his pewter mug. "Savages."

His gaze locked on a tall black man dressed in woodsman's clothes. Carrying in wood for the night, the man's skin glistened in the firelight. His powerful movements caused the Englishman to look away. Once he'd been just as strong—filled with the Mariah's power. Now he ached in his bones, his flesh flaccid and weak. The inn's greasy, rough fare rolled in his stomach.

The wayside inn had taken two days to reach in the snow, and the driver would not go on until the weather cleared. "St. Louie can wait," he'd stated when Mortimer-Hawkes demanded they continue.

The Englishman lifted the pewter mug and swilled the ale, which spilled down his frilled shirt. "Soon," he muttered, lifting his hand to the barmaid for another pitcher of ale. "Soon, my sweet Pagan."

Signaling the black man closer, Mortimer-Hawkes inspected his custom-made boots. When the giant loomed over him, the Englishman waved him to sit across from him. Within moments he'd given the man coin to locate Lord Covington's camp.

"Pagan, my sweet, sweet daughter," Mortimer-Hawkes

crooned as he watched a droplet of fat sizzle in the flames. "But then, you're not really of my loins, are you?" With that he laughed aloud.

REGINA slipped the horsehair through the hole she'd punched in the leather, fashioning an ear for Mose. Jack played within his pen, built of smooth willows. He cooed at her and waved a chubby fist in the air.

Would her baby have Jack's gleaming black hair? Would MacGregor's baby be a girl this time?

She wrapped her paisley shawl more tightly around her and ran her palm down her flat stomach. She'd missed her time by a week. . . . She would have to move quickly, leaving MacGregor before he knew. He'd want the baby, a part of her, and she couldn't let him bind her to a life that would make them both miserable.

"Baby or no, I've promised myself freedom. To stand on my own and make my decisions . . . deciding how to spend the rest of my life. MacGregor's theory that a man ruleth a weak-minded female isn't my idea of happiness. I have spent my time in that kingdom. When the time is right, Jack, and when Lord Covington's tentacles disappear, I'm afraid I shall have to go. I will miss you so, my lad," she whispered to the baby, who tried to stand but plopped down on his bottom.

"I've been trying myself on the snow. Watching Mac-Gregor and learning from him. I'll be ready to start off soon. . . ." She smiled tenderly at the baby. "Jack, when you are older and I am gone, try to understand your father's ways. He's been hurt deeply and wants to spare you the pain. He loves you deeply."

The leather ear was the same size as Mose's good one; leather thongs held it to the mountain man's craggy head.

At the evening meal Mose beamed, touching his new ear often as he sipped tea from Regina's china cup. "Right nice. Women will crawl all over me now for sure. My thanks, Miss Violet."

When Regina settled Jack for the evening, Mose picked up his Jew's harp and whanged away a few notes. "MacGregor's been wanting to ask you to dance, ma'am," he stated clearly before testing the harp again.

"Really?"

MacGregor glared at Mose, then turned to her and stood slowly. For all his size he looked like a reluctant schoolboy. "You'll have to teach me, Violet."

"I'd love to!" she exclaimed while Mose tried a few notes of *Greensleeves*. "How wonderful, MacGregor. Are you certain?"

He cleared his throat and stepped nearer. "Show me."

For the next hour Regina taught and giggled and looked up at MacGregor with all her happiness shining in her eyes. He grinned down at her, tugging her just a bit closer. "MacGregor, you're a wonderful dancer. You would cause quite a stir at a ball."

"Are you happy?" he whispered, tugging her closer and pressing her tightly against him.

"Wonderfully happy," she returned, lifting her arms around his neck to tug him down for her quick kiss that lingered sweetly.

She cried in her sleep that night, her tears sliding down MacGregor's bare shoulder. He stared at the flames and held her closer.

The next morning she was gone with his rifle. MacGregor stood looking at her snowshoe tracks, which led off to the mountain pass. Jack fretted in his father's arms, his fat cheeks warm. MacGregor kissed his son's hair. "She'll come back and you can snuggle into a softer chest than mine, boy," he whispered. "Reckon she smells a lot better than me, too . . . like cinnamon," he added softly.

Rocking his son while he stood, MacGregor frowned and tried to understand her tears. Delighted when they danced, Regina had spent a restless night, snuggling close to him. When Mose started screaming about eels feasting on his ear, she'd whispered urgently, "Hold me, MacGregor. Hold me tight."

By late afternoon Jack was flushed with fever and wouldn't be quieted. Mose jumped and wrung his hands when the baby cried, leaving the cabin to tend the sheep often. MacGregor cooled the baby's chubby body with a damp cloth and stared at the door, willing Regina to step through it. "I'll paddle that soft backside of hers for running off, Jack."

The moon skimmed across the snow, and within the cabin Jack wailed in pain, drawing his tiny body in a curve. Walking the floor with his son, MacGregor was frightened for Jack and the woman who had not returned. He wanted her safe, wanted to hold her close and feel her softness in his arms. Wanted to hear her speak in that soft, lilting tone.

A wolf howled and his pack joined the eery chorus. Laddie and Venus began stirring restlessly, and MacGregor's tall body went cold. A wolf pack worked their victim, tiring and hamstringing the prey in a deadly precision. Regina would be an easy kill. . . .

He scowled at the door. Covington's men or any of the renegades on the Taos would have Regina's tender body before they sold her.

Regina heard the baby crying when she was within yards of the cabin. Venus and Laddie barked, and MacGregor's deep voice snapped at them as she stripped off the snow-shoes and hung them on the outside of the cabin. Mose snored steadily in the background, and MacGregor cursed softly as Jack whimpered.

She'd proved herself today. Walked into the wilderness and survived one day without MacGregor. She'd hunted and killed her meal, roasting the birds over a fire she'd built. She'd met a passing band of Indian women foraging for wood and had made herself understood by gestures. Most important, she'd marked her way out of MacGregor's sheltered valley and plotted a course for the new mining town farther east in the mountains. Taking a deep breath, she opened the door.

MacGregor held Jack tightly as he pivoted to her. "Where the hell have you been?" he demanded as Jack began to cry again.

Jack turned to her, his tears rolling down his cheeks and his arms open. "He's wanting you," MacGregor said roughly as she slipped off her buffalo robe over pants. "Where have you been?" he asked more softly when she took the baby from him.

"Away. Hunting," Regina whispered, rocking the baby, who clung to her. She kissed Jack's damp cheek, and he clung to her. "MacGregor, Jack has the croup. Have you given him whiskey?"

He stared at her blankly, tall and unshaven, looking harried and frustrated. Dark circles slid beneath his eyes, and his hand made a scraping noise as it passed over his stubble-covered jaw. Rubbing his bare chest, he scowled down at her, the muscles tightening from his throat to his jaw. "What are you talking about? Of course I haven't given him whiskey."

He glanced at her feet and ordered, "Sit."

When she sat in front of the fire, MacGregor kneeled to take off her damp boots. He chafed her feet in his hands and looked up at her as he placed one foot in the warmth between his thighs and rubbed the other briskly. "Toes drop off after frostbite. . . . I ought to wring your scrawny neck. I reckon it makes you happy to have people go crazy worrying about that half-pint body of yours."

"MacGregor . . ." she began warningly as she rubbed Jack's taut stomach. Then she saw the pain in MacGregor's eyes and the deep lines around his face. Stroking his clenched jaw, she whispered softly, "I'm quite all right. I've been hunting. There's a sled loaded with game outside. You and Mose could smoke—"

"I was worried about you, damn it!" he exploded, wrapping his hand around her ankle. "You're cold clear through." He tilted her face to the firelight. "Your face is red as an apple. Noses drop off after frostbite, too. Even stubby little ones like yours."

"My face was covered until just before I came in—" Then MacGregor's hard, demanding mouth was on hers. The kiss bruised her lips, his hand cradling her face to his.

"Don't you ever do that again," he said unevenly, running the pad of his thumb across her cold cheek. "Jack was worried, so was Mose."

She stroked his jaw, feeling the tension race through him. "Mose is sleeping soundly. He isn't pacing the floor," she reminded him in a whisper.

MacGregor shrugged off her hand, then caught her palm to his lips and held it there for a moment. "Damn female," he muttered against her flesh. "Playing with a man's guts until he can't think straight."

The moment stretched and MacGregor looked up at her, waiting for a reply. Waiting for her to bend and give him just that fraction of herself that held her apart from him. He wanted more of her than she could freely give, and the thought sliced through her like a honed blade.

Jack whimpered, nuzzling Regina's breast, and she slid her hand away. She rubbed the baby's back, ignoring MacGregor's dark searching perusal. Vulnerable now, his appeal nibbled at her resistance. In another moment she'd commit herself to him, telling him of the new baby. Then her freedom would vanish untested.

Jennifer's voice whispered on the eery wind—*Remember the stories. The man who holds the Mariah woman. . . .*

Tucking her chin close to Jack's head, Regina closed her eyes and rocked him. She'd been owned by one man, and now MacGregor waited for her answer.

The frontiersman stood slowly, stepping back into the shadows. She'd hurt him by refusing to answer his silent question. "I came back," she said quietly, averting her head to study Jack.

"For Jack," he said slowly, probing, wanting more of her than she would give. Something in his deep voice caused her heart to tear.

IN the morning the two men drank coffee and Mose talked about Regina's hunting prowess. "She'll do. Birds and rabbits on that birch sled she made. Must have snared the birds, but shot the rabbits right through the head. Some nice fish, too. She must have ice-fished in some lake, by the size of 'em."

MacGregor studied the woman nestling on the cot with Jack. "She looks like a girl, laying there with Jack."

Mose chewed on a piece of white cake, licked his lips, then sipped his coffee. "She's a skimpy meal. But all the right woman parts are right pert—" He stopped when MacGregor turned to stare darkly at him. "She's damn tough, boy," Mose stated softly. "Hell, neither one of us could have hunted all day and stayed up all night with that cryin' young'un."

"Whiskey," MacGregor said, turning to look at Violet. "She put a drop of whiskey in his milk, and Jack eased up right away."

Sipping his coffee, Mose glanced at MacGregor's bearded face. "From the looks of you, you could have used a nip yourself."

Without answering, MacGregor moved to stand over Regina. After a moment he slid Jack into his arms and placed him in the crib. Then he eased into bed with Regina and held her tight. "Reckon you can manage things today without me, Mose," he said after a yawn.

TWELVE

A WEEK later Regina listened to the sounds of the night, her swelling breast cupped by MacGregor's large, warm palm.

She followed the firelight dancing in the shadows of the ceiling. MacGregor sought to bind her to him; his baby would accomplish the task. She sensed him waiting for her, tracking her for a sign of her commitment.

At an early age the marquess had given her a bitter lesson she'd never forget. He dominated, hurt, and possessed. Yet once he must have been appealing, for her mother had married him.

Regina's mouth firmed. She had a dream of a new life; to yield to MacGregor's demands would give her no more freedom than in England.

She had promised herself a new land and a new life, without the lordly bonds of male possession.

MacGregor's long fingers caressed her softness as he slept, and the tender crest tightened instantly. There were changes in her body, a heaviness in her breasts, and a constant desire to sleep. Her hand edged down to her stomach, resting on it. *MacGregor's child nestled within her.*

She'd been working hard, asking MacGregor questions a little at a time. "What woods will start fires easily?" . . . "How do you sleep when you're camped alone in the dead of winter?" . . . "What foods would you take on a winter trek of say two or three days?" . . . "How do you tell if the ice is thick enough to walk over?"

Yesterday MacGregor had announced his two-day absence to check traps and locate another snow-covered pasture for the sheep. The animals, tucked in their winter coats, thrived on small amounts of the wild grass dug from the snow.

Pierre lay in the bed Mose had vacated. The older man wanted to show off his leather ear to a prospective Indian bride. Jack's croup had passed, and he made smacking noises in his crib.

MacGregor's hand slid to her other breast, sliding a thumb over the peak. Curving his long body around her, he nuzzled her throat. "You wouldn't send me away for two days without a taste of you, would you, *Tsiso*?" he whispered as she stiffened in his arms.

"*Tsiso*?" His mouth warmed her skin, her body heating at his light touch.

MacGregor shifted, drawing them face to face, his hand sliding down her waist and thigh and back up to just beneath her breast. He kissed her nose. "Cheyenne for 'little' or 'little one.'"

Against hers, his body tightened, his desire probing the long shirt between them. His face was hot against her, his body trembling as he gathered her closer. "I want you."

On the other side of the blanket Pierre sighed hugely. Regina stiffened. "MacGregor—"

MacGregor's lips found hers, and he kissed her deeply, his hand easing the shirt higher. "Come with me today. Pierre will take care of Jack and the stock. . . ."

"Uh . . . What did you say, MacGregor?" Pierre asked sleepily. "You dreaming again?"

MacGregor breathed heavily, his fingers edging along the inner side of her thigh. Regina pressed her legs tightly together, fighting the urge to wrap herself around him. "I said the damned Frenchman had better find himself another nest after I get back," MacGregor stated sharply.

In the shadows over her he leaned down to find her grinning up at him. He shook his head and ran his thumb across her soft bottom lip. "It's a wonder I'm not dead from torture by now. It's getting damned hard to wear my trousers without permanent injury."

"Poor, poor MacGregor," she whispered, cradling his jaw in her hands. "What medicine would cure your ills?"

He shot her a hot look that answered her question. Looking hungrily at her mouth, he whispered roughly, "I'd settle for a kiss. One that tasted as though you wanted me." He ran his finger along her bottom lip and then leaned closer, looking into her eyes. "You're hiding something, Violet. It's eating you. Whatever it is, tell me and I'll try to help."

To expose the past to him would open her pain. When she turned her face aside, MacGregor watched her for a moment before he slid out of bed. She pretended to be asleep when he bent to kiss her a lingering good-bye. When the door closed behind him, she allowed her tears to begin. "Farewell," she whispered in a sob.

MACGREGOR crouched over the small snowshoe print, dusting away the loose snow from the hard crust. From Pierre's account, Regina had left at noon the day before in search of grass for her sheep. He scowled at the low-hanging snow clouds, the damp air freezing on his skin. She'd run from him, taking her fancy saddle and leaving him with an empty hole in the pit of his stomach. "Gutshot by a female. Left to rot in my own juices," he muttered, standing and scanning the trail she'd taken.

She'd glided over the frozen crust of snow easily, moving beside the sheep who followed and deepened a path used by Indians and game.

Anger stalked him, sweeping away the pain. Whatever she sought, Regina didn't want him near her. MacGregor shifted uneasily, tugging his hat low against the biting wind. Maybe he'd pushed her too hard. . . . "Fool woman. Headed straight for Teton Sioux ground."

He moved along the trail, reading Hercules's hooves and the marks of three sleds. She'd used ewes to pull them, taking the lambs and keeping to a trail that she'd marked. MacGregor stopped, listening to the sounds of the wind keening through the trees. Regina had planned her escape well, marking a trail protected from snow by high rock bluffs.

When he had returned, he had found Pierre washing Jack's cloths and hanging them to dry over the fire. Jack sat on a pelt, banging on a tin pot with a wooden spoon while Pierre complained of a headache. Jack lunged for his father and lifted his jam-covered face for a kiss.

The Frenchman had stared at MacGregor's grim face. "The woman *bébé* runs from you, my friend. She fears you."

"She should," MacGregor had answered, stuffing his pack with fresh supplies. "Any woman who runs from her husband—"

Pierre's hand had stilled him. "Take care. She is not ready for these bonds you place on her. There is something aching in her. Women have mysteries beneath their soft skin and sweet smell, *mon ami*. Perhaps you should not act like a bear with a thorn in his paw around her."

MacGregor shafted a dark look at his friend, who shrugged with Gaelic calm. "You scowl at the little one. Complain that she does not cook, and your eyes track her like a hungry wolf." Pierre shrugged again, turning to lift Jack on his knee. "You will have to work to keep that one at your side. She is not like the women who want your bed, though I have never understood why. Many would give themselves without trade to you . . . yet you keep apart, tossing a coin to them."

Over Jack's glossy head Pierre had met MacGregor's scowl evenly. "This one will not take a meager offering and remain at your side. She has pain in her heart and needs to heal."

"Women!" MacGregor had cursed. "Nothing but trouble. They'll do a man in once his back is turned. Stop grinning. My wife will do as I say."

Following her trail at a lope now, MacGregor glanced at a mountain sheep scampering up a rocky butte. Poised on a rocky shelf, the white craggy beast stared down at the man with lordly disdain.

By nightfall MacGregor's search had taken him straight into a Sioux winter camp. Away from the horses, Regina's ewes and lambs nestled beneath a low lean-to made of branches. He listened to a victory song coming from the main lodge and noted the markings of the Teton Sioux tepees nearby. The first guard watched MacGregor approach the camp and issued a bird trill to alert the others who nodded as he passed. Drawing aside the buffalo robe that served to keep the winter beyond the lodge, MacGregor stepped into the firelight. The song died as the painted faces of the warriors freshly returned from battle turned toward him. Black Buffalo's Teton Sioux shared the ceremonial fire.

Indian women sat against the walls of the lodge, and Regina sat beside Playing Wolf, a handsome young warrior. Her smile slowly died as MacGregor stared at her. "MacGregor!" she whispered, her eyes widening.

"Two Hearts, my friend," Black Buffalo greeted him. Fiercest of the warriors, the chief stood slowly. "Welcome to our fire, brother. Share our humble meat and fire. It is a poor kill, an old bull buffalo, *tatanka,* found in the snow. You are welcome, *kola.*"

"I have come to take my woman back, Black Buffalo," MacGregor said, nodding at Regina.

The young warrior Playing Wolf leapt to his feet. Livid with rage, he gripped his sheathed knife and stepped toward MacGregor. "*Epelo'!* I have said I will court the girl," he spat in Sioux.

"Speak the white man's tongue," Black Buffalo said quietly. "The woman must know what is being said."

"We are married in the white man's way. She runs from me." MacGregor stared at Regina, who rose slowly to her feet. Dressed in a short, beaded doeskin shift and leggings, her paisley shawl wrapped around her shoulders, she faced him across the flames and smoke.

Black Buffalo looked at her and then at MacGregor. He nodded slowly, his broad lips curving in mirth when the white woman faced Two Hearts defiantly. "*Ehan'kećon*— truly. I see in her face that she fears you, brother. A wife should fear her husband. That is good. You will beat her for disobeying you, then share our food this night."

Regina inhaled sharply, her fingers curling into a small fist. "MacGregor so much as raises his hand, and I'll take his thick black scalp."

"Ho!" a gnarled chieftain exclaimed, nodding his head. "I see that she shakes, fearing Two Hearts' hand."

"The little one has a warrior's heart. Two Hearts will bear her battle marks and fear *her* hand," Black Buffalo's wife murmured from the shadows.

"I claim the woman as my prize. It is my right after leading the raid on the trader who sold our people the bad whiskey," Playing Wolf stated loudly.

"No man claims me," Regina said quietly, facing MacGregor as the Indians turned to stare at her.

"Pah! She does not fear him. He is not her husband," Playing Wolf stated, spitting into the fire. His fist went to the heavy president's medallion resting over his breast plate of eagle bones and beads. "I claim her. Two Hearts is like the old bear foraging for a sweet berry bush."

The warrior's dark eyes swept to Regina, who blushed and looked down at her laced fingers. His voice softened. "When she is my wife, her cooking pots will always have antelope and buffalo. She will be warm in the many hides I bring her."

"I wear her mark in my ear," MacGregor returned flatly, touching his lobe. He wanted to tear the younger man apart. Pick him up by his throat and squeeze slowly. He wanted to jerk Regina into his arms and carry her to the first lodge. Lifting the gleaming ruby eardrop to the light, he said quietly, "We have mated, sharing the marriage bed and these red stones."

Playing Wolf leaned to Regina and touched her small earlobe curiously. "When I am her husband, I will wear the red stone, too."

MacGregor's hand slid to his knife. "A woman cannot have two husbands."

The younger man ran his hand along Regina's cheek slowly, thoughtfully. "We will fight. The winner claims the woman."

An Arapaho warrior leaned near the chief and whispered. Black Buffalo nodded. "The Arapaho is our brother and shares our fires. He offers to take the ugly woman from you, Two Hearts. You may have her sheep as his gift. In the old days he says, the people's custom was to eat the delicacy of the antelope udders. One day a chief came and asked to share the udder of a new kill. When he was refused, he asked then for the udder of the other side. Still he was refused. He took his people away. Buffalo Horn says to settle the matter of the woman's pale udders, he will take her as his second wife."

MacGregor smiled slowly, his eyes meeting Regina's dark purple ones. He spoke quietly. "The woman is scrawny, cold in the furs. But I claim my right to keep her. There are those who would cut off her nose. But there is not much there now. In the morning she will wear the mark of my hand."

Jerking her head up, Regina's steel-colored eyes slashed at him. "MacGregor, you put one finger on me, and you'll regret—" Moving quickly, MacGregor snared her wrist, bent and drew her over his shoulder. His open hand smacked her bottom, and the Indians chuckled at her outraged scream.

Black Buffalo placed his hand on Playing Wolf's shoulder. "Two Hearts will kill for his woman. It is in his eyes. *Nama' añon ye*—hear me. You will let him take the woman. You see he has the worst part of the bargain, for she is not an obedient woman." He smiled slightly as MacGregor stepped out into the night and nodded toward his wife. "Spotted fawn, Two Hearts and his woman will sleep apart from the people tonight. Take them to the lodge prepared for our Arapaho brothers."

The woman smiled knowingly and followed MacGregor into the night. "You big oaf. You brainless, possessive, arrogant . . ." the white woman's outraged voice cut through the night.

Later, MacGregor touched his bruised eye and winced. Lying on a thick bed of furs, Regina's stiff back was turned toward him. She'd scratched his pride, and when he'd tossed her to the lodge's fur mat, rounded on him like a spitting wildcat. Being attacked by a woman half his size didn't leave a man much fighting room, he'd decided just after her fist caught his eye. Small and agile, Regina nearly escaped the lodge before he caught her ankle to tug her inside. Taking her down to the mat and lying over her, MacGregor had caught her hands above her head. "Simmer down," he'd ordered roughly.

"You have embarrassed me for the last time," Regina whispered back, squirming beneath him. "You great, hairy, lewd, loutish beast of a man, get off me! This is exactly the reason I fled. You're a domineering, possessive beastie of a man. Throwing me over your shoulder like so much meal in a sack. I . . . am . . . a . . . lady of quality and breeding," she stated indignantly.

"You are my wife," MacGregor returned, fighting the need to drag up her shift and bury himself in her. "You stiff-necked little piece of baggage. Playing up to Playing Wolf . . ."

"*He* isn't the savage. He gave me a bundle of sweet braided grass and played a courting flute for me. You come sweeping in here as though you owned me. As though I was no more than a . . . a ewe strayed from your paddock."

"Hard to take when a man's wife runs off," MacGregor stated between his teeth. "Hold still unless you want me in you, ma'am. 'Cause riding you now would take the edge off this fierce need to paddle your backside."

Her violet eyes widened. "You wouldn't. You wouldn't dare, MacGregor. How you choose your words. Riding me as though I were a yearling colt, indeed."

"Might remind you of where you belong. With me. Under me."

"Oh! Oh! How like you. So coarse. . . . What's a *meshivotzis*? A Cheyenne woman said Playing Wolf wanted a *meshivotzis* with me."

The image of Playing Wolf's lean body coupling with Regina's paler one caused a lancelike pain to shoot through his stomach. "Baby. He wants a baby with you," he explained grimly. The idea of another man's child in her belly caused a bitter taste in his mouth.

The purple blue eyes widened within the heavy black lashes. "Oh, my . . . oh, my."

They stared at each other, barely breathing until MacGregor asked the question that had been burning his brain. His heart pounded heavily, slowly. "Why did you run, Violet? What have I done?"

Turning away from him, she closed her eyes. "My father tried to own me, too."

The single tear sliding down her cheek cut MacGregor's heart like a knife. "Own?" His throat was raw with emotion, the word choking him.

Running his thumb along the bluish veins throbbing beneath her inner wrists, MacGregor swallowed heavily. "*Own* isn't a word I like."

Turning to him, her lids lifted slowly. "Nor do I." The words slammed into him.

He wanted to stroke her pale cheeks, to soften the ache in her deep purple eyes . . . to tell her that he cared. Fearing that he could say the wrong words and deepen the agony, MacGregor left her for the safety of the men.

She cried in his arms that night, shuddering whimpering cries that shredded his pride.

IN the morning MacGregor studied Regina when she served his food, her head averted. She was too quiet, her cheeks pale. "Violet, I never wanted to own you," MacGregor stated before he knew he'd spoken.

"You don't," she returned quietly, meeting his hard stare easily. "I won't allow it."

Taking a deep breath, MacGregor tugged her down to his lap and carefully arranged the paisley shawl to keep her warm. He smoothed the soft cloth over her shoulders in a light caress while she watched him intently. Cradling her jaw in his palm, he lifted her face to his. "You're so small. Anything could have happened to you on this trip. There are renegades around who—" He didn't want to explain how these men would use and mutilate her. An image of a white woman's breast, tanned like an animal skin and used as a tobacco pouch, shot through his brain. "I worried . . ."

The admission cost him a measure of pride, but then her amethyst eyes looked straight into him.

Regina allowed him to intertwine his fingers with hers, studying the delicate lines and pale color against his larger, dark ones. "I've been taking care of myself for years, MacGregor."

"Not here. Not with white and red renegades torturing the countryside. There are soldiers who use their uniforms to cover murder and rape."

"Perhaps life with my father was more torture than you could imagine," she replied softly. "There are many ways to wound."

He frowned, gathering her slight body closer as if to protect her. "Tell me about your father."

Regina's soft mouth tightened, her eyes hardening beneath the heavy lashes. "Lord Mortimer-Hawkes? The darling of the *haute ton*? The man who caused my mother's suicide and tried to bend me to his will?"

Staring out into the mists and the campfire smoke encircling the lodge, Regina held MacGregor's hand tightly. Her other hand rested over her heart, smoothing the vibrantly colored shawl as if to soothe the pain of long ago. "The marquess is a most unpleasant man when in his cups."

She toyed with the cloth, the dark red fringes twining with her fingers like rivulets of blood. Her mouth tightened as she whispered, "A cruel, cruel man. He broke my mother's spirit with the pain of his fists and his cruel games. He'd married her for the power of her fortune, then tormented her until she leapt from a high turret window into the dry moat. Her name was . . ." The purple eyes looked straight into his, and she shuddered slightly. "Mariah."

MacGregor held her tighter, his lips against her damp temple. "The woman in the catwagon. Her name reminded you of your mother. That's why you've been saying the name in your sleep."

Nodding against his broad shoulder, Regina tucked her face against his throat. "I was only five when she died. But I remember her lying broken and bloodied at the bottom of the dry moat. My father made me look at her, kiss her torn lips before the burial in the family vault. Oh, MacGregor—she was so soft and fragile, and he destroyed her as surely as if he'd pushed her out that window."

Her small hand snared the vivid flames of the cloth, crushing it in her fist. "He hated her dark skin, yet made her dance for him when he drank. She was beautiful. . . . Then he started on me, calling me Pagan and terrifying me with his games. It's a wonder I survived until I was old enough to fight him on his terms. When Lord Covington offered the opportunity to escape my father's tyranny, I welcomed it. I plotted my own escape. I took what he valued most, a huge ruby named the Mariah Stone."

Staring into the smoldering fire in the center of the lodge, Regina whispered brokenly, "He'll hunt me until he dies. He feeds on the power he feels the stone—my mother's dowry and my grandmother's—gives him. I saw him feed . . . on her terror, grow wild with power. He wanted the same fear from me. . . ." She shuddered and he held her tighter. "I would not give him the pleasure."

When she shivered as though a freezing wind had just swept over her, MacGregor lifted her fingers to his mouth. "I wanted you, Violet. I still do. Never thought much about forcing a woman to stay with me . . . out here having a woman is a necessity. Jack needed a mother and I . . . I thought we could make a go of it."

Her fingers floated across his hard lips, then slid away. "MacGregor, you can be a lovely man when you try," she whispered sadly. "And at other times you are as dense as a castle wall. I must have the freedom I seek. I cannot allow you to own me, don't you see?"

IN Black Buffalo's tepee MacGregor shared the old warrior's pipe. A blend of white man's tobacco and the Indian's dried leaves, the *kinnikinnick* smoke curled upward with the heating fire.

"*Nama' ahon ye*—hear me, Two Hearts. Your woman is strong. She would choose her life's path," Black Buffalo stated after a long time.

MacGregor nodded, turning an ember with a sliver of wood. The sliver burst into a tiny flame. "She is my wife."

The elder man nodded solemnly, puffing on the long clay pipe. He studied the Cheyenne buffalo hide shield leaning against the side of his tepee. A deer filled the center of the burnt orange shield with tiny tracks decorating the outer perimeter. Four hawk feathers hung from the center, and leather thongs decorated the outside. "Young men often take a lonely path, seeking their dreams. A woman with a warrior's heart would follow her dream. Her journey is not from you alone, but toward her future and away from her past. She seeks her strength. . . . You cannot take this from her."

"She is my woman. I would have her at my side," MacGregor stated after accepting the ceremonial pipe and puffing on it.

He handed it back to the chief, who nodded, studying the white smoke above MacGregor's head. "A trapped heart will wither, leaving an empty shell, my friend. Let the woman seek her dream. Follow her, but do not keep her from her destiny. In time you will have what you seek. You wear her mark, the red stone. For now it is enough."

SHE'D hurt him badly, Regina decided as Mac-Gregor sat in the meeting lodge that night. Placing a wooden trencher of roasted deer meat and pemmican in front of him as the other woman tended their men, she'd caught the dark light of his eyes studying her before he looked away.

Black Buffalo's voice rose above the howling wind. "Before the whites, the people made arrows with sharp stones. Like the wolf, we hunted the buffalo, creeping up to him in the grasses. Close to him, we rose and shot him. Our knives were made with the buffalo's ribs, and we skinned and cut his meat, carrying it to the camp on our backs. Women cut his flesh into strips and smoked it on green striplings, smoking his hide to cover our lodges. When his hide was toughened, still we used the buffalo, making moccasins and winter clothing. We made snow sleds from his ribs, and our dogs pulled travois laden with *tatanka*."

The men nodded in agreement. MacGregor turned to look back at Regina, who sat in the shadows with the other women. "Come here," he whispered, reaching out his hand.

She shook her head no, and MacGregor stared at her, his expression hard. "You are my wife. Sit by me," he ordered quietly.

Black Buffalo continued his narrative, staring at the fire as Regina slid into the small place MacGregor had created at his side. Taking her hand in his, he listened to the ancient story of the revered buffalo.

"We made saddles of the raw buffalo hides, buried his stomach in the earth, and used it for a pot to make our soups. Boats of willow striplings covered with his hide take us down the rivers. Black paint worn in our victory ceremonies is made with his blood and cottonwood ashes. From the buffalo rawhide our women make the *parflèche*, bags to store our food. A bow made from his horns is stronger than wood. His paunch holds water when we are thirsty and is a cooking kettle for blood soup. His sinew is woven into bowstrings and sews our clothing and tepees."

With a wave of his hand Black Buffalo indicated the flames in the center of the lodge. "This fire began with soapweed and buffalo dung. Our young men place wood sticks through their skin and hang buffalo skulls from them to gain favor from the spirits. His skull rests outside our sweat house, and we smoke the pipe, asking him to return to life, giving us his meat and skin. To ensure he listens, our warriors slice bits of flesh from themselves in the sweat house and place it under his skull as sacrifice."

The men, young and old, nodded. An old man lifted his thin, scarred arm high. "This I have done many times, and the buffalo has come with his gifts."

Black Buffalo continued, speaking proudly. "We eat no meat of the white buffalo, for he will send away the rest."

"The whites kill our buffalo!" a youth shouted suddenly. "They massacre at Sand Creek and send our brothers to this dry place called a reservation. When the leaves fell, the Medicine Lodge Treaty called the people together for peace. Yet we kept our honor by staying in the lands of our fathers."

"Aiee!" a woman cried from the shadows. "My mother died at Sand Creek."

MacGregor held the small, fragile hand within his tighter, his jaw tightening. Of mixed blood he knew that bitterness could erupt into violence at any moment. In a sudden breach of formality, Regina could be hurt.

Black Buffalo held up his hand for silence and nodded when the people stilled. "The moon of the wolves running together is passing. For this meeting night we will honor Two Hearts and his woman by playing the hand-game—"

A fiery youth stood, shaking his fist at MacGregor and Regina. "White blood taints in this lodge—"

With dignity Black Buffalo stood his full height and wrapped his blanket around his aged shoulders. "Take your hatred into the cold night, Water-Too-Deep. Or stay and honor my brother, Two Hearts, as I have said." He sat and nodded, saying, "Begin the hand-game prayer."

A minor chief named High Hat nodded and moved to sit beside three other men near a drum. High Hat began chanting. MacGregor whispered an interpretation. "He is saying that he dreamed the placing of the tally-sticks and that a spirit has taught him how to play tonight. He is asking gifts of happiness and old age for the people. Their rules change with the leader's vision, and tonight they allow us to play."

Arranging themselves in two lines, the players began to sing, waving their closed hands in the air to confuse the opponents. A counter or marker was hidden, and one team guessed while the other hid the counter. Regina won several rounds and laughed up at MacGregor. "It's no more than the slight-of-hand shell games played in English fairs, MacGregor."

A dance began later, and she stayed by his side, allowing his arm to draw her close. For the evening the people enjoyed the feast of a new buffalo kill, placing their fears beyond the lodge. The old men told stories of their youth and their visions to the sound of the drum. Two women cried out their visions of happy fat children and the return of the buffalo. An old woman stood slowly and performed a shuffling dance in the manner of long ago. Swaying slightly to the drumbeat, Regina whispered, "I should like to dance, MacGregor."

MacGregor nodded, then leaned close to Black Buffalo. The chief nodded toward Regina and the dancers stepped back to allow her space. Taking the hand of the Indian beating the drum, she taught him a slower rhythm, watching him until he understood.

Knotting her shawl over one shoulder and beneath her other arm, Regina whispered to MacGregor, "This is what I see in my dreams. Tell them that, please."

MacGregor translated while Regina slipped off her leggings and moccasins, then stepped onto a large buffalo hide in the center of the lodge. Her short bleached doeskin shift and beads caught the firelight as she ripped a long fringe free. Taking four polished flat pieces of buffalo horn, she instructed MacGregor to tie them to her fingers and palms.

When he was done, she clicked the bits of horn together experimentally. "This will do."

Closing her eyes, she began swaying, moving slowly like the spring breeze sweeping through the reeds. The drum beat softly, and she hummed a song much like Indian flute music. Black Buffalo clapped his hands and a woman loosened Regina's long braid and spread the blue-black rippling mass until the ends danced at her hips.

He leaned near MacGregor. "Your woman seeks the vision that disturbs her. When she is at peace with the vision, her heart will be free."

Twining her arms high above her head, Regina clicked the horn pieces together slowly. Moving her hips to one side then another, she swayed, and the folds of the brilliant yellow and dark red cloth caught the firelight. The huge shawl clung to Regina's undulating body until it blended with the dancing movements of the flames.

Regina's shift drew higher with her movements, the slender muscles of her legs gleaming, though her soles had not moved from the tanned buffalo hide. A sweep of raven hair fanned out as she moved, circling the outer perimeter of the hide. Bending, turning, arching back until her hair swayed and brushed the hide, she moved in front of MacGregor.

Black Buffalo leaned toward MacGregor. "She is like the flame, burning, moving. She sees herself inside the flame and you outside. You trouble her heart, for there is something in you she fears, yet she cannot stay free. She fights you like a warrior. This is her battle dance."

Rotating her hips in a sensuous movement slowly, then faster, the purple eyes stared at him above the slender waving motions of her hands. The horn bits clicked slowly as she swayed, opening her thighs just inches from his face.

Slanting him a knowing look, she lifted the shawl to cover her face. Above the vivid cloth, a winged brow lifted, and her eyes half closed as though drowsy and sated from lovemaking. The horn bits clicked faster and the cloth swayed, clinging to a slender thigh. Turning slowly, keeping her heavy-lidded gaze on him, she allowed him to trace the sensuous swaying of her rounded hips beneath the light shift.

Above him her breasts shifted, quivering with the movements of her body.

MacGregor's throat dried, his body hardening as the shift tightened, presenting him with the flowing movements of her buttocks. "Damn it, Violet," he erupted, standing and catching her wrist.

Lifting her in his arms, he carried her the short distance to their lodge and placed her carefully on her feet. An old woman who was tending the fire nodded and slid into the night. MacGregor adjusted the buffalo hide covering the opening, then turned to Regina. "You were heating blood back there, woman."

Looking up at him sensuously, she began dancing again, following the beat of the drums from the meeting lodge. Nudging MacGregor with the brush of her swaying hips, she guided him to sit on their pallet.

Seconds later her shift lay at her feet, the flame-colored shawl barely concealing the curves of her body. Turning, clicking the bone bits faster, Regina's breasts quivered above him. The darkened tips peaked against the soft fabric, swaying as she danced. A pale soft belly and softer hips quivered near his face, her arms and hands weaving a sensuous story.

Turning, looking back at him over her gleaming bare shoulder, Regina's half-closed eyes sent him an age-old message. Her slender waist moved like a willow swaying in the wind.

MacGregor reached to stroke a quivering shapely buttock, caressing a slender muscled thigh, and her motions quieted. His palm ran higher on her inner thigh, just touching the fragrant nest of curls there before she moved away.

The cloth slipped, and firelight gleamed on a rounded breast, quivering and pale around the darkened nub that swayed close to his face. The taut crest slid along his cheek before he could touch, and she moved away, holding him with a promising gaze.

Easing lower to the skin covering the ground until her knees rested on a blanket, Regina lifted her arms and hands toward him, beckoning. Undulating her hips, her thighs spread within reach, she held his eyes.

The cloth slipped from her breasts, the pale gleaming softness quivering. Her hair spread around her, a single fat curl circling the dark tip of her left breast.

"Violet!" MacGregor muttered, unable to look away from the shadows playing within her thighs. The soft flesh across her stomach quivered and gleamed, the cinnamon and softer musk scent rising to tantalize him.

"You don't know what you're doing, woman," he whispered harshly, his body screaming for release.

For an answer she rose, clicking the bone bits faster, and the shawl slipped away to reveal gleaming pale curves, undulating, quivering faster and faster.

He wanted to be gentle. He wanted to give her the soft words and please her. But suddenly she was in his arms, her desperate kisses raining down his face to his throat and lower.

In another moment her small hand curved around him intimately, stroking his trousers from him.

She was all that her dance had promised. Hot, liquidy velvet, clinging to him, wanting more. Hungry for him.

Regina wanted this man desperately, wanted his trembling body sheathed in hers. Wanted his large hands holding her as though she were china and flower petals. "MacGregor," she whispered against his damp chest, licking at his hardened nipples.

"I'm trying to be a gentleman about this, Violet," he managed between his teeth, his tall body quivering in her arms. "You're so soft—"

Nibbling his bottom lip, Regina closed her eyes, reveling in the tender caress of his rough palm on her breast. She ached as his fingers foraged slowly down her stomach, then lower to her intimate damp opening.

He kissed her sweetly, his body shivering with the need to enter her. Clinging to him, she luxuriated in the hard muscles of his chest and arms tightening around her. MacGregor's lips nibbled at her lobe, and he whispered unevenly, "Hell of a way for a woman to come at a man."

He inhaled deeply and stiffened when she ran the tip of her finger across his erect manhood. "Damn, Violet—" he exclaimed breathlessly after a moment. "Watch those hands!"

Despite his passion, MacGregor took her carefully. At the last his teeth nibbled lightly at her breast, his tongue laving the sensitive tip before he suckled her deeply. Tightening around him, holding him close, Regina's body reached the heated summit, myriad colors bursting over her at the very moment MacGregor shuddered his release.

Later, curled around her as they watched the fire, MacGregor nuzzled her throat lazily. "*Tsiso*, that is no way to come at a man."

She smiled softly, placing her hand over his as it kneaded her breast beneath the shawl. "No? You seemed to enjoy it."

He snorted roughly. "Damn near killed me. It's a wonder the sweet grass beneath us didn't catch fire."

Turning slowly in his arms, she lifted her face for a long, sweet lingering kiss. Looking up at him through the shadows, she stroked his rough cheek. "I've been cold for two nights, sir. 'Tis your duty to warm a poor woman's flesh, you know." She arched against him, enjoying the crisp whorls brushing her breasts. "Aye, MacGregor, you are a lovely man."

Kissing her moist, swollen lips, he asked, "You'll stay with me, won't you, Violet?"

Then her small hand guided him inside the heat, holding him tightly, and he forgot she hadn't answered his question.

THIRTEEN

THE girl's innocence snared Lord Mortimer-
Hawkes like fresh blood drawing a shark. Within miles
of St. Louis the way station's rough customers framed
the serving maid's shy youth. The marquess followed the
movements of the tavern maid while he sipped on his ale.
He needed her fear, the tart taste of power seeping inside
his belly as she whimpered. Running his finger around his
mug, he studied the family crest on his ring. The golden
wings of a preying hawk glittered in the light of the crude
tallow candle.

"Martha," a customer called to the serving maid.
Mortimer-Hawkes's eyes slid to the girl as she balanced
a tray filled with platters of roast deer, baked potatoes, and
hominy. The heavy tray almost slid from her plump shoulder
onto the passengers' laps. Mortimer-Hawkes smiled leisurely at her; he needed Martha's soft brown eyes and rounded,
tempting body to sustain his strength until he found Alfred
Covington.

Lifting his mug with a smile, Mortimer-Hawkes signaled
the girl to him. The wretch's memory of his usage would
be soothed with a coin, he decided, smoothing his trousers
beneath the plank table.

Martha's luminous doe eyes warmed as she approached
him, reminding him of Mariah. At the end his wife wasn't
worth tormenting . . . a dull bit of trash, unaffected by the
pain he needed to bring him sexual release.

221

Pagan. The name stirred him afresh.

Pagan. Already in her mother's womb when they married, Pagan was destined to be his.

Mortimer-Hawkes's patrician features hardened, his molded lips curving in a cruel expression. Pagan was not the issue of his body, but that of a drunken cousin; a wealthy duke had paid him to marry the foreign woman. Then Mariah's immense dowry added to the attraction.

Pagan had taken the family's amethyst eyes; the resemblance to his shade was remarkable. But her eyes held a savage fire that burned despite her refusal to fight openly.

Pagan's flight had proved her worthy of his attention. Breaking her to his hand and body would be a pleasure he'd denied himself in England. Once tamed, he'd bring her back to the family estate as his daughter. No one would know how she served him.

Yes. Pagan's return could be easily explained, once Alfred Covington was dead. Everyone would believe that after mourning the earl's unfortunate accident in the American wilds, Pagan would choose spinsterhood and reside at her father's estate.

In a dark corner of the inn a frontiersman dressed in fringed buckskins talked quietly to an Indian wearing a blue uniform jacket. Mortimer-Hawkes studied them stealthily. The breed of the untamed country, they would know of ways to find Englishmen hunting in the western mountains. The Indian stared at him, and Mortimer-Hawkes nodded. When the black man returned, the marquess would approach these men or men like them to outfit and guide him to Covington and Pagan.

Pagan. Her quiet rebellions had begun early, marking her as a woman who could excite him. He'd brought her mother's costume with him, the gauzy heathen affair decorated with coins across the low bodice and hips. The costume left the woman's midsection and navel bare to incite passion.

Mariah's quivering, swaying body floated behind his

closed lids, and for a moment his breath caught in his lungs. She was beautiful, a flame to his passion.

He ached then. A quick stab of sadness that he pushed away with a long swallow of cold ale.

The marquess ran his finger around the cool moisture on the mug's rim. The heat in a woman's body rose when she was truly frightened, allowing him to harden. He used his manhood like a sword then, hurting, stabbing, heightening his arousal until the glorious explosion.

If the woman fought well, he could wound her again and again.

Pagan would fight him. With her and the Mariah returned to his grasp, his power would return.

The marquess's eyes swung to Martha. Tonight he would feed on the girl.

Later, he would savor Alfred Covington's terror.

MACGREGOR stared at the china cup's small curved handle and wondered if his finger would slide through the narrow opening. Two weeks after leaving Black Buffalo's camp, the afternoon tea party Regina had planned lurked ahead of him.

For the hundredth time, he glanced down at the tiny embroidered violet on his new shirt's cuff and swallowed the tight wad of emotion in his throat. In the past he'd paid for his clothing or traded an Indian woman for buckskins and moccasins. Regina's small hands had fashioned the shirt, studded with shell buttons and delicate stitches that fashioned pockets over his chest.

The shirt was a peace gift and the reason he'd agreed to the formal afternoon English tea.

Jack sighed sleepily in his cradle, and Regina bent to smooth his blankets over him. She'd wound her thick, twin braids over her head like a gleaming crown. Wearing a lacy blouse and voluminous plaid skirt drawn from her traveling chest, she fascinated MacGregor.

He eyed the ruffled blouse intently. Despite the full, muttonchop sleeves, the starched cloth stretched tightly across Regina's round breasts. Just thinking about her fancy lace underwear set his teeth together and caused his face to heat.

Damn. In his passion at the Indian camp he'd agreed to Regina's demands to leave at the first snow melt.

In the war MacGregor had seen men pushed too hard under fire. The aftereffects were deadly. When least expected, their emotions could erupt at any time. If Regina needed a small time to calm her nerves, she would have it.

Once she put this womanly nonsense behind her, they could begin their marriage.

He circled the fragile cup in the curve of his long fingers. Damn. *He didn't want to own her.* The thought turned his stomach sour and gnawed at his pride.

Taking a deep breath, he pressed his lips together and scowled at the cup perched in its fragile saucer. They'd made a fair bargain on the blanket. Marriage to Regina was like being caught in white-water rapids without a paddle.

He shifted on the chair, and the smooth cotton fabric tightened on his shoulders. The tiny purple violet on his cuff caught the lamplight. The fragile design fascinated him, and he touched it again.

"Goodness, what a scowl, MacGregor." Regina leaned to pour tea into his cup. "Is having tea such a torture?"

"It's damned silliness."

She smoothed a fold on the shirt, running a small hand over his shoulder, and MacGregor tensed instantly.

When she adjusted the collar, studying the fit around his muscular neck, he swallowed heavily. Her actions pleased him; they spoke of caring and possession. He shifted, uncomfortable with the depth of his feeling. "Stop fussing, woman."

Shadowed beneath her thick lashes, Regina's purple eyes darkened. She stared at him a moment, then winked and placed an ironed napkin across his knee. Smoothing the cloth high on his thigh, she winked at him again and slid into her chair. "You're a grumpy old bear, Mr. MacGregor."

"You're planning to pack up and light out as though a preacher's words weren't binding," he accused, watching her spread jam on a thick slice of freshly baked bread.

"Buzzard's wedding ceremony certainly wasn't formal," she answered quietly, handing him the bread. "Eat that and stop grumbling. You're ruining the lovely tea I've set out. . . . You might think of it in my terms, MacGregor. We were both in a bad situation—you needed help with Jack and I needed you to survive. Both ends of the bargain have been met. Now we've made a new bargain, and when the first snow melts you'll take me to a town. I intend to purchase a homestead of one hundred and sixty acres for my sheep."

"I have a claim right here. One hundred and sixty acres of mountain filled with game for trapping. You could use the bottoms for your sheep."

She smiled at him serenely, smoothing the paisley shawl across her breast. "I want my own land. I'll need more meadows."

MacGregor glared at her. "What kind of man do you think I am? Own you? Let my wife go chasing dreams alone? A woman alone is easy game to any man who wants her."

She returned the intent look. "I have found that to be true. I've learned from you since we met."

"I keep what's mine, Violet MacGregor," he stated flatly. "One way or another."

Arcing a narrow dark eyebrow, she said quietly, "I'm asking for my earring back. . . . I was never yours."

The flat of his hand struck the table, causing the china set to quiver. "The hell you say. We've mated. You are my wife."

Lifting the delicate cup to her lips, she sipped quietly, then looked at him. "There are moments when a woman is more vulnerable. She's easy prey—"

The cords in MacGregor's jaw hardened, fury running through him like fire. "You're saying that I circled 'round your backside when you weren't looking."

When she didn't answer, MacGregor took a deep breath and promised huskily, "You'll see me coming from now on, wife. I'll take you to that damn town on the condition that the first sign of trouble, you send for me. You're mine, and I'll be back to claim you. Jack needs you."

"You should hire Jack a nurse, or take a wife, MacGregor. We could easily overlook Buzzard's ceremony. Perhaps once I'm settled, I could look for someone to properly fill the position. I'd never bring bigamy charges if you did take a second wife."

"Violet MacGregor, you are as hardheaded as a mule, and you got that crazy promise out of me while—" He stopped and glared at her. "A man will say anything when a woman comes at him like that."

"And you, MacGregor, look quite handsome when you're dressed for tea," she returned easily. "I know you'll honor your promise to take me to a town and let me seek my dreams."

"Dreams. I have them every night until I hurt. When are you moving back to my bed?" he demanded, slashing aside her attempt at peace. "You cry in the middle of the night, enough to make a man ache."

Looking into the flames, Regina's expression was thoughtful. "I know. . . . Don't you understand, MacGregor? I've got to find a measure of peace from the past. I've been controlled and owned by one man, and now a second takes his place."

"Hell!"

After the evening meal MacGregor leaned against the cave's wall and stared at Hercules, who stood apart from the lambs and ewes. "Women."

He lifted Regina's book and studied it by the flickering light of a candle. "*The Poetry of the Romantics*," he muttered aloud. "Thees and thous. Talk about hearts fluttering and swooning. No man would talk to a woman like that. Words, just silly words. With their heads full of this fluff, no wonder women have strange ideas. Knights in a showdown wearing a woman's colors . . ."

Taking the purple ribbon from his pocket, MacGregor remembered how Regina had tied it on his arm before the Covington raid. "Damn. She dressed me up like her knight."

Running his finger over the tiny violet on his cuff, MacGregor leaned back and closed his eyes, thinking about the Englishwoman. He liked wearing her mark, signifying that she owned him—

Owned him? He owned her? He frowned, chafed at her remark. Was there more?

"Love, sweet love is a piece of buffalo dung," he muttered to Hercules. "Violet is messing in fluff that has no place between a man and a woman. A man and his wife," he amended curtly.

She was crying when he returned to the cabin. Her tear-spiked lashes widened around glistening deep purple eyes as she watched him strip from his heavy coat. "Oh, MacGregor . . ."

Dressed in her pantelettes, laced corset, and a frilly confection beneath it, Regina threw her small body against him, holding him tightly. "Oh, MacGregor. Where have you been?"

Her arms wrapped around his waist, her face burrowed against his chest. Holding her tightly and smoothing the tumbled, fragrant hair, MacGregor tucked her face into the shelter of his broad shoulder and throat. "*Tsiso*, what's wrong?"

Sobbing quietly, her hands ran up and down his back. "I've tried and tried . . ." A sob stopped her, and MacGregor waited, his heart thumping unevenly. "I just can't. No matter how I try, I just can't do it."

"Do what?" Leave him? Go back to England? Sleep at night when the dreams come haunting her? Share his bed and life? "What, *Tsiso*?" he asked, trying to keep his voice even.

"It's appalling. A woman of my age and experience should be able to handle the matter." Her small shoulders shivered, and MacGregor ran his hands down her back, warming her cold body.

"Your dreams . . ."

Against his chest her face moved side to side quickly. Fear gnawing at his entrails, MacGregor picked her up and carried her to his bed. Sitting down with her in his arms, he rocked her as he would Jack. Whatever her demons were, he wanted to protect her.

"Look. Just look," she murmured, leaning back from him, her eyes filled with tears. "How absolutely awful. This has never happened to me before."

MacGregor cradled her damp cheek in his palm, running his thumb gently across the tear trails staining the satiny skin. "*Tsiso*, tell me so I can help."

Her head went back, and she glared at him through her tears. "I'm not helpless. Don't you say that I am, or I'll never bake you that bread you consume a loaf at a time."

Shivering in his arms, she sobbed again and blinked. One fat tear rolled across the back of his hand. MacGregor kissed her damp lashes, her brows, and the tip of her nose. "Sweetheart . . ."

Squirming in his lap, she wrapped her arms around his neck and clung to him. She whispered urgently against his throat. "This never happens to me. If you laugh at me, MacGregor, I'll scalp that thick black hair of yours and then pluck every hair from your most sensitive parts. They do that in the desert for torture, you know."

He smothered a chuckle. "You've found other ways to torture me, *Tsiso*."

"Don't you dare laugh. . . ."

Leaning back, MacGregor eased her from him, tilting her chin up with his finger. "Tell me why you're crying."

She sniffed just once, a delicate reminder of her heavy sobs a moment ago. Pointing to her low lacy bodice, she whispered, "Look."

MacGregor's eyes gazed at the full shimmering bounty scantily covered by thin cloth and lace. Dark, rosy nipples shone through the cloth as Violet leaned farther back, giving him full view of her breasts.

He swallowed heavily, tantalized by rounded soft flesh pushing up at him. "I see," he said huskily, his hand sliding to touch the outer curve of her breast.

"You see what?" she demanded, brushing the back of her hand across her cheeks to dry them.

Soft, sweet skin and rosebud honey nipples, he answered silently. She shifted and allowed him a fuller view sweeping down to her tiny corsetted waist. Squirming slightly on his lap, Regina lifted one dainty foot, and MacGregor's hungry look swept down the long curve of her leg. Her soft buttocks slid from him as she stood, and MacGregor's body hardened instantly.

A lacy strap slid off her shoulder, the firelight gleaming on the satiny curve. Rounded above the corset, her breasts quivered as she pointed to her waist. "I've tried for a full hour and can't unlace my corset."

He stared at her tear-stained face blankly. "You've been crying because you can't get your underwear off?"

Tilting her head to one side caused a thick strand of hair to slide down her breasts, brushing MacGregor's hand. She scowled at him fiercely. "Of course! A lady usually has a maid to help her. I couldn't ask you. . . . You've been sulking about as though I'd taken away a beloved toy—"

"You've been crying because you couldn't unlace yourself?" he asked again incredulously. "Violet, you've faced Tall Tom, nursed a sick baby across a desert, dug a bullet out of me, and led a raid." He shook his head, running his fingers through his hair until it stood out in peaks.

"MacGregor, are you going to help me or not? If you don't, I'll cut the laces, and French cord can't be replaced in the American wilds," she stated haughtily.

He stared at her blankly for a moment, then sighed. His book had warned of women's shifting moods. Whatever Regina's current mood was now, it gave him an excuse to hold her. "Let me have a closer look."

MacGregor spread his legs, placed his hands on her rounded hips, and smoothed the curve thoughtfully. Then he drew her between his legs, until his face was just inches from her breasts. He kissed one shimmering tip through the delicate cloth, and Regina's body tensed as she inhaled sharply. MacGregor nuzzled the cloth lower over her other breast and kissed a slow trail to the rosy tip. This was what he wanted, the soft flesh flowing and heating beneath his touch. The scent of cinnamon rose from her skin as her fingers caressed the back of his neck. MacGregor tugged lightly at the cloth between her breasts. "The laces are fouled. This may take some time."

"MacGregor—" Her protest died as their lips met.

MACGREGOR'S dark weathered skin beaded with sweat, the areas around his mouth pale in the morning light. "You've been sick again," he said tightly. "Dropping weight until a good wind would blow you away."

Regina wrinkled her nose, trying not to smell the frying bacon. She pressed her palm over her stomach and swallowed uneasily. Jack babbled, fighting the length of toweling binding his fat tummy to the chair. Gnawing at his bacon strip, he held the thick slice up to Regina, a smile on his greasy chubby face.

Sitting weakly, she gripped the table for support while MacGregor grimly finished the bacon and placed sourdough biscuits on the table. In another moment he was sitting across from her, filling her plate and grumbling. Running the flat of his hand across his lean stomach, he looked at the bacon as though it were live snakes. "I'm not feeling that good myself."

Jack gurgled and threw his chewed rind at Regina. Instantly her stomach rose, and she ran for the door.

Leaning against the cabin, inhaling the fresh cold March breeze until her nausea eased, Regina closed her eyes. MacGregor's baby had caused her breasts to swell. That tiny life nestled in her as surely as England and her father lay in her past. She had to wrest free of MacGregor . . . and soon.

Before he discovered the baby.

MacGregor stepped outside and closed the door. "Jack's in his pen." Inhaling the air, he leaned against the cabin with her. "Violet, I've been thinking about your sickness. . . . In the war men's minds made them sick. I read in the book that women have queer urges and need time to sort them out."

"Your bloody book can go to—" she managed between her teeth.

His black eyes traced her pale face slowly. "I've seen trapped animals chew off a paw for freedom. Maybe that's what's happening to you. . . . At first light I'll take you to Primrose," he said stiffly. "Come back inside," he muttered roughly, taking her hand in his. "You're cold."

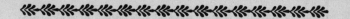

FOURTEEN

REGINA stepped from the brilliant March sunlight into the smokey gloom of Primrose's Last Dollar Saloon. She wiped her muddy boots on the grate, and the sunlight spread around her body, outlining it on the dirty floor. In the shadows the male inhabitants turned to her, grumbling. "Close the door!" "Damn! What's a woman doing in here?" "Sun can blind a man."

She smiled, closed the door, then dusted her hands on her trousers. "Mr. Pokey Wales, please. I understand that he wants to sell his farm."

A rough-voiced bartender nodded to a man sprawled over a table. "That's Pokey. Boys, pick him up and take him outside for the girl. Women can ruin business."

In the daylight and braced against a wooden barrel, Pokey's reddened eyes squinted up at her. "That land is worthless. Not a trace of color anywhere on it. Bought it from a tinker. Don't want to skunk you, ma'am." Pokey stared at her sheep drinking from the swollen stream coursing through Primrose's main street. He blinked. "Woollies. Big ones."

She crouched beside him. "My sheep and I need a home and quickly, Mr. Wales. They're needing shearing. How much?"

"Woollies." He stared at Je t'aime and the mule loaded with Regina's chest. "A woman with woollies. I reckon I can part with the land. The cabin is warm. Hauled in a black walnut, sassafrass, and wild cherry timber a while back. Settlers couldn't pay the price, so the wood is still

233

there, behind the house. Reckon that ought to add to the price. . . . How much are you willing to pay?"

"Ah. That is the problem, Mr. Wales. Would you take these diamond eardrops as payment?" The diamonds sparkled in the palm of Regina's embroidered kid glove. "They are genuine, I assure you."

"Pretties. There's a Chinese woman here that pays high for pretties. Reckon we got a deal, ma'am."

LILLY shivered with the pain burning across her back. Sold to her mistress at the age of thirteen, Lilly had tasted the lash often in five years. Madam Joy knew how to give pain and not leave marks on her prostitutes. Lilly's almond-shaped eyes slid to the small woman walking out of Primrose. Easing aside the dingy lace curtain covering the grimy window, Lilly wrapped her red silk gown tighter around her slender body.

The woman of the sheep walked alone, pride straightening her back. Dressed in men's trousers and a fringed Indian jacket, the woman carried a long rifle easily. There was something in the set of her jaw and in her shoulders that Lilly admired and wanted for herself. The woman led the big horse easily, the dogs obeying her commands to herd the flock of sheep out of Primrose. "A woman who is not afraid," Lilly whispered. "A woman who will rule her life. As I cannot."

Lilly's delicate fingers crushed the tattered curtain. At eighteen she knew her future. She had refused to work the opium den under the Last Dollar and had received Madam's lash. Lilly stretched a slender arm upward, allowing the loose silk sleeves to slide down her bruised skin. She studied the marks, her expression hardening. Once entering the den, many girls never saw the sun again. This beating had left marks on Lilly's small face and across her ribs. Aching, she rose unsteadily and slipped out the back door.

At the outskirts of Primrose Regina turned to the soft cry, "Missy. Missy."

The girl ran to Je t'aime, her slender hand touching the reins. Beneath the flowing silk gown embroidered with dragons, her willowy body was nude. A swath of sleek black hair slid aside to reveal a blackened eye and a swollen, cut mouth.

"My dear, what has happened?" Regina asked.

The girl clutched the robe around her, shivering in the cold wind that swept up her body. "I come with you, ma'am. Please? I am strong. I can cook and work. . . . I sleep outside and eat little."

Acting quickly, Regina wrapped a soft cotton blanket around the girl's thin shoulders. "You've been beaten," she said quietly, looking at the girl's horror-filled expression. "Of course you may come with me. We'll settle this matter when you're feeling better. Get up on my horse."

A heavy woman dressed in a tight indigo dress stepped from the shadows. "About time you pulled out, Lilly," she said, her worn face grim beneath the heavy white coating. "Good luck, girl."

Seated on Je t'aime, Lilly huddled beneath the blanket and tried vainly to smile. "Good-bye, Beulah, my friend."

The woman's bleached hair caught the sunlight in greenish tints. "Pah. You just remember where my crib is if things don't turn out. You can't stay 'cause of the madam's bad medicine, but reckon there's a hide hunter or two that would get you out of town . . . as a favor to me."

THAT evening MacGregor leaned against a birch tree and watched the smoke curl upward from the small cabin nestled in the trees. Leaving Jack with a settler, he'd followed Regina out of town and to her land. "Fool woman," he muttered, then tore off a piece of jerky with his teeth. Chewing on it, he watched Regina scavenge through the trees for dry branches while the dogs frolicked at her legs. Her sheep grazed on tufts of grass above the snow.

Another small woman dressed in Regina's clothes moved in and out of the cabin, dragging hides and litter out. Between them they unloaded Regina's chest. Watching the two women tug the chest into the cabin, MacGregor spat out the chewed meat. Picking up his rifle, he circled the cabin and noted the heavy wolf sign.

In the night the two women awoke to the sound of wolves howling and then rapid rifle fire. Twice more the wolves' eerie call sounded to be silenced by gun shots. Regina gripped MacGregor's rifle and stepped out into the moonlight, checking the flock. Laddie circled the sheep restlessly, a dark shadow on the snow, while Venus whined and stayed close to her side.

A rapid succession of rifle fire shattered the night, and then the silence stretched for endless minutes.

Standing beside Regina, Lilly's almond-shaped eyes widened, her small face turning pale as she wrung her hands. "Madam Joy . . ."

"Shh." Regina waited, but the starlit night remained quiet. "Go back to the house, Lilly."

"You come—"

Regina shook her head. "These are my sheep. You're ill. The night's damp chill won't help you to recover. Go along, now, Lilly. Take Venus—I'll need Laddie."

Regina propped the rifle across her lap as she sat on a log, watching the shadows around the meadow. Laddie acted calmly, circling the sheep to her orders, and the night quieted. When she entered the cabin an hour later, Lilly helped her from her jacket.

"Poor Miss Violet. So tired. You drink tea while Lilly comb your pretty hair?"

"I am so happy to have you near, my friend," Regina stated sincerely. "You are a treasure."

Lilly blushed shyly. "One is happy to serve Miss Violet."

Regina stroked Lilly's bruised cheek. "I am not your mistress, but your friend, Lilly. When you wish to leave, you may."

Later, Regina listened to the night slip away and the sound of doves greeting the dawn. When she closed her eyes, MacGregor's long, hard body lay near her. The fierce desire to have him ran through her like a flame. His body filled hers . . . then she opened her lids, the aching hunger quivering within her like a thin, tightly strung wire. Her hand foraged for the hair covering his chest and found nothing but the flannel sheeting of the cot. Rubbing her palms together, Regina turned to her side to watch the dawn slip through the window.

MacGregor. MacGregor . . . When she closed her eyes, she saw his face darken with passion. When she had danced for him, MacGregor had taken her fiercely, possessively. The flames danced in the shadows of the lodge, twining with their bodies wrapped in her shawl as they twisted seeking passion, his mouth tasting hers with sweet delight.

THREE days later Regina returned to Primrose alone and swathed in her finest dress. The paisley shawl caught the sun and shimmered around her shoulders. She eased her skirts away from a drunken miner lying on the boards scattered across the muddy street. After entering the dry goods store, she arranged payment with the manager, who held her emerald earrings to the sunlight and nodded. "Done. You have an account." He handed the earrings back to her. "Won't need those. Got no use for such things here. MacGregor said to give you anything you wanted. Said he'd come to collect you when he was ready." The balding man stared at Regina over his spectacles.

"MacGregor?" she asked ominously.

"Yep. Stopped by here. Said you was to have what you needed. Left a pack of green wolf hides against your account. Said they came off the Pokey Wales place. Said there would be a purple-eyed woman, talking funny, wanting to do business. Reckon you fit the bill."

"MacGregor?" she repeated softly. "Collect me? Like a piece of wayward baggage?"

"Yep. Said you was his wife and that he'd be moving in soon. Made a point to let the boys know that you was married and that he'd be mighty unhappy if they stepped over the line with you. Some young pup mouthed off about how a man should keep his woman, and MacGregor near killed him."

"That—" Regina pressed her lips together. She'd end MacGregor's claim to her at first chance. "Do you have a judge in town?"

"Judge Beauregard has arthritis. Won't be around till June or July when it's good and warm."

In the afternoon Regina found Beulah's tiny shack on the backstreet. Over a tin cup of tea Beulah asked, "That young Chinese girl, Lilly . . . is she healing?"

Regina sipped her tea. "She's taken a brutal beating. Apparently it wasn't the first. She was too frightened to come today. I thought it better that she rest in quiet. She has my dogs and my pistol for protection."

"None of the girls hereabouts will work for Madam Joy. She buys girls from China, brings 'em here. Nobody ever hears from them again, once they go down into the den. That's what Madam Joy was fixing to do with Lilly. She's too old to draw good money. Down in the den men don't care who takes care of 'em." Beulah poured tobacco into a thin paper square, licked an edge, then rolled it into a cigarette. "Poor little thing. She's tough and older than most. Couldn't do a thing for her, though. The madam would have my hide. She's got ways."

The "soiled dove" stuck a wood sliver into her small stove, lit it, and touched it to her cigarette. She inhaled and blew the smoke out her nose. "Miners and hide hunters want one kind of woman or they want another. Once in a while one of us girls gets a good man and a wedding ring. But Madam Joy's girls always end the same. Dead. Saw a dead one once, must have been all of seventeen. Looked like she was fifty. The madam is out to get you, Miss Violet."

"Perhaps I should visit with Madam Joy."

Beulah looked at her sharply. "You do and you might never have that baby you're breeding. She's got more potions—"

"How did you know?" Regina ran her hand across her flat stomach.

The other woman sat back in her chair and puffed on her cigarette. "You've got the look. Seen it often enough . . . and besides, any woman whose got MacGregor dancing around her skirts is likely breeding."

Regina flushed. "He isn't dancing around my skirts."

"He's the only reason the madam hasn't jerked Lilly free. He walked right into the Last Dollar and told her he didn't want anything happening to you. Bought Lilly for you. Said you needed company up there in that cabin. That anyone making trouble for you—"

"That man. That possessive bully. How dare he?" Regina stormed, tugging her shawl closer.

Beulah stared out her dirty window at the rainy mist for a minute, then spoke slowly. "Well, honey. MacGregor's a whole lot of man. He's the kind that sees one woman and wants her, no matter what. The thing is, no one can ever remember MacGregor wanting a woman for years. When he was a sprout there were plenty of quick turns on the blanket. Heard he had an Indian wife who died and left him with a baby. . . . Now you turn up married to him."

"He needed a woman for Jack. I needed help at the moment," Regina stated sharply.

"Sounds like a good bargain to me. You throw a man like that one into the blanket, and I'd take it in a minute."

TWO weeks later MacGregor glanced at Jack trying to pull up on a fallen log. When he stood upright, Jack grinned at his father and yelled, "Da! Da!" A big strong boy, Jack would soon be walking, chattering to a brother or a sister with big purple eyes.

Scooping him up, MacGregor hugged his son, who promptly bestowed him with a juicy kiss. Placing Jack on his shoulders, MacGregor unfolded Beulah's note and read it again. "Violet is with child. Beulah."

That night MacGregor lay in his bed, staring at the rafters above him. The firelight danced in the shadows, and he closed his eyes. *Violet.*

The thought of Regina with his child tightened the muscles around his heart and belly. She'd have known when she left . . . known that his child was growing in her. MacGregor's fist hit the cot.

Bastard child, she'd said. Bound for freedom, she hadn't shared her secret. His fist hit the cot again. *There were ways to rid a woman of an unwanted child—teas, potions . . .*

In a lithe movement MacGregor slid off the cot he'd shared with Regina. He ached to have her nestled against him, the womanly fragrances snaring him. Rubbing his palm along his bare thigh, MacGregor stared at the coals of the fire. "Violet will keep the baby," he murmured. "But what of the father?"

The sight of Regina's eardrops in Pokey Wale's grimy hand irked him. "Diamonds!" Pokey had exclaimed, turning his hand until the jewels sparkled. "Worked with a jeweler once in St. Louie. Them's real diamonds. That's a real ruby in your ear, too, MacGregor, as I live and breathe."

MacGregor's teeth ground together, and he forced himself to relax his jaw. He remembered the diamond she'd offered him on the flats. The size of an egg, the stone was worth more money than he could earn trapping. . . . Regina's jewels made her a wealthy woman.

Lifting Regina's purple ribbon from a peg, MacGregor ran it across his lips. "And I gave her boots and moccasins. Offered to keep her safe and well fed—she can buy men to work for her."

He crushed the ribbon. "She's carrying *my* child."

Two days later MacGregor placed Jack in a cradleboard and laced him in tightly. The baby chattered, excited about the routine trip outside to tend the stock and gather wood. "Well, son. Violet is on the run, and she hasn't made up her mind to have us yet. We can't let her stray too far while she's making up her mind. We've got to find ways of sweetening the pot."

Jack grinned up at his father, his new teeth shining. "Da. Da."

MacGregor picked up the cradleboard and eased his arms into it carefully. "What we have here, Jack, is a reluctant woman. A hard woman. Set in her ways. The thing is, I mean to have her. You're going to be my bait. Violet's got a soft spot for you."

Leaning against the cabin walls that night while Jack slept, MacGregor closed Regina's book of romantic poems with a grim thud. He ran his fingers through the hair on his chest slowly, staring at the fire. Regina's small hand had snared a portion of his heart and left him aching. Dark purple eyes stared at him from the shadows, drowsy in the aftermath of their lovemaking.

MacGregor's hard thumb ran across the purple ribbon marking the poetry.

"Violet MacGregor wants courting, does she?" he asked the shadows. "She dreams of storybook love and walks away from a marriage to me."

He threw the book against the wall. "I won't be bullied by a half-pint Englishwoman."

"TEAR it off," Mortimer-Hawkes demanded softly. "You've failed, Lord Covington. Regina isn't dead, or you would have her earrings. A few coins in the right hands and the story was mine. A miserable attempt and easily foiled. You tried to kill my daughter, Lord Covington, and for that you will pay dearly."

The marquess sliced a grim look at the other man's pale face. "You've failed to conquer her, and I shall have to take up the reins now. Tear off your fingernail as a sign of your allegiance and your apology for trying to harm Pagan. She was tempered for a stronger man than you, a miserable, spineless excuse of a man." He nudged the pliers closer to Alfred Covington's sweat-covered hand. "Now."

"She's with a madman. The two of them killed my guide. Regina's 'gone Injun,' as they say here. Taken to the wilds as if she were born here. You can't blame me for your daughter's savage ways. . . . She tried to kill me first. She—"

The marquess's amethyst eyes flashed angrily. "Regina is a lady. Say that she is anything but a proper lady, and I shall call you out."

When Covington's blue eyes widened, the marquess placed his Hessian boot on a velvet floor pillow to study the polish. "I've changed my mind. Pull out two nails. One as a pledge for your allegiance and one as an apology for your slur on my daughter. Or I shall gladly kill you."

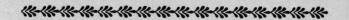

FIFTEEN

A COWBELL echoed through the June morning, cutting through the sounds of the grazing sheep and the mockingbird trill. Regina straightened from hoeing the small garden, tilting the broad brim of her straw hat against the bright sun.

A tall man walked toward her, and she immediately recognized the familiar sway of broad shoulders and easy long-legged stride. MacGregor's white shirt shone brightly in the sun as he led his Appaloosas and two heavily loaded mules across the lush meadow filled with flowers. His long switch reached out to tap a small mottled brown cow with curved horns and swaying udders.

"MacGregor . . ." Regina whispered, her hand raised to cover her rapidly beating heart. Dropping the hoe, she stood on tiptoe to better see the man coming toward her. A daisy tumbled down from the ribbon tied at the hat's crown, and she pressed the flower to her chest.

Striding through the high green grass, brushing aside a sea of yellow and purple flowers, MacGregor led his horses, the two heavily loaded mules, and the cow. Jack napped within the shadows of a small seat safely lashed to the back of a horse. Regina held her breath, jarred by the grim determination locked in MacGregor's rugged features. She instinctively smoothed his large shirt, covering the loosened waistband of her cotton skirt. The baby—MacGregor's child—nestled beneath her hand, and now

243

his father strode through the field toward her like a knight claiming his lands.

Cutting through the grazing sheep, he reached to rub Maude's forehead. Laddie and Venus barked frantically, jumping up on MacGregor's long legs. His black eyes never left her, the desire in them causing her to flush deeply. She ran the back of her hand across her hot cheek, brushing away the clinging tendrils.

His baby rested beneath her palm, and Regina took a deep breath. He'd find out in time, and she'd fight him for the child. But just now she hungered for the sight of him. Part of her ached to run into his arms.

Part of her ached in terror. MacGregor had the intent look of a hunter now, stalking his quarry. Something deep within her shivered in terror. *She couldn't be owned.*

He stopped in front of her. The angles of his face jutted against his dark skin, his hair almost touching the collar of the shirt she'd sewn him. Two tiny, fresh razor cuts slanted across his jaw, and droplets of water clung to his hair.

MacGregor tossed the switch aside and lifted his hat from his head; the ruby glittered in his ear. His lean brown fingers closed slowly on the hat's brim, the white knuckles showing for just an instant. He shifted on long legs, the gunbelt gleaming in the sunlight. " 'Morning."

She nodded. " 'Morning."

The grooves sliding down his cheek deepened as he smiled, and Regina's heart lurched. She blinked once, and his grin deepened, his eyes sparkling beneath the sooty length of black lashes.

MacGregor's smile . . . a beguiling, courtly, heart-stopping smile.

Her eyes widened. *MacGregor's courting smile,* she thought wildly, fascinated as he took a step closer to her and the reins slid to the dewy grass. MacGregor's black eyes swept slowly over her face, and she forced herself not to shiver. "You're looking well, MacGregor," she managed huskily, trying to keep her tone even.

"I tried to stay away longer. Tried to give you the time you need to heal," he stated softly, studying the daisies tucked into her staw bonnet and searching her face within the shadows. "Can't stay away any longer."

She tensed as he reached to stroke a fingertip across the heavy braid flowing down her left breast. Tracing the length slowly, MacGregor stared at her intently. "Jack's needing his ma, Violet. I'm needing my wife. I tried what you said, paid an Indian woman to tend Jack. But she said he was too ornery. Said I was ornery, too. That's why I've come to you. Seems like you're the only woman who can handle the pair of us."

Her eyes widened at his admission. "MacGregor, you know—"

He ran a fingertip across the sensitive tip of her swollen breast and up her inner arm before she stepped away. "You're a beautiful woman, Violet MacGregor. Enough to make a man lose his head like I did. . . . Maybe I went about it all wrong, but I reckon a man can make things right if he tries hard enough. That's what I'm here to do, Violet."

MacGregor's tone lowered, his hand cradling her hot cheek as he leaned down to brush a kiss across her parted lips. "So I've come to you, Violet. Sold my place—"

"You sold your homestead?"

He shrugged, scanned the lush meadows spreading across the valley, and nodded. "A man wants a home. You'll be needing help. I'll start plowing a cornfield at dawn if you'll let us stay." MacGregor turned to her, his expression still. He nodded to the cow, munching on the lush grass. "The cow is yours. Figured Jack will be needing the milk, too, maybe. The settler said the cow makes sweet milk with plenty of cream for butter. . . ."

Catching her breath, Regina crushed the daisy in her hand and threw it to the ground. "You've told everyone in Primrose that I'm your . . . your wife. You've set up my account without my permission and entered *my* affairs as though you—" Her hand slashed between them. "You have no right."

MacGregor locked his long legs at the knee and tilted his head arrogantly, his expression grim. "I wanted you safe. . . . Seems you've stirred up that Chinese whore . . .

woman who owns the Last Dollar. She thinks you've got something she owns. Offered a bag of gold dust to the first man who brought you in for her. They'd just started bidding on who would have you first when—"

MacGregor's jaw tightened ominously when he took a deep breath. "I'm asking this time, Violet. Asking if you'll let Jack and me stay."

"You've sold your property assuming that I—" Regina placed her hands on her waist, and his eyes skimmed down her body and the cloth tightening over her full breasts. She crossed her arms protectively over the sensitive peaks, willing her body to stop trembling. "MacGregor, I am not alone here. We are managing—"

"Divinely," he finished for her. "Two women. Two *small* women. One with the grit of a mule determined to go uphill when the going is easier downhill." He lifted a heavy black eyebrow. "That's you. Seems I've been taking the uphill trail since we met."

Taking a worn paper from his pocket, MacGregor hesitated and studied the tiny violet she had embroidered on his cuff. "Silly little thing. But it's your mark and makes me proud." He placed the papers in her hand. "You own Lilly now."

In the sunlight the bold Oriental brush strokes looked like whiplashes on white flesh. "Slavery," she spat the word at him as she tore the papers, tossing the shreds to the morning breeze. "You make a habit of buying women, don't you, MacGregor. You traded ten plew for my first time with you—"

"The madam," he said tightly, "was hopping mad. Short of killing her and setting a price on my head, I did the easiest thing. That first time in the cabin, when we bargained, I wanted you, virgin or not."

"We made an insane bargain, but one that served its purpose. I will repay you, MacGregor—" The hot look he threw at her stopped her.

Sunlight skimmed along his clean-shaven jaw, a muscle tensing beneath the dark skin. His fingers curled into a fist, the knuckles whitening across the darkly tanned back. He forced them to uncurl slowly. "The garden needs fencing. The cabin needs a room or two added. You'll need wood for the winter. I can make myself useful. The bargain stands—"

Regina's hand skimmed across her stomach and Mac-Gregor caught the movement, his expression darkening. "I've missed you, Violet. You're looking tired," he said, taking a step nearer.

"Da!" Jack's sleepy cry stopped him. "Da! Eat! Down!"

She turned toward the cry, her eyes lighting. "Jack— where is he?"

Hesitating a second, MacGregor took her wrist and slid a thin gold band on her finger. Lifting her hand to his lips, he whispered huskily, "I know you have better. The ring is from me, small and proper. Just like you."

Lifted from the horse, Jack rested in the crook of MacGregor's arm. He stared at Regina with big, black drowsy eyes. MacGregor straightened Jack's cloth shirt and trousers. "We cleaned up in the stream before coming here. Didn't want you to think we'd forgotten our manners."

"He's such a beautiful boy," she whispered, aching to hold Jack close. "Such a fine lad."

Regina tugged her hat off and toyed with Jack's chubby hand. He whimpered and clung tighter to MacGregor, staring at her solemnly. "Oh, Jack, how you have grown, my little man!" Regina exclaimed, leaning to kiss Jack's plump cheek.

"He walks now," MacGregor stated softly above her head. "You won't have to pack him very much." When she looked up, his dark eyes were filled with her reflection. The fierce longing wrapped around her, crushing her with a velvet fist. MacGregor's large hand ran down her shoulder to the back of her waist, urging her closer until her body touched his. His fingers trembled slightly as though he feared she would move away.

Entranced by the tender expression in his dark eyes, Regina closed her eyes as he kissed her lightly. The brief kiss promised a sweetness that made her ache for more.

"Da," Jack gurgled shyly, then pointed his finger at Regina's earlobe bearing the ruby stone.

"Yes, darling. Your father has one, too. They were my mother's." When she kissed his hand, he grinned and turned away, hugging his father tighter. "Oh, MacGregor. He's wonderful."

Stepping back from MacGregor's touch, Regina shivered and caught her lower lip between her teeth. MacGregor's son had her love in his chubby fist. His father was another matter. Taking a lacy handkerchief from her shirt pocket, she carefully wrapped his ring in it and slid it back into her pocket. "Don't think I'm keeping this, Mr. MacGregor. . . . Jack needs food and rest. If you want to stay a day or two, that will be fine. I'll keep Jack until you're settled in somewhere else."

When she reached for Jack, MacGregor stepped back. "He's heavy." Placing the boy gently on his moccasin-covered feet, MacGregor crouched while Jack clung to his fingers.

The boy took a tentative step away from his father toward the cow and squealed in delight as Laddie ran toward the sheep. "Da! Eat!" Jack cried, his tiny legs almost at a run.

Delighted with the boy's antics, Regina giggled and clapped her hands. "Oh, he's lovely." Without thinking, she stood on tiptoe to plop her straw bonnet on MacGregor's head. Lifting her skirts, she ran after the boy.

Lilly walked gracefully through the cabin's open door and smiled shyly at MacGregor. She nodded politely and stopped near him. "You are the keeper of Miss Violet's love," she singsonged in a melodic, soft tone. "Miss Violet's heart's delight."

" 'Heart's delight'?" MacGregor jerked off the bonnet and looked away, shielding his high color. He cleared his throat, trying to catch his breath.

Lilly smiled impishly. "One is happy for Miss Violet. One is happy you have come for the sun of your days and the moon of your nights."

He cleared his throat again, turning to unpack the mules with shaking hands. Over his shoulder MacGregor said quietly, "There's an English hunting party not far from here. I don't want Violet left alone, even for a walk." He handed the bundle of Jack's cloths to her. "A big man named Tall Tom is their guide. He's missing a toe and walks odd. Missing an eye, too. There's two Englishmen in the party. Both with light hair. They'll take Violet if they can. . . . Just as soon as Jack's settled in, I'm going after them."

Lilly's hand trembled as it lay on his sleeve. "But you cannot. You are her heart—"

That instant Jack's delighted squeal erupted behind them, his fists filled with Regina's red bead necklace. Balanced on her hip, he grinned and raised the beads to his sire like a trophy. "Da."

Regina's husky voice was dangerously quiet. "MacGregor . . . Lilly. Perhaps you might include me in this conversation."

Jack bounced on her hip, tugging at her braid as she looked up at MacGregor. "What's this about an English hunting party and Tall Tom?"

MacGregor turned slowly, his expression hardening. "You've learned how to hunt, haven't you, Violet? Enough to walk without making noise and creep up behind a man's back."

Deep purple eyes shadowed by her lashes met his. "Quite. Stalking game and spearing fish has broadened my training as a lady. You've come here to protect me, haven't you? I am not a damsel in distress now, MacGregor Two Hearts. Nor are you my knight," she stated flatly.

MacGregor ran the flat of his hand across his stomach. "Lilly, why don't you take Jack over to the cow? He likes to pick grass and feed her . . . watch he doesn't get under her feet."

Regina watched him intently. "Two Englishmen that I know have reason to be hunting me. Both have light hair—Lord Covington and my father, the Marquess of

Fordington." Her hand went to her stomach, flattening protectively over it.

Stripping off his shirt, he handed it to her. "I'm proud of this shirt, Violet. Finest thing I've ever owned."

He began unloading the mules' packs. "Covington and your father have paired up, hunting across the mountains and paying for word of a purple-eyed, half-pint English-woman. . . . They'll turn up sooner or later. That's why I'm heading them off."

Regina carefully folded his shirt. Faced with his broad back, she tried to avoid staring at the rippling muscles beneath the tanned, scarred skin. When he bent, loosening a rope, his trousers slipped fractionally from his waist to expose a pale strip of flesh. Regina's mouth went dry; unwillingly her eyes followed the hard shape of his buttocks and long, muscular legs. In the meadow the sheep bleated, and Jack squealed. A small hawk soared through the blue sky, and the cow lowed softly. The stream gurgled nearby, passing over a riffle, and her heart stopped.

Forcing herself to concentrate on MacGregor's mission, she cleared her throat. "Heading them off . . . exactly what does that mean?"

"I'll do what I have to do."

"You're hungry for the taste of blood, are you, Mac-Gregor? After all, it's been some time since you shot those men who kidnapped me, hasn't it?" When he didn't answer and continued to unpack the animals, she hit his shoulder.

MacGregor's hands gripped Kansas's saddle, then placed it over a sack of grain. He straightened to his full height, hooked his thumbs in his belt, and stared down at her. A muscle moved in his cheek, sliding down his throat to tighten across his chest. "What do you want me to do, Violet?"

"You will let me deal with my father."

"You're asking me to be less than a man. . . . That sounds like an order," he returned, the dark skin covering his high cheekbones tightening.

"It is. Manhood is not measured by killing, but by honor. If you kill my father . . ."

For the space of a heartbeat he stared down at her. Anger flickered beneath his lashes before he returned to his work. "We'll wait it out, then. Together."

Regina's trembling fingers crushed the cotton shirt. She ached to smooth MacGregor's strong back, the tense cords running beneath his dark jaw. Because of loving Jack, he'd plucked her from that deathly cabin. He wanted his son to have a woman's soft touch, a memory he'd been denied.

MacGregor. An orphan now a grown man seeking to protect those he loved. Scars from the mission beating glistened in the sun, and suddenly his skin rippled, beneath her palm.

MacGregor tensed and straightened slowly as her hand skimmed across his shoulders, following the hard contours. Her fingertip circled the healed bullet wound, then traced a long ragged scar slowly down to his lower back. Across the width of a heavily padded shoulder, she traced a row of scars—the mark of the cat she'd killed to the Sun Dance scars marring his gleaming chest.

A squirrel ran up a juniper tree, chattering to his playful mate. In that instant Regina realized her fingers rested on MacGregor's tense back. She jerked her hand back, crushing his shirt to her chest.

He turned slowly, the sun catching blue sparks in his black hair. "Touch me again," he ordered rawly, his eyes gleaming beneath his lashes. "Cure me of this ache—"

"MacGregor—" Regina edged back, frightened by the dark flush riding his stark, hungry face.

Taking her wrist, he placed her palm over his heavily thudding heart. "There. Feel that. You do that to me," he whispered huskily. "I'm flesh and blood, not ink and paper scrawled with pretty words of dreams and love."

     AT sunset a mist settled over the stream winding through the large meadow.

MacGregor tossed the last piece of chopped wood to the pile and sank the ax into a tree stump with all the force of his frustration. Regina had kept to herself in the house while doing her chores. Jack toddled happily at her heels, receiving her hugs and kisses freely. MacGregor scowled at the lacy underwear drying across the bushes and ran his hand across his bare chest. Regina's slender fingers had rummaged momentarily through the hair covering his chest before she'd run away into the house.

Lilly had brought him roast rabbit and bread for lunch while Regina scrubbed Jack's cloths on a washboard. She spread them over the brushes with her lacy underwear. MacGregor stared at a delicate scrap of lace, his mouth drying.

He'd wanted to kiss Regina until she clung to him. Wanted to tell her how his heart filled with happiness just thinking about the new baby.

Jack toddled out of the cabin's open door and promptly tripped. His wail brought Regina running to scoop him up in her arms. Balancing him on her hip, she cooed and kissed until Jack stopped crying.

"Hell of a thing to be jealous of my own son," MacGregor muttered darkly, stacking the wood.

"What did you say?" she asked, turning to him.

"You'll spoil the boy," he returned tightly, looking more closely at Jack. "You've put him in a dress." Sensing his father's dark mood, the boy clung to Regina and stared at MacGregor drowsily.

"Hum." She studied Jack, then kissed his damp hair. "He's bathed and dressed for bed. Lilly and I stitched him a gown—"

"Holy sh—Take it off. He sleeps in his drawers."

Regina's eyebrows lifted. "You brought him to me. We've agreed that I'll keep him until you're settled. I say he sleeps in proper night clothing. Lilly and I are making him new clothing tomorrow. For that matter, it wouldn't hurt you to sleep in a shift if you stay inside the cabin . . . not that I care about your sleeping habits." With that she swept Jack into the cabin and slammed the door.

He stared at the door. Just then it opened, and Regina placed a water basin on a bench outside the cabin. She straightened, handed him a folded towel, and met his eyes evenly. "Your shirt is on a peg next to the door," she stated coolly, primly. "We've arranged your things as best we could. We're having griddle cakes with wild strawberries in syrup. Thank you for the cow. I've named her Rosebud. In the morning we'll discuss the matter of your interference in my affairs. Because at this moment I am very, very angry with you."

MacGregor snared her wrist, staying her. "Damn it, Violet. You try a man's temper. I'll not beg for those meager kisses you dole out, nor the right to protect you—"

Her eyebrows lifted, challenging him as she slowly drew her arm back. "I'm perfectly capable of dealing with my life, MacGregor. You are not my black knight, protecting me from a demon sweeping out of the marshes. You would do well to remember that." With that she gathered the laundry and returned to the house. The door closed solidly in his face.

Regina's cool, polite tone answered his knock on the plank door a few minutes later. "Yes? Who is it?"

MacGregor took a deep, steadying breath. If Regina had set her mind to straining his patience, she had succeeded. "MacGregor," he said between his teeth.

"Oh. Mr. MacGregor. How nice. . . . Come in. You may leave the door open," she invited in the lofty tone of a grand dame bidding a visitor to enter her sitting room.

MacGregor entered the small cabin cautiously. A weathered ladder hung from the rafters, neat bundles of drying flowers and plants tied to it. Blue muslin curtains hung at the new windows. Another ladder led to a loft. Regina's china and various bottles stood on a shelf with her books. He'd been given a corner, his shirts and trousers neatly folded on a bench. His rifles and cartridges, knives and razor rested on a long shelf above Jack's reach.

Lilly knelt by Jack's willow bed, patting the drowsy boy on his back and singing softly to him.

Regina bent near a grate swung over a low fire, turning cakes on a griddle. She nodded to the rough table and chairs. "Please sit down. Lilly and Jack have eaten."

When she came to the table, her cheeks flushed by the fire, MacGregor swallowed the deep emotion rising within him. "You've learned to cook."

"I long for a proper stove," she returned stiffly, placing a platter of sourdough griddle cakes in front of him. "There's no butter. But the wild strawberry syrup is delicious."

He inhaled slowly, savoring the scent of a home.

After a moment he cleared his throat. "How are the sheep?"

"Very well. Lilly and I sheared a good measure of wool from them. It's washed and hung in the loft until we can experiment with dyes," she returned stiffly. "I have a measure of copperas for setting the color."

He nodded, searching for words uneasily. "That's good. Indians use clay for dye sometimes. Roots and bark. Flowers like goldenrod for yellow . . . barberry bush, peach leaves, onions, too. Berries for red . . ."

"Birch bark set with alum is supposed to make a beautiful nankin color—"

MacGregor caught the quick lift of her head before she averted her eyes. "In the war . . . a Reb granny-woman took care of me during a fever. We were out of quinine then, so she made me drink dogwood tea. . . . She had a loom. Used to weave all day. Kept her mind from the cannon shot in the next field."

Regina toyed with her fork as he continued. "A loom is a problem . . . but not one that we can't solve. Granny's took almost the whole room."

He glanced around the small cabin and nodded toward one end. "Wouldn't take much to add a couple rooms back there . . . maybe a big porch too, so you could sit outside in the shade."

"I've thought the same. Shall we eat?"

She ate voraciously. After finishing his meal, MacGregor settled back to sip his coffee and watch her. "Thank you for the dinner. It was good," he said simply, noting that she had reached for another cake. He glanced at Lilly questioningly.

The girl eyed him warily, then allowed a heavy swath of sleek hair to conceal her face. Lilly's giggle rippled through the cabin like tinkling bells in a gentle breeze.

Regina daintily licked a drop of syrup from her fingertips. "A salted herring or two would be lovely just now," she murmured. "Just the thing."

After placing a small wooden box on the table, she took out several dried herring fillets on a plate. "There. Have one."

MacGregor stared at her, then grinned slowly. "Believe I'll pass, ma'am."

That night Lilly slept in the loft; MacGregor counted the inches between his pallet and Regina's bed behind the flannel sheet.

Before dawn he left the sleeping household and walked to the creek. Standing in the knee-deep current and sluicing his hot flesh with the icy water helped ease the long, potent ache that had begun the day he took Violet MacGregor to his bed.

HER hands on her waist, Regina stared at the bucket beneath the cow's full udders. The cow turned and blinked at her with all the boredom of a seasoned royal lady at court. Her braided wreath of daisies slipped askew, and Regina sighed. "Lady Rosebud, you are every bit as difficult as that arrogant mountain laird, MacGregor."

The bluish-gray morning mist curled around the valley in layers at dawn, the dew dampening Regina's skirt. She traced her trail through the heavy grass back to the cabin and thought about MacGregor. Last night he had turned restlessly on the floor pallet.

Suddenly she'd awakened to the sound of her own crying.

Jennifer's cry had echoed through the night. *"Remember the legends. Mother to daughter—Mariah . . . Mariah . . . and the power. . . . "* Regina had wiped her wet lashes and curled into a ball, protecting her unborn child. In her dream she'd seen a daughter with MacGregor's jet-black eyes wrapped in the flaming color of the paisley shawl. . . . If she failed to remember, her daughter could lay within Mortimer-Hawkes's cruel fist.

MacGregor had drawn the sheet aside, staring down at

her through the night's shadows; hunger and passion burned in his black eyes. The bare light skimmed the breath of his shoulders, the angular length of his body. "Violet?" he asked huskily. "*Tsiso?*"

She'd pretended to sleep, fighting the need to open her arms to him.

Regina plucked a daisy from its stalk and ripped it apart. *What was the force binding her to him? What caused her to ache for his kiss, the strength of his body coupling with hers?*

Lifting her face to the swirling haze, Regina closed her eyes and shivered. A rippling length of silky hair slid across her flushed cheek, and she twined it around her finger. *Was it his daughter, nestling in her womb, who recognized the father's rights?*

Caressing the tight mound of her stomach nestled beneath MacGregor's loose shirt, Regina smiled whimsically. She wanted the baby desperately; the sweet feel of Jack had strengthened her desire to hold another MacGregor baby. . . . She stretched and yawned, enjoying the ease of her unbound breasts for a time.

MacGregor, dressed only in his trousers, suddenly stepped from the mist. Rubbing his damp hair with a towel, he asked, "Wishing for Rosebud to fill the pail by herself?"

Startled, Regina stepped backward. Her bare foot slid on the wet grass, and she half turned, her cheek brushing the warmth of MacGregor's broad chest. Shivering, she jumped back and scowled up at him. "Gads. You should wear Rosebud's bell."

She didn't want to see his hair rumpled and damp, the sensual curve of his mouth. She didn't want to look up into eyes stormy with desire. Nor ache to rub her palm across the night's growth of beard covering his hard jaw. . . . "I'm having a bit of a problem with Rosebud," she explained quickly, aware that her voice quivered like a drop of dew on the tip of a leaf.

MacGregor's special smile slid out; the devilish, beguiling heart-stalking smile. He rummaged through the black hair on his chest, and her fingers ached to repeat the deed.

Droplets of water clung to the hair veeing down his flat stomach. Regina stared at his unbuttoned waistband, following the muscular line of his stomach downward. Without his underdrawers MacGregor's heavy arousal pressed full length at the cloth.

He followed her stare and grinned wickedly, lifting an eyebrow at her widened eyes and parted lips. "Every morning it's the same, sweetheart. Aching for you."

"Gads . . . you've grown," she whispered, unable to draw her eyes away. Nor move from the warmth of his body as he stepped nearer.

"I'm hurting. The pain needs easing."

With that he bent and kissed her slowly, tasting the corners of her lips as though she were strawberries and honey. The cool mist clung to her hot face as the kiss deepened and his tongue foraged for the sweetness of hers.

With suckling and toying and heating desire, MacGregor drew her to tiptoe, her aching breasts pressing against him.

When at last their lips parted, Regina rested full length against him. Wide amethyst eyes met ebony as they breathed heavily, the mist sweeping over them. Startled by the emotions racing through her, Regina turned away quickly and shivered. "I . . . I just came to . . . milk."

MacGregor's soft chuckle brought her color rising, and she rounded on him. "Rosebud doesn't give milk easily. She's not used to me yet."

He lifted a thick brow. "You know how to milk?"

Regina studied a patch of daisies, white splashes against the dark green meadow. "Actually, I've always wanted to. My father didn't want a milkmaid for a daughter, and I was barred from the fields and the kitchens." She studied Rosebud's udders. "I squeezed, but nothing happened."

MacGregor walked to the creek and wet the towel, then returned to wash the cow's udders. He crouched and milked the cow easily, squirting the streams of milk into the pail. Looking over his shoulder at her, he said, "She's full. Come here, I'll show you how."

When she hesitated, he positioned the cow near a log and sat on it. He edged back, preparing room for her and spread his thighs. "It helps to sit. Come here."

In moments she was sitting between his thighs, bending to the cow's teats. MacGregor's strong hands took hers, demonstrating the pulling, squeezing motion. A stream of milk squirted into the pail, and Regina grinned up at him. "This is wonderful. Rosebud doesn't seem to mind at all."

"She's lost her calf. If she isn't milked, she'll hurt. Same as a woman full with milk." His voice had deepened against her temple, the muscles of his upper arms brushing her breasts.

His hands squeezed again, and another stream shot into the pail. Resting his chin on her shoulder, he kissed the side of her cheek. "You do it. Just keep up an easy pull."

Concentrating on her task, Regina adjusted her body position, scooting back against MacGregor. Within a few minutes the pail was full. Delighted with her accomplishment, she looked over her shoulder at MacGregor. "How wonderful!"

The angles and planes of his face caught her, his breathing slow and heavy. In the next instant she was lifted to his lap. His hand slid beneath the loose shirt to cover her bare breast, caressing it gently. "I wondered," he said rawly, reverently, as he traced the full, sensitive contour, warming her with his palm.

Caressing her, MacGregor bent to kiss her slowly, tenderly, and she curled her arms around his neck to draw him closer.

The steady plop-plop of the mist falling from the trees settled around them like a magical song. Regina pressed against the warmth of his hand, needing to be nearer.

A large cold drop splattered on her hot cheek, startling her from the velvety warm cloak of MacGregor's kisses. She opened her eyes to find herself lying across his thighs, the press of his arousal against her buttocks.

In a swirl of petticoats and skirts, Regina scampered from his lap, sending him to the damp grass. Rosebud snorted and stepped into the pail of milk, shook free, and galloped off a few yards to graze peacefully.

Regina shivered and jerked her shirt down, smoothing

it primly when she wanted to tug his trousers off and—
"Gracious MacGregor. Have you no decency? You're set
to rut at a moment's notice!"

His devilish grin stopped her, and she stared at him as
he stood lithely, brushing the bits of grass and dew away.
"With another woman and Jack in the cabin, I had to take
what—"

"Take what you could get?" she repeated, outraged. "You
use the faintest excuse to crowd me into a corner, ogle my
chest—" When he eyed that part of her and grinned widely,
she glanced down to find her hardened nipples thrusting at
the thin cloth. "Oh!"

Regina crossed her arms protectively in front of her. She
avoided looking down MacGregor's powerful body, staring
up at him. "You've made me very angry, Mr. Two Hearts
MacGregor. You've caused the first butter and milk we
could have had to be wasted. You swagger into my valley
as if you came to collect me, and you haven't the slightest
idea"—she tapped his chest pointedly—"about staying out
of my affairs."

"Your affairs?" he asked, running the flat of his hand
along his unshaven jaw.

The scraping sound slid across Regina's sensitive skin,
and she frowned up at him. Shaking her finger beneath
his nose, she continued. "You are not playing gunfighter
because Lord Covington and my father are lurking about
the woods. We're not in England now, and I'm perfectly
able to handle the both of them. I have not appointed
you my protector, nor do I appreciate your intervention
in matters that do not—I repeat, *do not*—concern you,"
she finished hotly.

MacGregor ran his fingers through his hair. "Damn it,
Violet. I want to protect you. Take care of you, like any
man wants to take care of his wife. Covington and your
father are running with Tall Tom, a bad mix. Yet you're
telling me to step aside? That's like waiting for a rattler
to strike before you stomp him!" he roared. "Women need
protecting. Wives let their husbands do the protecting—"

Her eyebrows shot up. "Really, Mr. Two Hearts Mac-

Gregor? You've decided all that on your own, have you?"

He stared down at her, the muscles in his jaw contracting. "Women," he stated finally. "They're like messing with whiskey. A little makes you feel good. Too much and you wake up with hammers in your skull."

"How sweet." Regina picked up her skirts daintily as though she were on a London street. She leveled a dark look at him over her shoulder. "MacGregor, you shoot anyone because of me, and I'll never speak to you again—"

"Violet." MacGregor traced her stiff back as she walked to the cabin.

The gentle sway of her hips drew his gaze. The high grass, laden with dew, brushed along her legs and dampened the cloth until it clung. MacGregor's gaze locked on the twin rounded curves flowing beneath the cloth. "Hell! I ache from head to toe," he stated between his teeth. Taking a deep breath, he stripped again and stalked into the stream's icy water.

SIXTEEN

MORTIMER-Hawkes intently surveyed the ram's trophy set of curved horns. Poised on a high bluff, the massive ram stared down at the hunting party winding through the firs and jutting rock shelves. Mortimer-Hawkes lifted the brass spyglass and nodded at Tall Tom. "Perfect set of horns for my lodge in England. Wonderful matched curl . . . tips intact . . . give me my rifle."

Easing the gun to the leather shoulder pad of his hunting jacket, Mortimer-Hawkes adjusted his cheek to the stock. He closed one eye, sighting in on the ram, and squeezed the trigger slowly. . . .

The shot echoed through the mountains, and a cloud of blue smoke drifted away into the lofty firs, the pungent odor of sulfur slicing through the juniper scents.

The ram stared down at the party with elegant disdain for an instant, then leapt unscathed to a higher bluff and out of sight.

That night Mortimer-Hawkes stared at the campfire, sipping brandy steadily from his tooled silver flask. Mariah taunted him from the dancing orange and yellow flames, her heathen fringed shawl rippling in the sparks shooting up into the night.

Pagan. Mortimer-Hawkes brooded and drank, lounging back on the Oriental carpet and satin pillows covering the pine needles. He crushed the gauzy dancing costume in his fist, then smoothed the embroidered bodice. After a proper beating, Mariah's satiny body had rippled when he made

261

love to her. The perfume of her terror had hardened his manhood into a weapon, slashing in her silky depths.

The marquess closed his eyes, remembering the sudden ecstatic gush of his juices . . . the bliss of turgid manhood. Abruptly he raised the flask to his mouth and drank to the dregs.

Pagan. Almost a replica of her mother, Pagan's dusky heritage and unique savagery made her a suitable mate for him. With her and the Mariah Stone in his glove, he'd never miss another trophy shot. . . . Power and wealth lay in possessing the woman of the Mariah Stone.

Pagan's power lay just within his reach. Tall Tom's Indian runners had brought word of a small Englishwoman who had settled outside the mining town of Primrose. "Violet MacGregor," he muttered, ignoring the startled looks of the other men. "You chose your name well, my dear. Yes, of course. Violet for the Mortimer-Hawkeses' unusual eye color, and MacGregor for that uncouth half-breed who's running with you. . . ."

Mortimer-Hawkes shifted on his luxurious pallet, narrowing his eyes at the sharp silver knife used to cut his meat. He picked it up slowly, studying the razor-sharp blade. "Yes, this will do nicely to slice his manhood away. Before he dies, I'll savor destroying him, inch by inch."

Mortimer-Hawkes cut a bead from the bodice carefully and stared darkly at Lord Covington, who had been fondling a half-white camp follower. "Eat this," he ordered quietly, handing Covington the bead. "Then show me and the rest of the camp how you can ride that slut like a man."

Minutes later Mortimer-Hawkes lashed Covington's white rump with a riding whip. "Faster—ride the slut harder!"

WRAPPED in her shawl against the night's chill, Regina sat on the bench outside the cabin. A cloud slid in front of the full moon, and she pressed her lips together tightly. The Mariah Stone heated her palm, filling it until she couldn't close her fingers.

Her daughter would not be served to Mortimer-Hawkes's cruel grasp easily.

With a fierce scowl MacGregor had taken to the mountains, salving his pride.

Two Hearts MacGregor could beguile her at the oddest moments . . . when he took Jack to bathe and play in the stream; when the two of them returned with matching wide grins; when he dropped a bouquet of tiny blue flowers—forget-me-nots—and pink primrose into her apron.

MacGregor's hungry black eyes followed her closely. His tender kisses flavored her lips, haunting her. MacGregor—she'd come a continent away from England to find him. Tall, strong, and oddly vulnerable—affected deeply by the simplicity of an embroidered violet on his shirt cuff. Touching her with his large, scarred hands as though she were lace. Shivering beneath her fingertips, his skin had rippled as she traced a trail across the scars. . . .

MacGregor acted like her knight, protecting her honor with his life.

MacGregor. Coming to her with his son. Giving her his daughter.

She caressed the baby nestled in her womb. He'd never leave her to settle the past alone if he knew. . . .

Regina sighed and looked up into the starlit sky. A meteor slashed downward suddenly, cutting a path across the inky sky as boldly as MacGregor had entered her life.

The Mariah's sharp edges cut into her palm, reminding her of her father looming in her past and thrusting into her future. The wings of an owl sailed across the moon; the breeze rustled the sumac bushes, and a woodrat scurried through the underbrush.

MADAM Joy lifted her long clay pipe and smoked deeply. The smoke made her feel young and desirable, causing her to forget for a time that her body was shriveled and her hair thinning. Drawing her long, curved lacquered nail across the black enamel of a small chest, she frowned. Her rival, Lacy's, a weathered-board tavern in front of the whores' cribs, enticed men admired in the wilderness.

The madam sneered, puffing her long stemmed pipe. Lacy's catered to a certain breed of man, while she offered more sophisticated entertainment for those wishing to pay. The madam sipped a heady wine and thought of Lilly. "The girl is willful and disobedient," the madam hissed, smoothing the enameled chest. "Stupid."

A woman riding an Indian pony on a sidesaddle eased through the muddy street and stopped near the dry goods store. "That Englishwoman," the madam hissed, leaning closer to the window. "She will regret taking Lilly."

The madam entered the dry goods store a few moments later, dressed in her best black silk gown. When Regina turned, the madam smiled coldly. "You are Violet MacGregor. The woman who cannot keep MacGregor in her bed. Perhaps soon he will bring both Lilly and you to me. I would pay well for you, my blossom," the madam crooned, leaning closer to Regina to hiss, "You dry English miss. MacGregor crawls between the legs of Lacy's women even now. The countryside knows you cannot keep such a man, even though you are breeding with his brat. If he rolls on another now, when you are big-bellied, he will laugh at you."

The madam leaned closer, reveling in her revenge when the Englishwoman paled. The unusual shade of her eyes fascinated the madam. "So that is why you are called Violet."

Regina straightened her shoulders, drawing up to her full height. Shopping for lengths of flannel for her baby had soothed her nerves momentarily. MacGregor's disappearance had cost her sleep, and the madam was the perfect person to encounter just now.

She smiled tightly. "Madam Joy, I presume." Placing her paper-wrapped parcel carefully on the counter, she tugged her kid gloves higher. Worn to keep MacGregor close, his ring circled her finger, and she smoothed it thoughtfully. "Lilly has recovered from your beating. I've often wondered what I would do if you crossed my path. . . . Now I know." In the next instant Regina stepped near the madam, swishing her skirts and petticoats aside. "Before you harm another innocent girl, please remember this—"

The madam staggered with the blow to her jaw, knocking over a display of dried herring boxes. She slithered to the floor and blinked up at Regina, who was dusting the madam's rice face powder from her kid gloves. She straightened her gingham dress primly. "I detest violence, but on occasion there is need."

Stepping over the madam's rumpled form, Regina picked up her parcel. "If you come anywhere near Lilly or myself, I shall repeat the performance. I've just gotten tea. . . . Lilly is baking cakes, and you are *not* invited to our ladies' tea on Thursday—however, if any of your . . . staff wants the shelter of my home, they shall have it."

"I would kill them," the madam hissed, slashing the straw brooms toppling down on her.

"Then I shall see you again. They tell me there is a slight pop when a scalp is jerked free of the skull. Yours should be very easy to trim," Regina returned calmly, then stepped out onto the boardwalk.

MACGREGOR leaned back in his chair and studied the whiskey in his glass. The smokey gloom of Lacy's had sheltered him for two days and kept the bright morning sunlight from burning the back of his eyes. A fresh breeze swept into the room from the open door, and MacGregor shuddered, his head aching. He ached from brawling with Peterson, who shared his table and his bottle. One of Lacy's girls sat on Pierre's lap and nuzzled his ear.

Nancy's purple dress reminded MacGregor of Regina's eyes, and he glared at the Frenchman from the bruised slit of his left eye. "Violet is a mean woman."

"Pah! She is one damn fine woman, my friend," Pierre answered easily, his hand running down Nancy's ample hip.

MacGregor slammed his glass down on the table. "She denies our marriage. Denies me her bed."

Another Lacy's woman slid her hand around MacGregor's chest, foraging for the hair beneath his muslin shirt. "Honey, anytime you want, you just come up to Belle's—"

"Violet MacGregor, she calls herself," MacGregor continued darkly, pouring another glass of whiskey. "Takes my boy to her cold heart. Spent the winter with me. . . . Takes my name and takes my baby in her belly. Takes everything but me. . . ." he brooded as Belle slid into his lap and draped her arms around his neck. Her ample breasts quivered over the top of her tight bodice, and she pressed them against him as she poured whiskey.

Shifting against the pain of his bruised ribs, MacGregor rested his hand on her waist. Belle's soft, voluptuous body nestled closer, and he thought of sweeter fare, the scent of cinnamon and musk and Regina's body arching in his arms. Pale thighs meeting his thrusts, the soft cries deep in her throat as she clung to him.

MacGregor swallowed the whiskey, waiting for the sharp bite to wash away his memories of Regina's eyes, dark with passion. The way the shawl clung to her like flame, tantalizing him with a length of long thigh, a shimmering thrust of pale breast. Her mouth was like hot silk, burning his skin. Her hair sliding across his skin with the scent of cinnamon—"Oh, hell, Pierre. Order another bottle."

Belle smoothed the beard covering his jaw and toyed with his hair. "Anytime, honey. My bed is fancy. A big man like you can stretch out nice and easy on it."

"My friend wants to suffer in pain alone," Pierre stated easily with a wry smile.

"The hell I do, you damned Frenchman," MacGregor threw back.

Peterson shook his craggy head and stared blankly at the three empty whiskey bottles on the table. "Woman trouble can drive a man insane. Bad for their man parts. I've heard of a man's balls shriveling away to the size of peas when—"

Belle ran her hand across MacGregor's jaw, toying with his black beard. "It's true," she added sagely, settling closer on MacGregor's lap and squirming against him. "The next thing happens is they get mountain fever. Go crazy."

Settling her massive bosom beneath MacGregor's chin, she urged his face into the deep crevice just as Regina stepped into the bar.

"Violet!" MacGregor stood, unseating Belle, who slid to the floor. "What the hell are you doing in a saloon?" he demanded, stalking over to her and placing his hands on his hips.

Cool purple eyes stared up at him, then slid to Pierre. "Lovely, just lovely," she said, swishing around MacGregor with all the disdain of her breeding to inspect the smokey depths of Lacy's. She pivoted to him with the air of a gunfighter. "You sulk about this . . . lair for two days, while I worry about your bloody life."

Tossing aside a long curling lock that had escaped her tortoise-shell combs, Regina sauntered toward MacGregor. Her gaze strolled down his hair, mussed by Belle's roving fingers, to his battered face. Her eyes swept slowly down his neck to the opened shirt, then upward to meet his.

MacGregor lowered his brows to glare back at her. Placing her hands on her waist, Regina returned the look. "This is a man's place," he stated roughly, when what he really wanted to do was sweep her into his arms and kiss her. "Wives aren't welcome."

Regina straightened her shoulders, and MacGregor's eyes immediately swept to her full bosom, thrusting at the dark gingham dress. A button had opened, and the swell of her breasts nestled in lace trim tantalized him. Fascinated by the small bit of soft flesh, he leaned closer only to be met by two dark amethyst eyes.

Belle's husky voice slid between them. "So this is your wife, MacGregor. No wonder you spent so much time this winter making that baby she's carrying. . . ." Her voice drifted off when Regina turned slowly to stare at her.

"It's true, then . . . Mr. MacGregor has been bragging about his prowess? Who says I carry his baby?"

Belle's thin penciled eyebrows lifted. "Honey, he's got baby maker written all over him. Says you spent the winter as his wife. . . ."

Regina turned slowly to MacGregor and reached to pluck a whorl of hair from his chest. She smiled as he grimaced and rubbed the painful spot. "Does he now? Did he tell you that he gave me the choice to marry him or freeze to death in a mountain cabin?"

She tapped his bearded jaw with her finger. "You've been

brawling and bragging and you smell like cheap perfume. I'll keep Jack, poor lad . . . until you can collect him like a proper gentleman. Pierre, you may come to the house for MacGregor's things."

She crooked a finger at Pierre who stood slowly, looking sheepish as a boy with his finger caught in the jam pot. "Come along, Pierre. The ride to the farm in the fresh air will clear your head. You shouldn't have let MacGregor lead you astray—evil, womanizing blackguard that he is."

She glanced at Belle and firmed her lips. "It seems that Mr. MacGregor boasts about this marriage and his ability to act as stud, then easily leaps into another bed. My child won't be reared by a man who tosses his vows away for"— she glanced at Belle's ample bosom—"a beautiful, desirable woman. You're invited to our first ladies' tea on Thursday. Beulah will give you directions."

With that Regina walked out into the sunlight, and MacGregor was left with the sight of her swaying hips and a raging hunger. Pierre glanced at MacGregor and shrugged, following her.

"She's mad as a wet hen," Belle stated flatly. "Can't say that I blame her. If my man had gone off for two days, drinking and brawling, and didn't let me know . . . especially with his brat in my belly, I'd kick him out, too."

Preening her curled locks, she glanced at the cracked mirror. "Beautiful and desirable, she said. Came from a real lady, too. . . . MacGregor, you'd better mend your ways to keep that one. Better start wooing her back right quick afore others get the idea that she needs a man around for that new baby."

MacGregor picked up his hat, jammed it on his head, and stalked out the door.

He caught Regina by the upper arm and turned her to him.

"MacGregor, go easy, my friend," Pierre warned softly, touching him on the shoulder. "Be careful. . . . She is *enceinte*—with child."

Her hand flew to her stomach to cover the babe, and MacGregor followed the action. "Violet, you're carrying my baby," he whispered unevenly, watching her eyes, twin purple pools, widen and fill her pale face. Then his hand covered hers, and the look of awe softened his dark face.

"Of course I am," she returned huskily. "You've made sure of that, haven't you? Proving yourself on any woman available?" She thrust his hand aside and glared up at him. "You wouldn't have come close to having me, MacGregor—"

"I haven't had a woman since you. . . . Can't remember any other women. . . . A man has rights," he stated darkly, his head throbbing as the sunlight burned his eyes.

Her eyebrows lifted. "Rights? With you in there"—she pointed at Lacy's weathered boards—"seducing a woman into your bed to prove your abilities? And the whole countryside laughing behind my back?"

MacGregor jerked his hat from his head and ran his unsteady fingers through his hair. "Damn it, Violet. I haven't wanted another woman. But if a wife doesn't provide for a man's needs, he's got a right to—"

The words caught in his throat as tears welled up in her purple eyes, spiking the black lashes. "Oh." The soft sound cut him like a knife.

PIERRE glanced uneasily at the tears rolling down Regina's cheeks. "My friend longs for you, *ma belle*. His heart aches for you every minute. . . . Because he is in the agony of love."

Regina threaded her fingers through Je t'aime's reins restlessly and wiped her cheeks with the sleeve of her dress. "Love . . . You don't need to lie for him, Pierre. I saw the way he was . . . was fondling that woman. Foraging like a hungry bear for honey between her breasts. The indecent way she was sitting on his lap—" She glanced at Pierre and blushed, looking away into a stand of shimmering aspen trees. "He's never said he loved me. Not once."

"My friend has love in his heart. But his life was hard and he finds words difficult."

Lilly ran to meet them, her long braid swaying down her back. She struggled with Jack's weight on her hip, then carefully placed him on his feet. Jack saw Regina and squealed in delight, toddling toward her.

Pierre tensed, entranced with the vision of Lilly's beauty sweeping toward them. "*Mon Dieu!* She is a goddess, a dream, a pearl—"

The Chinese girl ran to Regina and walked beside the horse, her expression concerned. "Miss Violet, you have found MacGregor? Does he live?"

Pierre swung down from his horse and walked beside the girl. The top of Lilly's head came just to his chest, her hair gleaming like black silk in the sun. Her fingers, clinging to Regina's dark skirt, were fragile and golden, delicate as flower petals. Beneath the long-sleeved, simple shift that covered her from head to toe, the girl's slight body caused his heart to beat faster. When she glanced up at him shyly, he fell into the soft, black almond eyes. "My name is Pierre. I'm a friend of MacGregor's and Violet's."

"Ah." Lilly nodded simply. "No MacGregor come back to house?" The sweet singsong tone drifted over him like gentle spring rain.

Regina sniffed, brushing away a tear. "I've banished him, Lilly. You should have seen him, looking like a pasha . . . burying his face in his harem girl's enormous bosom. Nuzzling her like a child looking for milk."

"MacGregor?" the girl asked softly, looking questioningly up at Pierre. "But, Miss Violet, his eyes say he loves you—"

"Posh! MacGregor is a plain-spoken man. He has a mouth—he can speak for himself." Regina sniffed and brushed away a tear, dismounting in a swirl of skirts and long hair. "He cuddles Jack, yet does he ever touch me without acting like a bull in heat? And when he's denied what he wants, to murder my father and Alfred Covington, he sulks like a spoiled child. At times his moods are no better than Jack's."

Tossing a rippling strand away from her breast, Regina looked at antelope grazing in the distance. The birdcalls and squirrels chattering filled the air as Lilly held her hand. Jack toddled closer, a grin on his jam-covered face. He lifted his arms to Regina, and she lifted him for a close hug. "Mama," Jack cooed, hugging her and studying a glistening black strand.

"My beautiful lad," Regina whispered huskily, nuzzling Jack's black hair. "I shall miss you." She turned to Pierre. "I want MacGregor's personal things returned to him today. I want no reminder—"

Jack's jam-covered lips smacked hers noisily. "Mama." MacGregor's image looked up at her with big black eyes and chubby cheeks, grinning widely to beguile her heart.

In the next instant Regina handed Jack to Pierre and raced for the shelter of the cabin, her skirts flying.

The next morning Pierre arrived in Primrose. He tossed MacGregor's clean folded clothes onto the cot at Beulah's. "Violet is good and mad," he said quietly. "She cried all night. She tore my heart. An *enceinte* woman must not be so upset. It is bad for the *bébé*. You must make amends and quickly, my friend."

MacGregor leaned back in the chair. "Amends? There's two mad men coming after her while she plans a tea party for the women. She wants my promise *not* to hunt them down. She's carrying my baby, damn it. A man wants to protect his own. . . . She thinks I'm bedding every woman in the territory."

Beulah placed his clothes on a shelf next to hers. "Women have pride, too, MacGregor. She's cut herself a place out there, settling the land. You'd best not do anything to make her want to lift that thick scalp of yours. Better try a little honey. Violet isn't the kind to let a man push her around. Wouldn't hurt you to court her. Let her know you think she's mighty fine."

The mountain man stared at her. "Court her? She's my wife, Beulah," he growled indignantly.

Beulah looked at Pierre. "You'd better start before that baby in her belly grows much more. Sweet talk won't choke you, MacGregor."

"Pretty hard to sweet-talk a woman with a baby in tow and another woman living in the cabin," he shot back.

"Two babies soon," Pierre corrected softly. "The beauti-

ful Lilly is mine, my friend. I will ask for her hand when
the time is right. I will assist you by entertaining my heart's
desire."

MacGregor muttered, " 'Heart's desire.' You throw words
like that around Violet, and she'd—"

"Melt," Beulah finished flatly. "Women melt."

THE marquess squatted by Covington's prone body
and smiled, clinically examining the slash across the younger man's throat. Blood seeped into Covington's linen shirt
and dripped down into the pine needles. The earl's blue eyes
looked helplessly up at Mortimer-Hawkes, blood welling up
from the cut across his throat as he tried to speak.

"A fitting end, Lord Covington," Mortimer-Hawkes
murmured, wiping his long thin blade on the dying man's
lace handkerchief. "You've bungled for the last time. Now
that I know Regina is settled near Primrose, I won't need
you anymore."

When Covington gurgled, his bloody hand reaching out
to Mortimer-Hawkes, the older man nudged it aside with
his boot. "Pagan isn't from my loins, you know. A distant,
wealthy cousin paid me to take her mother, Mariah. And
of course the heathen dowry. . . . Jewels, Lord Covington.
Worth more than you believe. . . . A giant ruby—the
Mariah—has a power that will make me a king. When
Pagan is mine and the jewels are safely in my hand, I shall
be all-powerful . . . a living god whose wishes are obeyed
without question. . . ."

The marquess settled down on an Oriental carpet and
lounged amid tasseled, satin pillows while Covington's life
seeped away on the pine needles. Lifting a flask to his
mouth, Mortimer-Hawkes watched the spreading stain with
slight interest. "She's carrying MacGregor's child now.
Nothing must harm Pagan until she has had the child. I'll
settle in Primrose, waiting for her to give birth. Pagan's
child will give me even more power."

A gurgle sounded from the dying man, and Mortimer-
Hawkes sipped more brandy. "Yes, you're right. My power
lies in the Mariah and the woman who owns it. Nothing can

happen to either one of them. MacGregor is another matter. She's bedded him, and I've found that there's a certain loyalty to the Mariah women. Their honor prevents them for taking another mate easily. MacGregor will have to die, of course. . . . Then I shall have the Mariah and Pagan to myself."

MACGREGOR lay on a blanket, his arms braced behind his head as he studied the stars. With the English camping to the north, he decided to spend the night near Regina. The summer night's breeze swayed the pine branches above him, the scent mingling with the fragrance of wild rose and Indian strawberry. The mountain daisies' sweet perfume reminded him of a more exciting fragrance . . . that of Regina's soft skin.

He wanted Regina for himself now. . . . MacGregor came off the blanket in a single lithe movement and bent to roll it tightly.

Cattails surrounding a small mountain lake swayed in the moonlight, reminding him of the way she'd danced with the shawl. The brilliant fabric had clung to her pale limbs, sliding down her thighs and beckoning him to the quivering softness of her hips. With her hair flowing around her, Regina had taken him into her heat, nipping at his throat with her teeth. Her nails had scored his back lightly, driving him deeper into the silky depths of her arms.

Her purple eyes stared up at him from the lake, the water rippling like the strands of her hair.

MacGregor brushed a daisy with his palm, the petals soft as Regina's skin. He'd felt the thrust of his unborn child when he kissed her, noted the changes in her swelling breasts.

Bending beneath a willow branch, MacGregor found himself standing in the meadow near Regina's cabin.

Regina lay on the blanket in the meadow, dozing lightly amid her bouquet of daisies. Tears dampened her cheeks, her long shuddering sighs of exhaustion sweeping along the evening breeze. She needed the time alone, away from Jack's needs and Lilly's worried eyes, and had carried a soft cotton blanket out into the field. When she dreamed, night black eyes gleaming with desire stared down at her. MacGregor's voice, deep and hoarse with need, whispered in her ear.

His mouth suckled each finger, playing with the simple ring before he inhaled unevenly and placed her hand over his heart.

Large, gentle hands swept down her legs, tugging the cotton shift higher, lifting it away from her body. Gently, gently, MacGregor's lips brushed her throat, finding the fast beating pulse beneath her skin.

Then the dream lay beside her, holding her close. His lips slid to tease her hardened nipple, his fingers slyly caressing the damp nest between her thighs.

Her fingers foraged through the whorls of hair covering his muscled chest, her fingertip tracing the flat male nipple until it hardened. MacGregor's cool hair slid across her stomach, his lips kissing the small mound of their unborn babe. With exquisite touch he lingered there, caressing the life they'd created.

A gentle hand swept the curve of her waist, raising to brush the tender swell of her breasts.

MacGregor. With infinite care he traced the swelling curve, then lowered his mouth to reverently taste the hardened tip. His face rested hot between her softness, tasting first one rounded globe, then the other with the tip of his tongue.

She ached from his sweet touch, his soft, passionate voice flowing into the night.

His fingers strolled down to her hip, testing the rounded curve, fitting it into his warm palm before moving down to her knee. Ever so slowly, he raised her knee, smoothing the sensitive back with his warm lips.

Beneath her fingers, the cords and muscles of his body rippled and moved to her caress. Floating in the exquisite dream, Regina's hands smoothed his ribs and moved downward to cup his hard buttocks in her hands. Lightly, stealthily she trailed her fingertips between his hard thighs, finding the soft treasure beneath.

"Violet, love me," MacGregor's rough, deep voice urged against her throat.

The dream's hand caressed her breast, molding it for the suckling of his hot mouth. The sweet pleasure rippled through her as he plied her tender breasts.

Then she was awake, and the dream became the reality of MacGregor, his strong arms quivering as he braced himself over her. The planes of his face caught the moonlight as she moved against him, desire sharpening his taut features. "Love me . . . take me, *tsiso*. End this ache I carry for you—" he urged unevenly.

With a cry Regina opened her arms to him and drew him against her. "Love me," he urged passionately, the beat of his heart heavy against her breasts.

In a moment he surged against her soft thighs, sheathing his desire within her tight, moist depths. His deep sigh brushed her flushed skin, his hand skimming down her flesh to seek her rounded hips.

Her senses ignited, exploding as the turgid tip of his manhood touched her deepest depths.

MacGregor stilled above her, the muscles of his back taut with the effort of reining his needs. When the sweet rippling pleasure slid away, she looked up at him. MacGregor smiled tenderly, his fingertip trembling as he swept a damp tendril from her cheek.

Resting lightly against her, he frowned, studying her mood as he arranged the wild disarray of raven hair away from her face. "I've missed you, *Tsiso*," he whispered huskily, winding a silken strand around his finger. Kissing it, he placed his hot face against her throat.

She shifted restlessly, still aching, and braced her foot on the back of his knee. The movement took his full length deeper, and Regina inhaled sharply, the heat beginning again within her. MacGregor shivered, his skin damp against hers as he lay so vulnerable in her arms. "There's never been another woman. You are my heart," he managed unevenly, smoothing her sensitive breasts. "For you to carry my child—" He eased away a bit and caressed the small mound of the baby tenderly.

His kiss enchanted her, brushing, tormenting, nibbling. "Sweetheart, you're still . . . needing," she murmured, caressing the back of his knees with her soles.

He lifted slightly, tracing the delicate lobe of her ear to find the ruby eardrop. "I can wait."

When she lifted her hips, he groaned suddenly and thrust deeper. "The baby—"

"Shh," she soothed, caressing his hot cheek and flowing against him.

MacGregor's taut body accepted her tentative thrusts, his face damp with perspiration. Then, with an unsteady sigh, he began to move. Caught in the wildfire, they climbed to the pinnacle of their passion to find release together.

Moments later Regina's cheek rested over MacGregor's unsteady heartbeat, her limbs nestled with his. The night sounds and the fragrance enveloped the lovers. Drowsy and sated, Regina slowly skimmed her palm over his damp chest and smoothed his flat, rippling belly. MacGregor shuddered, nuzzling her hair, and then kissed her forehead. He yawned and stretched, trapping her hand as it explored lower. "Unless you're ready to play again, sweetheart . . ."

"Mmm. Since the damage is done . . ." Daringly she touched him, amazed with the sudden velvety strength flowing beneath her fingertips.

"You do that to me, sweetheart," he murmured above her head. "Not another woman can stir me with a hot look or the slightest touch."

Easing her soft limbs over MacGregor's tall body, Regina allowed her fragrant hair to slide along his shoulders. "Did you mean that, MacGregor? Did you mean what you said about not having other women?" she whispered.

Running his fingertip across the hot peak of her breast, he nodded solemnly. "You've ruined me, ma'am. There's not another woman who could tempt me—"

Dark in the shadows, her eyes welled with tears. A single warm drop scalded his chest. MacGregor's hand swept the length of her back, caressing lower. Regina gasped as he boldly lifted her and slid, full bloom, into her depths. He tugged her closer, and they lay quietly joined, caressing each other, clinging to the tenderness before the heat.

Nipping his warm flesh with her teeth, Regina teased, "You lusty beast, ready to play when your baby tries to sleep."

MacGregor chuckled, and she listened, amazed at the rich, genuine sound rolling in his chest. "With ripe, sweet fruits such as this"—he gently squeezed her full breasts and lifted her to suckle the peak—"I could feast several times a night and wake ready for more."

Regina lifted up, staring at him with wide eyes. The moonlight skimmed down her body, providing him with a voluptuous view. "MacGregor, you've kissed the Blarney stone."

Adjusting her over him, he stroked her soft inner thigh. "Don't know what that is, but I'm dying for the taste of you again."

The birds began chirping just before the dawn, and Regina stretched against MacGregor's hard warmth. Her limbs tangled with his, his arms wrapping her tightly against the length of his body. In the night he'd covered them with another blanket.

Against her inner thigh his arousal began to shift, silky and hot, yet he slept on, holding her close. She whispered, smoothing back a wayward strand from his ear. "MacGregor . . ."

"Mmm? Come here," his warm hand swept down her thigh, urging her nearer.

"MacGregor, you should be ashamed," she teased and giggled. "You'll be damaged for life—"

He fondled her warm breast leisurely. "Stay with me. We'll hide out and make love all day."

Sitting up and easing herself away from him, Regina searched for her cotton nightshift. Damp with dew, the gown was wrinkled and needed smoothing. Taking care, she held the blanket to her chest with one hand and straightened the gown with the other.

MacGregor lay sprawled amid the blankets and his clothing, enjoying the sight of her shy blush. "We've seen each other before, sweetheart," he teased, toying with her hair and running a finger down the valley of her breasts. "Surely you wouldn't hide from me now."

"You improper, horny beast. You've dallied all night, keeping me from sleep, fondling and kissing and . . ." A length of hair hid her flushed face.

He chuckled. "And . . ." he prodded gently.

Regina's eyes widened, brilliant amethyst in the scant light. "Cover yourself, MacGregor. You should be ashamed—"

"Ah, but I'm not. I'm waiting for you to warm me again, to hear those soft little hungry cries. . . ." He slid his hand beneath the blanket to stroke her upper thigh.

Edging back, she eased into the gown. "You lusty black-guard. We can't lie out here all day. And you can't come back to the cabin. Neither one is proper."

MacGregor studied a pert nipple shining beneath the damp gown, tracing it with the tip of his finger. "I'm coming to court you today, Violet MacGregor. You are my heart's desire." He turned slightly; Violet gasped, viewing for the first time her teeth marks at his throat and shoulder, the long reddening scratches of her nails down his back.

"Oh, my . . ." She lightly touched the marks and found herself drowning in MacGregor's hot gaze.

He kissed her palm, then pressed it to his heart. "You'll do, Mrs. MacGregor. My heart's desire. . . ."

"Oh, my—" she managed before he kissed her sweetly, reverently, prolonging the moment when their lips would part.

SEVENTEEN

AT dawn Lilly hurried to answer the soft knock at the cabin door. MacGregor filled the doorway, holding a bucket of fresh milk in one hand and a bouquet of wild flowers in the other.

Lilly shielded her face with her small hand and giggled. "Miss Violet sleep late." She motioned him inside, signaling silence as she took the milk.

"Da!" Jack yelled from his willow crib, raising his arms to be held. "Da!"

Regina's sleepy voice slid across the shadows. "Hush, sweetheart. Mama's sleeping."

"Da!" Jack persisted as MacGregor picked him up. Taking his father's head in chubby hands, Jack surprised MacGregor with a moist kiss. "Da! Jack eat."

MacGregor cuddled his son, who kissed him again. Jack smoothed his father's freshly shaved jaw with his small hand and studied him with wide, unblinking eyes. Just then Regina murmured sleepily, "Jack, come sleep with Mama for a time."

Jack squirmed instantly, and MacGregor placed him on his feet. The baby toddled at a fast run toward the blanket shielding Regina's bed. When MacGregor eased the blanket aside, he found Jack curled against Regina's small body. Without opening her eyes she nestled him closer and kissed his head.

MacGregor's heart pounded unevenly as he crouched by the bed. Regina's long curls swept around her flushed face

279

and draped across her shoulders, spreading across the white pillowcase to snare MacGregor's hand. He toyed with a silky tendril as it coiled around his finger, enchanted by the beauty spread before him. The reminders of their love-making, the graze of his beard and the soft swell of her lips, enchanted him. Regina's scent, sweet and spicy and erotic, lingered in the shadowy nook.

She nuzzled Jack's glossy black hair sleepily. "Mama's little man . . . sweetheart." She sighed as Jack toyed with her ruby eardrop. Catching the chubby hand, she kissed his fingers. "Mama loves Jack."

The baby grinned up at his father and squirmed. The movement caught Regina's gauze shift, pinning it against her tightly to reveal the rounded shape of her stomach.

Snuggling closely with his son, his child nestling within her womb, Regina was the most beautiful sight of MacGregor's lifetime. He swallowed suddenly, fighting his fear and his joy.

He'd bound her against her will; she'd sworn not to "bear his bastards." Fear curled around him like icy fingers, tearing at his heart, for Regina's small hips cradled a life he had placed there.

The unborn infant stirred within his nest, and MacGregor's breath caught, his heart pounding. The babe repeated the tiny movement, and MacGregor placed his hand over it lightly, his fingers trembling. Suddenly MacGregor's eyes filled with tears, startling him.

Regina had snared his heart as surely as the dew clung to the meadow's lush grass.

Sensing his father's deep mood, Jack snared MacGregor's finger and held it tightly. "Da."

Regina's soft lips curled whimsically. "Mmm, yes. Quite," she whispered sleepily. "Your father is a beautiful man. He'll have two lovely children now."

Her expression slid into a drowsy sensuality as the tip of her tongue moistened her slightly swollen bottom lip. "MacGregor, beast that he is, is a beautifully formed, lovely mountain knight. You'll be just as handsome when you grow up. Yes . . ." She smiled dreamily. "Quite . . . breathtaking at times, my lad. Quite fascinating."

"Am I now?" MacGregor whispered huskily, scattering the wild flowers around her body. He grinned when her purple eyes opened suddenly.

"Egad, MacGregor," she whispered unevenly, brushing back a long curl from her cheek and throat. "What are you doing hovering about?"

"Da!" Jack announced firmly, grabbing a handful of bluebells and scooting off the bed. He ran toward Lilly, who was walking out the open door.

MacGregor bent to kiss Regina, inhaling the morning scents clinging to her. He nuzzled her throat, holding her to the bed easily as she tried to sit up. "You're a beautiful woman, Violet MacGregor . . . especially in the morning," he whispered against her flushed cheek.

She thrust at his chest, finding the hair covering it with her fingers and foraging slowly. "Gads, MacGregor. You can't just appear at dawn. . . ."

He kissed her breasts, then carefully lay his cheek over their child. A tiny limb thrust against him, and he kissed it reverently.

Regina inhaled suddenly, breathing quietly as MacGregor smoothed the small mound. He probed gently, then carefully lifted her gown away.

In the shadows of dawn his hard face softened with tender emotion. Eyes black and fierce in anger, now glistened with tears. His palm rested on the baby, caressing it. A teardrop clung to his lashes, soon slashed away by trembling fingers.

Lying quietly, Regina smoothed his cool, thick hair. Vulnerable now, MacGregor fought his emotions. The muscles of his throat contracted as he swallowed deeply. His heart raced beneath her palm as she waited for him to speak.

Another teardrop shimmered on his lashes, and she wiped it away with the tip of her finger.

Trembling with emotion, MacGregor caught her hand and lifted her palm to his lips. He kissed her wedding ring reverently as a shudder moved across his broad shoulders.

She stroked his jaw tenderly, waiting, sensing his need to talk.

Clearing his throat, he managed huskily, "You're so small. . . . Women die in childbirth. There's not a doctor within riding distance."

"I'll be fine, and so will your baby. Lilly is here, and she says Beulah is a skilled midwife."

MacGregor's large hand caressed their baby and trembled. "If anything happened to you—"

"Nothing will. You'll be there to see that it won't, just as you have always been," she soothed, caressing his tense shoulders.

"I'm wanting this baby with you," he stated roughly against her palm. "Will you love the baby, even though I . . . made you . . . ?"

She slowly traced the high cheekbones, the hard thrust of his jaw, and the vulnerable, sensitive shape of his mouth. "I love both your children, my handsome dark knight. The question is"—she tugged his head down to hers and brushed a kiss across his lips—"will you run at the sight of my swollen belly? Will you seek another cozy bed and play with another willing, hot lass?"

"Hot lass?" he repeated blankly, looking rumpled and disarming in his confusion. Then slowly his wicked grin met hers. "I've got my heart's desire, sweet and loving beside me. My hot lass nearly damaged my manhood in the meadow, her cries of pleasure echoed off the mountains . . . scared the bears into running away."

"MacGregor," she warned, grinning up at him. "You're a savage beast."

"A handsome, fascinating, breathtaking beast of a man?" he asked, bending to kiss her hungrily.

THE Marquess of Fordington counted his steps, marking the hunting lodge he would build overlooking Primrose. "While Regina is breeding, I intend to enjoy the wilds, Tall Tom. Plan a proper nursery, since the child will be living with us until it's old enough to travel safely. I'll want rooms with strong latches and good fires. See that the servants' quarters are on another wing from my rooms. I'll need privacy when Regina is under my roof . . . until she adapts to my reins again."

Tall Tom adjusted his eye patch and spat into a patch of Indian paintbrush. "She's carrying MacGregor's brat. The métis will fight to keep the bi—your daughter."

"He can be bought or killed. This métis is not a problem, he's my daughter's whim," Mortimer-Hawkes stated tightly. "He doesn't own her . . . I do."

Tall Tom stared at the pack mules laboring up the hill. When he was finished, MacGregor and the Englishwoman would be begging for a quick death. Mortimer-Hawkes was useful, setting his traps. But the mountain man intended to kill the woman known as Violet MacGregor. He drew his knife from its beaded sheath and slowly wiped it across his buckskin jacket.

MacGregor's woman had cost him a toe and an eye. He savored the promise of her agony, her screams before she died.

" . . . Nothing must happen to my daughter while she is breeding. I want her to have a healthy child. I'm sure we can all get along quite comfortably in these primitive wilds," Mortimer-Hawkes continued, tapping his quirt against his riding britches. He turned, striking Tall Tom across the chest. "You understand, don't you? Nothing must endanger my daughter now that she is breeding. I shall need MacGregor's baby, shall raise it as my own."

The mountain man stared at Mortimer-Hawkes with flat, blue eyes. The next instant his blade rested at the marquess's throat. The Englishman's eyes narrowed, his expression unchanged as Tall Tom breathed heavily.

"You won't kill me," Mortimer-Hawkes sneered evenly. "If I die, you'll never claim the gold deposited in St. Louis in my account. I've placed a bounty on the head of any man who harms me. The moment word of my death reaches my financier, he'll set the price . . . a very large price."

That night Tall Tom lay in Madam Joy's opulent bed. Mai, a young prostitute bearing Tom's bruises, caressed him while the madam talked. "These English I do not like.

MacGregor's woman struck me, and this I will not forget. To save face, I must kill her."

Tom swilled his whiskey and slapped the girl's slender back. "Get out of here."

The madam nodded her approval, and Mai slid from the room. Tom stood and stretched, careless that the madam studied his body. "Send Mai to Mortimer-Hawkes. She'll make a nice present from me," Tom said, pouring another whiskey.

"Agreed. The MacGregor woman is a thorn in my side. My girls whisper of her. I see disobedience in their eyes, placed there by this woman. Last week three girls disappeared, though one will not live long without the poppy. A Frenchman named Pierre sniffs around that ungrateful Lilly as though she were an unused virgin, when many men have had her. This Violet woman has torn the petals of my business and shall feel my wrath. A drink of my tea and the English miss looses her brat," the madam crooned, snapping her fingers.

"Mortimer-Hawkes will kill for her. She's more than his daughter somehow. Nothing can happen to the baby, either, according to him. He's crazy about the métis's woman. Sees her as a goddess. Almost like she was his mistress. I've known some men to take their daughters. Treat 'em like wives. One move on her and Mortimer-Hawkes will empty his pockets for revenge."

Madam Joy fondled the earrings she had purchased from Pokey Wales. "This miss has money, too." Her thin lips tightened. "She is worse than an Indian. A savage with purple eyes."

"I've promised myself her ears. Got the idea from an English lord friend of mine before Mortimer-Hawkes did him in. Still fancy taking MacGregor's woman's ears, though."

TINY, a black giant who had served with MacGregor in the war, loped into the valley after escaping carpetbaggers. He chopped and shaped the logs for the cabin's new rooms and silently salved the mental wounds he shared with MacGregor. Using the mules to drag in new timber, Pierre and MacGregor worked with Tiny from dawn until dusk. MacGregor continued his intent pursuit of Regina into the night, the courting flute's notes quivering above the night sounds.

Mose arrived at dawn one day, announcing that he intended to see Miss Violet in a proper house.

As Regina's body curved gently with his child, MacGregor investigated each new change with wonder. He presented her with starts of lavender and mint from a settler woman and sacks of dandelion flowers for yellow dye. Exclaiming with delight, Regina threw her arms around his neck and kissed him soundly. Then MacGregor caught her close, lingering until they were breathless and rosy. When she picked up a bucket of milk or bent to tend her vegetable garden, MacGregor swooped to lift her into his arms. Sitting on his lap, Regina received a lecture that turned into sweet, tantalizing kisses and a private walk into the forest.

When Regina soothed the mountain man's ruffled pride with a look or a kiss, Tiny roared with laughter and teased MacGregor about being tamed by a half-slip of a girl with purple eyes.

Sleeping near the cabin, MacGregor chafed at not sharing Regina's bed. The couple's daily play amused the other men, who shared a knowing wink when MacGregor stalked off to the stream, muttering about willful, mulish women.

Tension clung to the hot July days like a heavy, airless velvet cloak. Word of the marquess's hunting "palace" traveled quickly. A Spanish-Indian servant delivered Mortimer-Hawkes's letter to Regina.

My dearest beloved daughter—

How I have missed you. Soon we will be reunited. I have decided to spend a time enjoying the American wilds. You are welcome to return to my home at any time. Unfortunately, your fiancé, Lord Covington, has met his demise. We shall have to carry on without him. As is the custom, you are of course expected to serve as mistress of the Fordington family estate. Under my guidance we shall continue as before, though I shall not expect you to marry after the loss of our dear earl. I await your return to my loving arms.

—Nigel

The nightmares began immediately. Regina's cries filled with terror. Then MacGregor's dark, fierce scowl would appear in the night, his strong arms shielding her from the past as he carried her out into the clean, dewy meadow.

Wrapped in her shawl, Regina nestled against his sprawled, naked body and dreamed of their daughter.

Fearing for Regina, MacGregor demanded that she recognize and accept him as her husband. He snarled and coaxed and kissed her until she clung to him. Yet she refused to unleash his gunhand, to send him out as her protector.

Regina denied his possessive demands aloud, then hid her tears at night.

She ached for MacGregor, yet could not drive the fear of being possessed from her. The arrival of her father threw the past at her every day. She awoke at dawn with tear-swollen lids and Jennifer's whisper echoing in her ears. . . . *"Remember the legends. The Mariah Stone has the power. . . . the man who possesses. . . . "*

Once possessed by the marquess, Regina now fought MacGregor's demands with a strength born out of fear.

Yet she could not deny his sweet kisses, nor his claim to her babe.

In the hot July sun Pierre lifted the dipper of water over his head, dribbling the water down his sweaty body. Lilly traced the sheen covering his darkly tanned chest and, drawn to the water beads, reached to trace a tiny rivulet. When Pierre trapped her finger, bringing it to his lips, the girl blushed and lowered her eyes. *"Ma belle,"* Pierre whispered huskily. "Will you stay with me tomorrow when Two Hearts takes Violet to Primrose?"

Lilly looked away at a deer drinking from the stream. "Miss Violet says one must be a proper lady, even in the American wilds. Is this proper?"

Lifting her to his eye level, Pierre kissed the tip of her

nose. "*Chère*. There is no time for us. How can I ask you to be my wife when we have no privacy?"

Lilly's dark eyes widened. "Ah!" she exclaimed softly, placing her small hands on his bare shoulders. "You would ask me this after Madame Joy's use of me?" Her expression clouded. "I cannot. I am not pure."

He lowered her carefully to her feet. "You are my beautiful, sweet Lilly. . . . Stay with me tomorrow, *mais oui*?"

MACGREGOR lifted Regina from her sidesaddle carefully. Holding her against his chest, he frowned. "How do you feel? Riding a horse for miles . . ."

"Divine." She glanced at the busy, dusty street filled with curious onlookers. "MacGregor, put me down. Jack's entering the dry goods store. . . ."

"Damn." Carrying her easily, MacGregor stepped into the store. After gently placing her on her feet, he scanned the barrels and displays for Jack.

"Injun squawbaby," Tall Tom muttered in the shadows. Then Jack began to cry loudly. "Hey, storekeep. What are you doing letting redskins run around in here?"

Agile despite her slightly rounded stomach, Regina moved quickly through the narrow passages of barrels. MacGregor's bulk slowed him, and he was left to follow in the wake of her flying skirts. A loud whack preceded Jack's terrified screams.

Regina ran into the back room to see Jack dangling from Tall Tom's outstretched hand. Balanced on the back two legs of his chair, Tom spread his free hand on the table next to a Bowie knife. He shook Jack like a cat playing with a mouse. "I'll fix this brat good. So he can't spawn any more red blood," he drawled.

"I daresay you won't," Regina hissed near him. The Bowie blade flashed and his little finger lay apart from his hand. Regina's furious eyes slashed at him as she cuddled Jack against her. Then MacGregor's hand wrapped around Tom's throat to lift him to his feet. Slamming a series of hard blows to Tom's face and stomach, MacGregor forced Tom against the wall.

Regina quickly carried Jack out into the fresh air. "Da!" the baby cried, tears streaming down his chubby cheeks as he clung to her.

Soothing Jack while she trembled with rage, Regina looked up into the marquess of Fordington's cool amethyst eyes. "The gracious Lady Regina Mortimer-Hawkes comforting an Indian child," he murmured. "How droll."

The marquess's gaze wandered down her loose gingham blouse to the swell of the baby. "Dressing as a peasant now, my lady?"

"Father!" She hugged Jack closer, protectively.

Dressed in tailored hunting clothes, Mortimer-Hawkes tapped his riding quirt rhythmically against his polished Hessian boots. He smoothed Jack's glossy hair with his glove and smiled down benignly at Regina. "I have come to collect you. . . . When we are in private and settled in our own estate, you may call me Nigel, my dear."

In the brilliant sunlight her father's eyes were a shade of pale amethyst, set in puffy lids. His sallow skin hung loosely on the bones of his still handsome face. She had forgotten his strong, perfumed scent and the way her body tensed near him. "I will not be returning to England," Regina stated baldly.

The marquess's smile deepened. "We shall see," he murmured soothingly. He motioned for a heavily loaded pack train to proceed without him. Ten men, ranging from western toughs to burley English servants, waited impatiently on horseback. The marquess dismissed them with a casual wave of his hand. "What is this I hear about your breeding?"

MacGregor stepped into the sunlight, his hand resting casually on his gun butt. The same height as the sleek Englishman, MacGregor's heavier, powerful body made him appear taller. Regina caught his fresh soapy masculine scent and inhaled deeply.

Both strong men, they faced and gauged each other like knights preparing to battle. They towered over her, striking her with their differences.

Respected on the frontier, MacGregor's reputation had

not been built on greed or fear, as had the marquess's.

Cruelty marred her father's features. Hatred flickered for a moment before he shielded it. MacGregor's hand soothed Jack, then swept lightly down to rest at the small of her back. That instant she realized how often and how gently MacGregor's dark, calloused hands touched her. The marquess's slender fingers had left a trail of pain.

MacGregor feared for his child and for her, while her father enjoyed tormenting.

She leaned slightly against MacGregor, needing his strength and Mortimer-Hawkes watched the play, his mouth tightening.

Mortimer-Hawkes's gaze strolled down MacGregor's muscular body, lingering on the gun lashed to his thigh. "Ah, yes. This would be Tall Tom's nemesis, the indomitable Mr. MacGregor. Your current *paramour*."

Regina's eyes flashed at up at him angrily. "Lovely term, *paramour*. My lover is a better term, Father," she thrust at him coolly, then continued. "MacGregor, this is my father, the Marquess of Fordington, Lord Nigel Mortimer-Hawkes. His title does not require a bow." She stepped away from MacGregor slightly, lifting her chin and facing the marquess. "He wants me to return to England with him. I will not."

Amethyst eyes met and clashed as Regina patted Jack's back. The baby sniffed; wet with tears, his face pressed against her throat. "Father, this is MacGregor and his son, Jack. MacGregor is the father of my child."

The marquess smiled coldly. "How remarkable. The man who sired my daughter's babe also spawned a child by an Indian squaw. How many more children share the same sire, MacGregor?"

Regina stepped quickly between the two tall men. "That's enough, Father—"

"A fine, cultured specimen of noble blood, I'm sure," Mortimer-Hawkes prodded, angered by Regina's fierce protection of the man.

Mortimer-Hawkes's slashing eyes slid from MacGregor's ear to Regina's ruby eardrop. The Englishman quickly shielded his fury, just as Tall Tom slumped against the door frame. Blood seeped through the cloth wrapped around his hand, and he thrust out the other palm, opening it to reveal his severed little finger. "The bitch got my finger this time," he mumbled through swollen, bloody lips.

MacGregor's hand tightened on his gun butt. Regina's slender fingers touched his, and a dark knowing look passed between them. The marquess's narrowed eyes lingered on the thin gold band when Regina's hand slid away. He smiled tightly. "I shall take pleasure in correcting Tall Tom. He can be so gauche. . . . You're invited to tea at any time, Regina. My lodge will be quite comfortable should you want to visit without your entourage of half-breeds. I'm sure he has little use of you while you are breeding anyway. Though with your wealth, I can understand his motives."

Against her back MacGregor tensed, moving slightly toward the marquess. Regina quickly passed Jack to him. "There now," she soothed the baby while staring up at MacGregor's taut expression. "We'll be just fine, my love."

Nestled safely in his father's strong arms, Jack murmured, "Da. Mama." He shuddered with a last heavy sigh and stared at her with MacGregor's black eyes and sooty lashes. Her baby moved then, a tiny limb seeking more room and reminding her that MacGregor would love his children deeply.

Love. MacGregor loved her with his eyes and body, though he didn't say the words. MacGregor did not possess . . . he loved and protected.

Startled and filled with emotion, she placed her hand lightly on MacGregor's tense shoulder.

Slowly MacGregor's black eyes lowered to hers. "My love," she repeated in a whisper and kissed Jack's cheek.

The marquess slapped his thigh suddenly with the riding quirt. Then, taking his time, he bent to kiss Regina's cheek. "My dear, you are exquisite. You've positively bloomed," he whispered in a sensual drawl. "Just as exotic and beautiful as your dear, departed mother. My sweet Mariah. We shall have a marvelous welcome home party when you and the baby return to my estate."

When he straightened and stepped back, the marquess's cold eyes met MacGregor's flat black ones over Regina's head.

THAT evening MacGregor's open hand slammed against the log wall of the new room. "Violet, a man takes care of his family. He doesn't let anyone, not even her father, insult his wife."

"MacGregor," she warned tightly, pressing her hand against her stomach. "There will be no fighting."

He lowered his face to hers. "I'm asking you proper to share my bed. I'm asking you to bend that stiff neck and let me pay for our needs." He tossed his saddlebags on to the rough bench between them. "There's coin and nuggets in there. You do with it as you will. You've got a fine head for figures and business, but when it comes to common sense you're a far step below reasonable," he stated in a low roar, placing his hands on either side of her head.

Hoarse with emotion, his voice deepened. "You carry my baby, Violet MacGregor. He won't be treated like a bastard because you deny our marriage vows."

Regina looked up at him and arched a fine eyebrow. MacGregor stormed and ranted and yet she did not fear him as she had her father. She grinned impishly up at him, startling him. "Are you quite finished tossing out your orders, m'lord? . . . 'He,' you say. What if the babe is a girl?"

"A girl . . . ?" He frowned, startled at the thought and raking his fingers through his hair. "I reckon that would be even better. One with your curls and eyes, sweet to cuddle. . . ."

Then in a changing mood, MacGregor tilted his head arrogantly. "You smile and I forget my own name, but not this time. A girl needs the protection of a father's name even more than a boy out here. A lover, you called me. You wear my ring, yet deny my rights before the entire countryside. A métis, they call me . . . a breed. Has the English lady a poor pet dog following at her skirts? Or a man who protects her and shares her bed every night?"

His fingers tightened on her jaw, his frown savage. "Tell me, Lady Mortimer-Hawkes MacGregor . . . does the uncouth breed amuse you?"

"You know I don't think that—"

Moving closer, MacGregor ran his fingers around her smooth jaw. They trembled as they moved slowly across her lips. "Think about loving our baby and Jack and me. I want to know one thing. . . . Do you want to go with your father?" he asked unevenly.

"I will not return with him," she answered adamantly.

MacGregor studied her for a moment, then bent to brush his lips across hers. "Then stay with me, *Tsiso*. . . . Call me 'husband.' "

The next breath she stood alone in the moonlight.

EIGHTEEN

THE Marquess of Fordington braced his boot on a log and drank the last of his finest brandy. An antelope herd moved across a meadow, the white markings eerie in the moonlight. The marquess followed their progress into lush pines, his thoughts on MacGregor. "My mortal enemy. Only one of us may possess the Mariah woman," he said quietly, tossing the silver flask aside and dabbing his lips with a linen handkerchief. "I will own Pagan and your child in the end, Mr. Two Hearts MacGregor."

The baby growing in Pagan's womb carried MacGregor's Indian blood. She'd spread her thighs and allowed Mac-Gregor to crawl between them. . . . She wore the savage's cheap ring, protecting MacGregor with her body in Primrose. Mortimer-Hawkes's handsome mouth thinned. "Typical of the frontier breed. Illiterate, crude buffoon. Pagan has a history of being difficult . . . toying with sheep and mingling with the peasants. She is simply playing games. She couldn't possibly love this MacGregor."

He closed his eyes, hating the sight of Regina's slender fingers touching MacGregor's powerful shoulder. "The man is a savage, barely tethered by manners. Spawned by ancestors barely removed from animals, the bastard's lineage hardly compares with English nobility."

In Primrose he'd seen a passing woman stare at MacGregor with open hunger. The younger man's rugged, savage appearance would captivate any woman, Mortimer-Hawkes decided darkly. Once, he had been just as strong, just as devastating to female hearts, and he'd taken his pick of warm, pleasing beds.

MacGregor walked with an arrogant saunter, like a mountain cat prowling his domain. Mortimer-Hawkes recognized the way MacGregor's hand rested easily on his gun, the tense coil of his lean brown fingers. The younger man's deep-set eyes had ignited when Mortimer-Hawkes kissed Regina, then changed to the flat black eyes of a man who had killed and seen hell. He had the dangerous look of a wolf, protecting his mate to the death. Yet Regina tethered him easily with the light touch of her small hand.

Mortimer-Hawkes laughed aloud. "My fine MacGregor, you are the possessed. I shall have the Mariah soon enough. . . . Rather than kill you quickly, I choose to show Regina how you cower from your superior. A beating should do nicely. . . . Yes, a quick death would not show your weakness. . . ."

"*MARIAH . . . Mariah . . .*" Jennifer's eerie wail slid through the quiet cabin. Regina turned on her bed, stretching out a hand for MacGregor's solid body, and found nothing.

"*You are Mariah. Blood of my blood,*" her mother whispered. "*I am Mariah . . . you are Mariah. The stone's power is nothing without the woman who owns it. Nigel knows the secret of Mariah. He knows that he must have the woman and the stone to keep his wealth and great power. He must possess me . . . he must own you, my beloved daughter.*"

"*Shh,*" Jennifer crooned from the past, stroking Mariah's long black hair. "*The marquess will not harm your daughter, Mariah. I will see to it.*"

"*He will kill to keep his power. . . .*"

Mariah's deep sobs became the heavy beat of Regina's heart. In the next instant she sat up, her heart pounding violently. Damp tendrils clung to her cheek, her gown wet with fever. "*I am Mariah,*" she whispered into the shadows. "*I am Mariah. My father will kill MacGregor!*"

THREE days later Regina leaned against the cool, shaded cabin wall. In the hot afternoon sun the men strained to fit another log neatly into place. The two bedrooms and a kitchen grew slowly around new wooden floors. Taking pride in his labors, MacGregor patted Tiny on the back. MacGregor's white teeth slashed across his darkly tanned face as he grinned. Her ruby eardrop caught the July sun, sending out a brilliant shaft of light.

She touched the gold ring on her finger. She'd wounded his pride in Primrose. Now each time she approached him, MacGregor stared coolly down at her with rigid, masculine disdain.

His baby kicked within her, and she rubbed the movements with her palm. *If MacGregor stayed, the marquess would kill him.*

Jack ran to his father, lifting his arms. MacGregor chuckled and tossed Jack lightly, settling him on his bare shoulders as he talked to the other men. He pointed to a beaver dam, then to a lush meadow where they planned the new garden.

Lavender plant starts grew near the new rail fence, the large purple heads drooping slightly in the hot sun. Garlic and winter onions shared the fence, protected from Rosebud and the goat. The sheep grazed in a high meadow tended by Laddie. Regina inhaled and savored the scent of new lumber, enjoying the sweep of sunflowers rising over a rounded hill.

She twisted the ring and watched Lilly cook the evening meal over an outside fire. This was her dream, a new land and a new life. In three months time she'd give birth to MacGregor's child. Wrapped in her love and MacGregor's, the new baby and Jack would never know the torment of their parents' lives.

She frowned, suddenly remembering her father, sweeping out of England to hover nearby. Without warning the marquess could strike and shatter her dreams.

The baby shifted restlessly in its warm nest, and Regina hand smoothed her side. MacGregor knew the dangers of a bastard child well. A hard man, he was also gentle and loving. Fighting for his son, MacGregor had taken her as his wife. She twisted the ring again. MacGregor deserved better than her nightmares and her past.

His gunbelt hung from a peg near her head, the cartridges gleaming in the sun. *He could not die because of her.*

The Mariah Stone and other jewels filled a leather bag, weighing heavily in her apron pocket. MacGregor would soon know her frightening past. *And then he must leave. . . .*

Across the distance of sunlit grass, MacGregor stared at her. A muscle moved slightly in his jaw, his lips hardening as the stare held and heated. Then he turned to talk to Pierre, sharing a dipper of water.

Beside her, Mose spat a stream of tobacco into a tin. "He's damn mad, that MacGregor Two Hearts is. Not the rip-roaring fighting kind. But the kind that stays and eats at a man's guts. Ain't said a word about it, neither."

"We've had a slight disagreement, Mose," Regina murmured, smoothing the loose peasant blouse over their babe.

"Huh! MacGregor's hurting bad," the mountain man grumbled, walking past her toward the men. "I'd say it wouldn't take much to patch him up, Miss Violet. Do it quick. I want to keep my good ear."

MacGregor's eyes slashed at her, then he turned away, tilting his head at something Lilly was saying.

Rubbing Venus's sleek back, Regina traced MacGregor's tall body. She longed to press her lips against his bare chest, to rest in his arms. . . .

Moments later Regina walked toward the men carrying a light cotton blanket wrapped around buttered bread and jam. MacGregor's deep-set eyes traced her until she stood near him. "MacGregor, would you mind strolling with me into the woods?"

A muscle moved in his jaw, and his head lifted arrogantly. "A stroll?" The hard edge to his deep voice proved she wouldn't have an easy time salving his wounds.

Regina moistened her lips and ran a fingertip across the scars on his chest. "I thought we could dine out tonight."

"*Mon Dieu!*" Pierre exclaimed with a wide grin. "I think the lady has come to collect you, MacGregor Two Hearts."

But MacGregor was following Regina's small figure across the meadow and into the woods.

In a clearing Regina spread the blanket and sat in a swirl of skirts. MacGregor crossed his arms across his chest, enchanted with the feminine ways she prepared to hold court. Sunlight filtering down through the aspens tangled in her coronet of braids. Light and shadows played around her, a slender pale leg escaped the folds of her lacy petticoat and long skirt. Her loose blouse had slipped off one shoulder, the satiny curve fascinating him as she placed a leather bag next to the food. Slipping her moccasins off, she wiggled her toes and plucked a wood violet to tuck in her hair.

"It's so hot and still. I made bread early this morning in that lovely oven Tiny built outside, and Rosebud's butter is delicious." Regina arched, running her hands across the back of her neck, the movement drying MacGregor's throat. Unable to look away, he leaned against a birch tree and studied the flush rising up her cheeks. She glanced up at him uneasily. "Surely you can rest in the heat. . . ."

MacGregor sauntered to the blanket, looking down at her. "What do you want, Violet?"

"You could sit, my . . . dear," she whispered, placing her hand on his hard calf. MacGregor tensed, muscles ridging beneath the skin on his chest. He followed the slender length of her arm to the low blouse, tracing the hollow between her breasts. "Please?" she asked quietly.

His eyes narrowed. "You want something. What is it?"

"A bargain, nothing more. But in its own time," she whispered huskily, fearing that he would turn away.

"A bargain," he repeated grimly, crouching beside her. He touched the earring in her lobe. "On whose terms, wife?"

"MacGregor . . ."

He untied her braids, loosening them. Her hair fell around her, rippling to the blanket. MacGregor eased a tress away from her lush breasts, his expression hard. "You deny my rights as a husband, yet our baby grows in you." His hand smoothed across the baby, finding a small kicking limb. Gently MacGregor stroked the curve of her abdomen. "What bargain, dear wife?"

She stroked the planes of his face, caressing his taut jaw. "MacGregor, you . . . not I . . . are in grave danger. Jack could be hurt. . . ."

"Say it," he commanded, a dark flush of anger rising over his dark cheeks.

"I have what I sought," she whispered, sliding her arms around his neck. "More."

MacGregor bore her light kiss without moving. "Violet, you're pushing. . . ." he warned unsteadily. When she rose to her knees, tumbling him down on the blanket, he caught her gently. "The baby. . . ."

"The baby misses you, MacGregor Two Hearts," she whispered against his lips, her fingers smoothing his hair.

"Does he?" He breathed lightly, caressing the rounded curve of her hips and noting the new softness in her body. "Do you?"

She kissed his shoulder, and the sweet caress reminded him of his labors. Placing her firmly aside, MacGregor rose to strip his clothing away.

She followed him to the stream, admiring the broad sway of his shoulders tapering down to the narrow, muscular hips and the long length of his legs. Leaning against a birch tree, she enjoyed the sight of MacGregor bathing in the shallow water. He sluiced water over his head, rivulets of water tumbling down his darkly tanned skin to the pale, lean buttocks and strong legs. Sunlight skipped along the water, catching gold lights on the rippling water and on the man.

Slipping free of her blouse and petticoat, Regina waded into the stream dressed in her lacy camisole and pantalettes. MacGregor stood still as she cupped water in her hands, washing his back and shoulders. He trembled as her hands caressed his hips, standing still as her fingers slid to his navel and circled it lightly. She kissed his shoulder as her hands slid slowly lower, smoothing the hard aroused length of his manhood.

MacGregor inhaled sharply as Regina's hot cheek pressed against his spine, then kissed each scar with her parted mouth. In a swift movement he quickly turned and swept her up into his arms. "Violet . . ."

"My dear, beloved MacGregor," she answered softly, wrapping her arms around him as he carried her back to the glade.

Sitting with her in his arms, MacGregor leaned against a tree. His eyes closed when she kissed his throat, his ear, nibbling on the eardrop.

A man's lewd laugh slid across the clearing, and MacGregor's arms tightened before he eased her aside. In the next instant MacGregor stepped into his trousers and stood in front of Regina. She gripped discarded skirts to her chin as the marquess sauntered toward them.

"How droll," he mused, taking in Regina's wildly tumbled hair and the flush rising in her cheeks. His eyes slid down MacGregor's tensed body to his unbuttoned trousers. He raised an ebony cane near MacGregor's throat and touched the latch. A thin blade slid free, bringing a drop of blood. "Without your gun, I see. How perfect. Tall Tom tells me you are a deadly gunfighter and brawler. He's aching for revenge."

Tall Tom moved from the shadows of the trees silently, carrying Venus's body. Her front paw, cut and bleeding, clung to her leg by a slender tendon. Tom dropped the dog to the grass; Venus whined and struggled to stand. The woodsman's boot pushed her down and held her easily while he drew his gun, pointing it at MacGregor.

"Venus will lose the paw if not her life," Mortimer-Hawkes mused quietly. "Dreadful accident. Found her caught in MacGregor's traps. If she weren't your pet, my dear Regina, I would have been kind, putting a bullet through her head to end the agony. But because of my love for you, I've returned her to your keeping. Of course, if this interview goes awry, I can easily put her out of her pain. Your fine woodsman may meet his demise as well."

His eyes ran coldly down her bare shoulder. "Amusing . . . a woodland tryst. A beautiful nymph and a bold satyr poised on the brink of lovemaking. How delightful."

With a soft cry Regina started toward her dog but was stayed by MacGregor's arm. The muscles across his shoulder tightened, the cords standing out in relief. "Let her go," he said quietly. "You can have me."

Mortimer-Hawkes lifted the blade to Regina's dark hair and flicked the violet away. "Sorry, my good man. She would bring your Nubian friend and the rest of the ruffians. . . . Regina needs a reminder of who and what she is," he said, turning back to MacGregor. "Later, when we are finished, she will be free to go."

The knife slid across the younger man's shoulder, drawing blood. "She's breeding now," Mortimer-Hawkes murmured, studying Regina's small face framed by a sweeping river of raven hair. "Quite lovely, too. Has that hot, pagan look of her mother, blended with something stronger, wilder . . . almost tropical in its heat. Is it hate, my dear Regina? Or is it love?" he asked, taunting her.

"What do you want?" MacGregor asked too softly.

Fearing her father's answer, Regina slid her hand around MacGregor's lean side to press him against her.

Mortimer-Hawkes caught the movement, his expression brilliant with fury. "Regina needs a lesson. I've chosen you as an example."

He quickly shielded his anger, dusting a leaf from his hunting jacket. "Regina is quite wealthy, you know. Of course, her fortune was in my keeping, until she became a thief. . . . I trust you've placed the Mariah and the other jewels in a safe place, my dear."

His gaze slid down her body, hidden by MacGregor's powerful one. The point of his blade caught on the fragile lace brushing her bare arm. "Get dressed, Regina. Tall Tom is drooling at the mouth. We wouldn't want to expose those lovely charms to his friends who will be joining us shortly."

"Get dressed, Violet," MacGregor ordered quietly. Venus whined pitifully, and Regina's tears slid down his arm.

Mortimer-Hawkes followed the silvery trail with the tip of his knife, drawing a white line on MacGregor's dark skin.

"Father, please . . ." Regina pleaded as she quickly dressed.

"Because I love you deeply, Regina . . . and because I'm concerned for your future and the baby you carry, I've decided that MacGregor should pay the price for your dis-obedience. To kill him would be too easy. You would never see his weakness that way. Better for you to realize that he is our inferior, than a quick death. Yes, death would be far too simple. In time you'll realize that you must return with me. You'll see how ill-suited you are to this . . . breed."

"Father . . ." Dressed now, Regina stepped in front of MacGregor, only to have him place her firmly aside.

Mortimer-Hawkes's dark amethyst eyes met Regina's for a long moment before they wandered down her thrusting breasts to the swell of her baby. He breathed heavily, nostrils flaring, as he reached out to place his palm over the taut mound. "Exciting. Exquisite. A woman with child filled with passion . . ."

In that instant MacGregor was on him. Tall Tom's pistol butt crashed down on MacGregor's head heavily just as five rough men surged out of the brush. Two men caught the woodsman as he slumped, hanging in their grip. They looked at Regina, then at Mortimer-Hawkes, waiting his instructions.

Mortimer-Hawkes staggered back, wiping his hand across his torn mouth and staring at his bloody fingers. "Hold the bastard," he ordered. "Tom, please give MacGregor a lesson in manners."

Regina flung herself on her father, and he laughed in delight, quickly capturing her wrists. "You shall enjoy this, Pagan. It should suit your savage blood. . . . Easy now . . . you are breeding. We don't want the child harmed, do we?"

Tom's savage blows slammed into MacGregor as he fought the men holding his arms. His elbow hit one man in the ribs, breaking them just as he hit Tom in the stomach. The one-eyed giant fell to his knees, clutching his belly. The three other men moved in quickly, and Regina jerked away from Mortimer-Hawkes's grasp to fling herself on one man, scratching his face.

The marquess swept her back, pressing his arm across her chest until she struggled for breath. "There now, my savage Pagan," he crooned softly in her ear. "All in good time, my love."

Filled with rage, MacGregor faced him, blood running from the cut on his head. "Let her go," he ordered, panting for breath. "Let her go, or I'll kill you."

Mortimer-Hawkes lifted a small knife to Regina's taut throat. Then he laughed as a man hit MacGregor from the back, bringing him to his knees. "Tie him to a tree," Mortimer-Hawkes ordered softly, placing his hand over Regina's mouth as she squirmed against him. "Tom, take care of this rubbish. . . ."

When they were done, MacGregor hung unconscious from the ropes lashed to a birch tree. Mortimer-Hawkes released Regina, who ran to MacGregor. Straightening his jacket, the marquess sauntered to the unconscious MacGregor and pulled his head up by his hair. "A job well done," he murmured, securing the ruby earring between his fingers and ripping it free. He carefully wiped the jewel clean and tucked it in his breast pocket. "Your dear mother's jewelry in a savage's ear. Really, Pagan. The thought is disgusting. Perhaps you should give the jewels to me for safekeeping until you're ready to return to my care."

Regina shook, clinging to MacGregor's slumped body. Her eyes shimmered with tears and anger. "You will never have Mariah, Father," she spat the words at him.

"My dear, you are a lusty woman, but I am certain that by the time you are finished breeding, you will applaud my actions. *Noblesse oblige*, you know. Don't be surprised if MacGregor deserts you and his child after this. I shall await your return. You understand that Jack would not live long under your care—should you stay apart from me. You will have the best of care at childbirth. *Adieu*."

MacGregor struggled to crawl out of the murky, pain-filled haze, Regina's scents and soft kisses surrounding him like spring rain. "I didn't want to leave you to go for help," she whispered as a man's groan sounded far away. Pain enveloped him and he discovered that the sound was his own. Regina's unsteady whispers soothed the throbbing in his skull. "Oh, my darling, my love, my dear precious heart. . . ."

He lifted a swollen lid to have it closed again by a cold cloth. "My dear MacGregor, my own sweet loving knight. . . ." Regina cried, adjusting his head on her lap.

Kissing his bruises, she dabbed and inspected the cut placed there by Tom's gun butt. MacGregor lay in the soft tangle of arms and silky hair, his child kicking against his cheek. Regina shifted slightly, her tears dropping steadily on his cheek. "Oh, MacGregor . . . MacGregor . . . what will we do?"

He breathed cautiously, noting that his ribs were still intact. "We'll be just fine," he managed over swollen lips.

"Oh! Oh!" Carefully cradling his jaw with her palms, Regina eagerly kissed his face. "I should have told you sooner. . . . My father will stop at nothing."

A silky tendril slid along his cheek, and MacGregor closed his eyes, inhaling the scent. "Told me what?" he whispered, aware that his cheek rested on Regina's warm, soft breast.

Pale in the mist of the shadows and her hair, Regina's face bent over him. Her dark purple eyes shimmered with tears. "About the jewels, about everything. . . . You've got to go, MacGregor. I want you safe. . . ."

"And what of you and my child?" he asked carefully, frightened for her.

"He won't hurt me or the baby. He needs me. Jennifer, my nurse, told me about the legend. The Mariah Stone is the heart of an ancient idol and is the bridal dowry. The women in my family are symbols of power and united with the Mariah Stone. They will bring power and wealth to the man who possesses them both. . . . He must possess me. . . ."

"Violet . . . sweetheart . . ." MacGregor eased slowly upright, settling her a small distance away. Fearing that Regina's childbirth might come soon because of her wild emotions, MacGregor stroked her hair. "Easy now, sweetheart. . . . Those are only dreams."

"My father would kill for me and the stone," she stated bitterly. "He loved my mother, in his way. Yet he killed her, drained her of life by his cruelties. I won't have that happen to you. . . ."

She threw her arms around him, clinging to him tightly. "Oh, your poor head . . . your poor, precious ear . . . it's slit in two." In the next instant she sat back on her heels and tenderly wrapped his head in her damp camisole.

"You are my lover," she stated fiercely, tucking in a bit of lace and giving MacGregor a swift, possessive kiss on his lips. "The father of my baby and my own dear, loving husband. Father had no right hurting you, trying to bring me to heel. I am furious with him. I shall never forgive him. . . . In another moment I would have given him the jewels to leave. . . ."

While MacGregor dealt with pain and his new status— "my husband," she had said—Regina ripped open a leather bag. "A portion of my mother's dowry was here all the time. He could have had it easily."

Jewels tumbled from the bag, diamonds, emeralds, and a huge bloodred ruby attached to a heavy gold chain. Holding his hand tightly, Regina rummaged through the jewels to find a man's heavy gold ring, engraved with an elaborate 'M'. "M for Mariah," she said. "My father never knew the ring existed. Jennifer said it's for the keeper of the Mariah. . . . I don't want Nigel killed, MacGregor. He's the grandfather of our baby."

Sliding the ring on MacGregor's lean finger, Regina expression darkened. "There, my love. It suits you well. Wear it with my love as I wear your wedding ring."

MacGregor studied the intricate, heavy gold ring. "Does this mean that you agree to be my wife?" he asked slowly. "Is this part of your new bargain? Or is this to defy your father?"

"I hated him when he hurt you. More than I ever have before," she said bitterly, trembling in anger. "I've decided to make my stand here in the midst of all I've dreamed. Fighting him on his own terms. But you must take Jack to safety . . . and yourself." She bent to kiss the ring. "Wear this with my love. Take whatever you and Jack need—only leave. You saw my father—he is obsessed with owning me. He won't hurt me; he needs me too much."

"You want me to run." MacGregor's bruised and cut mouth spat the words into the sunlit air. The ring gleamed in the late-afternoon sun as he curled his fingers into a fist. His knuckles whitened. "Or are you buying your freedom?"

Her fingers paused, her eyes widening. "I want you and Jack safe. Wear the ring as a reminder of our love."

Venus whined, dragging her leg as she crawled to them. "My poor lovely . . ."

MacGregor soothed the greyhound gently, murmuring to her. "She'll lose the leg. Give me a strip of lace to bind it." Venus quieted instantly, allowing him to tend the leg. MacGregor stood slowly, then bent and picked up the dog to carry her toward the cabin.

Tiny, Mose, and Pierre ran to them. "*Mon Dieu!*" Pierre exclaimed taking the dog. "What has happened?"

MacGregor slumped into Tiny's huge arms, unconscious.

HE awoke in the cabin that night. Regina's soft body curved at his back, the unborn baby kicking him. Her hand rested lightly on his side, and her breath brushed across his throat. For a moment MacGregor lay quietly, enveloped by her scent. "My love, my sweet desire," she murmured sleepily, stroking the hair on his chest.

Venus limped to him, placing her head on his arm. MacGregor stroked the greyhound, noting the way Regina's small foot had slipped to rest on his. She sighed and whispered something in her sleep, her breasts pushing firmly against him.

Taking care not to wake Regina, MacGregor eased from the bed and padded into the clear moonlit night.

Regina's ring weighted his hand, and he lifted it to the moonlight, studying the intricate design. The shadows moved suddenly, and Pierre slipped into the moonlight. He patted MacGregor on the shoulder and handed him a bottle of whiskey. "So the little one's baby awakes, *mais non*? Violet would not let anyone tend you but herself . . . her precious MacGregor. Such a baby . . . you wear a woman's lace underwear around your head and faint at the smallest pain. That Violet, she stitched you up with silk . . . tiny little stitches and kissed every one. Even sewed your ear together."

MacGregor leaned against the cabin wall, and Venus limped out to lean against Pierre. The Frenchman petted the animal's head. "She lost the paw, but she is still one pretty dog, *non*?"

MacGregor touched his ear, smoothing the tiny stitches. He lifted the bottle and drank deeply, savoring the burning taste as he swished it around his bruised mouth. Spitting it out, he wiped the back of his hand across his lips. "Her father wants Violet like a man wants a woman. I've promised not to kill him."

"*Sacrébleu*! That one is crazy mean. When you are feeling better, perhaps we should visit this Englishman and draw his fangs. . . ."

"Tonight. He took something of mine." MacGregor touched his earlobe.

Pierre's hand weighted MacGregor's arm. "You are weak, my friend. Wait."

"Wrap my ribs if you want to help—and saddle Kansas. I'm going." MacGregor stared at him for a long moment, then slowly reached for his gunbelt, which still hung on the cabin peg. He strapped it to him slowly, painfully, then straightened. "Mortimer-Hawkes won't be expecting me tonight. Saddle Kansas for me will you? Then help me with my boots. . . . Stay here with Violet."

When Pierre helped MacGregor into the saddle, he warned, "The little one will be angry, my brother. She is very fond of your thick hide. If anything would happen to you, she would scalp me . . . I am coming, too. Tiny is awake. He will watch the women."

Wrapped in her paisley shawl, Regina walked into the moonlight. "Like hell," she said, her voice tight with anger. "MacGregor, you can barely move. It's insane to be on your feet now, much less counting coup on my father."

"*Chère* . . ." Pierre warned softly.

Regina's small hand gripped Kansas's bridle. Trapped in the moonlight and her shawl, her hair flowing around her, her beauty caught MacGregor. "Move away from the horse," he ordered. "I'm doing what has to be done."

"I see. Male pride must be appeased, regardless of pain or gentler emotions," she threw at him bitterly. Then her fingers caught his trousers at the calf, her face luminous in the night. "Oh, please don't do this."

"Wear your ring or not, Violet . . . but I won't run." Shadowed by his hat, the harsh planes of MacGregor's dark jaw caught the moonlight.

Regina breathed heavily, recognizing his set expression. Stepping back, she nodded. "Very well, then. If you must go, I insist on going with you. Pierre, please saddle Je t'aime."

"You stay put." MacGregor shifted on the saddle, his ring glowing in the night as he threaded the reins through his fingers. "I won't kill Mortimer-Hawkes, Violet," he said, watching her. "Take care of my babies."

Kansas's mottled coat slid into the dark shadows, and Pierre touched her shoulder. "*Chère*, MacGregor is a man of honor and one who must protect his family. Let him keep his pride. He does right, seeking the rattlers in their pit when they least expect him. He loves you. You must trust him now."

"I trust him completely. It is I who cannot be trusted near my father. Go with MacGregor and keep him safe."

NINETEEN

NIGEL Mortimer-Hawkes threw his tooled silver chalice into the fireplace of the main room. The goblet rolled out to the new lumber floors, and he kicked it with his slipper. "This heathen country. Not a civilized being within territories. . . ."

Pagan was civilized, he corrected as he adjusted the sleeves of his satin smoking jacket. The Mariah women were perfect mates for powerful English noblemen. The muslin drapes covering the windows shifted with the night wind, reminding the marquess of the gauze costume and Mariah's wonderful heathen shawl. The savageness of her Bedouin blood had excited him, but she could act like a lady when needed . . . just as Pagan would serve him.

Today had proved MacGregor's weakness. A quick death would make him a martyr. "Rather that he is brought to his knees in front of her. She'll soon see how weak he is. . . . I won't kill him at first."

Hawkes glanced around his room and grimaced. "How I miss Fordington. Galas and glass windows. Blooded horses and women with cultivated tastes . . . Once MacGregor is finished off, Pagan will be easily controlled. Her brat will ensure that."

MacGregor slid into the room, standing in the shadows as the marquess pivoted toward him. "MacGregor!"

"What's left of me." The mountain man's low drawl held the sound of a mountain cat ready to spring. In the half light MacGregor's tousled black hair and beard framed his rugged, bruised face. A long cut ran across his high cheek-bone, and Mortimer-Hawkes noted the tiny, neat stitches in MacGregor's lobe. His eyes darkened savagely, piercing the marquess. Surveying the room in a glance, MacGregor rested his weight on one long leg in a lazy stance. He opened and closed his right hand slowly, then rested it on his gun butt. "Don't bother calling for Tom. We palavered a bit . . . chatted, as Violet says, and now he's tied to a tree, resting. Tucked in a few of his men, too. The rest of your help didn't mind staying put in the root cellar. The door has a good latch from the outside. I guess that leaves us alone."

In an instant Mortimer-Hawkes grabbed a fencing foil from its stand, slashing the protective tip away. He sliced the blade through the air, a hissing sound filling the room. "So you came back for another taste, my savage friend. . . ."

MacGregor leaned against the log wall and leisurely poured wine into a silver goblet. Raising the glass, he drank slowly, then replaced the goblet on the silver tray. He surveyed the large, empty room leisurely, then sauntered to the cherry wood mantel. MacGregor lifted an ornate gold frame to the light, studying the small oil portrait of Regina and her mother. A young girl, Regina was dressed in a costume to match her mother's gauze-and-beaded one. "They look alike," MacGregor said, running his thumb over the heavy frame.

A heavy gold ring glowed against his dark skin, and MacGregor toyed with it while he studied his grazed knuckles. "Had to take off Violet's ring when Tom and I chatted." Then he carefully replaced the picture to the mantel.

"Pagan will surpass her mother, given time," Mortimer-Hawkes murmured. "How does it feel to bed a lady?" he prodded, circling MacGregor. "Did you enjoy her?"

The younger man smiled coldly, and for a moment fear clawed at the marquess. In a desperate show of confidence he slashed a velvet pillow with the foil, leaving it in shreds. MacGregor lifted an eyebrow and yawned.

"Do I bore you?" Mortimer-Hawkes asked mildly. Then the foil slashed across MacGregor's chest, cutting his shirt.

MacGregor stepped back slowly, drawing his gun before Mortimer-Hawkes could strike again. "Since this is a family matter, I'd like to keep this talk on friendly terms, Mortimer-Hawkes. Just so you'll know the rules."

The marquess laughed, lowering the foil to the floor and placing his free hand on his hip. "You amuse me, MacGregor. . . . Rules? Tell me, what are the rules to this game?"

MacGregor smiled slightly, then lowered his gun. The first shot splintered the foil at the handle guard. The second shot followed immediately, blasting a hole in the floor an inch from the marquess's left slipper. "Those are my rules."

"Pagan is mine!" Mortimer-Hawkes roared, shuddering with anger as MacGregor casually replaced the gun to his holster. In the next instant the marquess lunged at MacGregor.

The younger man moved easily, despite his pain, side-stepping and jerking Mortimer-Hawkes's arm up behind him. In the next movement the Englishman lay on the floor with MacGregor's Bowie at his throat. "You take one move toward Violet that I don't like, Mortimer-Hawkes, and you won't make another one," MacGregor stated quietly.

"I want the jewels," Mortimer-Hawkes muttered wildly, holding his head away from the blade.

"They're Violet's. Since they were her mother's, I reckon she'll want to keep them. She'd probably want that picture, too." He touched Mortimer-Hawkes's earlobe with the knife tip. "Violet thinks highly of my earring. Reckon you'll want to give that back," he drawled lazily, rising to his feet.

When Mortimer-Hawkes lay still, shaking in fear and anger, MacGregor threw the blade. It stuck deeply in the wood beside the marquess's severed blond lock. "Now."

After MacGregor slid into the night, Mortimer-Hawkes's scream of rage echoed through the empty lodge.

"They work in pairs," Tall Tom muttered, sagging against his ropes where MacGregor had tied him. "First her, then him. This time he's left the kill up to her."

REGINA pressed her hand to her side, caressing the baby. Night sounds of frogs and crickets echoed through the woods. An owl, spreading his wings against the stars, swooped to his prey in the meadow. Tiny and Mose spread their bedrolls near the cabin, sleeping with guns at their sides.

"Oh, please, Lord God, let MacGregor return safely," she prayed, hugging herself in the paisley shawl. Three hours passed, then four hours, and over the rugged mountains, dawn began to lighten the night sky. The moon clung to the heavens, fighting the day. A layered mist floated over the stream; the first mockingbird call ventured into the still morning, then another.

Regina watched Rosebud graze with two new longhorn cows as Ned and Daub moved through the stream's mist to drink.

"MacGregor's male pride will kill him," she whispered, tracing the pink dawn sliding over the jutting mountaintops. "Foolish gambol in the dead of night to prove a foolish point, whatever that is. . . . A man's lofty honor, indeed."

Dew dampened her cotton nightshift, and it clung to her bare legs. She remembered the morning in the meadow when she awoke to MacGregor's desperate need.

Bold, slashing knight of her dreams, swaggering a bit when he had his way . . . disarming her with his courting smile, and fretting about her approaching childbirth.

Scanning the sprawling meadows, Regina inhaled deeply. She'd sought a new land and a new life; she'd found them with MacGregor. She wanted his strength for their child.

MacGregor, spawned in the wilds by unknown parents, vowed to safeguard Jack against the horrors of an orphan. MacGregor, a woodsman, drinking tea with a napkin on his knee to please her.

MacGregor, playing his courting flute, his dark eyes watching her.

MacGregor, loving his son and anxious for the new child before its birth. A gentle man until roused, his eyes caught her with their midnight softness, trapping her heart when she would have it free.

MacGregor listened to her dreams and ideas for ranching, blending his thoughts with hers. He trusted his son and his fortune to her keeping, a gesture of faith that her father would scorn.

When had her love begun? With the bargain on the blanket? When he took her tenderly, despite his desperate need?

Regina plucked a fat lavender head as she passed the garden's fence row and smiled softly. She brushed the tiny flowers against her cheek. "Whatever he is, MacGregor is the man I love," she murmured, her smile deepening as her hand ran across the new life within her. "We've mated, after all."

Kansas whinnied, the ghostly white of his mottled coat sliding through the shadows at the edge of the meadow. Then Regina was running, picking up her skirts and flying to MacGregor.

Slumped in the saddle and holding his ribs, MacGregor allowed Pierre to lead Kansas from the woods.

"MacGregor . . . oh, my love . . ." Regina called, running faster as he straightened.

The pride, the honor, and the arrogance of MacGregor were in the defiant, wary tilt of his head. His deep-set eyes gleamed in the shadows, a tousled wave cutting across his forehead. "Stay back, wife," he ordered when she stood near his boot.

"The devil I will," she returned hotly, tears streaming down her cheeks. Then she added in a soft whisper, "Husband."

Tiny touched her arm, then bent to her ear. "Allow him his pride, missus. A fightin' man—"

She shook free, slashing the back of her hand across her tear-filled eyes. Stepping nearer, she touched MacGregor's leg, and his muscles tensed beneath the cloth.

The earring shone in his ear, nestled in the silk stitches. Her ring glowed on his dark skin, his knuckles swollen and grazed. Pride kept him upright, and she wouldn't take

that away from him. Clearing her throat, Regina stepped
back. "Did you accomplish your goal, Mr. MacGregor?"
she asked formally, her heart beating wildly as she noted
a bloody gash in his cheek.

"Yes, ma'am," he drawled, watching her. "Mortimer-
Hawkes is alive."

Aching to hold him, Regina straightened her shoulders.
If MacGregor's pride needed tending, she would not offend
him. "Of course. You kept your promise, as you always do.
Let me have your hat now. . . ."

She stepped back, enveloped with love for this tender
warrior. "Mose . . . Tiny. Put MacGregor in my bed. He'll
need his rest. . . . I intend to sleep with my husband tonight.
You have until then to make a larger bed of any sort. Pierre,
Lilly cried all night. You'd better tend to her."

She smiled softly up at MacGregor. "I am so pleased that
you returned safely, husband. I'll mend your shirt."

Then, wrapping her shawl around her tightly, Regina
turned and walked back to the cabin.

"That is one damn fine woman, Two Hearts," Pierre
murmured, watching her stiff back.

MacGregor allowed Tiny to help him to the ground.
"Violet's on the hunt," he stated tightly, then grimaced
in pain. "She's stirred up, the same as when we raided
Covington's camp."

Pierre dismounted and chuckled. "Beware, my friend,
this time you are the prey she stalks. From the light in
her eyes, I say the lady has decided to take a lover into
her bed."

Mose laughed aloud, easing his arm under MacGregor's
for support. "Going to be crowded in that bed for a few
months. You'll ache worse than you do now."

        REGINA restitched MacGregor's head wound, in-
sisting that he drink a relaxing herb tea before sleeping.
That night, in their new rope bed, she eased MacGregor's
head to her breast and stroked his hair as he slept restlessly. "My own dear heart," she whispered achingly, then
began to sing *Greensleeves*.

MacGregor's large palm settled over their baby, and he caressed a tiny, moving limb tenderly. "Violet, stay. . . ."

She lay quietly, savoring the gentle weight of his head on her breast. Venus whined softly in the shadows, and Regina bent to kiss MacGregor's hot forehead. "Sleep, my love. Sleep and heal. While you are resting, I shall deal with my father."

Before dawn Regina and Lilly spoke quietly outside the cabin. "He'll sleep this morning, and I will be back before noon. Will you please make certain that Jack doesn't disturb him? I don't want him to worry about me. . . ."

Pierre placed his arm around Lilly, kissed her cheek, then spoke to Regina. "Tiny said you want your horse saddled. That you want to have morning tea with Mortimer-Hawkes. I cannot allow this with MacGregor. . . ." He shook his head helplessly. "Wait, *chère*, do what you must with MacGregor at your side."

Regina tugged her purple kidskin gloves higher and smoothed the long lace blouse covering her child. "I'm simply having morning tea with the marquess. I don't want to be late." She glanced at Je t'aime and the morocco saddle. "Ah, lovely day for a ride, Pierre."

"I go with you—" he began, silenced by a small lifted finger.

"I have no less honor than my husband, Pierre. I intend to settle the matter before it worsens. MacGregor drank a healing tea in the night and will sleep until I return. Then I will tell him what has happened." She leveled a meaningful glance at the Frenchman.

"*Chère*, you are an *enceinte* woman. The *bébé* . . ."

Regina lifted a slender, winged eyebrow and looked up at him steadily with dark purple eyes. "Jack will have a beautiful sister, Pierre. Would you be her godfather?"

Two hours later Regina shifted in her sidesaddle. She strained for a first view of the marquess's hunting lodge, overlooking Primrose.

Seated on a velvet-and-horn chair, Lord Mortimer-Hawkes sat drinking morning tea and considering his next move. Tall Tom and his men had disappeared, licking their wounds. They'd come back in time, lured by his offer of gold. MacGregor was too powerful now, Mortimer-Hawkes acknowledged silently. Only a man possessing Pagan and the Mariah at the same time could have taken a bad beating, then acted out his revenge.

Regina entered the room in the same manner as MacGregor, easing aside the muslin drape. "Ah, Father. A cup of morning tea would be lovely."

"Pagan!" Mortimer-Hawkes was on his feet, his hand gripping her upper arm painfully.

"Loose me," she ordered too quietly.

The leashed fury in her soft tone startled Mortimer-Hawkes, and his fingers slid away. He bared his teeth in a smile. "Of course. I'm just so happy you've come at last. Tea?"

"Lovely." Sitting gracefully in a swirl of skirts, Regina plucked her gloves from her hand, finger by finger. After placing them neatly aside, she spread a napkin over her lap. She poured tea from the silver pot as though she were sitting in an English parlor. Mortimer-Hawkes sat, studying her expression.

"Tea in the morning is lovely, isn't it? Americans prefer coffee at every meal, you know," she said easily, then sipped the brew.

"I've missed you, Regina," Mortimer-Hawkes said, suddenly uncertain. "You've changed since yesterday."

"Yes. So I have. Yesterday was rather wearing." She replaced the cup on the saucer and folded her hands on her lap. "Indians are so interesting. For instance, the honor of the Cheyenne Dog Soldier is impeccable. He buries his lance at the front of the battle and lashes himself to it. He'll fight to the death rather than untie the tether or remove the lance."

"Interesting colonial tale," Mortimer-Hawkes sneered.

Regina's eyes gleamed beneath her heavy lashes. "You are vulnerable now, Father. You do not possess me or the Mariah. I've hidden it with a friend, who at a sign of any mischievous action from you will destroy the jewels. I suggest you return to England . . . but you will not come near me, my children, my husband, or anyone dear to me. Do I make myself clear?" she asked as her father stared at her blankly.

"You disobedient wench! I am your . . . father," he said when he could speak.

"Then I disown you," she said flatly, standing and carefully drawing on her gloves. "You should know . . . Mortimer-Hawkes, that when I was a child, Jennifer and my mother—Mariah—taught me something of the jewels and of my heritage. I'd forgotten, but your attack yesterday caused me to remember. I spent a poor night reliving the horrors suffered at your hands—the way you taunted my mother that she was soiled goods, the leavings of a cousin growing in her belly when you married her. I was only a child then, but I remember everything quite clear. Huddling beneath a bed while my mother was beaten and raped etched the details in my mind forever."

Regina straightened her shoulders. "I remembered every detail perfectly. One of your . . . ladies loved to send me off to bed with that lovely tale. Then when I was ten or so, one of your cousins decided to break me to his hand. He repeated the tale and Jennifer confirmed it while she was comforting me.

"MacGregor, my husband, is a powerful man. With him at my side, I could easily wrest Fordington from you. The estate is legally mine anyway, purchased for me by my real father, your cousin, to salve his conscience. You were in danger of losing everything before my mother's unfortunate marriage to you."

While the marquess dealt with her statement, Regina added quietly, "Pagan, you call me . . . perhaps I am. We never know what savageness rests in our very hearts until it is tried. Do not try my patience, m'lord."

"I could kill MacGregor's brat and you with a blow!" he shouted, leaping to his feet and trembling with anger.

Regally sweeping her skirt aside, Regina faced him like a tigress ready to strike. "You won't hurt me, Mortimer-Hawkes. You would lose everything. Even now you are a shadow of the powerful Marquess of Fordington that I remember. Take the shreds of your dignity and return to England."

When the curtain fluttered behind her, Mortimer-Hawkes dashed the silver service to the floor. "I'll have her brat soon. She'll crawl back to me."

Then he shivered in fear. "That bloody MacGregor! He has my power! I must have it back!"

THAT afternoon Regina napped at MacGregor's side and awoke to his tender kiss. When she yawned and arched against him, he groaned suddenly and stiffened. Taking her chin in his hand, he smoothed her bottom lip with his thumb. "If you ever count coup without me again, Mrs. MacGregor, your backside will feel my hand," he drawled, caressing the rounded shape of her buttocks.

"Promises, m'lord?" she purred, kissing a bruise on his bearded jaw. "My, you look handsome today. Like a knight of the realm at ease."

MacGregor studied the shape of her eyes, the inviting contour of her lips, solemnly. "Mortimer-Hawkes wants you, Violet . . . In his bed."

She shuddered, remembering a deluge of the marquess's sensual remarks and the way he held her against him as MacGregor was beaten. "I am the family secret, my dear. I remembered everything suddenly last night. The marquess was paid to marry my mother by my real father, his cousin. My mother's dowry was quite attractive, too. I realize now that he has wanted me for years. . . . How did you know?"

Holding her closer, MacGregor breathed deeply. "One man knows when another wants a woman. It was there when we met in Primrose—the way he looked at you, kissed your cheek. Yesterday, he held you like a man holds a woman he wants in his bed, not a daughter he loves."

She stared up at him drowsily and yawned. "But I'm in yours, aren't I? Who followed me to my fa—to Mortimer-Hawkes's lodge? Tiny? Mose? Or Pierre?"

"All three," he answered, before nestling his cheek on her breasts. "Soft and sweet here, my heart," he murmured before sliding into sleep.

AUGUST passed in hot, still days and loving, tender nights. Mortimer-Hawkes clung to his empty lodge like a spirit haunting a grave, his servants making necessary purchases in Primrose. Buzzard swept out of the mountains to marry Pierre and Lilly. The newlyweds occupied one bedroom of the MacGregor home for a week, then moved to a deserted cabin nestled nearby.

The wind sweeping over the territory echoed with fearful whispers, grief, and rage. Quanah Parker, Custer, Stone Calf, Dull Knife, Fetterman Massacre . . . Cheyenne, Kiowa, Sioux . . . The Union Pacific Railroad pressed westward; wild game fattened for winter and renegades sold whiskey and firearms, trading white and Indian captive alike in Mexico.

September entered with a blaze of orange and yellow, aspens brilliant amid the dark fir and pine. Ripening with MacGregor's child, Regina was delighted with Mose's gift of a spinning wheel. Mose spent hours carding the dyed wool as his mother had taught him while Regina began filling corn-shuck bobbins on her spinning wheel. They planned to spin the wool in the coming year, then dye and loop it into skeins. Tiny played his harmonica to the whir of Regina's spinning every night; Jack clapped his hands and gurgled excitedly on his father's lap. A Navajo family traded two ewes for coffee and cornmeal, then presented Regina with tiny, beautiful silver-and-turquoise buttons for her new baby.

Tiny and Mose hovered near Regina from dawn until dusk, and MacGregor scowled from the lack of privacy. The men insisted that she rest in the mornings and afternoons, while they worked outside.

From the men Regina learned how to dry green beans, pumpkin, cabbage leaves, and chili peppers. Garlic and onion braids hung drying on pegs, waiting to be stored. Regina experimented with cheese and minced meat for sausages to be smoked with jerked meat.

She insisted that their large larder be stuffed with bags of beans and barrels of cornmeal and flour. Regina plagued the men to harvest and identify native roots and healing herbs.

Custer continued the government's policy of Indian Removal, and for a few days a small band of Southern Cheyenne camped in a hidden glade on Regina's property. MacGregor visited the chief, Lean Deer, one evening, and they smoked Mose's best tobacco twist in a long pipe. When he returned late at night, he slid into their bed and lay quietly, staring up at the ceiling shadows.

Regina turned in her sleep and slid her arm around his shoulder, nuzzling his chest with her cheek until she slept again. Holding her in his arms, MacGregor ached for Little Beetle, who sang his death song, and for White Elk's woman, who cried and slashed herself over his death. The Indian babies had already seen slaughter and knew hunger, while Jack slept safely in his crib.

MacGregor stroked Regina's rounded stomach and thought of the food she'd sent to Lean Deer's people. Last week she'd sent Tiny to deliver a blanket, clothing, and lengths of new cloth to a settler's family, burned out by a drunken miner. The settler's wife accepted the gift with the condition that she sew and mend as payment. Emma Manson's first creation from the flannel lengths was a baby gown, edged with lace tatting. Regina had cried, throwing her arms around MacGregor and weeping against his shoulder. "I'm so happy, my darling," she had whispered when he sat, holding her on his lap.

Violet. Her scent and silky skin warmed him, her arm tightened across his shoulder, hugging him to her gently.

MacGregor closed his eyes, breathing lightly. *Violet.* Traveling from England to America to hold him in the night. To bear him a child . . .

"A dream," he whispered, awed by his fortune. "A dream that could end any time." So small, he thought, caressing her back and hips. Indian women squatted for hours in the birthing position, pulling on a branch, until the baby slipped into ready hands. Other women gave birth in the fields, placed the baby in the shade, and returned to hoeing corn.

So small. MacGregor's fingers wrapped easily around Regina's wrist, gauging her small bones.

In her last month Regina nestled in MacGregor's arms each night while he groaned and ached. The new walnut bed, exchanged for the makeshift pine one, creaked as he turned restlessly. "Darling." Regina sighed, her breath sweeping across his chest.

Her small hand moved and settled low on his stomach. Perspiration beaded his forehead, his body taut with passion as he slid quickly out of bed. Regina sat up slowly, staring at him sleepily, and yawned. "Is something wrong?"

Jerking on his trousers, MacGregor looked down at her. A button had come undone on her gown, exposing her full breast. The other breast pressed against the cloth, a dark circle beneath the muslin. Dark tendrils escaped her single, long braid, and she yawned again, stretching until the cloth strained against her chest. "Come back to bed, darling," she said with a sigh, lying down.

The gown boldly displayed a ripe nipple, and MacGregor's body tightened. "Violet," he said between his teeth. "I'm checking on the sheep."

Her eyes opened slowly. "Now? Something is wrong. It's hours before dawn." She listened intently. "The dogs aren't barking. . . ."

He bent to tug the flannel sheet and blanket up to her chin, concealing the intriguing rosy peak. Placing his hands on either side of her head, he nibbled temptingly at her lips. Working his way to the sensitive spot behind her ear, he stroked it with his tongue until she reached for him. MacGregor resisted her tug, smiling at her tenderly. "Violet, a man can take just so much. When a woman nudges and cuddles and strokes his privates in her sleep, he wants to do something about it."

She laughed, a low, seductive sound floating through the cabin. "Come back to bed. I can't sleep without you. I've grown fond of being cuddled every night. A dragon thrusts boldly at my thighs, nearly tearing my gown as he seeks shelter from the cold."

MacGregor rubbed her nose with his, savoring the soft arms enclosing his neck and the small hands soothing his taut shoulders. Regina's tongue slid along his lips. "I'd love one of those foolish kisses, my love. You've hoarded them lately and . . ."

She ran her hand down his chest, toying with the hair covering the padded muscles. "Come lie down, my love," she invited huskily, her fingers sliding beneath his trouser to enclose him gently.

"Violet, you're pushing. . . . The baby has dropped into the birthing position . . . ah . . ." MacGregor closed his eyes, taut with pleasure as she drew him down beside her.

"Shh," she whispered. "One of the best parts of our marriage, my love, is the freedom to fondle you every night in our own bed."

He inhaled sharply as her lips brushed his stomach. Then she was leaning over him, her expression fierce with love. "I shall expect a proper romp after the baby, Mr. Two Hearts MacGregor. I'm going to do things to you that a lady never thinks about. Like this . . ." Her fingers slid down and began caressing him as her tongue entered his mouth.

When he groaned, she bent to nibble his ear, her hand continuing its bold rhythm. "This is what I want to do after the baby comes, darling. . . ." she whispered, punctuating the bold verbal sketches with flicks of her tongue into his ear.

"That isn't possible," he rasped unevenly, his hips moving with her hand's rhythm. He smoothed her breast, careful of the swollen softness.

She smiled knowingly. "We'll have to explore the matter. We've all our lives. . . ."

"Violet," he said unsteadily, between his teeth, as she nibbled at his throat. He breathed unsteadily, his body taut. "A woman doesn't come at a man like that, taking him—Ah!"

Holding him tightly until his passion ebbed, Regina shook, enveloped with tenderness for this large, vulnerable man. The baby kicked strongly, and she lay down beside MacGregor, placing his hand over their child. "You've made me so happy, my love. . . ." she whispered, stroking his damp face.

He struggled for breath, his heart beating rapidly. "Violet . . ." he managed after a time. "Where did you learn that?"

"Lilly. She knows marvelous things," she answered sleepily as he gathered her close. "Hold me, MacGregor. You have my heart."

Lying quietly while she dozed, MacGregor laced his fingers with hers and wondered if his happiness was a dream soon to be shattered.

Regina snuggled her cheek to his shoulder, kissing it. "I love when you hold me, MacGregor," she whispered drowsily. "Kiss me."

He had what he wanted, MacGregor decided, his lips meeting hers in a gentle, lingering kiss. A woman who hugged and petted Jack, teaching him how to say his prayers and cuddling him when he hurt.

Her hand lay on his cheek, caressing him gently, and Regina whispered, "Don't worry so, MacGregor. Your baby will arrive bold and daring like her sire. I shall be fine. . . ."

In the evenings after supper MacGregor and Tiny worked in the tack shed, completing a huge loom of black walnut and wild cherry. Mose's cot served as a table to spread MacGregor's sketches while they worked; the sidesaddle lay beneath a tarp in a corner. The men considered the loom's complicated design as a challenge, their gift to Regina.

Mose pampered her by making a frothy chocolate drink every night from cacao bean flour mixed with corn flour. While Regina sipped from a dainty china cup, Mose drank deeply from his favorite *chocolatero*, a rounded copper mug.

In the next week Regina suddenly began cleaning and mending. MacGregor awoke to her sweeping the floor at midnight and embroidering by lamplight. Jack listened intently to explanations about the new baby, and Regina made him a velvet bear for his crib. "My baby? Mama?" Jack would ask, placing his chubby hand over her rounded stomach.

"Yes, my darling. Mama loves Jack . . . Jack loves Mama . . . Mama loves baby . . . Jack loves baby . . . baby loves Jack," she sang as she clapped Jack's hands with hers and kissed him until he laughed. "Jack loves Da . . . Mama loves Da . . ."

The first time MacGregor heard her sing the childish song as she played with Jack, he dropped the water dipper. Regina glanced up at him; the look held and warmed. "Goodness, MacGregor, you look stunned. What is it?"

He cleared his throat and blinked. "Violet. You just said you loved me."

"So I did," she said, shooting him a wide, happy smile. "My goodness. Don't look so shaken."

TWO mornings later Tiny carried Regina back from the woods, where they had been gathering herbs and roots. Mose ran from the garden, carrying Jack. MacGregor, seated on Kansas, left the mules standing in harness as they pulled timber for a shed. He raced the Appaloosa to Tiny's side and swung down.

"Her water broke," Tiny said as he handed Regina carefully to MacGregor. "Baby is coming fast."

"Mose, get Jack's things and take him to Pierre's," MacGregor began. "Ask Lilly to come—"

Regina's hand caressed his cheek as he strode to the cabin. "Just you, my fine husband. I want only you to be with me," she asked quietly, watching him before her eyes dimmed with pain.

MacGregor tensed and quickened his stride, holding her gently as her body tightened against the pain. She breathed heavily. "Tiny said you were better than a midwife in the war. That you helped with five babies, MacGregor. Something gentle and safe in the hands, he said. I want you. We've worked together before . . ." she whispered as he placed her gently on the bed and placed his hand over the baby.

"If anything happens—" he began grimly, probing the tiny life in her womb.

"It won't." She glanced at Mose, who was leaving the cabin with Jack and his bag. "Oh, Jack . . . come kiss Mama," she called, placing her hand over MacGregor's. Regina looked at MacGregor's taut face and kissed Jack, smoothing his rumpled hair. "You're going to visit Lilly, Jack," she said softly. "When you come back, your baby will be waiting for you. Go along with Mose now. . . ."

Her lips firmed, fighting pain until Jack left. In the next instant her body tightened beneath MacGregor's palm. "Goodness!"

"Violet, your pains aren't two minutes apart. How long have you been having them?" MacGregor demanded, holding her hand.

"Since before dawn. I'd heard that it takes a long time. . . ." She frowned when MacGregor cursed and stood, his fists at his sides. "It's my first child, for goodness' sakes. I'll know next time. And the next," she added tartly and began to push herself off the bed.

"That baby is coming damn fast," Tiny repeated at MacGregor's side. "She'll drop it on the floor if she gets up."

"Damn," MacGregor said quietly, kneeling by the bed. "Tiny, get water and cloths, then wait outside." He eased her down, then smoothed her hair away from her face. Her cheek nestled in his palm, and her gaze met his. "Violet, we need to change your clothes. . . ."

She clung to his hand as the next pain came. When it eased slightly, she opened her eyes and licked the fresh cut her teeth had made on her lip. "I love you, MacGregor. . . ."

The next pain washed over her, and he talked softly, easing her with his hands. She shuddered momentarily and then dozed.

He'd wanted love all his life, craved it as a child, crying long into the night. As a man he'd lost the dream, and suddenly a purple-eyed woman sauntered into his life. He claimed her, not expecting a measure of the happiness she'd brought to him.

The baby could take her life. . . .

His hands trembled as he adjusted the sheet over her knees to examine her. "Touch me with your marvelous hands, husband. . . ." she whispered, inhaling sharply as another pain went ricocheting through her and the baby's black head appeared.

MacGregor smoothed her taut stomach, pushing slightly and talking quietly to Regina. When he instructed her to push again, she groaned. "I will not obey your lordly commands, husband, until you tell me you love me. Damn you, Two Hearts MacGregor, do it now!"

"Violet! Push!"

She cried out in pain. "I refuse. Do it!"

"I love you, Violet. Always have," he rasped just as she pushed and Mary Rose MacGregor arrived in his waiting hands.

TINY and the morocco leather saddle disappeared early that afternoon.

TWENTY

"THE power of kings," the Marquess of Fordington said as he ripped open the heavy pommel of the morocco leather saddle. Tall Tom lifted the saddle, spilling the jewels onto the hard, earthen floor. Mortimer-Hawkes eagerly pawed through the stones. Jeweled facets caught the afternoon light coming from the old Spanish mine's entrance. "The Mariah isn't here!" Delving his hand deep into the opened pommel, he yelled at Tall Tom, "Cut open every part of that bloody saddle."

Tom's knife slashed at the tooled leather, exposing the padding. "Nothing."

Mortimer-Hawkes smiled grimly, then kicked the saddle aside with his polished boot. He handed Tom a large velvet pouch. "Put them in here. . . . I should have known. Regina is truly my match. She's kept the Mariah separately."

Tom studied a gleaming emerald and lifted a blue diamond, turning them in the bare light. "There's enough jewels here to live like a king. Let's take them and leave."

The Englishman turned on the mountain man. "You're afraid of MacGregor's gun hand," he accused, sneering.

Tall Tom straightened to his full imposing height and stared down at the slighter, older man. "Say that again and I'll—"

"What did you do with the black man's body?"

"Left it in the woods. Had him carry the saddle to my horse, then did him in nice and quiet. He was the only one outside the cabin. Mose left with MacGregor's brat, headed for Pierre's."

The marquess's dark blue eyes glowed in the shadowy cave. "That could mean Regina is in childbirth." He methodically slapped his riding quirt against an ancient supporting beam of the tunnel. He smiled slowly. "Imagine the stir Regina's half-breed brat will create in England. . . ."

Turning to Tom, he reached for the bag of jewels and tucked them into his pocket, buttoning the flap safely. "Regina needs time to recover from childbirth. MacGregor can tend her and the child for a time, my gift to him before he dies. . . . Take care of Tiny's body. I don't want it found."

"You're afraid of the woman and MacGregor, Mortimer-Hawkes. Why not move in now while they're busy with the birthing and grab the woman? I can kill MacGregor—"

Mortimer-Hawkes stared at him coldly. "He's too powerful now. Can't you feel it? He's got the Mariah woman and the stone. My sweet Regina needs to recover—I don't want anything to harm her now. Just after birth, anything could happen to her or to the child."

He touched a patch of blood on the saddle with his quirt. "Too bad about the black man. He found Covington for me. He disappeared shortly after and turned up at MacGregor's."

Tall Tom laughed, crouching to slice off pieces of intricately tooled leather. "Tiny served with MacGregor in the war. Before he cashed in, he said he discovered who Covington was hunting and decided to throw in with MacGregor. The métis promised his woman he wouldn't come for you, and Tiny stayed to protect him. He didn't make it."

"I see. Take care of the body tonight. I want MacGregor to think he's alive."

"I thought of that. Had him write a note before he passed on. Says, 'I need you. Spanish cave. T.' 'Course 'T' means Tom, and I need to do MacGregor in."

Tom laughed again, joined by the marquess. "You show promise, my good man. Make certain that you stay out of sight for the next month."

"And you?"

"I'll stay in comfort at my lodge, hunting and enjoying the wilds, waiting for spring, when I may leave. With winter settling in soon, I can't be expected to leave."

Mortimer-Hawkes sauntered to the mouth of the mine and thoughtfully prodded a dented, antique Spanish breast-plate with his quirt. "You've found a wonderful lair, Tall Tom. Pack it with foodstuffs and firewood. MacGregor may be our guest in a month or so."

He pivoted to Tall Tom. "I have to see his power over Regina. . . . Test its strength, so that mine can be even greater. Can a woman make it up the trail leading here if it snows?"

Tall Tom touched his eye patch with the stub of his little finger. "That woman can run on snowshoes like a man. She'll make it."

"She's small . . . and after childbirth—"

"MacGregor's woman would crawl to him over a bed of live coals. She's not an ordinary female."

The marquess slashed the quirt across Tall Tom's chest. "Of course she's not ordinary. She's the Mariah woman. Don't call Regina 'MacGregor's woman'—and she will crawl to *me*!"

THE morning after her birth, Mary Rose MacGregor suckled at her mother's breast. Regina nestled back in the bed's pillows, easing aside her lace gown for Jack's special viewing. Jack perched on MacGregor's knee, holding his velvet bear. "Baby?"

"Yes, darling. Your baby sister, Mary." Regina kissed the infant's glossy black head and looked at MacGregor's dark, emotion-filled expression. "You're a lovely man, Mr. Two Hearts MacGregor. I'm so proud of you," she whispered huskily, slipping her hand into his.

"Baby?" Jack persisted, scrambling down to peer at the baby's rosy, fat cheeks and black curls. Then he climbed up into bed and snuggled on Regina's free side. She kissed his forehead. "Mama loves Jack . . . Mama loves Mary . . .

Mama loves Da . . ." she sang, looking at MacGregor's tears.

His hand tightened on hers, the rough calluses familiar against her palm. "Thank you, Violet," he whispered in a husky, unsteady tone.

"Thank you, m'lord," she returned, tugging his hand until he bent for her long kiss. Against his lips she whispered, "I love you fiercely, Two Hearts MacGregor. I shall expect you to sire another baby soon."

He brought her palm to his mouth. "I never believed . . . hoped for all this, Violet," he whispered.

"Neither did I," she admitted, trailing a fingertip across his damp eyelashes. "I hoped to find peace in this new land, but I found more. I found love."

"Love," he repeated, tasting the word slowly, fearing that his happiness was a dream.

"Love, my handsome woodsman. . . . My husband. . . ."

Jack squirmed at her side and slipped to the floor, running for the door to open it.

MacGregor touched the baby's fat cheek softly. "She's so perfect, so tiny. . . . I was afraid . . ."

"She's beautiful. Every bit your daughter," Regina said softly. "She was in a rage when my milk didn't start immediately, wanting things her way."

MacGregor's finger slid from the baby's downy cheek to Regina's milk-swollen breast. "You fill my heart," he said simply, watching her blush rise. "You're even more beautiful after a baby."

"Posh. Here I am in my dishabille after having a child, and you're—"

"Loving you," he said quietly, his eyes glowing.

Mose, Jack, Pierre, and Lilly filled the cabin, exclaiming over Mary Rose. But the long look MacGregor and Regina shared held and warmed. "I love you," she mouthed silently.

Then the baby yawned and stretched and nestled to her side to sleep.

Later, Pierre held the baby and Jack while Lilly brushed Regina's hair. The big Frenchman cooed and made noises, and Mose grumbled. "Here, you old bear," Pierre said finally. "You hold the *bébé*. I will cook. That Two Hearts MacGregor, he looks like he is tuckered."

Mose's eyes widened fearfully, and he grabbed Jack for protection. "Can't trust nursing babies. No telling what comes out of their drawers. She's mighty pretty, though. Mary was my mam's name."

MacGregor stood and yawned. "Reckon we've got something to bring in the house, don't we, Mose?"

The three big men moved the huge loom into the cabin in pieces. They placed it in a corner of the front room, where Regina could see them assemble it. "Oh, my!" Regina exclaimed repeatedly, craning for a better view through the bedroom doorway. "How marvelous."

"Divine," MacGregor said, then chuckled. "Lovely."

"Oh, my," Regina whispered, awed by the huge loom. "It is so beautiful. I can't wait."

Mose beamed by the loom. "Lots to do to prepare a loom for weaving. Helped my mam do this plenty of times. Takes a knowing hand."

When Regina threw back the covers and began to sit up, MacGregor was at her side, scowling. "Get back in bed, woman."

She glared up at him. "My lover or not, Two Hearts MacGregor, you're not keeping me from my loom."

For a moment he stared at her, locked in his thoughts. Then he smiled slowly, arrogantly. "Lover is it?"

She wrapped the paisley shawl around her gown. "You're my husband, lover, father of my child . . . children," she corrected. "Jack's mine now, too. . . ." Then stretching out a hand, she smiled up at him as she sat carefully. "You're a beguiling, handsome man, Two Hearts MacGregor."

In an instant he was on his knees, his arms holding her tightly against him. His damp lashes pressed against her throat, and she held him as he shuddered. "If anything happened to you . . ."

She smoothed his rumpled hair and held him close. "You were wonderful. I had nothing to fear."

For a long moment she rocked him in her arms and soothed away his tears with gentle kisses. "There now, husband. Our guests and my loom are waiting," she murmured, tugging on his earring.

"It's been a long night," he grumbled gently as he picked her up in his arms.

With a loving smile she nestled against him, smoothing the muscles of his taut neck with her hand. "I feel just wonderful. You'll recover with a good night's sleep in our bed." She rubbed her nose against his and kissed him. "Everyone's here. Where's Tiny?"

MacGregor eased her through the doorway, his expression still. Regina frowned, stroking his tense shoulder. "You're hiding something. Where's Tiny?"

"He's gone. So is your saddle," he answered tightly as the others surrounded them.

Regina's fingers tightened on his shoulder. "You must find him. The marquess—"

MacGregor met Mose's eyes, then spoke grimly, "Men who came through the war act funny sometimes. . . . Mose couldn't find sign of Tiny anywhere, or of a fight. When he left, he took the saddle. It was hidden so that only one of us knew where it was—"

"Oh, MacGregor, surely not."

"Tiny can wait, but right now, we're celebrating Mary Rose's birthday."

"But—"

"Hush, woman. I had enough of your orders while we were birthing my baby."

Pierre slapped MacGregor on the back and grinned widely. "Lilly has my *bébé* soon. We make another loom, *mais non*?"

MARY Rose and Jack and joy filled the next weeks, and then the first snowfall came in early November. Madam Joy's Last Dollar was quiet, the windows covered with boards. Lilly and Regina rescued the girls the madam had left to forage for themselves.

Pierre, in a stroke of brilliant gallantry, opened a marriage market. The ten girls stayed at his home while he interviewed the prospective grooms. Two girls were gone the first week and three the next week, each with the option to return safely if they were not treated according to Pierre's standards.

Though unspoken, Tiny's disappearance troubled everyone. His gear lay waiting in his shed, occupied by Mose.

A cold mist preceding snow clung to the mountains like an icy god waiting to descend. Mose hunched down in his heavy coat, walking to MacGregor, who was carrying wood into the cabin. "Hey, there, sweet darling," he teased the younger man, reminding him of Regina's endearments. "Just came from town. Someone tucked a note marked 'for MacGregor' under Beulah's door." He delved into his heavy coat and pulled out an envelope.

"Let's go inside," MacGregor offered, scanning the sheep in the meadow. "Good thing we've finished the shed for the new lambs. They won't have such a time as that first crop. Jack's down for his nap and Mary Rose, too."

Laddie jumped up on Mose's leg, and Venus licked his hand. MacGregor signaled Mose to be quiet and unloaded the wood. He poured coffee, heating on the new iron stove, into mugs and sat them on the table.

Mose sighed longingly and inhaled the scent of the freshly baked bread on the table. "Where's Violet? You run her off yet?"

"She's hunting," MacGregor said tightly. He sat and sipped his coffee. "I thought a woman would stay in the house in the winter." He nodded at the loom. "She weaves in the morning and evening. But in the early afternoons she hunts nearby. Just until she thinks Mary Rose needs feeding. She caches her milk in the snow, in case she's late for a feeding. I'll be the laughingstock of the territory . . . my wife providing food on the table," he grumbled. "Violet's happy as a lark . . . wants another baby soon as she can."

Mose laughed outright. "Damn. That sounds fine to me."

"Let's see that note." MacGregor turned away, but not before Mose caught his grin.

After tearing open the envelope, MacGregor's expression slid into a dark frown. He tossed the note to Mose, who eyed it suspiciously. "You know I can't read. What's that scribbling say?"

"Tiny is at the Spanish cave. Says he needs me."

"You leaving?" Mose asked as MacGregor began packing a *parflèche* with ammunition and food. "Violet won't like if you leave before she gets back. . . ." His eyes rounded. "You can't leave now—wait! I'll go with you. Damn it, pup! You're planning to leave me with those babies, aren't you?"

"Mary Rose's milk is cached in a wood box nailed to the aspen out front. Heat it in hot water until just warm. Don't forget to pat her back."

"Great buffalo balls, man. What if her drawers need changing?"

TWO hours later MacGregor stared up at the rugged snow-covered mountain. Brush grew over the trail leading to the old mine. MacGregor bent to brush away new snow covering a big man's tracks. The heel was worn like Tiny's army-issue boots, a man's heavy weight taking the boot deep into the snow.

MacGregor unsaddled Kansas, then slung the *parflèche* over his shoulder. "Stay, boy," he ordered the horse, feeding him a lump of sugar.

The wind whistled through the aspens, an eerie sound as though the Indian slaves of the Spanish conquistadors were keening. According to legend, the Indians of long ago haunted the cave. Children had worked and died in the mine, and finally the Indians rebelled, killing every Spanish soldier and worker within the territory. Bear Robe of the Southern Cheyenne wore the finger bones of a Spanish soldier on his necklace of eagle talons.

Kansas's breath shot into the frigid air, and he stamped impatiently. "That's a good hour walk up the mountain and another down. Reckon you can wait." MacGregor looped the reins across a bush that the horse could easily snap if frightened.

Halfway up to the mine's entrance, MacGregor noticed a shred of cloth with blood dangling from a small bush.

A trail of blood mottled the new snow, and MacGregor moved quickly, carrying his rifle in his hand.

Tiny appeared at the shadowy mouth of the cave, holding his arm and bending as though he were hurt. Beneath the brim of his hat, his dark jaw was covered with blood. He leaned against an entrance beam and crumpled to the ground.

"Tiny!" Hurrying up a slight embankment, MacGregor stumbled on a snow-covered rock and twisted his ankle.

The blow hit him from the back of the head, and he fell facedown into the snow.

"There now," Tall Tom crooned as he sat on MacGregor. He lashed the unconscious man's hands. "Mortimer-Hawkes's playacting did the trick after all. Soot and bear grease and blood and a dead man's shirt brought you to die. The big man wants your bitch to crawl, and after that you are a dead man."

MacGregor awoke slowly, his skull pounding to the sound of Mortimer-Hawkes's roaring laughter echoing off the mine's walls. Lashed to a supporting beam of the Spanish cave, he struggled against the rawhide expertly tied around his wrists. Night swept by snowflakes veiled the mouth of the cave. "Look at the almighty, powerful MacGregor, Tall Tom. He looks too weak to possess the woman and the stone of the Mariah!"

Mortimer-Hawkes slashed his quirt across MacGregor's face, bringing a welt. "Regina's spawned your brat, you bastard. I've let her have time to heal before playing out our charade. I'll make her beg for your life, then destroy you as she watches. . . ."

MacGregor strained against his bonds, then glanced up as rocks fell from the roof of the cave. Testing the ancient beam supporting the cave by shaking it gently, he dislodged a spray of pebbles. The timbers overhead creaked and groaned ominously.

Mortimer-Hawkes sneered, running the quirt across the new welt. "Easy on, my good man."

Sprawled on pelts, Tall Tom sipped from a silver flask.

"You promised to let me finish him when the woman arrives, Mortimer-Hawkes. What makes you think she'll come, anyway? A female just finished whelping is weak."

Mortimer-Hawkes trailed the quirt along MacGregor's jaw slowly. "If he has this great power of the Mariah Stone, she'll seek him out. My . . . woman of the Mariah is very strong-willed. She'll come. Regina will do what I want because I am reclaiming my powers. With you gone she'll obey my every wish in order to keep . . . Mary Rose, is it? . . . alive."

"Violet won't leave the baby to hunt me, Mortimer-Hawkes," MacGregor taunted softly. "She'll send Pierre and Mose."

"Then they'll return empty-handed. We've got enough food to wait for an eternity." Mortimer-Hawkes shrugged carelessly. "She'll hear your screams, and she'll do what I want. It's a simple matter, really."

"I get that big egg of a diamond and your boy, MacGregor," Tall Tom added. "He caused me to lose this." He held up the stub of his missing finger.

MacGregor tested his bonds again, and the beam creaked. "I could bring this down on all of us. I will if Violet does come."

The marquess dusted his hands and lounged on a length of red velvet near the mouth of the cave. He kicked Tiny's boots aside, then tossed the bloody shirt into the fire with the tip of his cane. "The entrance of the cave is well braced by rock, very sturdy. You are the one in danger, not we, my fine friend."

He sank into a heavy quilt and stared at MacGregor across the fire. The smoke rose to the blackened ceiling and followed a course to the entrance, escaping into the night air. "I've always wondered what a woman of the Mariah Stone would do when put to the test. Regina's mother lacked her spirit. Oh, she'll come for you, her *paramour*. . . ."

"They've mated. Like wolves," Tall Tom stated and rose to step outside the mine. Relieving himself, he scanned the snow-swept valley sprawling beneath the mountain. "I figure she won't leave the cabin until first light. Give her two or three hours, and she'll be coming up the same trail as the métis."

REGINA returned to find Mose frantically trying to feed Mary Rose her milk. She saw the note and crumpled it into a ball. "Tell me the way to the Spanish cave, Mose. I'm going to my husband."

"Why? MacGregor hasn't had time to get back yet. It's only been three or so hours. Give the man time—"

Regina leveled a dark frown at him. "Tiny is dead. I just found his body . . . or what was left of it. I fear my father—Mortimer-Hawkes—is up to his tricks."

"Tiny? Damn that skunk for dyin'! Now, Violet . . ." Mose began heatedly. "Two Hearts would scalp me if I let you go. I calculate it'll be full dark in no time. How are you going to tell which way is north?"

"The North Star. You start me out and draw the shape of the mountain. The moonlight will be good tonight—"

Mose lifted Mary Rose. "You take the baby. I'll go."

"The Marquess of Fordington wants me. He won't hurt me, Mose."

"Wolves are hunting now—"

"So am I. I'm going to MacGregor, Mose." She kissed his cheek. "I'd appreciate any instructions you could give me."

He studied her for a long moment, then bit off a fresh chew of tobacco. "When a skunk lays out a trap, take the back door in. If'n I was you, I'd be doing just what you're doing . . . hittin' 'em afore they was expectin' me. If'n I was you, I'd keep to the shadows since the moon hits the face of that mountain. The snow makes a crust that a half-pint like you can walk right over. They won't be expecting you until a few hours after dawn. Hit 'em before light . . . hit 'em fast and hard."

Taking care to instruct the mountain man on how to feed the baby, Regina emptied her breasts in privacy, preparing another jar of milk. "I'll put this in the cache, Mose," she said, delving into a china teapot to pull out an enormous bloodred ruby.

Slipping the heavy chain over her head, she crouched by Mose, who was grinning widely and rocking the baby. Caressing the baby's plump cheek and soft black curls, she met Mose's worried stare. "I'm going to my husband. If anything should happen . . . you, Lilly, and Pierre are our family now. The children and the land are yours."

Mose blinked hard, a suspicious tear oozing out of his eye. "You'll be back. So will that sprout, MacGregor. I'll be wanting my *chocolatero* filled to the brim every night for changing all these wet drawers—female ones at that. You been promising me you'd teach me how to knit. You die out there, and I'll never know how," he grumbled. "Take my handgun. Sling the belt and cartridges across your shoulder. Shoots a mite to the right. If Tall Tom's tied up in this, save one for him."

She kissed his gnarled hand. "I love you, Mose. Don't forget to pat Mary Rose's back, and don't let Jack eat too much jam."

REGINA, dressed as a boy, circled the base of the Spanish mine mountain on foot. MacGregor's footprints followed the trail leading to the mine. Smoke drifted out of the mouth of the mine, and firelight outlined a man's brawny body. "Tall Tom," Regina whispered.

Keeping to the shadows at the side of the path, she startled a deer nibbling on dried berries. Regina's shoulders ached from dragging the buffalo robe and supplies; her heart ached from terror. Mortimer-Hawkes had nearly killed MacGregor once; given a second chance . . .

A short distance away from the trail she found a stand of brush and made a lean-to. Kansas and Je t'aime were loosely tied nearby and would signal danger. Snuggling down inside the buffalo robe, she forced herself to eat. Her breasts had filled, dampening her camisole beneath layers of clothing. Easing and cleaning herself as best she could, Regina settled down to sleep.

The Mariah Stone, warmed by her skin, reminded her of the past tormenting her future. Mortimer-Hawkes's greed for the bloodred stone had ruined her mother's life, and now it endangered MacGregor, the dark knight who had loomed out of the mountain's mist to claim her. Craggy and wounded by life, he fought to keep his son safe. A man who lived by his gun, leashing his hand for her. MacGregor . . . courting her with his heart, wooing her with his gentleness. MacGregor, delighted by freshly baked bread and a tiny, embroidered violet on his cuff. Dozing lightly, she hummed *Greensleeves* and dreamed of MacGregor, her love. "I'm coming, my love," she whispered sleepily and nestled to the warmth of the red paisley shawl.

In the cave MacGregor's blood dampened the rawhide thongs around his wrists, loosening them slightly. A spray of dirt and pebbles sifted down to his shoulders as he moved against the beam. Tom snored loudly and the marquess slept beneath layers of velvet and buffalo robes as the beam creaked ominously.

MacGregor's jaw tightened. He'd been tied and beaten before, but never used as bait for the woman he loved. Love . . . a dream for others and never for him . . . until the Lady Mortimer-Hawkes flashed her purple eyes at him. Regina, her hair spreading around her bare shoulders, her cheeks flushed with lovemaking . . . taking him that first time on her own terms. A hungry, loving woman, fierce when defending her own.

Mortimer-Hawkes knew of Regina's deep loyalty to those she loved and played on it.

Regina would be coming after dawn. Mortimer-Hawkes and Tom could spot her easily as she rode across the flats to the mountain.

He had to stop them, even if it meant killing himself in the bargain.

Bargain. He'd made a bargain on the blanket with an Englishwoman.

He'd found warmth and joy, basked for a time in the glow of her love.

Regina would love again.

The rope around his ankles had numbed his feet, and MacGregor planned how to throw himself without the use of his legs. He turned his head slightly, and the tight raw-hide bit into his throat.

Violet . . . Violet . . .

Another spray of dirt hit his head, and MacGregor stilled. He had to live, to stop Tom and Mortimer-Hawkes from taking Regina and the babies.

Mose and Pierre would rush the mine. Or snare the first man's neck that stepped out onto the small shelf in front of the cave.

A bird chirped, signaling the coming dawn, and fear snaked through MacGregor. The weight of either Mose or Pierre would throw them into Mortimer-Hawkes's covered pit in front of the cave.

Another bird chirped, and MacGregor tensed. A long trill sounded, then another, and his heart pounded heavily, beating against his chest.

Violet.

A small branch snapped. Then another.

Then quiet.

Another long, soft trill swept over MacGregor, raising his flesh. He remembered the night they lay in the meadow after lovemaking, practicing Indian calls. . . .

Dawn sifted through the night, and suddenly Regina's small body stood outlined at the mouth of the cave. The scant light traced the long, thick braid snaking down her shoulder. The fringes of the shawl slid along her leather leggings, catching the dawn in fiery tints.

In the hazy depths of shadows and smoke, her eyes sought his.

Then Tall Tom surged out of his blankets, taking two steps toward her. Regina lifted Mose's heavy gun, pointing it at his stomach. "Back," she ordered quietly. "Step back, please. Over there by Mortimer-Hawkes, and away from my husband. Mose tells me that a shot in the stomach makes a man die slowly, painfully."

"Mortimer-Hawkes, the *métis*'s woman!" Tom hissed. Hawkes stiffened in his layers of heavy robes, turning his face toward her. Filled with terror, his lips opened wordlessly . . . then he whispered, "Mariah!"

"Get up, Mortimer-Hawkes," she ordered, her voice crisp. "Free my husband."

The marquess smiled coldly and stood to smooth his clothing. "If you fire that gun in the cave, you'll bring tons of earth down on all of us. Your precious MacGregor included."

"Nothing will happen to my husband if the Mariah legend is true. He possesses the Mariah Stone and me."

"Let her go," MacGregor ordered. He tugged at his bonds and the old beam swayed. "Let her go—Violet, get out of here!"

Mortimer-Hawkes's stiletto blade lifted MacGregor's chin slightly. In that moment the Mariah ruby hung, glistening, from Regina's other hand. Bloodred in the rising dawn, it swung from the heavy gold chain in an lazy arc.

"Let my husband go, or I shall throw this bauble into the gorge. It could shatter into a thousand pieces or be lost forever. . . . Perhaps a bird will fly the Mariah to its nest, or a woodrat will drag it into a burrow. Just think . . . Nigel. All your power resting beneath bird droppings."

She swung it side to side, taunting him, and he shrieked in horror. "Don't let it go. All my power—"

Tom bent to toss a burning coal into the brush near MacGregor, and it ignited.

The Mariah sailed out into the clear mountain air.

Terror bound Mortimer-Hawkes for a moment, then he screamed, "Mariah! I must have the Mariah!" and swept out of the cave entrance. He crashed through branches and snow covering the pit. The earth rumbled and the bottom of the pit broke loose, sending Mortimer-Hawkes and tons of rock plummeting down the face of the mountain.

The canyon echoed his scream of death, boulders tumbling after him.

The brush fire grew, crackling as a splinter of the beam ignited. "Violet, get out of here," MacGregor ordered as the smoke curled around his legs.

Tall Tom cursed, running at Regina with his hands outstretched. "Wolves, the pair of you. MacGregor mated with a purple-eyed witch. . . . You'll die within feet of each other. I'll have those damn rubies in your ears yet!"

A tall man, Tom's head hit a beam, stunning him. He staggered, reaching for Regina. She danced aside, escaping his grasp. Tom's foot slid on a loose rock, and he went over the cliff, tearing a dead bush from the rocks.

Fire encased the ancient beam, and MacGregor coughed, squinting through the smoke to see Regina. "Get out of here, woman. This whole mountain will come down any time."

"Then it will come down on us together," she said, placing Mose's gun in the holster and running to slash his bonds.

MacGregor cursed, stepping free. He stared down at her, then tenderly brushed a tendril from her cheek and smiled slowly. "How's Mary Rose?"

She stood on tiptoe to kiss him, the gentle caress lingered. "Hungry. We shall have to make fast work of our escape, dear heart."

Taking her hand, MacGregor scanned the shimmering layers of cold mist beyond the cave. An empty space yawned between the cave entrance and the first rocks of the trail. "Damn it, Violet. You should have stayed put," he snapped, drawing her into his arms for a quick, hungry kiss.

"I wanted you home for supper," she whispered, stroking his cheek. "Darling . . . my love . . ."

MacGregor crushed her to him, breathing hard. "Violet, you're a hard woman," he said, grinning widely. "I love every ornery inch."

"My own dark knight rescuing his lady in distress," she returned, holding him tightly.

"Uh-huh. When we're safe, you're getting a talking to." MacGregor tugged her braid. "We've got to get out of here fast."

"What are we going to do?" Regina's husky voice barely sounded over the crackling flame behind them. He brought her hand to his mouth, then held it firmly.

"See that rock?" He nodded toward rock ledge skirting the mountain to the trail. "Move slow and easy, Mrs. MacGregor."

In the next moment they were sliding, skidding down the trail, racing to outdistance the avalanche.

They reached the horses just as dust and smoke boiled out of the mine. MacGregor lifted Regina to Je t'aime's saddle before swinging up on Kansas's back. Racing back across their trail to the mine, they slowed the horses at a safe distance. The mountain rumbled and shuddered. Boulders, tinted fiery red in the dawn, rolled down the sheer face of the mountain, sweeping trees aside as if they were matchsticks.

Regina and MacGregor halted the horses at a safe distance and watched the mountain settle into peace.

MacGregor dragged Regina from Je t'aime and into his lap, kissing her hungrily. He framed her face in his palms, kissing her nose, her eyes, her cheeks, her lips. "Violet . . . MacGregor . . ." he whispered urgently between kisses. "You could have been killed. . . ."

"My heart . . . my own precious, dear husband. I would follow you into hellfire and back again. . . ." she answered, kissing him as eagerly.

"Violet . . . Violet . . . my life . . . my love. . . ."

REGINA curled on the walnut bed, snuggling to the warmth of the spot MacGregor had just vacated. When he thought she was asleep, he slipped from bed for his nightly ritual. The moment was a private one, between father and children . . . a bonding that MacGregor treasured with infinite respect.

The gold frame with the Mariahs' portrait lay wrapped in the gauze dancing costume, deep in the traveling chest. Finally at peace, Regina snuggled in her marriage bed, holding the past and the dreams at bay.

MacGregor bent over Mary Rose's crib to kiss the baby's cheek lovingly. Toying with the infant's tiny hand, MacGregor's hard face softened as her fingers curled around his.

The firelight caught his body, tracing it and sending his

shadow against the white clay chinks of the cabin logs as he moved to Jack's small bed. He crouched beside his son and tucked the velvet bear beneath the covers. The November wind howled outside, the windows lashed by fat snowflakes, as MacGregor smoothed Jack's rumpled black hair.

MacGregor's love ran deep, as did the fear that his happiness could be shattered in a moment.

Regina's hungry gaze traced a muscular thigh beneath the long nightshirt. A thatch of dark hair gleamed in the opening of her husband's nightshirt, a concession to Mary Rose's recent birth and a shield concealing his blatant desire.

Padding across the shadows, MacGregor stopped by the bed and stared a full moment at the rumpled garment at his feet. Bending slowly, he lifted Regina's ruffled nightgown. He studied it, smoothing the cloth with his hands thoughtfully, as though he molded his wife's soft body, then placed it at the foot of the bed.

Taking care not to disturb her sleep, he slipped into bed gently. Regina reached for him and snuggled close, capturing him with her soft limbs before he could move away. He tensed, his hand brushing her full breast. His fingers caressed the softness for a brief instant before he muttered a strangled, "Violet!"

"Yes, my love?" she answered innocently, snuggling closer.

"Violet . . . you're pushing your luck," he muttered unevenly. "You're newly healed from Mary Rose. . . ." he protested as she began kissing his throat. "A lady doesn't ambush her husband—"

"A lady can ambush her *lover*, can't she?" she asked, savoring the hard warmth of his body.

Reaching for her, MacGregor grinned in the shadows. "Reckon so."

"We've mated, Mr. Two Hearts MacGregor. Bound to each other for life."

"We've mated for life," he drawled arrogantly. "But not lately."

Regina's hair spread around them as she lifted an elbow to prop it on his chest. "You've been overlong in attending your husbandly duties, Mr. Two Hearts MacGregor. Oh, how I love you," she whispered, trailing her finger across his lips.

"You're playing with fire," MacGregor warned between his teeth. His large hands trembled, stroking, discovering anew. . . .

Regina rested her thigh over his, nudging the nightshirt higher on his hard thigh. She toyed with a strand of his hair that crossed his forehead. "It's been over a year since you swept out of the mists to rescue me. . . ."

"Those purple eyes caught me then and now. Bound me until I couldn't think straight." He kissed her palm, then placed it over the heavy beat of his heart. "You've taken the heart of me. . . ."

MacGregor's hand stroked the length of her silken back then slid to fondle her full breast, thrust against his chest. He toyed with a fat curl, resting on her slender arm. "Every day brings more. . . . You've brought me peace, Lady Violet MacGregor. Soothed the pain and gave me love . . . a child . . . a home."

"Love," she repeated slowly, savoring the word.

"Love," he repeated. "You wanted more. . . ."

"Yes, my darling. I've found more than I sought," she whispered as he turned her boldly beneath his taut body.

THE winter snows swept through the open windows of Mortimer-Hawkes's deserted hunting lodge, piling against the inner walls. Beneath tons of rock, the legendary Mariah found peace.

"Mariah" . . . *a woman crooned softly in the winter night. The sound slid through the pines, soaring over the rugged mountains.*

"Mariah . . . "

SNEAK PREVIEW

. . . of a spellbinding new novel
by Nora Roberts!

No one combines suspense and romance
as brilliantly as Nora Roberts, the *New
York Times* bestselling author of *Carnal
Innocence* and *Genuine Lies*. Her newest
novel unveils the dreams and schemes of
an unforgettable family—who turn fantasy
into fame and risk everything for love. . . .

Honest Illusions

Following is an exclusive excerpt from this
tantalizing new novel, available in July
from G.P. Putnam's Sons . . .

THE Lady Vanishes. It was an old illusion, given a modern twist, and never failed to leave the audience gasping. The glittery crowd at Radio City was as eager to be duped as a group of slack-jawed rubes at a dog and pony show.

Even as Roxanne stepped onto the glass pedestal she could feel their anticipation—the silvery edge of it that was a merging of hope and doubt glued together with wonder. The inching foward in the seat ranged from president to peon.

Magic made equals of them all.

Max said that, she recalled. Many, many times.

Amid the swirl of mist and the flash of light, the pedestal slowly ascended, circling majestically to the tune of Gershwin's *Rhapsody in Blue*. The gentle three-hundred-and-sixty-degree revolution showed the crowd all sides of the ice-clear pedestal and the slender woman atop it—and distracted them from the trickery at hand.

Presentation, she'd been taught, was often the slim difference between a charlatan and an artist.

In keeping with the theme of the music, Roxanne wore a sparkling gown of midnight blue that clung to her long, willowy form—clung so closely that no one studying her would believe there was anything under the spangled silk but her own flesh. Her hair, a waterfall of flame curling to her waist, twinkled with thousands of tiny iridescent stars.

Fire and ice. More than one man had wondered how one woman could be both at the same time.

As in sleep or a trance, her eyes were closed—or seemed to be—and her elegant face was lifted toward the star-pricked ceiling of the stage.

As she rose, she let her arms sway to the music, then held them high above her head, for showmanship and for the practical necessity that underscores all magic.

It was a beautiful illusion, she knew. The mist, the lights, the music, the woman. She enjoyed the sheer drama of it, and was not above being amused by the irony of using the age-old symbol of the lone, lovely woman placed on a pedestal, above the common worry and toils of man.

It was also a miserably complex bit of business, requiring a great deal of physical control and split-second timing. But not even those fortunate enough to be seated in the first row could detect the intense concentration in her serene face. None of them could know how many tedious hours she had put in, perfecting every aspect of the act on paper, then in practice. Unrelenting practice.

Slowly, again to Gershwin's rhythm, her body began to turn, dip, sway. A partnerless dance ten feet above stage, all color and fluid movement. There were murmurs from the audience, scattered applause.

They could see her—yes, they could see her through the blue-tinted mist and spinning lights. The glitter of the dark gown, the flow of flame-colored hair, the gleam of that alabaster skin.

Then, in a breath, in a gasp, they could not. In less time than it takes to blink an eye, she was gone. In her place was a sleek Bengal tiger who reared on his hind legs to paw the air and roar.

There was a pause, that most satisfying of pauses to an entertainer when an audience held its stunned collective breath before the applause thundered, echoing as the pedestal descended once more. The big cat leapt down to stalk stage right. He stopped by an ebony box, sent up another roar that had a woman in the front row giggling nervously. As one, the four sides of the box collapsed.

And there was Roxanne, dressed not in shimmery blue but in a silver cat suit. She took her bows as she'd been taught almost from birth. With a flourish.

As the sound of success continued to pound in her ears, she mounted the tiger and rode the beast offstage.

"Nice work, Oscar." With a little sigh, she bent forward to scratch the cat between the ears.

"You looked real pretty, Roxy." Her big, burly assistant clipped a leash to Oscar's spangled collar.

"Thanks, Mouse." Dismounting, she tossed her hair back. The backstage area was already hopping. Those trusted to do so would secure her equipment and guard it from prying eyes. Since she'd scheduled a press conference for the following day, she would see no reporters now. Roxanne had high hopes for a bottle of iced champagne and a stingingly hot whirlpool bath.

Alone.

Absently she rubbed her hands together—an old habit Mouse could have told her she'd picked up from her father.

"I've got the fidgets," she said with a half laugh. "Had them all damn night. It feels like someone's breathing down my neck."

"Well, ah . . ." Mouse stood where he was, letting Oscar rub against his knees. Never articulate under the best of circumstances, Mouse fumbled for the best way to phrase the news. "You got company, Roxy. In the dressing room."

"Oh?" Her brows drew together, forming the faint line of impatience between them. "Who?"

"Take another bow, honey." Lily, Roxanne's onstage assistant and surrogate mother, swept over to grab her arm. "You brought down the house." Lily dabbed a handkerchief around the false eyelashes she wore onstage and off. "Max would be so proud."

The quick twist in Roxanne's gut had her willing away her own tears. They didn't show. They were never permitted to show in public. She started forward, moving into the swell of applause. "Who's waiting for me?" she called over her shoulder, but Mouse was already leading the big cat away.

He'd been taught by the master that discretion was the better part of survival.

Ten minutes later, flushed with success, Roxanne opened the door of her dressing room. The scent hit her first—roses and greasepaint. That mix of fragrances had become so familiar she breathed it in like fresh air. But there was another scent here—the sting of rich tobacco. Elegant, exotic, French. Her hand trembled once on the knob as she pushed the door fully open.

There was one man she would forever associate with that aroma. One man she knew who habitually smoked slim French cigars.

She said nothing when she saw him. Could say nothing as he rose from a chair where he'd been enjoying his cigar and her champagne. Oh, God, it was thrilling and horrible to watch that wonderful mouth quirk in that very familiar grin, to meet those impossibly blue eyes with her own.

His hair was still long, a mane of ebony waving back from his face. Even as a child he'd been gorgeous, an elegant gypsy with eyes that could freeze or burn. Age had only enhanced his looks, fining down that compelling face, the long bones and shadowy hollows, the faint cleft in the chin. Beyond the physical, there was a drama that shivered around him like an aura.

He was a man women shuddered over and wanted.

She had. Oh, she had.

Five years had passed since she'd seen that smile, since she'd run her hands through that thick hair or felt the searing pressure of that clever mouth. Five years to mourn, to weep and to hate.

Why wasn't he dead? she wondered as she forced herself to close the door at her back. Why hadn't he had the decency to succumb to any of the varied and gruesome tragedies she'd imagined for him?

And what in God's name was she going to do with this terrible yearning she felt just looking at him again?

"Roxanne." Training kept Luke's voice steady as he said her name. He'd watched her over the years. Tonight he'd studied her every move from the shadows of the wings. Judging, weighing. Wanting. But here, now, face to face, she was almost too beautiful to bear. "It was a good show. The finale was spectacular."

"Thank you."

His hand was steady as he poured her a flute of champagne, as hers was when she accepted it. They were, after all, showmen, cast in an odd way from the same mold. Max's mold.

"I'm sorry about Max."

Her eyes went flat. "Are you?"

Because Luke felt he deserved more than the slash of sarcasm, he merely nodded, then glanced down at his bubbling wine, remembering. His mouth curved when he looked back at her. "The Calais job, the rubies. Was that yours?"

She sipped, the silver sparkled on her shoulders as she moved them in a careless shrug. "Of course."

"Ah." He nodded again, pleased. He had to be sure she hadn't lost her touch—for magic or for larceny. "I heard rumors that a first edition of Poe's *House of Usher* was lifted from a vault in London."

"Your hearing was always good, Callahan."

He continued to smile, wondering when she'd learned to exude sex like breath. He remembered the clever child, the coltish adolescent, the irresistible bloom of the young woman. The bloom had blossomed seductively. And he could feel the pull that had always been between them. He would use it now, with regret, but he would use it to gain his own ends.

The end justifies everything. Another of Maximillian Nouvelle's maxims.

"I have a proposition for you, Rox."

"Really?" She took a last sip before setting her glass aside. The bubbles were bitter on her tongue.

"Business," he said lightly, tapping out the stub of his cigar. Taking her hand, he brought her fingers to his lips. "And personal. I've missed you, Roxanne." It was the truest statement he could make. One flash of sterling honesty in years of tricks, illusions and pretense. Caught up in his own feelings, he missed the warning flash in her eyes.

"Have you, Luke? Have you really?"

"More than I can tell you." Swamped by memories and needs, he drew her closer, felt his blood begin to pump as her body brushed his. She'd always been the one. No matter how many escapes he'd accomplished, he'd never freed himself from the trap in which Roxanne Nouvelle had caught him. "Come back to my hotel." His breath whispered over her face as she went fluidly into his arms. "We'll have a late supper. Talk."

"Talk?" Her arms wound sinuously around him. Her rings flashed as she dipped her fingers into his hair. Beside them the makeup mirror over her dressing table reflected them in triplicate. As if showing them past, present, future. When she spoke, her voice was like the mist she'd vanished into. Dark and rich and mysterious. "Is that what you want to do with me, Luke?"

He forgot the importance of control, forgot everything but the fact that her mouth was an inch from his. The taste he'd once gorged on was a wish away. "No."

He dropped his head toward hers. Then his breath exploded as her knee shot up between his legs. Even as he was doubling over, she slammed her fist onto his chin.

His grunt of surprise, and the splintering of wood from the table he smashed on his way down gave Roxanne enormous satisfaction. Roses flew, water splashed. A few slender buds drifted over him as he lay on the dampening carpet.

"You . . ." Scowling, he dragged a rose from his hair. The brat had always been sneaky, he remembered. "You're quicker than you used to be, Rox."

Hands on her hips, she stood over him, a slim, silver warrior who'd never learned to sample her revenge cold. "I'm a lot of things I didn't used to be." Her knuckles hurt like fire, but she used that pain to block another, deeper ache. "Now, you lying Irish bastard, crawl back into whatever hole you dug for yourself five years ago. Come near me again, and I swear, I'll make you disappear for good."

Delighted with her exit line, she turned on her heel, then let out a shriek when Luke snagged her ankle. She went down hard on her rump and before she could put nails and teeth to use, he had her pinned. She'd forgotten how strong and how quick he was.

A miscalculation, Max would have said. And miscalculations were the root of all failures.

"Okay, Rox, we can talk here." Though he was breathless and still in pain, he grinned. "Your choice."

"I'll see you in hell—"

"Very likely." His grin faded. "Damn it, Roxy, I never could resist you." When he crushed his mouth to hers, he tossed them both back into the past.

The sizzling new novel by the bestselling
author of <u>BLACK TIE ONLY</u>

Julia Fenton
BLUE ORCHIDS

"A dazzling page-turner. I was swept away by all the
glamour, fame and rivalry of two unforgettable sisters."
    —Maureen Dean, bestselling author of <u>Washington Wives</u>

"Delightfully decadent...kept me turning pages late,
late into the night!"   —Rex Reed

It was the most eagerly awaited, star-studded premiere of
any Broadway musical ever. But for Valentina and Orchid it
would be much more. Each found success as recording
artists; Orchid had always struggled for stardom, but Valentina
captured the spotlight with her dark exotic beauty and
crystal voice. A bitter jealousy tore them apart, but tonight
they will reunite, and once again the eyes of the world will
be upon them, at a performance that will make or break
their dreams, and determine their destiny, for once and for
all . . .

__0-515-10875-8/$5.99 (Available July 1992)